KISSING THE RAIN

From the Chicken House

Kevin Brooks is a proper writer. He never lets you stop *thinking*. Caught in brilliant dialogue and tense situations, his characters fumble and stumble with real-life dilemmas, just like us. But for them the threats are frightening and all too close.

No easy endings, no bland half-truths – Kevin is the real thing.

Barry Cunningham
Publisher

KISSING THE RAIN

kevin brooks

2 Palmer Street, Frome, Somerset BA11 1DS

High Praise
for
MARTYN PIG

WINNER OF THE BRANFORD BOASE AWARD 2002
SHORTLISTED FOR THE CILIP CARNEGIE MEDAL 2002

Martyn Pig *is dark, funny and with a neat twist in the tale. This is very good stuff indeed. Watch this guy, he's good.* MELVIN BURGESS

The most exciting debut by a UK author since Skellig *by David Almond ... a hugely promising first novel.* MICHAEL THORN, LITERARY REVIEW

Page turning and thoughtful ... NICOLETTE JONES, SUNDAY TIMES

This could become a cult novel. NICHOLAS TUCKER, INDEPENDENT

A frankly brilliant first novel. ANNE JOHNSTONE, GLASGOW HERALD

A confident, compelling debut novel. LINDSEY FRAZER, GUARDIAN

Martyn Pig is a character you will never forget. The comic awfulness of the events which overtake him will keep you gripped. Kevin Brooks is a welcome new voice. KIT SPRING, OBSERVER

Tense and twisty ... SARAH JOHNSON, TIMES

... a very classy read. DINAH HALL, SUNDAY TELEGRAPH

In a word ... genius! ANGIE SIMPSON, WATERSTONES HEAD OFFICE

I thought Martyn Pig *was tremendous, one of the most original books for young people that I've ever read ... I found it compulsively readable ...* TERESA SCRAGG, SOLIHULL LIBRARIES AND ARTS

Fresh and edgy, Martyn Pig *will have tremendous teen appeal.* SCHOOL LIBRARY JOURNAL

High Praise
for
LUCAS

SHORTLISTED FOR THE GUARDIAN CHILDREN'S FICTION AWARD 2003

Brooks maintains a terrific suspense, clarity and warmth of writing that makes this novel outstanding. KIT SPRING, OBSERVER

A particularly moving and unusual love story…
ADELE GERAS, GUARDIAN

It gets to you. Then when this has passed, you want to tell everyone how good it is. NICOLETTE JONES, SUNDAY TIMES

A gripping story that confirms this new writer's undoubted talent.
JILL SLOTOVER, FINANCIAL TIMES

This is wonderfully assured and insightful writing.
ANNE JOHNSTONE, GLASGOW HERALD

Brooks' writing is of the highest quality: he creates an almost tangible sense of place and strong central characters. He tells his story with confidence and has created a novel that can't be put down.
WENDY COOLING, BOOKSELLER

This is a powerful evocation of the terrible power of ignorance – deceptively simply delivered. LINDSEY FRAZER, GUARDIAN

This is a powerful novel to be savoured by all who appreciate fine writing and a gripping read. SCHOOL LIBRARY JOURNAL

Its combination of big ideas and forthright narrative make this novel likely to linger in readers' minds. PUBLISHERS WEEKLY

Caitlin's overpowering feelings of love and loss will resonate with teen readers. HORN BOOK

Thanks

To Bob Colover and Eric Frank for answering my questions.
To all the Chickens - that's Rachel, Alison, Laura, Elinor, and Imogen – for being so wonderful. To Mary, for taking care of me and being a friend. And, finally, to Barry, for a million good things, but most of all for opening the door and letting me into my life. It's a pretty good feeling when your dreams come true – and I'll never forget who made it possible.
Thank you.

First published in Great Britain in 2004
The Chicken House
2 Palmer Street
Frome, Somerset BA11 1DS
United Kingdom
www.doublecluck.com

Cover design by Ian Butterworth
Designed and typeset by Dorchester Typesetting Group Ltd
Printed and bound in Great Britain

3 5 7 9 10 8 6 4 2

British Library Cataloguing in Publication data available.

ISBN 1-904442-19-6 HB
ISBN 1-904442-39-0 PB

Contents

1 The Sta[illegible]

You wanna know the TRUTH [illegible]
I'm sick of it. Sick of [illegible]
Who and the bridge and the [illegible]
and the words and the lies [illegible]
GOD.
I wish I'd never [illegible]
Yeah, THAT's what I wish [illegible]
ing. [illegible]
[illegible] RIGHT.
[illegible] now I know it.
Now I [illegible] things [illegible]
Bad [illegible]
[illegible]
[illegible] TRUTH [illegible]
[illegible] TRUTH [illegible]
The world [illegible]
I'll tell you the TRUTH [illegible]

[illegible]
[illegible] about [illegible]
cold hands and smoky skies [illegible]
tonight and we got heavy [illegible]
on down the garden path [illegible] about
halfway down [illegible]
me from the back door.
'You got your gloves, Mo[illegible]

1/ The Start of the TRUTH

You wanna know the TRUTH? I'll tell you the TRUTH – I'm sick of it. Sick of all the FAT stuff and Callan and Vine and the bridge and the road and the cars and the eyes and the words and the lies . . .

GOD.

I wish I'd never been there . . . never got INVOLVED . . .

Yeh, THAT's what I wish. Din't see nothing, dunno nothing. Me? I shoulda kept my big mouth shut. I DIN'T SEE *NOTHING*, ALL RIGHT?

Yeh, **now** I know it.

Now I gotta fix things. Do things. Bad things.

Bad = good.

Good = bad.

TRUTH = lies.

Lies = TRUTH.

You wanna know the TRUTH?

I'll tell you the TRUTH.

OK, let's see what we got. It's early November last year, nearly Bonfire Night, about 5 o'clock in the evening. We got cold hands and smokey skies and earlybird fireworks ripping the night, and we got heavy breaths misting the air as I stomp on down the garden path, heading for the shed. I'm about halfway down, just zipping my coat, when Mum calls out to me from the back door.

'You got your gloves, Moo?'

'Yeh.'

'You sure?'

'Yeh, I got em.'

'OK – don't be too long. It's gonna freeze up later.'

I wave a hand over my shoulder.

The back door shuts – *clunk.*

I get my bike out the shed and wheel it round the back of the house, down the path, and out the front gate. I pull on my gloves, pull up my hood, yank the gate shut, then scoot the bike along the pavement, swing a leg over the saddle, sit down, get it going, stand up, whack it into gear, hit down hard on the pedals, up through the gears, getting faster and faster, then I'm hopping off the kerb at the end of the road, and I'm gone, I'm away, riding the evening streets.

Here we go – around the back of the village, away from the houses, away from the people, into the small country lanes, then down into the dip and up the hill, pedalling hard, puffing BILLY, sweating like a pig . . . GOD, I wish I din't sweat so much. It's so cold and sticky, like freezing blood, and the icy air's burning the back of my throat, hurting like a bastad, and the tips of my fingers are getting all numb . . . but I don't care. I don't give a TOSS about none of it. Cos I'm going where I wanna go. I'm going to the bridge . . . MY bridge. And that's all I EVER want.

The bridge.

Oh yeh . . .

The bridge.

The railings – dit dit dit – the steps, the concrete, the dull grey steel. The shape of it, the angles, the colours . . . the tide of traffic on the road below . . . the sound of it . . . the background *uuuurrrrhhhhhsshhhhmmmm* . . . the *swoo-ooosh-swoo-ooosh-swoo-ooosh* of the cars . . . trucks . . . lorries . . .

The song of the road.

I can hear it now, getting louder as I push on up the hill – *swoo-ooosh-swoo-ooosh-swoo-ooosh* – getting closer all the time, getting inside me. The song, the road, the bridge . . . I can FEEL it, doing its THING, making me smile, emptying my head . . . and now I'm nearly there. The hill's levelled out and I'm freewheeling, taking it easy, swinging my leg over the saddle and jumping off – landing pretty light for a FAT guy (if only they could see me now) – then bouncing a stride or 2, then wheeling the bike to the foot of the steps and letting it go – *clank*. Just like that. Just leave it. It's all right – ain't nobody here but me.

Just me and the bridge.

Me and the road.

MY bridge.

MY road.

It's the same road from 5 years ago, the same road we came in on. I din't know it then, but I know it now. Know it? Do I KNOW it? Yeh, I know it. I know it every Day. It's my release. My PLACE. My shelter from the RAIN. I got no idea where it starts from or where it goes . . . from some place to some other place, I guess. It don't matter . . . it's IRELLI . . . IRRILA . . . it don't matter. It starts and ends as far as I can see. The rest of it . . . who cares about the rest of it? The rest of it ain't got nothing to do with me. And the bridge? What about the bridge? What's it for? What's it DO? It don't GO nowhere. It goes from here to there, from this side of the road to the other side. And what's on the other side? The same as on this side – not much. Lanes, roads, little places, fields, hedges and stuff . . .

What's the bridge for?

For ME.

For every Day . . .

Cos back then every Day's the same – Oneday, Twoday,

Threeday, Fourday, Fiveday, Scatterday, Dumbday . . . every Day's just another day . . . same as the Day before, same as the Day before, same as the Day before. Ain't nothing much happens, just the same old stuff, over and over again . . .

You know how it goes.

You gotta do *some*thing, right?

OK – so every Day, after school, after the RAIN, after tea, I get on my bike and ride to the bridge – puffing and gasping, too FAT to breathe – and when I get there I wheel the bike to the foot of the steps and let it go – *clank* – just like that. Next thing I do, I stand there for a minute or 2, just looking up at the bridge, taking it all in, getting my breath back, getting the tingles under my skin, and then I start climbing the steps – 3 zigzag flights, 12 steps each, dimpled, grey, boingy, zig, zag, zig – and every Day they take me where I wanna go. Up on the bridge. Above the road. Looking down. Watching the traffic – 2 lanes north, 2 lanes south . . . *uuuurrrrhhhhhsshh-hhmmmm . . . swoo-ooosh-swoo-ooosh-swoo-ooosh* . . . the grey river . . .

GOD, it feels GOOD up here.

The air, the wind, the feel of the bridge beneath my feet . . . it's made from some kinda grippy, grey, non-slip stuff, and it feels good when you walk on it – nice and scuffy and dry and safe. I walk it every Day – *tump*, *tump*, *tump* – along the bridge, sometimes *bing*ing the railings with my finger, sometimes not – till I get to my place . . .

MY PLACE.

There it is, look – 8 steps along, that bit there, where one of the railings has a knee-shaped kink, and the cross-rail's worn and shiny from 5 years' leaning . . .

MY PLACE.

And now, with the updraught of traffic ruffling my hair, and the pulse of the bridge buzzing in my feet, now's the moment to sink down into my position – arms crossed . . . leaning over . . . looking down . . .

Listening . . .

Watching . . .

Watching the traffic.

Every Day . . .

I watch the traffic.

That's what I do.

I watch the traffic.

Day after Day, hour after hour . . . one hour, 2 hours, 3 hours, sometimes 4 at the weekend. 4? All right, 5 . . . 5 hours. It ain't long. Not when you think about it . . . or DON'T think about it, which is the whole POINT. Cos up here you DON'T think about it. Up here you don't think about NOTHING. Yeh, all right, you THINK about *some* kindsa stuff, like non-thinking stuff, but that ain't the same – that's THINKING thinking. And you don't NEED time for that. You don't need NOTHING, which is the whole POINT. Cos, up here, the time just flows, like the river of traffic on the road below – never-ending, always there – *swoo-ooosh-swoo-ooosh-swoo-ooosh* . . . cars, trucks, vans, lorries, bikes . . . heading north, heading south, rumbling, racing, roaring, screaming, silent as nothing . . .

It takes me away.

Every Day.

It takes me away.

From the bridge, the road runs straight for half a mile, and then it starts to curve. A slow downward curve to the right, to the east, down down down and away, like a long black ribbon in a falling breeze, down beyond the crown of a hill and away outta sight. On a clear day I can follow it for just over a mile.

That's a fact.

I know – cos I measured it one Day when the road was closed for repairs. I ain't gonna tell you ALL the details, cos it's too SAD and boring to talk about, but basically what I did was this – I walked the road, from the bridge to the bit-where-you-can't-see-it-no-more, counting my (pre-measured) steps all the way, and then I went home and worked out all the distances on a calculator. So I KNOW it's 1204 steps to the big green signpost where the curve starts, which is 797 metres (or nearly half a mile), and I know it's 1422 steps from the big green signpost to the gate in the hedge opposite the pylon, which is as far as I can see, which is 941 metres (or just over half a mile).

So, all in all, I got about a mile of road to look at. A mile of watching traffic. A mile of anything I want. And it IS anything I want – cos it's MINE. I can do whatever I want with it. And that's what I do – whatever I want. I watch it. I listen to it. I feel it. I think things. Secret things. I play games in my head. I wonder. I make things up. I go places. I DREAM. I breathe the fumes. I soak up the movement.

Sometimes, I just drift away.

Headgames.

Counting the colour of cars is a good one. What you do is . . . well, it depends how busy the road is. When it's busy, which it usually is, it's best to stick to one lane. If it's quiet you might use both . . . but that can get tricky. So let's say it's busy. OK – what you do is, you take the cars in the north lane . . . that's your field of play, if you like. You take the cars in the north lane, and you pick some colours. You can have as many colours as you want, but the more you pick the trickier it gets. So let's start with 2 – red and blue, say. What it is, see, it's like a race, a competition. Red cars V Blue cars. Who's got the most? It's dead easy. All you gotta do is watch the cars and count the colours. Use your head. There's a red one, that's 1-0. Another red one, 2-0. Blue, 2-1. Red, 3-1. Course, you gotta pick a finishing line before you start, else it goes on for ever. The finishing line's up to you. You can have sprints – first to 20 is the winner – or middle-distance races – first to 50 or 75 – or, if you want, you can have marathons – first to 100, 200, 300 . . . 1000. It's up to you. You can do whatever you want.

Red V Blue.

Winner plays Green.

Blue V Green.

Winner plays Grey.

Blue V White.

Blue V Red V White . . .

Whatever you want.

It's YOURS.

It's ALL yours.

You can do whatever you want. You can watch faces in the windscreens. Watch em talking. Give em names – BIG NOSE, DREAMY GIRL, TWITCHER, TOUGH GUY. You can guess their lives – MISERABLE, BORING, BOOZY, BAD, SUNNY, TWISTED, LUCKY, SAD . . . You can watch em drive – slow, fast, faster . . . 50mph, 60mph, 100mph, 155mph . . . whooee! HE's got somewhere to go, he's a *FASTMAN*. You can watch the lorries and trucks full of stuff you dunno nothing about, going places you dunno nothing about, coming from places you dunno nothing about . . . Bergen? Rotterdam? Hamburg? Harrogate? I dunno. You can watch the coaches full of bored kids or old people eating sandwiches – WHERE THE HELL ARE *THEY* GOING? You can watch motorbikes, cranes, tractors, cop cars, wide-loads, breakdowns, spillages, things thrown outta windows . . . there's ALL kindsa stuff going on. I saw a nude guy once in the back of a Ka, just sitting there, flashing past all flabby and white . . . a Ka 1.3i, it was, lilac, with 6-spoke alloy wheels and a rear spoiler . . . oh yeh, I KNOW cars. I ain't PROUD of it. It's just how it is. I know em all – Mondeo, Legend, Jaguar XK8, Peugeot 106, 206, 306, 307, Micra, Clio, Punto, Saxo, Cruiser, Korando, Wrangler, Cherokee. Lexus RX, Space Wagon . . . show me a car and I'll tell you what it is.

I see em all.

Riding the river.

Swoo-ooosh-swoo-ooosh-swoo-ooosh . . .

Sometimes, once in a while, you see BIG things, things that make a splash. Things that disturb the flow. Like a screech of brakes, a swerve, a horn, then a hubcap rolling across the lanes and clattering into the verge. Or a car stopping, pulling up at the side . . . someone getting out, a guy in a sleeveless T-shirt . . . what's HE doing? . . . looking around, walking over to the hedge . . . nah, it's OK, ain't nothing, he's just taking a leak. Or another screech of brakes, another swerve, another horn, and this time *CRASH!! KRUMP!!* – that dull lump of metal on metal, you know, the sound that stops the air – *CRASH!! KRUMP!! SCRUURRR . . . DUNK!!* Then smoke and steam . . . voices . . . tears . . . dazed drivers . . . then maybe the crash-cops . . .

Yeh, I seen a few crashes. They're pretty good to watch. It's like someone throwing something big in the river – the big *SPLASH*, stuff flying all over the place, then the waves, the ripples, hitting the bank, bouncing back, disturbing the flow . . . then after a while it all calms down again and the river gets back to what it was.

Yeh, big splashes are OK.

This though . . . today, this Oneday . . . 7 months ago. This was different.

After this, nothing calmed down.
Nothing got back to what it was.

It's gone midnight **now**. It's a warm night and the world is quiet and I'm pausing for breath – breath and biscuits. I keep em in a tin by the bed. Biscuits, that is – not breaths. I got Hobnobs, Fig Rolls, Custard Creams, Strawberry Creams, Chocolate Digestives . . . I got em all. Anyway, like I said, it's gone midnight and everything's quiet. The window's open, letting in the summer dark and the distant rush of the road, the night-whisper of midnight traffic, singing its song . . . calling out to me – *get it done, Moo . . . get it done, get it done, get it done . . .*

Yeh . . .

Get it done.

It's OK. Time-wise, I mean. I ain't gonna sleep **now**. Not with this to tell. I got all night for this.

OK – so I'm on the bridge, facing north . . . I always face north, towards Wickham. Never south. I dunno why. Maybe it's cos south is where we came from . . . yeh, maybe that's it. Back along the road, back towards Moulton, about a hundred metres south, that's where the road turns off to the village. It ain't much to look at – just a crummy little junction, a hole in the hedge, a crappy little lane, 2 crabby white fingers on a pole, saying – THIS IS IT, THIS WAY . . . and I don't wanna look back there. I KNOW back there. It's SMALL. I don't wanna look SMALL, I wanna look BIG. I wanna look forward to something else. Something out there . . . I dunno what. Nothing in PARTICULAR. Not Wickham – GOD no. Wickam's just a place 10 miles up the road. It's probly *OK* . . . I mean, I dunno, I ain't never been there . . . well, I been there ONCE . . . but that ain't the point.

The point is, Wickham's just a place. And I ain't looking at PLACES. I'm just looking – that's all. Just . . . I dunno . . . it's just . . . look, I ain't LOOKING looking, I ain't looking AT nothing. I'm just looking down, dead-eyed and blind – just losing the RAIN in the river.

Anyway, like I said, this Oneday, I'm on the bridge and I'm facing north. It's around 6 o'clock now. I been here nearly an hour, just doing my thing – watching the river, the flow of lights, watching the fireworks tracing the night, cracking the air with *zips* and stuttered *bangs* . . . lights above and lights below. In the dark you can see bits of fire and village lights and glowing beads of red-and-white where the lines of distant roads dissect the Essex plains. This is my world. Up here, down there . . . watching the lights . . . watching, watching, watching, just doing my thing . . .

It's getting pretty cold now, and I'm thinking about getting back. But I'm also thinking – yeh? getting back to *what*? To Mum and Dad, the house, the front room, the TV, the hissing gas fire that sends us all to sleep . . . 3 fat Nelsons slumped in a small front room, grunting and snoring and farting along to *Hollyoaks* . . .?

You want that?

Is *that* what you want?

Maybe not. Maybe I'll just stay here for a while. Yeh, maybe the cold ain't so bad after all . . .

Nah, I'm thinking, the cold's OK.

THAT's when it happened.

Right then.

The start of it . . .

The TRUTH.

OK – so I'm watching the tail-lights streaming past the pylon and disappearing down the hill. I'm watching, watching, watching . . . I'm drifting away . . . HIPPONOTISED by the trail of lights . . . moving . . . glimmering . . . merging into one . . . falling away . . . fading . . . I'm watching . . . watching . . . eyes closed . . . watching . . . when – *KA-BOOOM!!* – a volcano erupts in the sky, a fountain of blue, a mushroom cloud, and my eyes jerk up and scan the black horizon. It's OK . . . ain't nothing – just a firework. But now I'm awake . . . now I'm alert again . . . now I can SEE. I can see 2 FAST cars speeding up the south lane towards me. And when I say FAST – whooee! – I mean *FAST*. I can't make em out just yet, they're maybe half a mile away, all I can see is 2 pairs of glaring headlights, one behind the other, 4 blazing eyes, bombing like mad up the outside lane.

Now THIS is worth watching . . .

A quarter of a mile away – just past the lay-by – the second car, the one behind, swings out into the inside lane, accelerates hard, zips past the other car, then cuts back in front and dabs the brakes – *EEEEEEEeeeeeee!* The other car screeches and screams, nearly ramming the one in front, and then they're both off again.

Here they come . . .

Here we go . . .

BIG stuff.

They're getting pretty close now, close enough for a rough ID. The car in front is a light blue – or grey – BMW, probly a 328, and the one behind is a black 4x4 . . . a Discovery? Nah . . . it's a Range Rover. A good one. Top of the line. Big and FAST. Look at it GO . . . lights flashing, horn blaring, swerving out alongside the BMW . . . and the BMW speeds up and cuts in front again . . . then the Range Rover rolls back into the outside lane and races up alongside the BMW . . . and starts to SHOVE it off the road. Look at

THAT! Nosing, slowing, nudging . . . he's SHOVING him off the road . . . RIGHT IN FRONT OF ME. I can see it all. It's BIG . . . it's disturbing the flow. Cars behind are slowing down, backing off, giving these 2 maniacs plenty of room, and traffic in the north lane is backing up too, the drivers slowing down to eyeball the show, like – *hey! look at THAT! what's going on there? look – look at THAT!*

And this is the TRUTH, don't forget. This is the TRUTH.

The 2 cars bump and grind and skid to a halt about 20 metres from the bridge, both of em arrowed into the dusty gravel of the verge, shining in the dull orange glow of a roadlight. There's dustclouds and tyre-smoke all over the place, and the BMW's half-hidden behind the Range Rover, and everything's weirdly shadowed in the orangey light, but I can see things well enough.

The BMW . . . it's a 328ci. Newish, pale blue, maybe grey. Driver: male, white, wearing a black Nike cap. The Range Rover's a Vogue SE, 4.6, V8. Brand new. Shiny black. All the trimmings. Driver: male, white, wiry black hair, kinda tough-looking. No passengers in either car, not that I can see. (Remember that – NOT THAT I CAN SEE.) OK – so the 2 cars are pulled up at the side of the road, about 20 metres from the bridge, and I'm looking down at em, watching for all I'm worth. The driver of the Range Rover gets out first – gets out, leaves the door open, and marches through the gravel-dust to the BMW, looking mad as hell. He's tall, over 6 foot, wearing a long leather coat and shiny black shoes. The BMW guy gets out to meet him – loose T-shirt and jeans, trainers, gloves, not so tall as the other guy, but wide. Range Rover stops in front of him and starts shouting. The traffic's pretty loud, so I can't hear what he's saying, but I can see his shouting mouth, his bulging eyes, his pointing finger, his clenched fist . . . he ain't happy. The

BMW guy don't say nothing, just stands there looking at him, calm as you like. Range Rover keeps on yelling. The BMW guy looks around, eyeing up the faces in the passing cars, then he glances over his shoulder . . . like he's looking at his car . . . looking FOR something. Range Rover shouts again to get his attention. I still can't hear him too well, but I reckon he's shouting pretty loud – HEY! HEY! *HEY!* Now BMW turns towards him with a weird kinda *half*-smile on his face, like he's got it all worked out, and then he steps up and shoves Range Rover in the chest. Just like that. It ain't much, just a half-hearted shove, like a playground shove, but it takes the Range Rover guy by surprise. He takes half a step back, looking at BMW like he can't believe it – *you shoved me? you SHOVED me?* – and then his anger kicks in, his face gets hard, and he steps up and whacks BMW in the head – *THWACK!* I can't actually *hear* the thwack, but you know what I mean – *THWACK!*

BMW staggers back, holding his hand to his mouth, half bent over, like he's gonna be sick or something. Then – and this is where it starts getting weird – he throws another quick look at his car, wipes some blood from his gob, and jumps at the Range Rover guy. He don't hit him or nothing, just kinda leaps at him and grabs him tight with both arms, like a mental person giving someone a hug. Range Rover squirms and struggles, trying to break free, straining like a madman, but he can't do nothing cos his arms are pinned to his sides . . . but then, all of a sudden, BMW jerks back, doubling over with his hands to his belly, like he's taken a good hard dig in the guts, like Range Rover's busted him one right in the belly . . . and THAT's what's so weird . . . cos Range Rover never touched him. I'm telling you, he NEVER TOUCHED HIM.

Anyway, BMW goes down, clutching his belly and screaming like a pig . . . and then it gets even weirder. Range

Rover's just standing there, right, looking all puzzly-eyed, shaking his head, like he dunno WHAT's going on, just standing there watching BMW writhing around in the dirt, when – lookee here – 3 guys are getting out the BMW. 2 from the back and one from the front. And I'm going – Uh? *UH?* Where'd THEY come from? The one who gets out the front looks like a caveman on drugs – a heavy-headed guy, kinda big and loopy, wearing a baggy white T-shirt and gloves. The other 2, the 2 from the back . . . one's kinda half-bald, wearing a zip-up jacket and gloves, and the other one's BMW's size, wearing a loose T-shirt and jeans . . . the same as BMW . . . and a black Nike cap . . . JUST like BMW . . . UH?? I look at him again. *UH????* I mean, is this confusing or WHAT? Cos now look what's happening. The 2 guys who got out the back of the BMW – Half-Baldy and Twin BMW – they're standing between the 2 cars, so I can't really see what's going on, but it looks like they're struggling or something . . . like Half-Baldy's got a hold of Twin BMW, grabbing his arms and pulling him down, and then the Caveman runs round and joins in the fight . . . and I don't get it. Why're THEY struggling? They're from the SAME car . . . THEY ain't got nothing to fight about.

Then it all gets *REALLY* confusing. The BMW guy, the REAL one, the one who went down without getting hit, he's on his feet again. He's got up off the ground – WITHOUT his Nike cap – and he's getting hold of Range Rover and slamming him up against the car. Range Rover's too shocked to fight back, he dunno WHAT's going on. Then Caveman runs up and joins BMW, so now there's 2 of em holding Range Rover against the car, holding him tight, and then the other one, Half-Baldy, he runs up too, looking over his shoulder, and the 3 of em get Range Rover down on the ground, scuffling and whacking and grabbing and shoving –

and just for a second something glints in the orangey light, something shiny . . . and then I can't see what's going on no more. It's too messy. I can't work it out. They're all down on the ground, a writhing mess of arms and legs . . . and I dunno who's doing what to who . . . or why . . . and I dunno where the other guy's gone, the one who looks like BMW . . . he ain't there . . . where's HE gone?

That's when *I* shoulda gone. Then. Before the cops showed up, before it all went splashy. If I'd left em to it then, just got off the bridge, got on my bike and gone home . . .

Yeh, **now** I know it. But what good's **now** to then? Then was different. Then I was lost in the show of it all, the EXCITEMENT, the DRAMAAH . . . and don't go telling me YOU wouldn't like it – cos we ALL like it. *CRASH BANG BOOF* . . . ELECTRIC in the air . . . sirens . . . *oww-woww-woww-woww-woww* . . .

Oh yeh, and that's another funny thing . . .

The sirens.

This is less then 5 minutes after it happened, right? A couple of minutes after the 2 cars first screwed to a halt in the verge . . . and here's the crash-cops already. How'd they get here so fast? You know what I mean? How'd they KNOW?

Beats me.

Anyway, here they come, screaming up the south lane – a Ford Explorer traffic car and, behind it, one of the new Mitsubishi Evos. Essex cops, I reckon, from Wickham. They pull up where it's all going on, and a bunch of cops in yellow coats get out – 2 from the Explorer and 2 from the Evo. Looking hard and fast. Doing the quick walk. Taking control. One of em moves off to cone the scene, and the other 3 draw their sticks and get over to the guys on the ground. Blue lights are strobing from the cop cars, the flashes mixing with the orange of the roadlights, giving everything this muddy-grey electric look, like pictures in an old magazine. Plus there's fireworks going off in the background, rockets in the sky, headlights and tail-lights trailing the road, like shining bugs, or shooting stars . . .

It's a hell of a thing – and I LIKE it.

It's BEYOND things. It's HOT. It's OUT THERE. It's . . . I dunno . . . it's just a different world, I guess. It's something else.

OK – so I'm still watching, but I dunno what's going on no more. I ain't got a CLUE. The cops are talking to the BMW guys . . . one of em's pointing at something on the ground between the BMW and the Range Rover . . . the Range Rover guy's got over his shock and he's yelling his head off and struggling like mad, trying to take a swing at the Caveman . . . but 2 of the cops have got a hold of him, and the other one's between the 2 cars, looking at what's on the ground down there. He's got his torch out . . . bending down . . . outta sight for a minute or 2 . . . then he's up again, talking on his radio . . . talking and looking around . . . serious as hell.

It goes on like this for a few minutes – all of em milling around, doing their cop stuff, busy busy busy. Lights flashing, faces shouting, bodies scuffling and pushing . . . then the Range Rover guy gets cuffed and shoved in the back of the Explorer, the cop putting his hand on his head, just like they do on TV . . .

Why'd they do that, anyway?

What's the point?

I dunno . . .

But, anyway, there he is, the Range Rover guy, sitting in the back of the Explorer, tight-mouthed, cuffed and angry, and I guess things are starting to calm down a bit now . . . and it's starting to get REALLY cold . . . and I'm kinda thinking of going. I don't really WANNA go, but I'm getting this itchy feeling in my feet, something creeping up on me, a head-whisper – *time to go, Moo, time to go, time to go . . .*

Why?

Cos something's GOING ON, you fat-arsed TWAT.

(Yeh, even my schizo-voice RAINS on me.)

Anyway, I step back from the railings, not sure if I'm stepping back to go, or just – you know – stepping back, and then I step forward again as another siren splits the night. This one's an ambulance. I can tell by the tone. And I says to myself – right, ambulance . . . I'll just wait for that, see what happens, and THEN I'll go.

So I'm looking down, looking out for the ambulance . . . and that's when I feel the eyes on me. You know that feeling? When someone's giving you the stare? I know it . . . GOD, do I *KNOW* it. I know it so well I can feel it when it ain't even there. It's a DIRTY stare – a FAT stare, an UGLY stare, a YOU'RE *DIFFERENT* stare . . . a stare that says – MY *GOD*, LOOK AT THE STATE OF *THAT*. It burns your skin, like a laser. You can FEEL it cutting into you. And you don't WANNA know where it's coming from, but you can't help it, you GOTTA turn to the heat to see what's coming . . . and what's coming this time is one of the cops from the Explorer. The driver, I think. He's standing at the side of the road – radio, coat, blue-flashed yellow – with his laser eyes fixed on me. Looking up, a granite face morphed in the weird mix of lights . . . and, just for a second, I see what he sees. I see a fat kid standing on the bridge. A fat face framed in a hood. Fat head, fat troozies, fat trainers . . . And you know what? He don't look so bad. Not to me, anyway. He's FAT, yeh, but he ain't GRUESOME or nothing. He ain't the

WORST thing I ever seen. But that's to me. To him, to Laser Cop, the fat kid looks like a fly in the oinkment.

Know what I mean?

Yeh, and the thing is, now he's got me in his sights, now he's burning me, I can't see nothing BUT him. And, cos of that, I can't move. All I can do is look. I see him turn around and call out to the other cops. I see em look up at me. I see Laser Cop wave em over to the ambulance as it pulls up (adding more flashing blue to the mix), and then I see him look back at me and raise his hand, palm out, like – STOP, DON'T MOVE, STAY *RIGHT* WHERE YOU ARE. Then he's striding over to the bridge, up the steps on the other side – zig, zag, zig . . . *boing*, *boing*, *boing* – and here he comes, adjusting his hat, looking around, adjusting his eyes to fix on me . . . here he comes, across the bridge . . . across MY bridge . . . *stomp*, *stomp*, *stomp* . . . and I don't LIKE it. It ain't RIGHT. It shoots a spark of ANGER through my head, cos he's INVADING my space. This is *MY* bridge mister – what d'you think you're *DOING*?

The anger lasts all of half a second, snuffed out by FEAR.

'All right, son?' Laser Cop says, still 10 strides away. I watch his eyes flick to the side, looking down at the scene below, then – *stomp*, *stomp*, *stomp* – and he's right in front of me, doing his cop thing – head up, eyes down, flexing his neck. 'All right?' he says again.

I nod.

He looks around. 'What you doing up here?'

'Nothing.'

'Going somewhere?'

'Not really.'

He gives me a look – come *on* . . .

'Just hanging around,' I tell him. 'You know . . .'

'You live round here?'

'In the village.'

'Where's that?'

I flick a thumb over my shoulder. 'Back there – down the lane. About half a mile.'

He gazes off into the darkness, nodding his head, like he UNDERSTANDS what I'm saying. He rubs his chin, looks at me, then looks down at the cars and cops and flashing lights below, where 2 paramedics are carrying an empty stretcher back to the ambulance.

He says, 'You see what happened here?'

'Yeh.'

'All of it?'

'Yeh – they was coming up over the hill—'

'Hold on . . .' He pulls a notebook from his pocket. 'I'm gonna need some details first . . . you OK?'

'Yeh.'

'You wanna sit down or anything?'

'I'm all right.'

'Sure?'

'Uh huh.'

'OK . . . just a second.' He flaps through his notebook and finds a fresh page. 'Right – what's your name, son?'

'Moo Nelson.'

'Moo?'

'Mike . . . Michael Nelson.'

'What's this *Moo*?'

'Nothing – it's just what they call me . . . you know – fat, cow, moo . . .'

He shakes his head, giving me a crumb of PITY . . . yeh, like *he* cares.

'Address?' he says.

I tell him.

He writes it down.

'Phone?'

Ditto.

'How old are you, Mike?'

'15.'

'You live with your parents?'

'Yeh.'

'They at home now?'

'Yeh.'

'They gonna be in tomorrow?'

'Probly.'

'OK,' he says, folding his notebook away and looking down at the road. 'Look, I gotta get back to it now, but we're gonna need a statement, find out what you saw, what happened and everything. D'you understand?'

Duh, I think.

'Yeh,' I say.

'We'll get someone round to see you as soon as possible. If not tonight, probly tomorrow. All right?'

'I got school tomorrow—'

'What time d'you get back?'

'About 4.'

'OK,' he says. 'You're gonna need your mum or dad with you when we take your statement. Is that gonna be all right?'

'I spose . . .'

'Good.' He looks off into the darkness and rubs his chin again, like he's thinking, or he wants me to *think* he's thinking . . . I dunno. I don't really care. I just stand there looking at him. He's tallish, kinda ruggedy-looking, a bit like what's-his-name from *Emmerdale*. Or the one who used to be in *Heartbeat* . . . you know, the guy who used to be in something else? Like him, but a bit older . . . but not much older . . . I mean, Laser Cop ain't ancient or nothing, he's just kinda ruggedy-looking. Ruggedy skin, flat grey eyes, a slitty little scar on the side of his nose . . .

'You see anyone else?' he says.

'What?'

'You see anyone else?'

'Who?'

'Anyone. Was there anyone else around who might have seen what happened?'

'I dunno,' I shrug. 'People in cars . . . there was a lotta cars went past.'

'I mean here. On the bridge.'

'No.'

'What about the road, down there, the fields . . .?'

'I don't think so.'

'Sure?'

'I din't see no one.'

His radio crackles. He snatches it up, spouts some cop talk – *alfie bravo coca cola* . . . then turns his back on me and looks down at the road. 'Yeh,' I hear him say, 'yeh, yeh . . . a kid . . . right . . . yeh . . .'

Yeh yeh yeh.

The ambulance is moving off now, nice and quiet, no siren, and another cop car's pulling up at the side of the road. This one's an unmarked Rover 600. Maroon. Driver: male, white, T-shirt, jacket. Passenger: male, white, waxy coat. He's the boss, the waxy coat guy. When he gets out the car, everyone watches him. I watch him. He walks over to where the other cops are standing, the spot where something's on the ground. He looks at the ground. Asks questions. Looks around. Points at the BMW, then the Range Rover . . .

People Watching You + Questions + Plenty Of Pointing = BOSS.

Beneath the bridge, the river's starting to flow again. It ain't too disturbed. The north lane's pretty much the same as usual, maybe a bit slower with all the flashing lights and everything. Traffic in the south lane's edging slowly round the cones, drivers rubber-necking, seeing what they can, looking out for blood and bones and bits of bodies, then speeding up and streaming off under the bridge and on towards Moulton. I guess they'll have something to talk about when they get home tonight.

'OK, Michael,' Laser Cop says, turning back to me and slotting the radio into his collar. 'How you getting home? You need a lift or anything?'

'Bike,' I tell him, pointing it out.

'Right. Well, off you go then. We'll be in touch.'

I don't move.

He stares at me. 'What?'

'Nothing.'

'Well, like I said, we'll be in touch.'

'OK.'

And that's it. No *thanks*, no *mind how you go*s, no explanations, no nothing. I turn around and start walking, thinking to myself – right, it's gonna be like THAT is it? *We'll be in touch*, he says, *we'll be in touch* . . . dumb-arse din't even check my address. What if I made it up? He wouldn't be so cocky then, would he? Nah . . . he ain't gonna be so cocky tomorrow when the boss man gives him a bolloxing for not checking the witness's address . . . you know, like in a TV cop show when the big fat Chief Super calls in the renegade cop and balls him out for messing up – WHAT'S THE *MATTER* WITH YOU, LASER COP? YOU DIN'T CHECK THE WITNESS'S *ADDRESS*? HOW WE GONNA GET A STATEMENT NOW? EH? GOD*DAM* IT, MAN, YOU'RE OFF THE CASE. GIMME YOUR BADGE AND GET OUTTA HERE . . .

Heh heh heh . . .

It takes me a couple of minutes to realise I DIN'T give Laser Cop a false address . . . so he AIN'T gonna get blasted by his boss . . . so it AIN'T funny after all . . . it's just embarrassing.

Back home, Mum and Dad are sitting in the front room eating toasted sandwiches and watching *Crimestoppers* on TV. There's a reconstructed raid going down in a High Street jeweller's. Bad actors looking shifty . . . a photofit . . . a quick picture of some necklaces on a tray . . . then a skinny woman talking to the camera, trying to make out like she really cares . . .

'Hey, guess what?' I say. 'There was a fight on the road tonight, a road rage thing—'

'That's nice,' says Mum, wiping crumbs from her mouth, staring at another photofit on the TV. 'God, look at *him*. Look at his *eyes*—'

'No, listen . . . Mum?'

'Hmmm?' *Chomp, chomp, chomp* . . .

'I *saw* it. I was *there*. I saw the whole thing.'

'What's that, love?'

'On the *bridge*. The police were there. Police, ambulance, everything . . . these 2 cars, right, a BMW and a Range Rover, they was doing about *130* . . . at *least* . . . it was like in a film, a car chase—'

'Police?' coughs Dad.

'Yeh, all over the place. Traffic cops, CID . . . they talked to me.'

'Who?'

'The cops.'

'When?'

'Tonight. I was on the bridge—'

'What they want?'

'Who?'

'The *cops*.'

'A statement . . . I saw what happened.'

'When?'

'To*night*. I was on the bridge . . .'

I sit down and start all over again, going over what happened bit by bit – the cars, the guys, the fight, the police, then Laser Cop coming up to me, talking to me, asking for my name and address and stuff . . .

When I get to the bit about the cops coming round to take a statement, Dad groans.

'What?' I says.

'Come on, Moo,' he sighs. 'How many times I told you not to get involved?'

'Yeh, but—'

'There's no yehbuts about it. I told you before – keep your nose out and your mouth shut.'

'But he asked me, Dad. He *asked* me . . .'

'So?'

'I couldn't *lie*, could I?'

'Why not? You think it's gonna make any difference? The only *difference* it's gonna make is a bunch of coppers coming round here asking questions.'

'What?'

'You know what I mean. Look – it ain't lying, anyway. Not LYING lying. You ain't saying this or that did or din't happen, you're just saying you din't see nothing. That's all you gotta do. You din't see nothing. You dunno nothing. All right?'

'Yeh,' I mumble. 'Sorry.'

He sighs again, then looks at me and smiles. 'Ah, it's all right . . . don't worry about it. They probly won't bother coming round anyway. What time'd they say?'

'I dunno . . . tonight or tomorrow some time, probly after school.'

He looks at his watch. It's nearly 7.30. *Crimestoppers* is just finishing – *duhh, duhhh, duhhhhhh . . . DUHH-DUH-DUH . . .*

Dad starts flicking through the channels to see what else is on.

'What should I do?' I ask him.

'Uh?' *Click, click, click . . .*

'About the cops . . . you know, the statement. If they *do* come round – what should I tell em?'

He shrugs. 'The truth, I spose. It's too late for anything else – you might as well tell em the truth.'

The night goes on – sandwiches, *Coronation Street*, Pop Tarts, *EastEnders*, hot chocolate, a lawyer thing on ITV, one of them boring thrillers with that Irish woman who used to be the woman who cut up dead bodies for the cops . . . and I dunno what I'm sposed to be DOING. I dunno if I'm waiting for the cops to come round or not. Laser Cop said they'd get someone round as soon as possible, if not tonight, *probly* tomorrow . . . but what's that sposed to mean? How probly is probly? *Very* probly? *Quite* probly? D'you know what I mean? And what they gonna do? They gonna let me know if they're coming or not? They gonna ring me or something? Or've I just gotta wait?

I dunno . . .

So I just sit there, eating and drinking and watching TV, not knowing if I'm waiting or not . . . then it gets to about 10 o'clock and Dad turns over for *Death Wish V* on Channel 5, which is all right, but I already seen it on ITV about 2 weeks ago, and I'm getting kinda tired anyway . . . so I get myself a glass of milk, say goodnight, and go to bed.

And that's it – 7 months ago – that's the start of it. Another Day on the bridge . . . just another Day . . . the start of the TRUTH.

That's it . . .

Or is it?

Cos **now** I'm starting to think about it . . .

I dunno.

Maybe I'm wrong?

Maybe that AIN'T the start of it, after all . . .

2/ The TRUTH of the Start

Maybe the REAL start of it is 5 years ago, when we first moved out here from our old place. 5 years ago . . . GOD. I musta been about 9 or 10 at the time . . . getting on for 11 . . . I dunno. It's kinda hard to remember that far back. I don't mean it's HARD hard, you know, like when old people can't remember stuff cos their brains is all shrivelled up, I just mean it's hard to remember cos I don't WANNA remember . . . cos remembering them Days makes me kinda sad. Cos it was all right back then – the old place was all right. It was a PROPER place, you know? Not some piddly little village in the middle of nowhere. It was a TOWN, with places to go and things to do – Burger Kings, train stations, bus stations . . . stuff like that. Yeh, all right, so maybe it was a bit dirty, a bit rough – but at least it wasn't DEAD. It was OK. And I was OK, too. Yeh . . . I was OK back then. I wasn't SKINNY or nothing – I ain't NEVER been skinny – but I wasn't no 17-stone FAT kid. And I wasn't Moo, neither – I was Mike. Mike Nelson. And Mike din't get RAINed on all the time, Mike din't get stared at and beat up and laughed at . . . yeh, I LIKED being Mike. Being Mike was all right. I ain't saying it was PEACHY or nothing . . . but it was all right.

Then stuff happened.

1) Dad got done for fiddling the benefit.

2) We owed on the rent.

3) Mum got itchy feet.

4) Little Mike got a bad throat.

Time to go.

It was raining the Day we moved, rainy and cold. We'd been up half the night, packing our stuff into crates and boxes, and it was still early morning when we left . . . 5 o'clock, 6 o'clock . . . something like that. It was still dark. The van was a borrowed Talbot Luton with a tail lift, and it din't have no heating. It was REALLY cold. Which is kinda funny, cos I was hotter than HELL, cos of my throat . . . I was burning up with a fever, all sweaty and buzzy and bug-eyed, my neck puffed up like a red balloon. I was probly crying, too, moaning and crying . . .

'It hurts, Mum . . . it *hurts*.'

'I know, love. I'm sorry – but we can't stop now. You'll be all right. It's just a virus or something. We'll see the doctor when we get there.'

Yeh, when we get there.

When we get there . . .

When we get there . . .

I guess I musta drifted off soon after we left. Zonked out – *zzzzzzzzzzzzzzzz* – fever-dreaming to the sound of the rain on the roof, the furniture rattling and clonking in the back of the van, the wipers clacking, the tyres zooshing on the miles and miles of wet road. I din't know how far it was – 50, 60, 70 miles – or the names of places we went through – Thingford, Thingdon, Thingwood . . . I knew Moulton, where we stopped for petrol and crisps ('I can't eat *crisps*! My *throat* hurts. I need *jelly* or *ice-cream* or something . . .'), but we din't stop for long. Petrol, crisps, a coke and a wee, and then we're off again – rain, rattle, clack, zoosh . . . *zzzzzzzzzzzzzzzz* . . . driving sounds, dreaming sounds, the wordless sound of Mum and Dad talking . . . *nuh nuh nuh n-huhn nuh nuh* . . . you know, that sound you heard SO many times it don't mean nothing? And then, some time later, the van slowed and the furniture clonked, waking me up to a raging throat and a hole in a hedge and a crabby white signpost.

'Here we go,' says Dad. 'This is it.'

I'm looking out the window, still half-asleep, half-thinking – This? *This is it?* This is *WHAT*? There ain't nothing *HERE* . . .

I'm too sick to speak.

'Looks nice,' Mum says doubtfully. 'Nice and quiet.'

Quiet? This ain't quiet, this is *DEAD*. This is decom*POS*-ing.

The village is flat and grey and pocked with squatty little houses and scrawny little roads that don't go nowhere. There's a few little shops, an offy, a couple of pubs, a petrol station, a flat grey school, houses, bits and pieces . . . and over there, hanging at the bus stop, a bunch of leery-looking tough kids spitting through their teeth and giving us the welcome stare, like – *Yeh? What you looking at, fresh-meat? You want it?*

Great.

The van rumbles on through the village and along a potholed track, and I look around at broken barns in scrubby fields and bare trees blurred in a crystal wind, and all of it moves against a black-and-white sky . . . an UNKNOWN sky . . . a sky that ain't MINE . . .

GOD, my throat is THROBBING.

Through the village, around the houses, along a track, then down along a high-banked lane that opens out into a stumpy little street with a row of terraced houses on either side. 6 houses, 6 houses, 12 houses – all grey and grubby, apart from one, which is *green* and grubby.

Now Mum brightens up, cos green's her favourite colour.

'Is that it?' she goes. 'The little green one?'

Dad grins. 'That's it.'

And it was.

That WAS it.

Cos it was around then I started getting fat. I dunno WHY . . . it coulda been anything, I spose. All the ice-cream and stuff they gave me after they took my tonsils out . . . the STRAIN of moving and starting a new school . . . new things . . . things I din't want . . . nothing to do, nowhere to go . . . nothing to do but EAT EAT EAT . . . I dunno. I'm probly just making excuses. I probly started getting FAT cos I'm a FAT greedy bastad. I mean, I LIKE eating, OK? It makes me feel GOOD. Is that so bad? I mean, *you* wanna FEEL GOOD, don't you? We all wanna feel good. The trouble is – you feel good, you feel bad . . . good, bad . . . good, bad . . .

My trouble is – I can't stop eating.

MY trouble is . . .

Apart from all the *MOO*s and the *JABBA-THE-HUT*s and the *ENORMOUS-MILLION-POUND-TUB-OF-LARD*s – and a thousand other bits of RAIN, which I might or might not tell you about later – MY trouble really hit home for the first time when I was around 12 or 13 years old. It was at school, at dinnertime . . . some girls were talking about me in the playground. There was 3 of em, just sitting around yakking, like they do . . . you know, picking on people, tearing em apart . . . that kinda thing. They din't know I was listening.

One of em goes, 'What d'you rather do? Kiss Moo or eat dog poo?'

Another one says, 'Yeh – kiss Moo or die?'

And the third one goes, 'I'd kill him, then I wouldn't have to do neither.'

YA YA YA YA YA YA YA YA YA YA . . .

After that – which, by the way, girls, I'm thinking about right

now – after that . . . I dunno . . . that's when things started happening, I spose. I musta been fat all along, I guess, or getting fat, I just never noticed. The fat stuff – the RAIN, the poking and joking . . . that's all I thought it was – joking. You know . . . like mates, messing around, having a LAARRF . . .

I din't get it. The sound of it – *YA YA YA* – I din't hear it right. I heard it *HA HA HA* . . . like a FUNNY sound . . . but it ain't got no FUNNY in it. Not one bit. Never did. Never never never never NEVER . . . nah, I just din't GET IT. And that's something else . . . realising how DUMB you are . . . you just wanna crawl into a hole and DIE.

Once I got it, though, I REALLY got it. Cos when it hurts, it works – you know what I'm saying? When it works you can't go back, you can't get it back, it's gone. YOU, I mean. You ain't YOU no more – you're just THE FAT KID. FAT FAT FAT . . . that's ALL you are. You're gone to the RAIN for ever . . .

Get it?

Gone.

Yeh, so maybe THAT's when it REALLY started – 5 years ago, when we first got here . . . or the time in the playground with the girls . . . or maybe just afterwards . . . I dunno. I don't spose it matters, really. I mean, it started some time, somewhere . . . what difference does it make? I ain't got time to tell it ALL, anyway. So maybe it's best if I just stick to the other start, the one I started with, 7 months ago, when every Day's the same . . .

3/ The RAIN

OK – so it's 8 o'clock Twoday morning, the Day after the Day it happened, and I'm doing the same old morning stuff – getting up, going to the bathroom, getting dressed, going downstairs – and everything's pretty much the same as it always is. The kitchen's hot, sizzling with the smell of bacon-smoke and eggs . . . Dad's at the table in his XXXL Homer T-shirt, trying to fix the knob on the radio . . . and Mum's wiping cooker-sweat from her face.

'Hey, Moo,' she goes. 'You all right?'

'Yeh.'

'Breakfast's nearly ready – how many you want?'

'How many what?'

'Bacon.'

'4.'

'4?'

'All right, 5.'

Bacon, eggs, fried bread, a bit more bacon – NOSH NOSH NOSH – get it all down . . . then a big mug of tea, then back upstairs to the bathroom . . . and all the time I'm WISHing the cops'd turn up to take my statement *now*, cos then I'd get to stay off school – WISH WISH WISH – but I KNOW it ain't gonna happen. I KNOW the cops ain't coming round till tonight. I can feel it inside me. I can SMELL it – I got a hard-luck stomach. So I sit down and sort that out, which takes up a few more minutes, then I waste some more time spraying myself with anti-sweat stuff, coughing on the fumes . . . wiping my face . . . washing my hands . . . drying my face . . . drying my hands . . .

And then it's time – I can't put it off no more.

I gotta go to school.

I gotta face it.

I gotta leave the house and walk the lane, I gotta walk on through the funny RAIN – *HEY MOO! LOOKING SLIM TODAY! SHAKE IT, FAT BOY! WHOO-HOO! HERE COMES THE FATSTUFF!* It's the same every Day. The RAIN of words, the boys on bikes spitting their spite, the PITY looks from parents in cars, the girls in short skirts with *their* spite and *their* PITY . . . GOD . . . I dunno what's worse – the spite or the PITY. Spite ain't NICE . . . GOD no. It sticks a rusty knife in your guts and jabs so hard you wanna SCREAM . . . but at least it's just a one-off kinda thing, done and forgotten . . . well, it's *sorta* one-off, anyway . . . one-off in an over-and-over-again kinda way . . . so it ain't never *really* done . . . and it ain't never *really* forgotten, neither. In fact, it ain't NEVER forgotten at all . . . but what I mean is, spite-wise, it's the kinda thing that don't hang around too much when it ain't actually there. PITY, though . . . PITY lingers, like a bad smell. It hangs around in your head making you feel dirty and bad all Day, cos there's a bit of you that WANTS it, a bit of you that tries to kid the other bit that the PITY looks are TRUE. But the other bit knows they ain't. The other bit knows you DON'T want it like that, cos when it's like that you ain't nothing but a sick dumb animal.

But what you gonna do?

I'll tell you what you do – you do what you do. You walk through it all with your eyes down. Umbrellarise it. It's the only way. What else is there? Go BLUBBING to someone? Be PROUD? STAND-UP-AND-FIGHT? Don't make me laugh. That kinda stuff don't work. Ain't NONE of it works.

Mum told me once – 'If you don't get upset when they make fun of you, they'll stop' – but that was 3 years ago, and I'm STILL waiting for em to stop. I mean, I got patience, but 3 years waiting for something that ain't gonna happen? That ain't *patience*, that's world-record STUPID.

So now, today, what I do – I live in my head. I umbrellarise em. It's the only way. Down the lane, through the grey of the village, through the funny RAIN – *MOOO-OOOVE OVER GIRLS, CHUNKOSAURUS IS COMING! HEY HEY VANESSAAAH!!! DONG! DONG! DONG! IT'S THE EARTHQUAKE BOY!!!* – yeh, yeh, yeh, umbrellarising all the way . . .

It's the ONLY way.

Then I get to school, and I get some more, and the Day goes on. Maths, Engerlish, break, Snickers, Biology, sex, sniggers . . . dinnertime – mash, beans, some kinda pork, fruity pie and custard for afters. Pile it on. Pile it up. Pile it in. There's 4 long tables down the middle of the dinner-room, and some smaller ones round the edge, and that's where I sit – on the edge . . . on my own . . . getting WATCHED all the time. I ain't gotta SEE em to know they're watching me – big kids, little kids, girls giggling to their boyfriends – *lookatimdarren . . . lookattheSIZEofim* – staring and giggling and whispering so loud they might as well SHOUT – nah, I ain't gotta see em. I can FEEL em. But what do I care, eh? What do I care? Let em stare. LOOK AT ME. I'M FAT, OK? I EAT A LOT. I *LIKE* FOOD. IT TASTES GOOD! Yeh, all right, so I'm just gonna get more fat . . . so what? Who cares? Fat's fat. What's it to you? What you gonna do? KILL ME?

Anyway, the Day goes on – French, Physics, break, Twix, Maths again . . . and the afternoon dims, the light starts to die, and pretty soon it's time to go home. Time to raise the umbrella again, but this time I'm smiling inside cos it's nearly time for the bridge. It won't be long now, I'll get to it soon. Soon soon soon . . .

But then I remember the cops.

Shit. The cops are coming round tonight . . . I probly won't even GET to the bridge.

So then I'm walking back through the village WITHOUT a smile inside, keeping my head down but my RADAR turned on, and I'm half-looking out for Brady . . . not that I really WANNA see him, but – there he is, look, crouched at the bus stop getting gobbed on by a dog-eyed lump called Bowker . . . Dec Bowker and the boys . . . the monkeys in boots. They're always around, always taking it out on someone, Brady or me, me or Brady . . . and he's taking it hard today, his starry eyes lit in the scream of a rocket flash – oh yeh, the firework stuff's really happening now. We got air bombs going off all over the place, whizzes and booms, kids with bangers . . . which is tough times for kids like Brady and me, cos DWARFY and FAT's good targets – WHIZZ BOOM *BANG!!!* . . . GOT IM *RIGHT* UP THE ARSE AAAHHH AH AH AH!! – too good to miss. Anyway, Brady's there, getting it good – *whack whack whack* on the arm, knee in the thigh . . . and it GETS me a bit, you know, it GETS me . . . cos he looks so small and PATHETIC, crouched down on the ground, all curled up and stumpy, like some kinda 15-year-old embryo or something . . .

But what can I do?

I can't help it – I just do what I do. I don't do NOTHING. I just leave em to it and walk on by. It's all right. I mean, I ain't WORRIED about it. I ain't ASHAMED or nothing. Why should I be? What for? What's it to me? Brady's all right. He can take it, he knows how it goes – dead leg, flobby hair, smack in the face if he's gobby . . .

Better him than me.
Better him than me.
Better him than me.
Better him than me.
That's the way it goes.
See you later, Brady.
I'm going home.

Home – my house. HERE. I'd draw it for you if I wasn't so bad at drawing. What I'd draw – like a square with a triangle on top – you'd think I was backward, like I got bits of dee-en-ay missing or twisted genes or something. And that'd be WHOLLY unfair. So I'll just tell you. Not that there's much to tell. It's a house – number 4. It's got a kitchen, a front room, 2 bedrooms, a bathroom, a garden out back, and a shed. OK? It's a house.

So I get home to my HOUSE and put the umbrella away for the night and go upstairs to pee and get changed. Same old clothes – big check shirt, big hoody hood, big baggy troozies . . . and when I'm all togged up, when I got myself looking OK, then it's that time again . . . a DIFFERENT time this time. This time it's time for my moment, my small reward, my time to take a good long look at myself and say – *OK . . . you made it, Moo. You got through another Day. You made it . . .*

It ain't much.
But it's something.
D'you know what I mean?
It's something . . .

I mean, don't get me wrong, it ain't got nothing to do with feeling sorry for myself or nothing . . . not that I don't feel sorry for myself, cos sometimes I do, same as everyone else.

Which is all right, cos there ain't nothing wrong with feeling sorry for yourself, is there? As long as it's REAL, and you don't make a BIG DEAL of it, what's the problem? It ain't like you're ASKING no one for nothing, is it? You ain't BOTHERING no one. Like with this, for instance – whatever *this* is – I mean, I ain't asking you to feel sorry for me, I ain't looking for PITY or nothing, all I'm doing is showing you the RAIN, letting you feel what it's like, cos you gotta feel stuff to understand it, don't you? So, if I'm gonna be telling you stuff about ME – which it looks like I am – then you gotta feel what it's like to be ME, else you won't understand it. And I know that probly ain't nice – feeling like ME. I mean, if *I* was you, *I* wouldn't wanna feel like ME . . . GOD no, not in a thousand years. But that's by the by, cos I *ain't* you, and, besides, I already know what it feels like to be ME. Crap is what it feels like. RAINY WET DIRTY COLD CRAP. Like when you wake up every morning wishing things was different, wishing you was someone else, wishing you din't have to go to school, wishing you din't even EXIST, and all the time you know you're wishing for stuff you ain't gonna get . . .

It does your head in.

But, like I said, I don't wanna make a BIG DEAL of it, cos I KNOW it ain't nothing to moan about really. Not REALLY. I mean, it ain't like I'm getting tortured every Day, is it? I ain't getting shot or stabbed or burned alive or nothing, and I know there's loads of people got it a million times worse than me, like disableds and people with diseases and stuff . . .

I KNOW that.

I KNOW I got it all right, really.

It's just . . .

It's just CRAP, that's all.

Getting RAINed on ALL the time, Day after Day after Day after Day . . .

IT MAKES YOU FEEL SO CRAP.

Downstairs, the kitchen's thick with the smell of hot pastry and meat. It's just gone 4.30. Dad's still sitting at the table, still trying to fix the knob on the radio, and Mum's wiping oven-sweat and flour from her face.

'Hey, Moo,' she goes. 'How's school?'

'All right.'

'Any trouble?'

'Nah . . .'

'Good. Tea's nearly ready – how many you want?'

'How many what?'

'Pies.'

'What size?'

'Pie-size.'

Dad laughs.

Mum looks over her shoulder and smiles at him. 'You like that one?'

'Yeh,' he says. 'Huh-yeh . . . uh-huh huh huh . . .' His laugh turns into a hacking cough and his face turns red. After a bit more coughing, he puts down the radio, wipes the radio-dust from his hands, and wipes his mouth.

'You all right?' I ask him.

'Yeh – just a tickle.' He clears his throat and slaps his belly. 'You hungry?'

'Yeh.'

'OK . . . let's eat.'

He turns on the TV and we eat to the sound of coughing and *Countdown*.

4/ The Wiggies

Later on that night, when the cops come round, Dad's *conveniently* disappeared. I dunno where he's gone – probly the allotment, which is where he goes when he wants to be somewhere else, if you know what I mean. It's HIS PLACE. It ain't for growing stuff or nothing, he ain't got no veggies or flowers up there, it's just a pile of weeds and sticks and a padlocked shed. It's one of them cronky old sheds, the kind that's held together with bits of old board and sheets of plastic, but he's got it fixed up nice and cosy inside – deckchair, radio, beer, dust and wood, cobwebs, tins, boxes, stuff hanging on the walls . . . it's a pretty good place.

Anyway, that's probly where he is when the cops come round.

Ding dong.

Mum's in the kitchen doing some vollervons, so I get the door. There's 2 of em – a guy in jeans and a fleece, and a black lady standing behind him. The guy waves a wallet at me.

'DS Bowker and DC Dorudi,' he says. 'Moulton CID. About the incident last night?'

I dunno if that's a question or not, so I just says, 'Right.'

He says, 'You're Michael Nelson?'

'Yeh.'

'Can we come in?'

'OK.'

He breezes past me into the hall, and the black lady

follows him. She's OK – she gives me a non-fat smile (I can tell), but Bowker's got these big starey monkey eyes that gimme the creeps. Plus he's wearing aftershave – a spiky smell of glass and chemicals that reminds me of sick. When he goes along the hallway it's like I can SEE this cloud of pong surrounding his body, like a giant see-through teardrop.

'Which way?' the lady-cop asks.

I take em into the front room.

There's a few things bothering me already. Like, how come they're from Moulton and not Wickham? Wickham's closer. Not much, I spose . . . and I don't spose it makes much difference. And . . . what else? Oh yeh, Bowker's jeans – they're them pre-dirtied ones, you know? All mucky and faded like you been working on a building site for 3 weeks without getting changed . . . you BUY em like that. Which I guess is OK if you're like 16 or something, but this guy's about 40, 45 . . . you know what I'm saying? He's OLD. What's he doing wearing dirty jeans? And another thing . . . his name – Bowker. That's kinda odd, ain't it? DS Bowker . . . Dec Bowker . . . what's THAT all about? Nothing, probly. I mean, there's plenty of Bowkers live around here, it's some kinda local thing, so it *probly* don't mean nothing, but still . . .

He says, 'Your mum and dad around, Michael?'

'Mum!' I shout. '*MUM!*'

The lady-cop – DC Dorudi – she's looking round the room, taking a folder out of a briefcase, still smiling, a bit fidgety, like you're sposed to be when you're in someone else's house. But Bowker don't care. He just unzips his fleece and plonks himself down in Dad's chair like he owns the place. I give him a quick look. His hair's kinda thin on top, and he's got this wispy little curl half-sticking up at the front, like a hairy horn.

Mum comes in wiping her floury hands on a tea-towel. DC Dorudi goes up and shakes her hand.

'Mrs Nelson?' she says. 'I'm DC Dorudi and this is my colleague DS Bowker. We're here to take a statement from Michael about what happened yesterday evening. Has he told you about it?'

Mum nods, looking at Bowker.

'You're Declan's dad,' she says.

He smiles. 'That's right.'

Yeh . . . I shoulda known. The shape of his head, the eyes, the way he walks . . . JUST like Dec Bowker. Shit. He's Dec Bowker's dad. The lump's dad. The gobber's dad. The dead-legger's dad . . .

He's looking at me now. 'You know Declan from school?'

'Yeh . . . well, not really . . . he's in the year above me . . .'

Bowker goes, 'Hmm, yeh . . . he would be,' and I look at him, wondering if he KNOWS. D'you KNOW what your son's like? D'you KNOW what he does? D'you KNOW how he gets his FUN?

DC Dorudi has sat down now. She's perched on the edge of the settee with her briefcase on her knees, looking at me. There's some bits of paper resting on the briefcase. She's clicking a biro. She's wearing a narrow skirt, a black jacket, a slinky top, and tights. Her hair's nice and shiny and tied in a ponytail.

'OK, then, Michael,' she says. 'If we could start with yesterday evening . . .'

The whole thing takes *AGES*. First I gotta tell em what happened – what time it was, what I was doing, where I was standing, what I saw . . . the whole thing, basically. While I'm telling em everything, they just sit there listening and nodding, going – *right, right, yeh, right* . . . which is OK. I mean, telling what happened ain't exactly DIFFICULT. It's just like telling a story . . . a pretty *boring* story – *I came home from school. I had my tea. I got on my bike. I went to the bridge. Dah dah dah. Dah dah dah* . . .

After about 5 minutes of this, Mum slopes off to check on her vollervons.

'Back in a minute,' she says.

But she ain't back in a minute, she's back in about half an hour. Which I ain't too pleased about at first, but when she comes back she's got a tray full of tea and chocolate mini-rolls . . . so I let her off. She pours the tea, hands round the mini-rolls, then scarpers back to the kitchen again. Bowker and Dorudi eat ONE mini-roll each, like they're trying to be POLITE, which leaves 5 for me . . . which ain't really a lot, cos they're pretty small . . . but I KNOW the kinda looks I'm gonna get if I scoff the whole lot . . . so I just eat 2 . . . all right 3. And then I get back to the story – *I saw the cars. The Range Rover did this. The BMW did that. The driver got out. Dah dah dah. Dah dah dah* . . .

Like I said, it's a piece of cake. But then it gets to the bit when all the scuffling was going on, when all the guys got out the cars . . . and it ain't so *dah dah dah* no more. It ain't *dah dah dah* at all. It's REALLY hard to explain. I keep getting lost. And Bowker keeps stopping me, making me go back over things.

'OK,' he says. 'So when you first saw the cars, you din't see these other men? The ones in the BMW.'

'Yeh . . . I mean, no. They musta been hiding in the back or something.'

'In the back of the BMW?'

'Yeh.'

'What about the Range Rover?'

'What about it?'

'Was there anyone hiding in the back of the Range Rover?'

'I don't think so.'

'Just the BMW?'

'Yeh.'

'OK – then what?'

'They get out the car—'

'No,' he says. 'Before that – the other 2. The fight.'

I tell him about the fight, how Range Rover whacked BMW, then that odd bit when BMW went down without getting hit.

'What d'you mean – he *din't* get hit?' says Bowker, leaning forward.

'He din't get hit – the Range Rover guy never touched him.'

'Are you sure?'

'Yeh, definite. He never touched him. Not the second time.'

'You're absolutely *certain* about that?'

'150%,' I says.

Bowker looks at Dorudi. She raises her eyebrows, like – well, well, well. Bowker nods, looking pleased with himself, then looks at me.

'What'd they look like?'

'Who?'

'The men in the cars – whoever you saw. What'd they look like?'

So I *describe* em. 1) Male, white, wiry black hair, tough-looking, tall, leather coat, shiny shoes. 2) Male, white, wide, Nike cap, T-shirt, jeans, trainers. 3) Caveman on drugs. 4) Half-Baldy, zip-up jacket. 5) Twin BMW, T-shirt, jeans, Nike cap . . .

'Hold on,' says Dorudi. 'Which one had the cap?'

'They both did.'

'Who?'

'The BMW driver and one of the guys in the back. The one who looked like the driver. But later on . . . the driver *din't* have a hat.'

'When?'

'After it happened.'

'After *what* happened?'

After the *confusing* stuff happened . . .

I'm getting fed up with it now. It's getting too hard – trying to REMEMBER everything . . . trying to see it all in my mind – it's all getting blurred. Flashing lights, fireworks, cars, hats, people, fights . . . who's who, who's where, what's this, when's that . . . it's getting me all mixed up. And I can't stop thinking about what Dad said. Not so much the stuff about lying and keeping your mouth shut – although I'm thinking about that too – but more the other stuff, when he said – *It's too late for anything else – you might as well tell em the truth.* I dunno why I keep thinking about that . . . it don't MEAN nothing . . . but I just keep thinking about it – *you might as well tell em the truth . . . you might as well tell em . . . you might as well . . .*

I dunno.

Anyway, I get there in the end. I tell em what happened. Start to finish. I tell em the TRUTH. And you know what? It feels OK. Like it's the RIGHT thing to do . . . like I'm being really HELPFUL. I'm being USEFUL. It's a GOOD feeling.

But then, just as I'm starting to feel OK again, after *not* feeling OK for a while, old Bowker goes, 'Did you see the body?'

Body? BODY? *BODY? What* body?

'Michael?'

'Uh?'

'Did you see the body?'

'What body?'

He glances at Dorudi. She glances back at him, then turns to me, all *carey* and soft.

'A man was stabbed,' she says. 'One of the men from the BMW.'

'Which one? Who did it?'

'That's what we're trying to find out,' Bowker says.

'I din't see no one get *stabbed*.'

Bowker gives me a long hard look, then he gets up and walks over to the window and stands there with his hands in his pockets peering out at the street, like he's thinking really hard about something. I'm thinking pretty hard myself, thinking about this body (what body?) . . . this guy who got stabbed (what guy?) . . . and suddenly my brain goes *CLICK*, and I'm thinking – oh yeh, the thing on the ground, after the scuffle, the thing the cops were looking at . . .

Oh *yeh* . . .

'The man in the Range Rover,' Bowker says, turning from the window. 'When he hit the other one in the stomach—'

'No, I told you – he *din't* hit him.'

'Did he have a weapon or anything?'

'No, nothing . . .' – then my brain goes *CLICK* again – '. . . no, hold on . . . yeh, there *was* something. Yeh, I remember now . . .' (*something glinting in the orangey light, something shiny* . . .) '. . . one of the others had something . . . the baldy one, I think. Yeh . . . after he got out the car and the other one in the hat disappeared . . . when he run up to the Caveman and Range Rover . . . he had something shiny in his hand—'

'A knife?'

'I think so . . .'

'You sure?'

'I *think* so . . .'

This goes on for another half hour or so – over and over and over again – till I dunno what I'm saying no more. My brain's had enough. Bowker keeps asking me the same old stuff . . . I keep scratching my head . . . getting more and more confused . . . then after a while Bowker decides to give it a rest and he goes upstairs for a pee, leaving me on my own with DC Dorudi.

After all the talking we been doing, the room's TOO quiet now. I mean, it's REALLY quiet, like someone's just died or something. I look at DC Dorudi, looking for sympathy, I guess, or maybe just cos I dunno what else to do. But she don't look back at me. All she does is sit there, nice and cool, reading her notes.

I look away, looking at the floor.

Waiting.

Thinking.

The whole thing feels different now. I dunno *how* or *why* . . . it just FEELS different. Like it's getting SERIOUS. And the thing is – I dunno what it means. I dunno if it's SERIOUS serious, like serious to ME, or just serious serious, you know, POLICE serious. I dunno, cos I dunno how it all works. All this police stuff – I dunno nothing about it. I dunno how it goes. I dunno how it's going. I mean, are we done yet? Can I ask questions? What's happening? What's *gonna* happen?

I dunno . . .

Then the toilet flushes upstairs – *kshuoooarrRHH . . . shh . . . shh . . . shhh . . .*

And I look at Dorudi again.

She smiles and says, 'Excuse me,' then she gets up and walks out into the hall. I hear Bowker coming downstairs, and then I hear the 2 of em talking quietly in the hall. I lean forward and sneak a quick look at Dorudi's notes – but her writing's too squiggly to read, and it's all upside down, and I don't wanna touch nothing in case they fingerprint me or something. So I just slump back in the chair and wait.

It's getting on for 8 o'clock.

I'm *STARVING*.

You can blank stuff with food – blank out the bad stuff. Think of GOOD things – CHEESE, CAKE, CHIPS, KFC, MARS BARS, EGGS & BEANS, MCMUFFINS, PIES, TWIXES, PIZZA, PORK CHOPS, ROLLS, KING CONES, TOAST, diet coke, SQUIRTY CREAM, BURGERS, CHEESECAKE, CHIPS . . .

After a couple of minutes, Bowker and Dorudi come back in and we start all over again. This time, Dorudi's writing it all down, word for word, on a special bit of paper with boxes and dotted lines and stuff. I guess this is THE STATEMENT – the REAL thing. And it takes AGES. First I say something, then Dorudi repeats it, makes it sound right, and then she writes it down. I say something else, Dorudi repeats it, makes it sound right, then writes it down. I say something else, Dorudi repeats it, makes it sound right, then writes it down . . .

And on and on and on . . .

Then, when we're finally finished, she makes me read it all the way through again, telling me to take my time and point out anything I'm not happy with. I ain't sure what that means – *not happy with* – but I read it through anyway. It sounds all right. It don't sound much like ME, but it's pretty much what happened.

'OK?' says Bowker, when I'm done.

'Yeh.'

'Did you read this?' He points out a bit of writing near the bottom of the page, one of them things you gotta sign to say it's true. It goes – *This statement is true . . . it ain't been beaten outta me or nothing* . . . or something like that, anyway.

'Yeh,' I tell him.

'You're happy to sign it?'

What's all this *HAPPY* about?

'Yeh.'

So I sign it, and I think they probly do, too. I can't remember. Then they get Mum to read it and sign it as well. She reads it in about 5 seconds. She don't care – she'll sign anything. And that's about it. They start getting their stuff together, putting all their papers away, getting ready to go . . . Mum and Dorudi are chit-chatting about the weather or something . . . Bowker's poking around in his pockets . . . then he starts saying something to me about the school football team, like he's suddenly really INTERESTED in me, like we're MATES, you know, we're GUYS, so we talk-about-football, like GUYS are sposed to . . . but after about 10 seconds he remembers the SIZE of me and realises – *du-uh . . . HE ain't no socceroo* . . . Yeh, I can see it in his eyes – FAT FAT FAT – and he gets a bit flustered. Not flustered for ME – flustered for HIMSELF, like he wants to laugh but knows he can't. THAT kinda flustered.

So it's – chit-chat, chit-chat . . . edging out the front room into the hall . . . getting to the front door . . . and I still don't KNOW nothing. I still dunno what it all means. I still dunno what's gonna happen . . .

'Um . . .' I says.

No one hears me.

I cough. 'Uh . . . yeh – hello?'

Dorudi looks at me like she's forgotten who I am. 'Yes?'

'What's gonna happen?' I ask her.

'When?'

'Now . . . you know – what's gonna happen now?'

'Well,' she says, 'it all depends . . .'

'On what?'

'All sorts of things – whether anyone's charged, how they plead, what the other witnesses say, if the case goes to court . . .'

'Yeh, but what about *me*? What's gonna happen to *me*?'

The air stops dead for a second. Bowker and Dorudi stare at me like I just told em I'm a NAZI or something. I know what they're thinking – SELF SELF SELF – I can see it in their eyes . . . FAT – GREEDY – ALWAYS THINKING OF ME ME ME . . . or maybe that's just me, how I'm seeing ME in their eyes?

I dunno . . .

Probly not.

It's just – you know – what's their PROBLEM? I mean, I was only *ARSKING*. What *ABOUT* me?

'Like I said,' says Dorudi, all cool and narky. 'It all depends . . .'

'Yeh, we'll be in touch,' adds Bowker, opening the door. 'OK?'

OK, I know it all **now**, of course – or most of it anyway – but I din't know nothing then. Bowker was Bowker – the lump's dad. Dorudi was Dorudi . . . actually, I *still* dunno about her. But Bowker . . . I dunno. I din't know if he was good or bad. I din't even know if there WAS a good or bad. Yeh, **now** I know it . . .

Bad = good.

Good = bad.

. . . but then was different.

Now = then.
Then = now.
Same = different.
Different = same.
Now . . .
It's one o'clock in the morning and the air's getting cold.

Dad gets home about 10 minutes after the cops have gone. It's just gone 9. First thing he says is, 'They gone yet?' Then, 2 seconds later, 'What's for supper?'

It's vollervons . . . with fruitcake for afters.

We don't talk much when we're eating, just shovel it down, shovel it down – YUM YUM YUM – get well stuffed up, then slap our bellies and slurp some tea. Then, after thanking Mum with a couple of good burps, Dad shifts his bum and turns to me.

'So,' he says, 'how'd it go with the wiggies?'

'The what?'

'The wiggies . . . wiggums . . . *Chief* Wiggum . . . the police, stupid.'

'Oh . . . right. Yeh, it was OK.'

'They treat you all right?'

'Yeh.'

'Who was it – Wickham?'

'Moulton CID. A man and a lady—'

'Paul Bowker,' Mum says.

'Who?'

'You know – Dec Bowker's dad. From the village.'

Dad looks surprised. 'What – him with the buggy eyes?'

'Yeh.'

'He's a *copper*?'

'Detective Sergeant,' I tell him. 'There was a black lady with him – DC Dorudi. That's Detective Constable—'

'What's CID doing with it?' says Dad, looking at me. 'I thought it was just a road rage thing?'

'Someone got stabbed.'

'Who?'

'I dunno – I din't see it.'

'They dead?'

'Dunno – I spose so . . . they said there was a body.'

'A body?'

'Yeh.'

'A dead body?'

I give him a look, like – you know any *other* kindsa bodies? He looks back at me for a second, his eyes blank, then his face cracks and he starts laughing . . . HO HO HO . . . then he stops, looking at me again . . . then he starts laughing again – HO HO HO HO HO . . .

And it's OK, cos it *is* pretty funny when you think about it.

9.30, upstairs in my room, I switch on my PC and run AOL. After 5 minutes of *tickitty-tickitty-durr-tick-tick-teck* . . . *dung-dung-dung* . . . *DURRR-DURRR-DURRR* . . . *dee-doo-dee-doo-di-di-di-da-da-du-di* . . . *eeeeee-iicchhhh-eeeee-AAAHaaah-eeee* . . . I finally get a connection.

'*Wel*come to AOL,' Joanna Plumley says. 'You have *e*mail.'

It's from Brady:

```
hey moo – my dad was down the pub & some
guys siad u was at the cops about a crash.
what crash? u c it? ne bods? give it upguy!
jicky collins got me afer gim today – sat
on my bastad head! made me latefor art.
then bowker done me after scholl again.
b
```

I click on *REPLY*:

yeh b – there was a thing at the bridge last night. 2 cars had a bustup & there was a fight & some guy got stabbed. i saw it. the wiggies come round for a statement. guess what? teh cop is dec bowkers dad! yeh. looks like him 2 – big monkey eyes and monkeyfied legs! ooh ooh ooh. hey – u shoulda bit jc on the arse!

10.35, downstairs in the front room, watching TV. Mum's in the kitchen, rattling pots and pans, and me and Dad's watching the local news. It ain't that interesting – stories about murdered old people, cops V gypsies, a squinty old doctor caught fiddling with the ladies – but it's something to look at. I'm just sitting there staring at the screen . . . drifting away . . . thinking about stuff . . . wondering if I can get back to the bridge tomorrow . . . I dunno . . . maybe . . . maybe not . . . it's probly crime-scened, you know, sealed-up, taped-off . . .

And then Dad says. 'Hey, Moo, look at this.'

'What?'

'There,' he says, pointing a toe at the TV screen. 'That's the thing, innit? The bridge . . .'

At first I don't recognise it. A TV lady is standing at the side of a road, talking into a furry microphone . . . traffic *swooshing* past behind her. Behind the traffic – sorta *diagonally* behind it – in the background, there's a bridge. Dull grey steel, concrete, steps, railings – dit dit dit . . . cars, trucks, lorries . . . *swoo-ooosh-swoo-ooosh-swoo-ooosh* . . . but across the road, on the other side, there ain't no traffic. The road's closed off. Blue-and-white tape, cones, barriers

. . . and at the side of the road, on the verge, there's a big green tent thing and some police vans – 2 marked Ivecos and a plain white Transit. Uniforms are standing around looking bored, and there's a couple of guys in white rubber suits going in and out the tent.

'Moo?' says Dad.

'Uh?'

'Is that it?'

Yeh . . . yeh, that's it. The road . . . the bridge. MY road . . . MY bridge. It looks small, kinda squashed up, and wrong. The angles are all wrong, the whatsit . . . the perspective. It's all outta whack. I'm seeing it from down there at the side of the road, that's why . . . I ain't used to seeing it from down there. It looks different. But it's mine all right.

Or it was . . .

'. . . and a number of men are being questioned by the police,' the TV lady is saying. 'In a statement issued earlier today, the dead man was named as Lee Burke, a father of 2 from Essex. Detective Inspector John Callan from Moulton CID is leading the inquiry.'

The picture switches to a sharp-looking guy in a dark suit standing on the steps outside a dull brick building. He looks familiar. I lean forward to get a better look . . . and, yeh, it's him all right. Last time I saw him he was wearing a waxy coat and getting out of an unmarked Rover 600, pointing at things, asking questions . . . being the boss. Now he ain't wearing his coat and he ain't pointing at things and he ain't *asking* questions, he's *answering* em . . . but that don't make no difference – he's still the boss.

The TV lady says to him, 'Can you confirm reports that one of the men being questioned about the incident is Keith Vine?'

Callan smiles. 'Several men are helping us with our

enquiries.'

'Including Mr Vine?'

'I'm afraid I can't comment at this stage.'

'Has he been charged?'

'No one's been charged.'

'In view of past experiences, Inspector, are you confident of bringing Mr Burke's killer to justice?'

Callan don't answer straightaway. He smiles again, his eyes all icy and hard, looking at the TV lady. Then he turns his head, giving the TV camera a tough-guy stare, and says, 'Yes.'

Just like that – yes.

Confident as hell.

You know what it's like when you're watching TV with your dad? There's YOU, the TV, your DAD . . . like 3 points of a triangle – dot dot dot – and the triangle's got little arrows on it, and the arrows go round and round – from YOU to the TV, from the TV to DAD, from DAD to YOU, from YOU to the TV – and vicee verso, too, in the opposite direction – from YOU to your DAD, from your DAD to the TV, from the TV to YOU . . . and all the time these little arrows are picking up stuff from the 3 of you, moving it around, passing it on, making REACTIONS . . . d'you know what I mean?

No?

Me neither . . .

All right, it's like this – I dunno NOTHING then, OK? I'm in the dark. I don't KNOW Lee Burke or Keith Vine or Detective Inspector John Callan. They ain't nothing to me, just names, TV names – Blah Blah . . . Blah Blah . . . Blabblahblah Blahblahblah Blah Blahblah . . . nothing but noise. **Now** it's different. **Now** I know who they are (ain't THAT the TRUTH) – but THEN they're nothing. OK? But – and this is the big BUT – even though I dunno nothing then, I know that things don't FEEL right. The bridge and everything . . . it don't FEEL right. The reporter's questions, the stuff about *past experiences* . . . it don't FEEL right. And most of all – Dad don't FEEL right. There something wrong with the arrows that's gone from the TV to him and from him to me. Yeh, THAT's what I'm saying. The arrows have picked up some kinda bad stuff from Dad.

I dunno what it is.

What it is, when the TV flicks back to the studio for the weather, Dad coughs and sniffs and wipes his mouth and gives me a funny look – a kinda shaky-faced I-*told*-you-so look . . . like – GOD, now you REALLY gone and done it. But there's something else there too, something worse, something in his eyes . . . like he's *scared* of something.

'What?' I ask him.

'Nothing . . .' He blinks a couple of times and nervously waggles his fingers. 'That's it then?' he says.

'What?'

'What they're talking about . . .' He nods at the TV. 'That's what you saw. You was there?'

'Yeh.'

He nods again, his chins wobbling, his eyes gazing over my head. 'Looks like it's pretty big stuff . . . on the news and everything . . .'

'I spose.'

His eyes settle on mine and he tries a smile, missing it by a thousand miles. 'Well,' he goes. 'On the news, eh? Fancy that.'

And that's about it.

Well, well, well . . . fancy that.

I think he knows more than he wants to say. I think he's CONFLICTED about something . . . and I think I need to take his bent arrows, take em somewhere quiet, and take a closer look at em.

When I say quiet, I mean noisy. Noisy like LINKIN PARK, MY VITRIOL, SLIPKNOT, SLAYER, KORN, BUCKCHERRY, SPINESHANK, FEAR FACTORY, KILLING JOKE, SOULFLY, SEPULTURA . . . stuff like that. Nu stuff, thrashy stuff, noisy metal stuff, stuff that takes you places. I like going places. As long as they're on-my-own places – like in my room, in my head, on the bridge – it's OK. I can DO things there – I CAN BE ME. Anyplace else is too RAINy.

So that's where I take Dad's arrows. Upstairs, into my room, where I rattle down the CD rack and pick out . . . I dunno . . . something . . . something LOUD . . . like FEAR FACTORY . . . yeh . . . *Soul of a New Machine*. Stick it on – *Martyr . . . DAAHUNDAAH DEEUNDAAH DAAHUNDAAH DEEUNDAA DAAHUNDAAH DEEUNDAAH DAAHUNDAAH DEEUNDAA . . .*

'TURN IT *DOWN*!'

I turn it down, sit down, and think about arrows . . .

I think . . .

I dunno.

I think it's probly nothing. Maybe Dad knows the names . . . Vine, Callan, Burke . . . or *half*-knows em. He half-knows a lotta things . . . names and stuff. Not so much round here, but Essex names . . . you know? NAMES. FACES. OPERATORS. He don't know em PERSONAL, but he knows OF em, if you know what I mean. He knows enough to know who's who and what's what . . .

That's what I'm thinking.

Maybe . . .

Let's see.

CLICK.

Sign on . . .

Let's see what Google's gotta say – *tickitty-tickitty-durr-tick-tick-teck . . . dung-dung-dung . . . DURRR-DURRR-DURRR* . . . beating in time to FEAR FACTORY – Track 3 *Scapegoat – DUHDUHDUHDAHDUHDUHDAHDUH-DUHDAH* – and the modem – *dee-doo-dee-doo-di-di-di-da-da-du-di . . . eeeeee-iicchhhh-eeeee-AAAHaaah-eeee* . . . and *Scapegoat – DUHDUHDUHDAHDUHDUHDAHDUH-DUHDAH* and Joanna Plumley again.

'*Wel*come to AOL . . . you have *e*mail.'

2 from Brady:

`yeh? whats a wiggie?`

and:

`u c it on tv? VINE man! u c vine stab himup? heeehooo! u best watch out – hes a BADASS`

Brady's an idiot sometimes . . . most times, actually. A small ugly idiot. I don't mean that in a bad way . . . just in a real way. Cos that's what he is – an idiot. Not that I mind . . . I don't mind one bit. Idiots are OK with me.

I write back:

`b – its WIGGY – wiggies. you know? wiggum. chief wiggum . . . the cops stupid. what u mean – watch out? for waht? vine?`

Then I get back to Google and put in *keith vine* and – *BAM* – 0.13 seconds later I got 106 results. Most of it's crap – other

Vines, stuff I ain't got the right BROWSER for, repeat stuff – but there's a couple of good hits, and one that's bang on the nose. This is how it goes:

Keith Vine, aged 51, operates what appears on the surface to be normal business activities, dealing in cars, property, leisure facilities, and jewellery. Amongst his associates are many respected figures, including senior politicians, judges, lawyers, and policemen. But behind this facade he is in the top league of criminals, a multi-millionaire whose empire is founded on an elaborate network of crime, including fraud, drug smuggling, and extortion. In 1988, Vine received a 12-year prison sentence for his part in an armed robbery in which a security guard lost his life. On his release from prison in 1994 he was subsequently charged with the murder of a prosecution witness at his previous trial. The victim, Jonathon Bardin, suffered fatal stab wounds in the car park of an Essex hotel. At the trial, however, crucial evidence was dismissed and Vine was found not guilty of the charge. After his acquittal he was soon back in the crime business with his financial empire flourishing more than ever . . .

. . . followed by a load of stuff about where he was born, his family, his youth, growing up, stealing apples, blah blah blah . . . then we're right back into his *villainous empire . . .*

`. . . Scotland Yard . . . stolen goods . . . £££ . . . Freemasons Lodge . . . contacts . . . profits . . . evil and corruption . . . single-minded predator . . . vast wealth . . . drugs . . . £££ . . .`

The writing's really small and the screen's gone all flicky . . . and I ain't too hot on reading at the best of times . . . and right now I can't be arsed with it . . . so I scroll down to the bottom of the page where there's a little picture – like one of them little passport photos – showing this hard-looking mug with wiry black hair, his skin all tanned and orangey, like he's dried up in the sun . . . and I KNOW all along it's the Range Rover guy, but it still kinda hits me – WHACK – in the head. Cos Brady's right – this guy's a BADASS. And I can see what's gonna happen – I can SEE myself getting dragged into a whole heap of BADASSery.

And NOW I know what bent Dad's arrows.

Later, still in my room . . . I dunno what time it is. Pretty late, I think. FEAR FACTORY's done for the night and I'm sitting in the QUIET quiet looking out the window towards the road. There's only half a whisper tonight – half the river, half the road-rush calling out to me . . . I can't hear what it's saying. The sky's all dark and moony, the black night cut with orange lights, and I'm breathing hot breath on the window and thinking about Brady.

He emailed me again about an hour back:

`i KNOW its wiggy i aint stupid. i KNOW what it is. i ment what SORT. like cid or what?`

& u HAD better watch it cos vine if you dont know is a GANGSTA OK? he stabbed some guy & pools out teeth & stuff. i read about it. sleep tight HAHA!
b

Now it's **now** again. I could do with a bit of FEAR FACTORY **now** to help me through these long hours, but I don't guess Mum and Dad would like it too much – 2 o'clock in the morning . . . *DUHDUHDUHDAHDUHDUHDAHDUHDUHDAH . . . what the HELL'S THAT????* Dad'd probly fall outta bed – *KABOOM!!* – wake up the whole damn village. And that ain't what I need right **now**. Not with the stuff I gotta do. No way . . .

No . . .

So . . .

I guess I'll just have to sit here in this QUIET quiet, telling tales till the morning comes.

If it ever does.

5/ Brady

Going to school the next morning was kinda weird. I had that extra-nervous feeling you get when you go back to school after you ain't been in for a Day or 2, you know, when everything feels NEW again and you get that squitty feeling in your guts . . . the squits of starting a brand new school. GOD knows WHY I felt like that, cos I HADN'T been off school for a Day or 2, but the feeling was there all right, I could feel it bubbling around in my belly as I walked down the lane, through the grey of the village, and up to the school gate – the feeling of NOT KNOWING. You know, when you don't KNOW anyone, you don't KNOW where nothing is, you don't KNOW what to say or what to do or where to go . . . GOD, I hate that. Everyone LOOKING at you, sussing you out, giving you the hard eyes and the dirty looks . . . and you can't stop wondering what they all think of you. THINK THINK THINK – what do I do? what do I say? what do I look like? how do I WALK? WHAT DO THEY ALL *THINK* OF MEEEEEE?

And the worst of it is – you can't be alone, can you? There ain't NOWHERE to be alone . . . and there ain't no one to rely on, neither. Not then, not now. Friends? What's a friend? One minute they're this and the next minute they're that. Friends ain't nothing. And even if they ARE something – which they ain't – you still got no CHOICE. You get what you're given . . . you get what you DESERVE. Like with me, right? When I first got here I wasn't FAT or nothing, but I was probly a bit on the *podgy* side. You know – large-*ish*, a bit *chubbo* . . . a bit *soft and round*. Yeh, that's it – SOFT and ROUND. You know what I'm talking about. Soft and splodgy, round-faced . . . yeh, I guess I always been one of them *round-faced* kids . . . which ain't surprising really – I got a round-faced mum and a round-faced dad . . .

But anyway . . .

It ain't what you IS that puts you in your place – it's what you AIN'T. I ain't COOL, I ain't LEAN, I ain't HARD, I ain't MEAN . . . I ain't even got a NICE PERSONALITY. So, friends-wise, that puts me about as low as it gets. It puts me right down there with the bottom-of-the-barrel kids – the GOBBEES, the BUTTS, the RETARDS, the MONGS, the CREEPS, the PUKERS . . . the WEAK, basically.

The WEAK.

When I first got here there was 3 of us WEAKos – me, Brady, and a kid called Keenan. Keenan was the resident fat guy. Fat, short, Welsh, with horrible wavy hair and sharp little teeth . . . GOD, he was *REALLY* something. Even *Brady* din't like him. Dinnertime, right, Keenan used to go over the shop and buy tons of sweets and stuff then come back and start giving it all away. He'd just stand there in the middle of the playground dishing out stuff from a carrier bag – *there you go, there you go . . . you want one? . . . there you go*. All the other kids – me included – we was nice as pie to him for about 5 minutes, crowding round him, trying to catch his eye, *smiling* at him . . . but as soon as the Mars Bars ran out he was nothing again, just a fat Welsh kid standing on his own in the middle of the playground with an empty carrier bag in his hand. You'd think he wouldn't bother – Day after Day after Day, giving out Mars Bars like they're going outta fashion . . . GOD, he musta spent *TONS*. And for what? 5 quid a Day for 5 minutes' fake-friendship . . .? I spose he thought it was worth it. I dunno . . . maybe it was? You'd never catch *me* doing nothing like that, though. If I had 5 quid a Day to spend on grub, I'd scoff it all myself.

Chocolate friends might not last any longer than fake ones, but they sure as hell taste better.

Keenan left school about 6 months after I started. I ain't sure why . . . his dad topped himself, I think, stuck his head under a heavy duty fence-post hammer or something . . .

I dunno . . .

I don't even know why I'm *talking* about it.

But, anyway, going to school the next morning . . . this'd be Threeday . . . the Day after the Day after the Day it happened . . . and, like I said, it's kinda weird. I'm nervy, squitty, but I dunno why. I guess it's cos I dunno what to expect, cos I KNOW they're all gonna know about the bridge and the cops and everything. I mean, I know Brady knows about it, and Bowker probly knows about it, too, and them 2 ain't exactly FAMOUS for keeping their gobs shut, so there's a pretty good chance the whole damn school's gonna know about it by now. And, cos of that, I dunno what to expect, but I expect I'm gonna get the usual, the RAIN RAIN RAIN . . . but I'm kinda thinking it might be different today COS of the cops/bridge/killing thing . . . but, then again, I could be wrong. It might *not* be different. It might be exactly the same. It could go either way, I guess. It might be the same or it might be different . . . same or different . . . same or different . . . I dunno. I don't even know which way I WANT it to go. Course, I don't WANNA get RAINed on . . . but the funny thing is – I ain't sure I WANT it any different, neither. I *KNOW* the RAIN . . . I don't LIKE it, but I *KNOW* it. I know what to do with it. But DIFFERENT? I dunno about that . . . DIFFERENT's different. I dunno different. I ain't sure I can cope with different.

Different = scary.

Scary = scary.

So, I says to myself – what you gonna do?

Nothing, I guess – just the same as usual, walk through it all with your eyes down. Umbrellarise it. It's the only way. Down the lane, through the grey of the village, up to the school gates . . . *tump*, *tump*, *tump* . . . here we go . . . there they are . . . the monkey-brains, the boys on bikes, the eyes, the looks, the parents in cars, the girls in short skirts . . .

And you know what?

You know what I get?

I get SMILES is what I get. I get looks that DON'T hurt. I get *INTEREST*.

I get –

'Hey, Moo – what's it all about?'

'What's happening?'

'You been down the cops yet?'

'What they say?'

'What's going on?'

– and it DOES ME IN. It conflicts me. It stirs me up and splits me right down the middle. Cos there's me, right – the FAT guy, the RAINman, the COWboy, the chunk who took over from Keenan – and there's all these blubber-hunters, all these monkeys in boots and sniggering girls who spend all Day RAINing on me – Day after Day after Day – and now, all of a sudden, they WANT me. All right, so they don't want ME, they want what I GOT, what I KNOW. . . but what's the difference? They want something OF me.

And that's what splits me in 2.

Part One – the Mike part, I guess – is 1000%FURIOUS. He can't *BELIEVE* it. He's burning up, fit to bust – YOU WHAT? he's thinking. YOU *WHAT?* YOU THINK YOU CAN *SMILE* AT ME? YOU THINK YOU CAN *TALK* TO

ME? WHAT D'YOU THINK I AM? YOU THINK I'M *STUPID* OR SOMETHING? YOU THINK I'M JUST GONNA *FORGET* WHAT YOU *DONE* TO ME? YOU SKINNY *BASTADS!!* YOU THINK A SUDDEN *SMILE* IS ALL IT TAKES? – and he's right, of course. He's right as RAIN, he's RIGHT RIGHT RIGHT . . .

But . . .

There's another Part, Part 2 – the Moo part – and HE's getting warm. This sudden INTEREST is making him go all warm and soft inside. He's lapping it up, he's loving it. He's thinking – HEY . . . *THIS* IS ALL RIGHT. THIS IS *NICE*. I COULD LIVE WITH *THIS*. MMMMMM! OH, YEH! THIS IS *GOOD* . . . I'LL HAVE SOME OF *THIS* . . .

And I dunno whose side to take.

Nice or right.

Good or bad.

Be yourself or kid yourself.

Cos you know it ain't gonna last. As soon as the Mars Bars are gone you're gonna be nothing again, just a used-up fat kid standing on your own in the middle of the playground with an empty carrier bag in your hand.

Is that what you want?

Think about it.

Listen to em . . .

'Come on, Moo, give it up.'

'You talking or what?'

'Come on, Moo . . .'

'I can't,' I says, 'I ain't allowed to say nothing.'

'Eh?' goes one.

'Why not?' goes another.

'I dunno,' I tell em. 'It's what the cops said – I ain't sposed to say nothing about it.'

'Come *on* . . .'

'Get out of it . . .'

I shake my head. 'Ask Bowker if you want – he'll tell you.'

Their eyes flick to Dec Bowker who's leaning against the wall clicking a cheap cigarette lighter – *chick chick chick* – making out like he don't give a toss.

'What?' he says, lifting his eyes from the lighter, cool as hell.

A kid called Nish – sitting on a bike – grins at me, then leans over the handlebars and leers at Bowker. 'Moo says he can't say nothing bout what happened cos the cops won't let im.'

Bowker sniffs. 'So?'

'He says to ask you bout it.'

'Bout what?'

'If it's true.'

Bowker turns slowly and looks at me. There's spite in his eyes, spite and want. He WANTS to whack me. He WANTS to make me squirm. He WANTS to push my face in the dirt. It's in his eyes. I can FEEL it. I dunno what IT is – hate, monsterosity, BADness – but whatever it is, whatever he's got, he WANTS to take it out on me. The thing is, though, even though I'm shaking, and even though I got the taste of puke in the back of my throat – I'm doing all right. I'm actually feeling OK. Cos I'm thinking to myself, I'm thinking – not today, Dec . . . not today. Cos, just for once, I got you where I want. I GOT you. See – your dad's the cop, right? I din't know that before, but I reckon everyone else did. So now we all know it – your dad's the cop. And who's been talking to the cops? Yeh, that's right – ME. Moo Nelson. ME and the cops . . . in MY house. YOU? You dunno nothing. You dunno what they said to me. You dunno what's what. And even if you do . . . well, so what? You still can't DO nothing, can you? You can't take the risk. Yeh, OK, so you're *hard* – but your dad, the cop, he's *HARD*. And I'm pretty sure you're shit-scared of him. In fact, I'm betting on it. So you can look at me all you want, cos today I'm looking right back at you and finding nothing . . . and for a sweet little moment we're equals – nothing and nothing.

THAT's what I'm thinking.

Bowker – meanwhile – is still staring hard. Without taking his eyes off me, he leans to one side and spits on the pavement, then steps forward and casually smears the gob into the pavement with the sole of his trainer.

'What you saying, Biggie?' he says.

'Uh?'

'What you *saying*?'

'I ain't saying nothing.'

He stares some more, all DARK and BLACK and RED and SCARY . . . and then he winks – he WINKS! – and looks away.

'Hear that?' he says to the others.

The school bell's ringing.

No one moves.

'You hear that?' Bowker repeats. 'The Tub says nothing.'

I dunno if I'm smart or not. I mean, I ain't no muttonhead or nothing, and I can be pretty *sneaky* when I want – but sneaky ain't smart. Sneaky's just something you need, like when you gotta get something you ain't sposed to get and you gotta work out a way to get it. I can do THAT. But I dunno about smart. Smart's something else. Smart's what you got when you THINK you're being smart, when you THINK you know what you're doing, when you THINK you GOT someone for a sweet little moment, and then they go and do something that turns you upside down – but it's OK, cos you

KNOW what to do about it. THAT'S what smart is. And I guess I ain't got it.

Cos I din't have a CLUE what Dec Bowker was all about. Taking the piss? Having a laugh? Watching his back? Looking out for me? Looking out for himself? Turning things around? Setting things up? Straightening things out? Knocking me down? Picking me up? Diddlee dah? Diddlee dum? Diddlee dee?

Who knows?

Not me.

I ain't got a clue.

I'm still trying to work it out 7 hours later when I come across Brady in the corner shop after school.

The shop's OK. It's a shop, you know – *confectionery, soft drinks, beers/wines/spirits, news, videos, crisps & snacks, biscuits, health & beauty* – walls of cheap coke and soap powder, security mirrors and dayglo cardboard stars – *BEANS! MILK! BREAD! PIES! BEER!* There's a magazine rack and trays of beer on the floor, and an old Muslin guy who sits on a high stool by the stock-room door, mumbling through a little black book, while his daughter works the till. She's called Zarina, his daughter. She's all right. The whole thing's all right.

It's OK.

It's a shop.

It's where it happened with me and Brady a couple of years back. IT being not much . . . well, not really. Not so's you'd notice. I guess IT was one of them things that ain't much of a muchness, but mean a lot anyway . . . but you ain't sure why . . .

You know what I'm saying?

OK, it's like this –

I'm 12 or 13 then, just starting to get it bad. Getting the FAT stuff, getting the RAIN, getting the YA YAs . . . and I'm in the shop after school getting some stuff to get me home – crisps, probly, or maybe Monster Munches . . . yeh, it's Monster Munches. Pickled Onion flavour. OK? So I'm in the shop, and Brady's with me. He ain't WITH me like we're MATES or nothing, we ain't TOGETHER, he's just kinda *with* me. And I guess I'm just kinda *with* him. The fat guy and the dwarf. Safety in numbers, I guess . . . not that 2's much of a number, but it's better than one. And even if it AIN'T better than one – which is kinda what I'm talking about – it's still better than nothing.

Anyway, me and Brady's in the shop, and we ain't saying much to each other, we ain't shooting the breeze or nothing, we're just hanging out, in the shop, getting some scoff, and getting ready to go.

'All right?'

'Yeh.'

Up at the till, Zarina's painting some stuff on her fingernails. She don't smile, but that's OK, cos she's one of them girls who look better when they don't smile. Brady pays first, getting a packet of Polos or something (one of them I-don't-really-want-nothing-but-I-don't-wanna-make-you-feel-bad kinda things . . . yeh, like I'M gonna feel bad if he don't buy nothing), then he stands to the side and I move up and put 2 bags of Monster Munches on the counter. Zarina plays the till, jabbing the buttons with her knuckles so she won't mess up her nails, and I'm just digging some dosh outta my pocket – when it happens. A poke in the back. Not *that* hard, but low down, in the kidneys or liver or whatever it is down there – and it hurts like hell. I yelp a bit and jerk around to see Dec Bowker and Jicky Collins and a couple other kids leering at me – all devil-eyed and ready to rock. I'm looking at em – kinda bent over to one side, clutching the pain – trying to make out like it don't hurt, it's just a game, a laugh, a BIT OF FUN . . . but we all KNOW it ain't.

Bowker says, 'What?'

'Nothing,' I says.

'What you looking at?'

'Nothing.'

Then Jicky steps up and brings his hand down on my Monster Munches – *whack*, *crunch*, *whack*, *crunch* – squashing em flat.

'You paying for these or what?' he says. 'We ain't got all Day.'

I look around, looking at Brady and Zarina, looking for someone to say something, but they don't wanna know. Zarina's doing her nails and Brady's just standing there like he's kacked his pants, like he ain't never SEEN me before . . . and I dunno if it's that or something else that gets me stupid-angry for half a second . . . I dunno . . . I just lose it, I guess. I dunno *what* I'm doing. My hand whips out, grabs a squashed-up bag of Monster Munches from the counter, and before I know it I'm chucking the bag in Bowker's face. Whip – chuck – *splat* . . .

Then, sudden silence . . .

Oh shit.

WHAT HAVE I DONE?

GOD . . . I mean, how PATHETIC can you get? Pathetic, weedy, pointless, thoughtless, stupid, brainless, DUMB DUMB DUMB . . .

Bowker grins, cold and happy.

'Ooohh,' he says. 'Vicious.'

'I din't mean—'

'Shut up.'

Then him and Jicky are walking me out the shop, followed by the others. I dunno who they are – a couple of monkeys from Bowker's year and a chubby girl in a skirt that shows her arse . . . Mandy Something, I think. Anyway, they take me out the shop, round the back to the little parking place near the field, down behind some bottle banks, and then they beat me up. It ain't too bad. Up against the bottle bank, couple of whacks in the belly, then Bowker grabs my head and cracks it hard against the bottle bank wall and I go down. I dunno if I *need* to go down. I'm a bit black and woozy, and I got dizzy-stars in my eyes, but it don't hurt that much and I could probly stay up if I wanted, but it seems like a good idea to go down. So down I go, into the broken glass and pools of stale booze, curled up like a ball, hands over my head, knees over my belly . . . and I take another whack or 2 – or 3 or 4 – including a high-heeled stomp in the giblets from Fat Mandy that makes me squeal like a pig . . . and that's about it.

Anyway, the IT of it is – the what-it's-all-about – is Brady doing nothing. Nothing to help me. Nothing to say. Nothing at all. Zero action. Looking out for himself. Once Bowker and the rest get busy with me, he's gone – ZZZZIPPP! Get out of it quick. Get away. Get home. Get safe. And the IT of it is – it's OK with me. I don't BLAME Brady for doing nothing, cos I'd do the same. I DO do the same. One for one and one for one . . .

Better him than me.

That's the way it goes.

See you later, Moo.

I'm going home.

OK?

Yeh, it's OK.

2 minus one is better than one minus nothing.

Now – then – we're here again, in the shop. This time Brady's already in there when I go in – he's over in the corner looking at the computer magazines. I can't see his face cos he's standing with his back to me, and he's got the hood of his parka pulled up, but you don't have to see Brady's face to recognise him. He's about 2 feet tall . . . well, OK, maybe a *bit* taller than that. I mean, he ain't a dwarf, exactly . . . but he's pretty damn short. Short and squat. Stubby little arms. Stubby little hands. And a head that's way too big for his body. Yeh, that's Brady for you – pretty as sin. Anyway, there he is, flipping through the computer magazines, checking out the TECHS and SPECS, and every now and then he's looking over his shoulder, looking around, then turning back and looking up at the top shelf, checking out the SECHSY PICS of FOCHSY CHICS . . .

'See anything you fancy?' I say, sneaking up behind him.

His head whips round and I'm hit with a pair of bulging blue eyes. 'I was just—' he starts to splutter, holding up the magazine. Then, 'Oh – it's you,' and the panic's over. 'Shit, Moo,' he says. 'Don't *do* that.'

'You wanna be more careful,' I tell him.

'Uh?'

'Nothing – you all right?'

'Yeh . . . you got any money?'

'Some.'

He shows me the computer magazine. 'Wanna buy me this?'

'No.'

'Fair enough,' he shrugs, chucking the magazine back on the rack. 'I din't want it anyway.'

I get myself a big Twix and a Double Decker and 2 cans of Diet Coke, then me and Brady get out the shop before the rest of em show up – cos they always do. Like lions at the watering-hole, waiting for the wildy-beasts . . . they know we're gonna be there. So we get going – around the back of the shop, across the parking place, and into the little park. I give Brady one of the Cokes and open up the other one – *pop*. Brady thinks about opening his, then changes his mind and stuffs it in his parka pocket.

'Don't you want it?' I ask him.

'Saving it for Ron,' he says.

'Who's Ron?'

'Later Ron.'

Hur hur hur.

He's like that – funny as hell.

We don't talk much, we never do, just walk the walk, you know, just keep on going. I open up the Twix, scoff it down, stick the wrapper in my pocket, and drink some Coke. I think about the Double Decker, wondering if I oughta save it till later . . . but then I think – nah . . . if I want one later I can always get another one . . . so I open it up, scoff it down, stick the wrapper in my pocket, and drink some more Coke.

'Rots your teeth,' says Brady.

'What?'

'Coke – it rots your teeth.'

'Who says?'

He shrugs. 'I dunno, I seen it in a magazine.'

'What magazine? *Bad Teeth Monthly*?'

He snorts.

'Anyway,' I says, finishing the Coke. 'If I get bad teeth, I'll get em fixed.'

'Right,' he goes.

We're about halfway across the park now, both watching our step, watching out for dog shit, watching out for lions, watching out for monkeys down at the swings at the end of the field. There ain't no one there.

Brady sniffs and jerks his head. 'So,' he goes – sniff,

sniff. 'What was all that with Bowker this morning?'

'When?'

'This morning – at the gates.'

'Was you there?'

'Yeh.'

'Where?'

'Behind the wall. What's it all about? I mean, how come Bowker din't do nothing?'

'I dunno – cos of his dad, I spose.'

'What – the bridge thing?'

'Yeh.'

He don't say nothing for a while, just shuffles along, twitching his nose, rubbing his eyes . . . he's always fiddling with his face. He can't leave it alone – poking, picking, rubbing, scratching . . .

'What about the rest of em?' he says.

'What about em?'

'They do anything?'

'Nah . . .'

'Why not?'

'I dunno . . . it's kinda funny, really.'

'What?'

'I dunno . . . it's like they din't do nothing all Day. None of em. I got a few names at dinner . . . but that was the girls, you know . . . whatsername, the fancy one with the big shoes—'

'*Becka*,' Brady spits, 'Becka and *Charlie* . . . the Tick-Tock Twins.'

'Toxic.'

'Uh?'

'It's Toxic – not Tick-Tock. The *Toxic* Twins.'

'Right – Toxtic.'

'Yeh . . . anyway, that's all I got. A couple of names from

the Toxic Twins. And they only do it cos they ain't got no one else to pick on.'

'Yeh . . .'

'Apart from you.'

'Right.'

'So it was a pretty good Day, really.'

'Yeh, for *you*.'

At the swings now, we walk on past, down a little slope, through the gap in the hedge, up the other side and onto a grass bank that runs above the road. Now Brady's gonna turn left along the bank and head for his house, and I'm gonna cut down the bank and cross the mini-roundabout and head down the lane to mine. This is as far as it goes for us.

This is as far as it goes.

Brady's standing there, scratching his head through his hood, looking down at the traffic on the roundabout. I'm watching it too. It ain't as good as MY traffic, nowhere NEAR as good. But I ain't been getting mine for a couple of Days now . . . my endless river . . . my *swoo-ooosh-swoo-ooosh-swoo-ooosh* . . . my cars, my trucks, my vans, my lorries, my bikes . . . rumbling, racing, roaring, screaming . . . always there . . . silent as nothing . . .

God . . . I really NEED it.

'So is that right what you said?' goes Brady.

'What?'

'You know – about the bridge thing . . . not saying nothing. . . you said the cops told you not to say nothing . . . is that right?'

I knew all along he's gonna ask me about it. I been waiting for it. I been WANTING him to ask me about it, cos I gotta tell SOMEONE, and Brady's all I got – but then, when he asks, when I hear the tone of his voice, I know I CAN'T tell him nothing. I can't tell him about IT. Cos IT's something I got that GIVES me something. I dunno WHAT it gives me just yet, or why, but whatever it is – it makes the Day pretty good. It makes me something more than just the FAT KID. And that's gotta be OK. But the thing is, whatever it is, it ain't gonna work no more if I give it up. If I give it up to the rest of em, then I ain't got nothing left, and if I give it up to Brady . . . well, I can tell by the sound of his voice what *he's* gonna do with it. If I give it up to Brady he's gonna use it to get him*self* a pretty good Day. Which is fair enough, as far as it goes. But he'll use it all *wrong*. He'll give it up cheap. Waste it. And I ain't having THAT.

So I says to him, 'Yeh . . .' (like I'm *really* sorry) '. . . it's some kinda legal thing. Something to do with witness . . .' (what's the word?) '. . . witness . . . I dunno . . . witness something. *Com*-something . . .'

'Witless *com*-something?'

'Yeh . . . something like that. Some legal word. It's all signed and everything – I gotta keep my mouth shut. I ain't got no choice.'

'Right,' he says, tilting his strange head and lowering his eyes, knowing I'm lying, but also knowing there ain't much he can do about it. 'Yeh, well . . .' he goes, sniffing again, pinching his nose. 'Maybe later then?'

'Yeh.'

'OK.'

And off he goes along the bank. Dragging his feet, head down, stuffed full of ugliness . . . thinking bad stuff about me, no doubt.

Can I live with that?

Yeh, I reckon.

Now I'm thinking about it – doing the GUILT stuff . . . cos if I'd told Brady everything then, maybe he wouldna done what he did. But I ain't gonna let it GET to me. Brady's Brady – I'm me . . . there's a difference. If I was him I wouldna done what he did, and if he was me he wouldna done what I did. So what am I sposed to do? I ain't telegraphic. I ain't no magicman. I ain't GOD, for GOD's sake. I dunno what no one's gonna do, do I? And even if I did . . . I ain't even sure that Brady did what he did cos of me anyway. He's a weird kid. He does weird stuff. I can't help that, can I? It ain't MY fault . . . I din't do nothing. I din't MAKE him do it . . .

IT AIN'T MY FAULT.

So the Days go on and nothing much happens. The INTEREST at school dies down a bit, but it's still there, and it's still working, keeping the RAIN away, keeping me dry, keeping the Days pretty good. I don't get beat up, I don't hardly get laughed at, I don't get rocks thrown at me . . . so, yeh, the Days are pretty good. I still don't get it . . . I mean, I GET it . . . sort of . . . I know what I got and I know what it's doing, and I know it's got something to do with the bridge and the cops and Bowker's dad . . . but I ain't sure how or why. I dunno the DETAILS, if you like. But the way I see it – who cares about details? I dunno the details of *most* things – TVs, bodies, houses, telephones – but that don't stop me *using* em, does it? Who *cares* how they work? As long as they work . . . who cares? So forget about it, I keep telling myself, forget about the HOWs and the WHYs, just enjoy it. And I do . . . I DO enjoy it. But – there's always a BUT – I can't stop thinking about it. I can't stop thinking about what I saw, what it means, and what's gonna happen. Like these names I dunno nothing about – Vine, Burke, Callan, Dorudi – and the ones I do – Bowker & Bowker. What's their angle? Where they coming from? What do they want? The TRUTH? Lies? Nothing?

I dunno.

I ain't got the place to THINK no more, that's the trouble. I ain't got the bridge. The road's open again by Fiveday, the tent's gone, the crime tape's gone, the cops are gone, so there ain't nothing STOPPING me getting back to the bridge . . . nothing outside my head, anyway. Cos THAT's what's stopping me – the stuff in my head. I dunno what it is – the schizo-voice, the reason, the beasty-brain – but I know I gotta listen. *Just leave it for a bit*, it says. *See what happens. See what DEVELOPS. Just wait and see. The FLOW's still disturbed. You gotta give it time to settle down again. It won't be long. Couple of Days, a week tops. Yeh, I know it's hard – but you gotta let the river get back to what it was – OK?*

Yeh, OK.

It *is* hard, though, cos the bridge is where I KNOW myself. It's where I'm ME. Yeh, I got other places and other things – I got my room, my music, the net, computer games, FOOD, TV, a ton of books I never read . . . I got loadsa stuff. And it's all OK. It's all right. It keeps me OCCUPIED. But it ain't the same. Nothing's the same as the bridge.

Nothing.

But, anyway, that's how the Days are going – pretty good, YES YES YES, no bridge, NO NO NO. Good YES, no NO. Good YES, no NO . . .

Then, Fiveday night, the NOs are interrupted by a name.

The name is DI Callan.

6/ Callan

It's about 9 or 10 o'clock, maybe a bit later, the kinda time when the TV's full of *Friends* and *Fraser* and crappy sex stuff on Channel 5. I'm sitting in the front room watching it on my own . . . well, I ain't really *watching* it, I'm just kinda staring at the pictures and flicking around to see what else is on. There ain't much. Nothing I really wanna see. It's all a bit . . . I dunno . . . a bit SAD. Like they're all ACTORS, these people, they're ACTING. They're just pretending. Funny, sexy, tough, beeyootifull . . . they're all just pretending. And they're all so bloody THIN.

Anyway, I'm on my own. Fiveday night is Mum and Dad's night-at-the-pub. They won't be back until 11.30 or 12, and I dunno if I can be bothered to stay up. They're always full of it when they get back – all happy and smiley, like it's Christmas or something. It's OK . . . I mean, they ain't boozed-up or nothing, just enjoying themselves, but I dunno if I feel like it tonight. So I'm thinking about that, thinking – maybe I'll get a bacon sandwich and play some *Hitman* for an hour or 2 . . . and that's when the doorbell goes.

Ding dong.

I could leave it, I spose. Just sit here and wait for em to go away, whoever *they* are. But they'll have seen the lights are on . . . they'll know *some*one's in . . . and I guess it *could* be something really important . . . like . . . I dunno . . . Mum and Dad's been killed in an accident or something . . .

So I'd better get it.

So . . .

Into the hall . . .

Open the door . . .

And there he is – the man from the TV. The waxy coat guy. The man in the Rover 600. The Bossman. DI Callan, standing on my step, smiling that smile, icy and hard.

'Good evening, Michael,' he says. 'Detective Inspector John Callan, Moulton CID. I wonder if I might come in for a moment.'

'Mum and Dad's out,' I tell him.

'It won't take a minute.' He holds up a slim black briefcase and taps it with his finger. 'I'd just like to go over your statement again – clear up a few little details.'

'What details?'

He gives me a knowing smile, like we're secret buddies or something. 'Best if we don't talk out here,' he says. 'Why don't we go inside for a minute – all right?'

I dunno . . . I don't KNOW if it's *all right* or not . . . and I dunno if it makes any difference if I DON'T think it's *all right* . . . cos he's halfway through the door anyway . . . and I seem to be moving to one side . . .

'Thank you,' he says.

And in he comes.

Into the front room, a dirty look at the TV, then he takes off his waxy coat and folds it over the back of a chair and sits down.

'Do you mind?' he says, nodding *painfully* at the TV.

'Uh?'

He mimes a switch, meaning – turn it off. Turn it off? Can you believe it? Just like that . . . *turn it off* . . . like he owns the damn place. And you know what I do? Yeh, that's right. I turn it off.

'Now,' he says, unzipping his case and taking out a cardboard file, 'what I'd like to do, Michael – you don't mind if I call you Michael, do you?'

'You can call me what you like.'

He don't smile, just looks at me. 'Why don't you sit down?'

Nice of you to offer, I think, sitting down. Now we're both sitting down. He's on the settee, I'm in Dad's armchair, and there's a coffee table between us . . . well, it ain't really a COFFEE table, exactly, more like a RUBBISH table . . . you know, the kinda table that gets piled up with plates and newspapers and stuff. Callan opens his file, clears a space on the table, and starts laying out a load of papers – photocopied notes, some typewritten stuff, a copy of the statement I gave, and some photographs in a clear plastic wallet.

He picks up the statement and glances through it. I look at him. He's got big hands, kinda big and flat, and a big silver ring on one of his fingers. He's wearing a dark suit, white shirt, blue tie . . . his skin is white – like hard white plastic – and smooth, but not as smooth as it looked on TV. And he's older than he looks on TV, too. He's . . . what? I dunno . . . 45, 50, 55 . . .? Old, but not *old*, if you know what I mean. Silvery hair, cut and combed, very NEAT. Grey eyes. Steel mouth . . . Don't Mess With Me.

'Right,' he says, leaning forward, still holding the statement. 'I'm OK with everything up to here – the bit where you see the cars – but then I think you got it wrong.'

'Wrong?'

'The BMW,' he explains. 'You say there was only one person in the BMW – the driver.'

'At first, yeh.'

'At *first*?'

'When I first saw it there was only the driver. The other 3

din't show up till the car had stopped.'

A little smile. 'They appeared out of *nowhere*?'

'They was in the car.'

'But you only saw them when they got out?'

'That's right.'

'You're sure about that?'

'Yeh.'

'Well, that's strange. Because it's not what I'm hearing from the other witnesses. Everyone else seems to think there were 4 people in the car all along.'

I shrug. 'I only saw the driver.'

He looks at me. 'Well . . . it's an easy mistake to make. Night-time, the lights, the fireworks . . .'

I don't say nothing.

He gives me that smile again, then looks back at the statement. 'OK,' he says, running his finger down the page, 'this bit here – both the cars have stopped and the driver of the Range Rover is approaching the BMW.' He looks up. 'We'll be arranging an identity parade at some point, but for now I'd like you to look at this.' He slips a photograph from the plastic wallet and places it on the table in front of me. 'Is that the man you saw driving the Range Rover?'

It's the same photo I saw on the internet, only bigger. The hard-looking mug with the wiry black hair and the tanned skin.

'Yeh, that's him.'

Callan nods. 'This man—'

'Keith Vine.'

He looks at me with narrowed eyes, all thoughtful, like he's wondering how I know the name. Then, realising I probly got it off the TV or something, he nods again.

He says, 'Mr Vine admits he was driving the Range Rover. He's the registered owner. We don't have a problem with that.' Another look at me. 'The problem is, Michael – what happened next?'

'You got it there,' I tell him, pointing at the statement. 'The black lady wrote it all down—'

'Why?'

'What?'

'Why did DC Dorudi write it down? You can write, can't you?'

'Yeh, I can *write.*'

'So why did DC Dorudi write your statement for you?'

'I dunno . . . I never got asked – she never said nothing, she just started writing. I ain't *done* nothing—'

'OK, OK,' he says, all calm and *nice*. 'It's no problem. I was just wondering, that's all.' He glances at the clock. It's 10.35. He gets some more photographs from the wallet and lays em face down on the table – 1, 2, 3, 4.

'All right?' he says.

'Yeh.'

'Good. OK.' Another quick glance at the statement. 'So, Mr Vine gets out of the Range Rover and approaches the BMW. Yes?'

'Yeh.'

'He starts shouting and gesticulating at the BMW driver?'

'Yeh.'

'Like this?' Callan shakes his fist.

'Yeh.'

'He's been cut up. He's angry.'

'Yeh.'

'The BMW driver gets out?'

'Yeh.'

Callan turns over the photographs – 1, 2, 3, 4. 'Which one is the driver?'

I look at em. 3 black-and-white shots and a colour one. #1

= BMW man. The driver. He ain't wearing the hat, but I know it's him – kinda wide-looking, empty eyes, a bit mad, crazy-tough. #2 = the caveman on drugs. Longish hair, like a shaggy bowl, whacked out, wearing a flowery shirt. #3 = Half-baldy. Round face, pig eyes. And #4, the colour photograph, I *think* = the other one. The one who got out the back of the BMW wearing the same hat as the driver. The one who looked the same as the driver. The one who got in a struggle with the other 2 and then disappeared. He ain't wearing the hat in the photo, and his hair's nothing like the driver's hair, so the 2 of em don't look *so* much the same as they did before . . . but they still look pretty much the same . . . sort of . . . I mean, they ain't *totally* different or nothing.

I point at photo #1. 'That's the driver.'

Callan nods slowly, then looks at me. 'You're sure?'

'Yeh – he was wearing a Nike cap. That's him. He was driving the BMW.'

'What about the other 3?'

'This one (#2) was in the front. These 2 (#3 and #4) got out the back.'

'And this was after the fight?'

'Not *after* . . . sorta during it. As it was going on. When the BMW driver went down.'

'After he was stabbed?'

'I din't see no one get stabbed. This one (#1) shoved Vine, then Vine hit him, then he grabbed Vine, then he went down. No one *stabbed* him.'

'That's because he wasn't the driver.'

'What?'

He taps the colour photograph. 'This is the driver, Michael. Lee Burke. It was his car. He was driving. He was the man you saw in the Nike cap. He was the man who fought with Mr Vine. He's the man that Mr Vine stabbed.'

'No—'

'Yes, Michael.'

'No – he was in the back of the car. He din't even get out till the other one had gone down.'

'That's what you're saying?'

'That's what *happened*. I was *there*. I saw it.'

Callan tilts his head at me. 'You were on the bridge?'

'Yeh.'

'How far is that from where the cars were?'

'I dunno . . . not far – 20 metres, something like that . . . 30 metres.'

He smiles. '20 or 30?'

'I dunno – I din't have a tape-measure with me.'

He ignores that and looks at the photocopied notes, running his finger over some little drawings and figures. 'From your position on the bridge . . . here,' he says, jabbing his finger, 'to the spot where the cars were parked . . . just here . . . is . . . let's see . . . here we are – 22.6 metres.' He looks up, a smug grin on his face. '22.6 metres, Michael. What's that in feet?'

'I dunno.'

'More than 50?'

'I spose.'

'More like 70, wouldn't you say?'

I shrug.

He looks at the clock again. It's getting on for 11 now. It's getting on . . . I'll tell you what – it's getting on my nerves is what. All this – all this . . . I dunno. What IS all this? What's Callan up to? What's his game? I mean, I dunno much about the wiggy business – not the REAL wiggies, anyway. I know how they do it on *The Vice* and *Taggart* and stuff, but that's just pretending. That's TV cops. This is REAL. But still . . .

I'm pretty sure there's stuff going on here that ain't right. Like Callan shouldn't be alone, for one thing. Me neither. And he shouldn't be coming round here this time of night . . . and he shouldn't be telling me names and showing me pictures . . . and – most of all – he shouldn't be doing all this YOU'RE WRONG stuff. That ain't right, is it?

Or maybe it is.

I dunno . . .

Anyway, now he's staring at me again – the tough-guy stare from the TV, all icy and hard – and it's hard to take. It's a different kinda stare than I'm used to. The ones I'm used to – the FAT stares – they ain't as HEAVY as this . . . they ain't got the same INTENSITY. FAT stares I can handle. They ain't got no PERMANENCE, if you know what I mean. This, though – Callan's stare . . . this is a look that lasts for ever. His eyes are frozen dark.

I wish I had something to eat.

Callan blinks, breaking the stare, then he gets up and starts getting his papers and stuff together. 'All right, Michael,' he says. 'That's all for the moment, thank you.'

I look at him, waiting for him to say something else, but his mind's off me now. I ain't nothing to him. I'm like . . . what am I like? A bit of jigsaw puzzle. Yeh, that's it – a bit of jigsaw puzzle. He's picked me up, turned me over in his fingers, had a good look, and now he's putting me to one side for later. Yeh, I'm like a bit of jigsaw puzzle . . . one of them muddy little brown bits that could go anywhere.

Callan puts his coat on. Buttons it up. Checks his pockets. Tucks his briefcase under his arm, then turns around and looks at me.

'I'd like you to think again about what you saw, Michael. Take your time, have a really good think – OK?' He smiles. 'And don't worry about anything. There's nothing to worry about. We all make mistakes now and then – it's perfectly understandable. Things happen so fast in the heat of the moment, don't they? It's easy to get confused. But that's OK, confusion's nothing to be ashamed of . . . as long as the truth comes out in the end. That's the main thing, Michael – making sure the truth comes out in the end. Do you understand?'

'Yeh.'

'Good.' He looks around the room, sniffs, then wipes his nose and looks back at me. 'OK,' he says. 'So you get your thinking cap on, then, and I'll be in touch in a few Days – all right?'

'Yeh.'

'Good lad. I'll see myself out.'

And he does – out into the dark, into his Rover 600, away down the street, and he's gone.

7/ Back on the Bridge

Like a GOOD LAD, I did what I was told – I thought about it. I thought about what I saw at the bridge. I took my time, had a really good think. Days, Days, Days, hitting the REWIND button, playing it back, REWIND, play it back, REWIND, play it back . . . we all make mistakes, don't we? confusion's nothing to be ashamed of . . . the main thing's the TRUTH. Yeh, right – I thought about that. The TRUTH, the TRUTH, the TRUTH, the TRUTH . . . and what I came up with was this:

Vine's a bad guy. 3 of the BMW boys are bad guys. The other one, Burke, he ain't nothing, just a right-shaped piece of meat. The BMW bad guys wanna take Vine OUT. I dunno why . . . it don't MATTER why . . . they just wanna take him out. So they rig up this road rage thing, stick Burke themselves, and make it look like Vine done it. And there you go – bingo! Vine's stitched up, sent down . . . the cops are happy, the BMW guys are happy, everyone's happy.

What d'you think?

It fits, don't it?

Maybe . . .

I dunno.

Anyway, that's what I thought.

I thought about other stuff, too. Like – maybe I oughta talk to Dad? And – what's the MATTER with you? This ain't no DAD thing, this is a YOU thing. And – why don't you just take the easy way out? Why don't you do what you always do – walk through it all with your eyes down. Give em what they want. Don't rock the boat. They want some lies – give em some lies. What's it to you? You ain't got no PRINCIPLES or nothing . . . you don't even know what a principle IS. You don't give a toss. Why not TAKE IT EASY?

Yeh, why not do that?

Do it.

Yeh.

OK.

Give em what they want.

Just do it.

OK, so that's what I'm gonna do . . . as soon as Callan gets in touch, I'm gonna tell him whatever he wants me to tell him. Yeh, Vine had a machine-gun . . . yeh, he chopped the other guy's head off . . . yeh, he fried him in butter and ATE HIM . . . that's right. That's what happened. I saw it with my very own eyes . . .

It ain't no problem.

So come and get it.

I'm waiting.

Oneday – I'm waiting.

Twoday – I'm waiting.

Threeday – I'm waiting.

Fourday – I'm still waiting.

What did Callan say? *I'll be in touch in a few Days . . .* What's a *FEW*? 2? 3? 4? What's it now? How many Days now? Fiveday = Zero. So Fourday = 6 Days from Fiveday.

6 Days?

6 ain't a FEW. 6 is nearly a *week* . . .

I HATE that – when people say they're gonna do something and then they don't do it. It really ANNOYS me. Why not just say you ain't gonna do it in the first place?

Anyway, there ain't much I can do about it, so I just carry on waiting . . . waiting, waiting, waiting . . .

Then, about a week later, which is a week after the first week of waiting, which makes it about 2 weeks after Callan came to see me, STUFF starts happening. I've just about given up on Callan by then. I'm still waiting, and I still got the goodies if he wants em, but I ain't so *hooky* about it no more. You know what I'm saying? It ain't bothering me so much. I ain't thinking about it ALL the time. And that's mainly, I think, cos I'm back at the bridge again.

It's kinda weird the first time I go back to the bridge, you know, that GOING BACK feeling – the NEWness, the squits . . . a banging heart . . . the evening streets . . . the country lanes . . . pedalling hard . . . puffing BILLY . . . sweating like a pig . . . but it's OK. I mean, it's still there. The bridge, the railings, the tide of traffic, the song of the road, the grey river . . .

It's all still there . . .

But now it's different.

I dunno WHY it's different . . . nothing's CHANGED. Like I said, it's all still there, it's just . . . I dunno . . . there's something else . . . something there that wasn't there before. I can't SEE it, but I KNOW it's there. I can FEEL it . . . like it's down below, beneath the surface . . . yeh, that's it. Like something's IN the river, something sunk. It's down there somewhere, hidden from sight, resting on the river bed, doing nothing . . . but it's doing *some*thing. The water's running round it, over it, changing the flow . . . yeh, that's it. Changing the FLOW. Not the bit you can SEE, but the bit below – the undercurrent.

The undercurrent's changed.

It's still the river, though. Still the bridge and the road . . . it's still MINE. And it's still good. Maybe not as good as before . . . not 100% yet . . . but that's OK. I can wait. And, anyway, a little bit less than 100% of something good is a whole lot better than 100% of nothing.

OK – so it's about 2 weeks after Callan came to see me, and it's Fiveday afternoon, which is HELL-TIME for me. Cos Fiveday afternoon is PE, which – for a FAT kid – is the WORST of the WORST of the WORST. PE, running, games . . . all that kinda stuff . . . it's the WORST THING IN THE WORLD. You can't climb the ropes, you can't jump the jumping thing, you can't touch your toes . . . you can't even SEE your toes . . . then there's basketball or 5-a-side or whatever – Shirts V Skins. And guess which side *you're* gonna play for. Yeh, right – Skins every time. EVERY time – *GET THE TENT OFF, MOO! LET'S SEE WHAT YOU GOT UNDER THERE! YAAAAA!! LOOKIT THAT!* And then the showers afterwards . . . in the showers . . . naked and blubbery bare . . . I don't even wanna THINK about that.

PE = **P**ain **E**xhibition.

ROLL UP! ROLL UP! SEE THE PAIN EXHIBITION! – EVERY FIVEDAY AFTERNOON! – ROLL UP! ROLL UP! SEE THE FUNNY FAT GUY! WATCH HIM SHAKE HIS CAKES! IT'S BLUBBER-TASTIC!!!!!

Today it's cross-country running . . . around the football pitch, out the back gates, down the streets, across the park, along the bank, through the estate, then back around the football pitch again . . . slopping through the mud . . . last as usual . . . gasping for breath, legs and belly on fire, tight shorts riding up your arse . . . with the rest of em waiting at the end, sitting there pointing at you and laughing or – worse – cheering through PITY . . .

GOD.

You think I'm doing that?

No chance.

I got a note from Mum. I got asthma, apparently. There's a lot of it about. Mad Johnny Jago – the guy who takes PE – he don't believe a word of it, but there ain't much he can do. I got a note. I got asthma, look – it says so right there. So what Jago does, after giving me a look like he wants to punch me in the belly, he says if I can't do cross-country I gotta go visit an OLD PERSON. *Community service*, he calls it.

'Do something useful for once,' he says.

'Right,' I says.

He gives me instructions. Get the old person's name and address from the headmaster's secretary. Go visit. Talk to em, be nice, ask em if there's any JOBS need doing . . .

'And don't even *think* about not going,' he says. 'Cos I'll be checking up. And if I find out you never showed up, I'll have you running round this field till you're thinner than Posh Spice – asthma or no asthma. You understand?'

'Yeh.'

'Go on, then.'

20 minutes later, I'm on the bridge.

It's all right. I mean, Jago ain't gonna check nothing . . . and so what if he does? This old person I'm sposed to be seeing, they're probly mad as a bat anyway, probly got Old Timer's disease or something . . . so even if Jago does check, even if he does ring em up and ask em questions, they ain't gonna know what he's talking about, are they? *Was there a what? a what? speak up . . . a boy? who's boy? when? oh, yes . . . when? who is this? hello?*

Yeh . . .

So I'm on the bridge, just watching the river, drifting away . . . drifting away . . . and I'm pretty sure I'm thinking about a little dig I got from one of the girls at school that morning. Debbie Mason, it was – she's one of the 3 I heard that time in the playground, the kiss-Moo-or-die thing. Course, she's older now, older and bigger and curvier . . . and does she know it? Yeh, you BET she does. And she likes to make sure everyone else knows it, too. A very POPULAR girl, is Debbie . . . POPULAR as a bike. Anyway, she was hanging round outside the toilets with this kid called Deon. It was after dinner. I was still hungry. I had this big bar of nougat and I'd just nipped into one of the cubicles to finish it off in peace . . . yeh, I know it ain't *nice* . . . but it's not like I dipped it in the bowl or nothing. The thing is, when I came out I musta got some bits of nougat stuck on my face, cos Debbie started pointing and giggling at me, showing off to Deon. I din't make nothing of it, though. Just walked past. And she din't like that.

'Hey, Moo,' she calls after me. 'What you been doing in there? You find it all right?'

'What?' I says.

'HEE HEE HEE,' she goes. 'Must be like looking for a worm in a big bag of fat.'

'You're the bird,' I says. 'You tell me.'

Which she don't get – which ain't surprising, cos it don't make sense. It does the trick, though – shuts her up for a second. Then Deon laughs, like a little snort through his nose, and he's probly laughing at me, but Debbie takes it like he's laughing at HER, and that makes her mad. I can see it in her eyes, and I start walking off.

'Hey, Nelson,' she calls out, all nasty and spitty. 'You getting any yet? You ever done it when you ain't on your own?

Have ya? Nah . . . course you ain't. I mean, how's that gonna work? That's what I wanna know. Who's the hell's gonna do it with YOU? Christ, you'd KILL em . . . YA YA YA . . . squash em flat . . . YA YA YA . . . splat em all OVER the shop . . . YA YA YA . . . YA YA YA . . . YA YA YA . . .'

Anyway, THAT's what I'm thinking about when I'm standing on the bridge, while the traffic sings its song. That's what I'm MULLING OVER. Thinking up things I coulda said to Debbie Mason. Funny things. Smart things. Nasty things. Thinking how the TRUTH hurts . . . how it creeps up behind you and drops a blanket over your head – a cold, black, greasy old blanket. And then you can't move. You ain't never been able to move. And you ain't never been nowhere else but here. You been stuck in this stinking darkness all your life and you're stuck here for ever. You can't do nothing. You don't wanna do nothing. You don't care. Who CARES?

THAT's how it hurts.

And the only thing that makes it better is the thing that makes it hurt in the first place.

Eating.

Food.

FAT.

You feel bad cos you're FAT, so you eat to make yourself feel better, which makes you get FATTER, which makes you feel badder, so you eat some more to make yourself better . . .

Bad = good.

Good = bad.

But at least I ain't been beat up for a while, and that's something, I guess. *You're still making it, Moo. Making it through the Days. You're still making it . . .*

Yeh, so that's me, just MULLING things over, thinking

up things I coulda said, knowing I ain't never gonna say em, cos I ain't got the GUTS, feeling sorry for myself, feeling sick of feeling sorry for myself . . . and then I hear something, something WRONG, and suddenly I ain't MULLING no more, I'm tingling, I'm buzzing, I'm a BUG-EYED BEAST. My head jerks around and I stare down the lane, listening HARD. It's a car . . . the sound of a car coming slowly up the lane. It's a different sound to the traffic below – TOTALLY different. Different road surface. Different air. Different speed. Different direction. It's as different as the sound of a trickling tap is different from the sound of a river. It's DIFFERENT. It don't BELONG here. It's outta place. Cos cars don't come up the lane – the lane don't go nowhere but the bridge. And the bridge is a footbridge, not a road-bridge. So what's a car wanna come up the lane for?

I step back from the railings and watch it pull up beside the steps – a light green Vauxhall Omega. The engine dies, dust blows in the air, then the door opens and DS Bowker gets out. He's on his own. No DC Dorudi this time, no one but him – and somehow that makes him look kinda scarier. He's wearing faded black jeans and a scuffed leather coat . . . he's slamming the car door . . . jangling his car keys . . . looking around at nothing . . . then he's slipping the keys in his pocket, raising his head, and looking up at me . . . his coppery eyes cutting through the dust and the afternoon light . . . shining hard, like animal eyes.

He starts up the steps.

For about a squillionth of a second, I think to myself – hey, don't worry about it, it's nothing, it's probly just . . . yeh . . . Jago's probly found out you din't go to the old person's place and he's sent the cops after you . . . but I KNOW I'm just trying to kid myself. Jago wouldn't do that. And even if he did . . . what's the cops gonna do? Laugh at him is what.

Like they got the time to go chasing after fat kids for not visiting old people . . . yeh, right. And anyway, it's Bowker, you dumb-arse . . . it's DS Bowker . . .

'Michael,' he says, reaching the top of the steps, looking over his shoulder. 'How you doing?'

'All right,' I grunt.

He comes up to me, looking around at the view – the road, the traffic – like he's seen it all before, like he's the KING of the WORLD or something. He stops beside me and runs his fingers through his wind-blown hair.

'You OK?' he says.

'Yeh.'

'What you doing up here?'

'Nothing.'

He grins, Mr Nice Guy. 'Afternoon off?'

'Yeh.'

'Don't blame you,' he says. 'I used to *hate* school.'

I don't say nothing.

He takes a deep breath and looks around again, sucking in the air like he's on the beach or something. Then he puts his hands in his pockets and looks at me.

'So,' he says, 'I hear John Callan's been to see you.'

'Yeh.'

'You have a nice chat?'

I shrug. 'It was all right.'

He nods his head and gazes around, looking kinda bored, like he's trying to make out he don't care too much, you know, like he ain't really interested in what I'm saying. Without looking at me, he says, 'This was a couple of weeks back, yeh?'

'Yeh.'

'Seen him since?'

'Nah . . . he said he'd be in touch, but he ain't.'

'Well, he's a busy man. There's a lot to do.' He takes his hands from his pockets and studies his fingernails. 'Did you wanna see him about something?'

'He wanted to see me.'

'About what?'

'I dunno . . . my statement, I spose.'

'What about it?'

'Din't he tell you?'

Bowker smiles. 'Like I said, there's a lot to do. It's a major investigation, Mike, there's a lot of people involved, and we're all covering different areas . . .' He scratches his head. 'To tell you the truth, the right hand doesn't *always* know what the left hand's doing . . .'

'Right.'

'Anyway, I'm sure Mr Callan hasn't forgotten about you.' He puts his hands back in his pockets and gazes down at the verge, looking at the spot where it happened. I take a look, too. The grass at the side of the road is scuffed and flattened and you can still see the tyre tracks of all the cars and ambulances and stuff. There's a metal pole there, stuck in the ground, leaning over – a rusty old black thing with a twisty little loop on top. A scrap of blue-and-white tape is tied to the loop, fluttering in the breeze, and bunches of flowers are scattered round the base of the pole, all wrapped up in cellophane, looking limp and dirty and wet.

Bowker says, 'I can pass on a message, if you like.'

'What message?'

'To Mr Callan.' He clears his throat. 'What was it he wanted to see you about, exactly?'

'Just some stuff in my statement . . . stuff he thought I might've got wrong.'

Bowker's eyes sharpen. 'Like what?'

'I dunno . . . the guys in the BMW . . . the thing about not seeing em till they got out the car . . .'

'That was right, though – wasn't it?'

'Well . . . yeh . . .'

'You *din't* see em till they got out the car. They were hiding in the back.'

'I know, but—'

'That's what you saw?'

'Yeh.'

'So what's the problem?'

'I dunno . . .' I'm getting confused here. 'Mr Callan said—'

'Listen, Mike. Lemme tell you something. When I took your statement I got the impression you were a pretty smart guy. Jenny did, too – DC Dorudi. She reckons you're one of the best witnesses she's ever come across – observant, precise, detailed . . . you know what I mean?'

'Yeh.'

'You just told it exactly as it happened – right?'

'Yeh.'

'So what's all this about changing your mind?'

'I dunno.'

'Smart guys don't change their minds. Not if they *know* they're right. You know you're right, don't you?'

'Yeh, I guess . . .'

'Good.' He sniffs hard, coughs up some snot, and gobs it out. Then he wipes his mouth and turns back to me. 'Anything else you're thinking of *changing*?'

'It wasn't me—'

'What else?'

'I dunno . . .'

'Don't gimme that. Come on . . . what *else*?'

'Well, I dunno . . . the stabbing thing, I spose . . . like who it was and what happened . . .'

'Vine din't have a knife.'

'No.'

'He din't stab anyone.'

'I know.'

'And the man who got stabbed wasn't the driver of the BMW.'

'I din't see *no one* get stabbed.'

'OK . . . but Mr Vine – he *definitely* din't stab anyone?'

'No.'

'That's how it was?'

'Yeh.'

'So the statement you made is true. That's how it happened. There's no need to change anything.'

'I spose not.'

'So don't change it.'

'What about—'

'Don't worry about anyone else. *I'm* the one you gotta worry about.'

'Why?'

He smiles hard at me. 'Cos I'm your conscience, Mike. I'm your truth.' He stares at me for a bit, then runs his fingers through his hair again and starts buttoning his coat.

The wind's getting cold.

And I'm getting mixed up good.

This guy's invaded MY PLACE. He's spat on my bridge. And now he's getting me so I dunno which way to turn. I dunno WHAT he's doing. I dunno who's SIDE he's on. I dunno WHAT he is. Good or bad. Friend or foe. Threat or promise. THAT's how he's got me.

And now . . .

He sniffs again, pulls up his collar, then reaches out and gives me a friendly poke in the belly . . . you know, one of THEM friendly pokes – hard enough to hurt, but not quite hard enough to LET ON that it hurts. One of them pokes that FAT guys don't mind cos they ain't got no feelings.

'OK?' he says.

'Yeh.'

'OK – so don't worry about anything. Don't worry about the statement, and leave Mr Callan to me. I'll have a quiet word with him and get it all sorted out – all right?'

'OK.'

'You probly won't hear from him again, anyway.'

'Why not?'

He sighs – like, it's really *complicated* . . . I gotta explain *everything*? – and I know he don't care and can't be BOTHERED with it, but I know he ain't gonna NOT tell me neither, cos NOT telling me's probly more bother than telling me. So I just look at him and wait. I watch him thinking . . . weighing things up, doing the thoughtful stuff with his face . . .

Then – *deedle-dee, deedle-dee, deedle-dee* – he's saved by the bell. He reaches into his pocket and pulls out a mobile phone and checks the caller ID. Nods his head, presses a button, slips the phone back in his pocket.

'I gotta go,' he says, searching for his car keys.

'Yeh, but what about—'

He holds up his hand – shut up. Finds his keys, rattles em, then looks at me. Quick and hard. I know what he's gonna say. And he says it.

'Look, I gotta go. I'll be in touch – OK?'

Yeh, yeh, yeh ..

Then he moves right up close to me, leans down, looks me in the eye, and lowers his voice. 'And don't forget what I said.'

'About what?'

'The truth.'

He holds it there for a moment, the heat of his face against mine, the breath of his words on my skin, a vision of me in his eyes . . . and then – *click* – the moment snaps and he's gone, striding away along the bridge and down the steps, with his leather coat flapping in the wind.

So, there you go . . . that's the way it's starting to look. Clear as mud, eh? **Now** I know the shape of things, but then it wasn't nothing but rolling clouds. Nothing . . . something . . . I just din't GET it. There wasn't nothing TO get. There was just one time, one place, one thing . . . one STUPID LITTLE MOMENT . . . and the next thing I know I'm slap-bang in the middle of something MENTAL . . . something I ain't got a CLUE about. Yeh, I got my GUESSES . . . but it's another world, don't forget, I'm guessing blind. I'm just making it up as I go.

Now it's getting on for 2 o'clock and I'm tired to death.

It's OK.

I think I'll be all right . . .

It's just THAT time . . . you know, the dead of night. The coldest and darkest and stillest time. The time when time stands still and nothing moves and your blood is black as hell.

See? It GETS to you.

8/ The Volvo Guy

A couple of Days after the stuff with Bowker, there's a thing about Keith Vine on the local TV news, just a short bit saying he's been charged with murder . . . and that's about it really. No details, no INFORMATION, no nothing. Apart from that, the rest of November is mostly just waiting to see what happens. The Days are still pretty good. They ain't GREAT or nothing . . . I mean, I still ain't PART of nothing. I'm still the FAT KID. I still get the LOOKS and the WHISPERS and the SNORTS and the MOOS . . . but that's about as far as it goes. It's like the RAINclouds are still *there*, looming in the air, keeping me cold and dark, but at least they ain't RAINing down on me. And that's OK, cos cold and dark ain't great, but it's a whole lot better than cold and dark *and* WET.

I still don't GET it – *why* thing's have changed – not for sure, anyway. I still don't GET why the kids at school ain't beating up on me no more. But I know one thing – it ain't got nothing to do with THEM. THEY ain't changed. It's me. Or something to do with me. And that's a definite. Cos, all right, they mighta stopped RAINing on me, but they ain't stopped RAINing on Brady. Hooo . . . NO. He's getting it good. Every Day, near enough. Every which way. Whacks, gobs, the funny RAIN, monkeys, girls, the dirty names . . . he's getting it ALL. And I think – I KNOW – he's getting it for me, too. He's getting my share. *Double* whacks, *double* gobs, *double* RAIN . . .

It's a shame . . .

I know.

But what can I do? I mean, it ain't MY fault, is it? I din't ASK em to lay off me and take it out on Brady. I never ASKED for it, did I? That's what I tried telling him . . . Brady . . . I *tried* telling him . . . after school one time . . .

'Brady! Hey, Brady, hold up . . .'

But he won't even LOOK at me, just limps away across the park holding a hand to his face, like he's the Elephant Man or something. And he don't reply to my emails neither . . . except once . . . yeh. One time . . . this is when he first started getting it hard, end of November maybe.

I wrote:

b – i know u getting it bad but dont blame me alright? – ithink is something to do with bowker and his dad and the cops and that . . . i dunno. something like they keeping me sweet or something. anyways – just dont get mad at me about it ok?
moo

And he comes back with this:

whose mad? i aint mad. u said u cant talk about it so dont talk about it – u think i give a shit?

Yeh, I do, ACTUALLY. I think you give a whole lot more than a shit . . . but I ain't gonna make a big deal about it. You wanna be funny? OK – be funny. See if I care. I got better things to do than flop around after you – I got my own turds to flush.

Turds like this –

Every morning for the last week there's been a guy in a Volvo 340 parked at the end of our road. Same guy, same car, same place, same time every Day. 8.25 in the morning. End of the road, on the other side, parked behind number 9's cronked-out Transit. An F reg Volvo 340 – old and grey and scratched and dirty, with bust-up doors and green stuff growing on the trim. The guy in the car's kinda old and greyish, too. About 50, I guess. Raincoat, hat, glasses, ratty little moustache. He don't DO nothing, just sits there, looking like he's *sposed* to be doing something. One Day he's waiting for someone – reading a newspaper. Next Day he's got a clipboard. Then he's fiddling with a map or a bag or a packet of fags or something . . .

It's pretty creepy, and I don't like it much – but what am I gonna do?

Knock on the window, say – who're you?

Tell the cops?

Watch him? See what he does?

Follow him?

How?

On my *bike*?

Nah . . . I ain't gonna do NOTHING, am I? I'm just gonna walk on by every Day and wonder what's up. I'm gonna get to school and think about it . . . but not *too* much, just a bit . . . cos mostly I'm just gonna ease on through the Day, soaking up the absent RAIN, making the most of it, wallowing in the silent drought. I'm gonna eat, sit, drink, listen, walk . . . all nice and easy . . . Maths, Engerlish, break, Snickers, Biology, sex, sniggers . . . dinnertime . . . mash, beans, pork, fruity pie and custard for afters, pile it on, pile it up, pile it in . . . and the Day goes on . . . French, Physics, break, Twix, Maths again . . . and the afternoon dims, the day starts to die, and pretty soon it's time to go home again, and I'm smiling inside cos it's nearly time for the bridge. It won't be long . . . soon soon soon . . . and then I'm walking back through the village, half-looking out for Brady – not that I really WANNA see him, but . . . yeh, all right, I WANNA see him – and there he is, look, bent over a brick wall at the back of the shop getting a face full of dog shit . . . getting it good from Dec Bowker and the boys . . . and there's Jicky Collins, giving me the wink, like I'm on THEIR side now . . . and I dunno what to do . . . cos half of me's sad for Brady, but the other half's glad for me . . . so I just stand there for a bit, half-watching em, half-thinking I oughta do *some*thing . . . but I know I ain't got it in me . . . I ain't got the GUTS . . .

So I just start walking again.

Half-hearted.

I walk on by with my eyes down.

Back home the Volvo's gone and everything's NORMAL. House, bathroom, bedroom . . . go upstairs and get changed . . . big check shirt, big hoody hood, big troozies . . . go downstairs . . . and the kitchen's hot with the smell of fried eggs and bacon and chips and beans. Dad's sitting at the table snorting at Carol Fordaman's hair, and Mum's wiping chip-fat sweat from her face.

'How many you want, Moo?' she says.

'How many what?'

'Eggs.'

'How many you got?'

Dad laughs . . . coughs . . . turns red. He wipes his mouth and coughs again.

'All right?' he asks me.

'Yeh.'

'Hungry?'

'Yeh.'

We eat to the sound of coughing and *Countdown*.

He's something, my dad. I ain't sure what, exactly . . . but he's something all right. Too much for **now**. Too much for this. Too big, too many stories, too much to tell. But I'll tell you this much. He might not be perfect – in fact, come to think of it, he ain't nowhere NEAR perfect – but he's MY DAD, and he's always THERE. No 2 ways about it. He don't SAY much, and he don't DO much, and he don't make a big FUSS about nothing, but he's always been there. Always . . . for as long as I can remember. And when I say always, I mean ALWAYS. Not just evenings and weekends. ALWAYS. Every Day – mornings, afternoons, evenings, weekends . . . EVERY SINGLE DAY. Money-wise, I dunno how he does it. I mean, he ain't never had a JOB, exactly. He ain't never done nothing with a NAME . . . you know – like Postman or Milkman or Accountant. He just . . . I dunno . . . he just *meets* people now and then . . . does a bit of this, a bit of that . . . know what I mean? He does enough to keep us going. Plus there's always the benefit money he gets for his dodgy heart . . . which ain't much . . . but, all in all, we do all right. I mean, we ain't loaded or nothing, but we exactly ain't starving, neither. Well, we're *starving*, but not in *that* kinda way. We ain't starving cos we're poor-and-ain't-eaten-for-a-week, we're just starving cos we're FAT and HUNGRY and we WANT SOME MORE . . .

So, anyway, there's some of Dad, as much as you need to know, and there's me, and there's this mysterious Volvo guy . . . and then there's the return of DI Callan.

And this is how it all comes together.

I don't remember what Day it was . . . it don't matter anyway

. . . but it was a school Day. The week after the Volvo guy first showed up. Actually, now I come to think about it, I DO remember what Day it was. It was a Threeday. Yeh, cos I remember the Volvo guy wasn't there Oneday and Twoday and then he *was* there again Threeday morning. Same place, same time, same car, same guy, only this time he ain't got a map or a clipboard or a newspaper, he's just sitting there giving me a good long look. Which normally I'd avoid. But I got me some front now. What with not getting RAINed on all the time, I'm getting a bit more COCKY. So instead of looking away, I look back at him . . . like – yeh, what you looking at, Wrinkly? And that's when I realise he ain't so old and weedy after all. He's *old*, yeh . . . but he's kinda tough, too. Kinda cold and meaty . . . like he wouldn't think twice about pushing you off a cliff. And I ain't got enough front for THAT. So I drop it. Look down, look away, and walk on.

Forget it.

I'm pretty good at forgetting things. I can take a bad taste, wrap it up tight, and swallow it down. I can put it away. Lock it up in a box. Pretend it ain't there. I can do that . . . easy.

So I do it.

Forget it.

But later on, after school . . . I'm out through the gates . . . still forgetting . . . and I'm walking down the school road . . . still forgetting . . . and then *BOOF!* A flash of dirty grey stops me dead. The damn Volvo's parked at the end of the road, and suddenly I ain't forgetting no more. I'm stopping, staring, burping up the bad taste, staring at the Volvo guy standing on the pavement, smoking a cigarette . . . watching me with his cliff-killer eyes.

Waiting for me.

And I think to myself – why not walk back the other way today? Around the back of the shop and through the park.

Yeh . . . why not?

So I turn around, bumping into a bunch of kids behind me –

('Watch it, Moo!'

'Chrissake!'

'Sorry.')

– and head for the park.

It ain't like I'm SCARED or nothing . . . not really. I'm just being WARY is all. I'm used to it – being wary. It comes natural to me. And I'm good at it, too. I'm an *expert* in wariness. I got a black belt in it.

Right now, heading for the park, I'm waried stiff.

I wanna look back and see if he's still after me, but I know better than that. I KNOW the rules – don't look back, don't run, don't panic, don't stop . . . just keep going, keep your eyes down, melt into the ground. Make yourself NOTHING – Me? Nah, you don't wanna bother with me. I mean – look at me. What's the point? I just ain't worth it, am I?

That's the way to do it. Make yourself NOTHING.

It even *works* sometimes.

Not today, though. Cos today's different.

I'm about halfway across the park, eyes to the ground, walking fast-but-not-too-fast . . . *tump, tump, tump* . . . and I'm risking a quick look up to make sure I'm heading in the right direction, heading for the swings, the gap in the hedge, and that's when I see him – DI Callan, perched on a swing, with his hands in his waxy coat pockets and his eyes fixed on me. I slow down and start to turn around – and then I get it. I KNOW what I'm gonna see before I see it . . . I KNOW who's gonna be there – and there he is, the Volvo guy, standing at the top of the park with his back to the shop, hands in his raincoat pockets, staring at the sky, blocking my exit. Oh yeh, I get it. It's like I'm the thingy bird . . . the peasant or phartridge or grouts or whatever. The Volvo guy's the whatsit . . . the beater, the guy who flushes the birds out and sends em flying off in the right direction. And Callan's the posh knob waiting at the other end with a loaded shotgun in his hand.

POW!

He takes his hand from his pocket and beckons me over.

I don't move.

He flicks a look at the Volvo guy, then looks back at me and nods his head – come *here* – NOW.

I could run, I spose, but I ain't exactly the zippiest guy in the world. I ain't no Limford Christy or nothing. And anyway, where the hell am I gonna run *to*? There always the phone box at the other end of the field, I guess . . . but who'm I gonna ring? Mum? Dad? The cops? Yeh, right, the cops . . . tell em I'm trying to get away from DI Callan . . . they're gonna love that, ain't they? And anyway . . . Callan IS a cop . . . he's a police *officer* – a good guy. He ain't gonna EAT me, is he?

So, what the hell . . .

I start walking towards him – *tump, tump, tump* – watching him grow with every step I take. Watching him watching me, taking aim, ready to shoot . . .

'Michael,' he says, nodding his head. 'How are you?'

'I'm all right.'

'Sit down,' he says, indicating the swing beside him. 'Take the weight off your feet.'

I look at him to see if he's taking the piss . . . but it's hard to tell. The Daylight's nearly gone. It's half-dark, dusky, blurry . . . that colourless time of Day when everything looks the same. Callan's face is as blank as a rock.

'I'm all right here,' I tell him.

'Suit yourself.' He looks down, flicks at something on his coat, then looks up, giving me the tough/silent treatment.

I take it for a while, but then my mouth gets the better of me.

'Who's your friend?' I ask him.

'Hmm?'

'The guy in the coat . . .' I start to say, turning round to point him out – but of course he ain't there no more. There's just an empty space where he was standing, just empty crisp packets blowing around the car park, like no one's EVER been there . . . like I'm crazy . . . but I know I ain't, cos I can see his ghost in the winter dark. I can see his OUTLINE.

I turn back to Callan. 'There was a man . . .'

'What man?'

I look at him, look into his dead-eyed face . . . he thinks I'm stupid. OK, I think . . . all right. You want stupid? Here's stupid. Mouth shut, staring dumbly at the ground . . . how's that?

'Michael?' Callan says.

Stupid says nothing.

'*Michael.*'

'What?'

'Look at me.'

Stupid raises his head. 'What?'

Callan looks at me, all THOUGHTFUL and WISE, like he's trying to work out what to DO with me. Then, after half a minute or so, he takes a deep breath and says, 'So . . . you're sticking to your story then?'

'What story?'

'Your statement.'

'It ain't a *story* . . .'

'No?'

I shake my head, thinking – here we go again . . . this

way, that way . . .

Callan goes, 'There's still time, you know.'

'For what?'

'For you to do the right thing.' He arches his neck and scratches his cheek. 'Vine's been charged with murder,' he says. 'There's going to be a trial. I've got solid witnesses, forensic evidence . . . I've got just about everything I need. He's going down, Michael – guaranteed.'

I shrug. 'So?'

'So it'd make things a whole lot easier for me if you stopped pissing about. I know what's going on—'

'Ain't *nothing* going on—'

'What's DS Bowker saying?'

'Uh?'

'What's he giving you?'

'He ain't giving me *nothing*—'

'Listen,' he says, pointing a finger. 'I don't *need* you for this – you're not *necessary*, d'you understand? I can get what I want without you. You're just an irritant. Like a piece of grit in my eye.'

'Thanks a lot.'

His voice softens. 'You think I'm the bad guy here?'

'I dunno.'

'Let me tell you something,' he says, smiling. 'Compared to Keith Vine, I'm an *angel*. Believe me – you think *I'm* bad? Vine's *made* of bad. He *breathes* bad. If *he* thinks he needs you – he's going to take you. He's going to chew you up and spit you out. Is that what you want?'

'I don't *want* nothing.'

He pauses, looking at me – and from here and **now** I can see myself standing there being LOOKED at . . . staring at the ground, surrounded by dark and grass and not-knowing . . . and I feel like reaching out and getting hold of myself, shaking myself, shouting at myself – HEY . . . HEY! WHY THE HELL DON'T YOU *TELL* HIM? TELL HIM YOU DUNNO WHAT HE'S *TALKING* ABOUT . . . WHY DON'T YOU JUST OPEN YOUR MOUTH AND *TELL* HIM?

Cos I DON'T know, that's why. Cos I probly don't care. Cos I KNOW that don't-caring is the easiest way out. Don't care . . . it'll go away . . . don't care . . . it'll go away . . . don't care . . . it'll go away . . .

'Do you know what a *dilemma* is?' Callan says.

'Some kinda car?' I suggest, suddenly the smart-arse. 'A Fiat Dilemma?'

His mouth twitches, like he's trying to grin . . . or trying *not* to. 'OK,' he says, holding up 2 fingers. 'You've got 2 things. You don't want to do either of them, but you've got to do one. OK? That's your problem. A difficult choice. A dilemma. Understand?'

'Yeh.'

'One thing's right, but the outcome is wrong. The other thing's wrong, but the outcome is right. What are you going to do?'

'I dunno. I dunno what you're talking about.'

'Don't you?' He smiles, looks down at his shoes for a bit, then raises his head and looks at me again. 'OK,' he says slowly, 'let's put it this way. Let's say your dad's doing something wrong—'

'What's he doing—'

'Nothing—'

'He ain't doing nothing—'

'No – I said let's *say* he is . . . just for argument's sake. Let's say he's doing something wrong, but it's something and nothing, something stupid, something that doesn't actually *harm* anyone.'

'Like what?'

He rubs his chin. 'Ohh . . . I dunno . . . some kind of small-time fraud, maybe. Benefit fraud . . . something like that.' He stops speaking and smiles at me, and a bell starts ringing somewhere in the back of my head. An alarm bell – *dingalingalingalinga* . . .

'You with me?' says Callan.

'Yeh.'

'OK . . . so what are you going to do? You find out your dad's doing something wrong, and you *know* it's wrong, you *know* it's against the law, and you're a law-abiding citizen . . . but you don't want to grass him up, do you? He's your dad . . . you don't grass on your dad.' He looks at me. 'See? It's a problem, isn't it? A difficult choice. A dilemma. You see what I'm saying?'

'Not really.'

He sighs, giving me one of his LOOKS – not sure now if I'm dumb or just making out I'm dumb – then he shakes his head and looks up at the darkening sky, like he's praying to the stars. And I think to myself – is he THREATENING me? Is that what he's doing? Nah, I tell myself, it's nothing . . . don't worry about it . . . he's just giving you a yank, a tug, a push, a warning shove, a watch-it poke in the arm . . .

That's all.

Callan gets up off the swing and stands in front of me, looking down, looking tall and cold in the dark, making me take half a step back.

'Sometimes,' he says, 'sometimes you've got to do what's wrong to make things right.'

'Right.'

'And sometimes,' his voice getting hard, 'sometimes, getting it right can hurt.'

'What about getting it wrong?'

'That's up to you,' he says. 'But if I were you, I'd make damn sure I got it right.'

'Right.'

His head and shoulders move back, like he's trying to get me in focus, then he reaches out a hand – and just for a second I think he's gonna whop me . . . but no . . . it's all right, he's just . . . *CHRISSAKE* . . . he's RUFFLING my HAIR, like I'm 8 years old . . . then hup-*CUFF* . . . and *whooo!* that's better – a good old clip across the head. Not hard, not even close . . . just a CUFF . . . a man-to-boy thing . . . that's all . . . one of them friendly clips-across-the-head that puts you in your FATBOY place.

'Think about it,' he says, man-to-boy. 'You got 7 Days.'

The thing about this is I KNOW IT. I KNOW what's going on. But it's hard to know if I'm giving it out right. It's like I got all the stuff in my head, the REASONS and stuff – the WHYs and the WHOs and the WHATs – but it's all kinda jumbled up, cos that's how it happened – all jumbled up – and I dunno if I'm giving it out too *jumbly* . . . or if I should maybe make it a bit more straighter . . .

If that makes any sense . . .

Probly not.

Anyway, I dunno . . . I think jumbly's probly all right. At least it's HONEST. And as long as I get it straightened out in the end . . . that's the MAIN THING, I spose . . .

I dunno . . .

I'll have to think about it.

Right **now**, I gotta go to the bog.

9/ Donut

The Days and weeks go by. November crawls into December, the weather gets colder, school breaks up, and Christmas comes and goes. I get some new games, CDs, vids, a new black hood, some car books . . . the usual kinda stuff. We EAT a lot. Watch TV. Then it's off to Uncle Dave's at Southend for a couple of Days . . . more food, boozy New Year parties, midnight singing and drunk uncles fighting . . . and then pretty soon it's back home and back to normal again. January Days – cold and wet and dark – back to school . . . back to whatever it is.

Days, the bridge, nights.

Days, the bridge, nights.

Days, the bridge, nights . . .

Callan don't show his face, and neither does Bowker, but the Volvo guy's still around. Not as much as he was before, not every Day, but he's definitely still around. I seen him. In the village, around the lanes, here and there, now and then . . . I even seen him in Southend once. I'm pretty sure it was him, anyway. I dunno, though . . . it's hard to tell, cos once you start looking out for crappy grey Volvo 340s, you can't *stop* seeing em. They're *every*where. And the drivers are all the same – they're *all* old and grey and raincoaty. It's like they're a SPECIES or something . . . *Oldus Greyus Raincoatius* . . . the Volvovians. And I see em so much now, or I see *him* so much – whichever it is – I'm actually getting used to it. I'm getting like one of them monkeys you see on

TV, the ones they follow round for years with cameras and that. Like, I KNOW I'm being watched, and I dunno why, but as long as I ain't getting HURT or nothing – who cares? If they wanna watch me – let em watch. Ain't no skin off *my* arse.

Which is mostly a LIE, of course. Cos I ain't no MONKEY. I got stuff going on in my head that'd make a monkey SCREAM – know what I mean? I got PONDERINGS . . . I got POSSIBILITIES . . . I got POTENTIALITIES . . .

Nah, I ain't no MONKEY.

I wish I *was*.

But I ain't.

OK, so what happens next is, a couple of weeks after New Year we get this phone call from a guy called Clark. It's a bit confusing at first. It's just after tea and I'm on my way out to the bridge when the phone rings. Mum gets it, says hello, then waves me over as I'm halfway out the door. She's wiggling her finger in the air, rolling her eyes, pointing at me, then pointing at the phone . . . I dunno *what* she's doing, but I guess she wants me to wait, so I sit down on the stairs and wait, listening to one end of the phone conversation.

It goes like this:

–

– Who?

–

– Clark? Clark *who*? What solicitor?

–

– Sorry? You're *whose* Clark?

–

– Oh, right . . . *clerk*. Like a sales clerk?

–

– Yeh, that's gotta be confusing.

–

– Right . . . yeh . . . I see . . . right . . . uh-huh . . . hmmm . . . yeh, well, he's here if you wanna . . .

–

– No, OK.

–

– What for?

–

– I dunno . . . I spose so . . . when?

–

– Well . . . I dunno about that—

–

– Oh, right . . . right yeh . . . no, I'm sure he won't . . .

–

– Of course . . . yeh, OK. Thanks.

–

– All right then . . . g'bye.

–

She puts the phone down and looks at me.

'Who was that?' I ask her.

'Solicitors,' she says, like that explains *everything*.

'What solicitors?'

'Well, he's called Mr Clark . . . and I think he said he's the solicitor's clerk. Like a secretary or something, I spose . . .'

'*What* solicitors, Mum?'

She frowns. 'Horse Something, I think he said. Horse's Moulding? Horse and Poldy? I dunno . . . something like that . . .'

'Horse and Poldy?'

'He had a lisp.'

'Who?'

'Mr Clark – the solicitor's clerk. He said they wanna see you about that road rage thing.'

'Me? Why?'

'They're sending a car . . .'

This goes on for about 5 minutes – me asking questions . . . Mum not answering em . . . or answering em in the wrong order . . . so you dunno what she's talking about. She's like that sometimes. A bit scatty. Like she's never quite *with* you – she's always either one step behind or one step ahead. It gets on your nerves a bit sometimes, but it ain't so bad once you get used to it. All you gotta do is keep on going. So that's what I do – I keep on going. I keep asking Mum what the guy on the phone said, and in the end I get there. I get the story.

Apparently, the guy on the phone, Mr Clark, he works for these solicitors in Moulton who're working for Keith Vine . . . they're *defending* him, OK? And they wanna see me about the statement I gave the cops. They wanna go over some *details* . . . have a little chat . . . no problems, no worries . . . they'll even send a car, with a driver, to take me and Mum to their office in Moulton – *and* back again – tomorrow morning, if that's *convenient*. Which, according to Mum – who'll do anything for a cheap Day out – it is.

'Do I get the Day off school?' I ask her.

'I spose.'

'What about Dad? Is he coming with us?

'No.'

'Why not?'

'He's allergic to solicitors.'

Next morning then, about 9 o'clock, this VERY nice Audi Quattro 4.2 Twin Turbo comes rolling down the street and stops outside our house. The guy who gets out and rings the bell is a tough little cookie dressed up smart in a dull black suit. He's got no hair, a thick chin, and a short fat neck. He looks like a midget weightlifter. Mum, who for some reason is wearing her best purple ski pants, gets the door.

'Good morning,' she says, like she's a princess or something. 'You must be Mr Clark. Would you care for a cup of tea?'

'Best if we just get going,' the little guy grunts. 'Fanks all the same.'

And off we go – me and Mum in the back, the midget tough guy lost in the driver's seat. He's so small I can't even see his head. GOD knows how he can drive. He must have special pedals or something . . . or platform shoes. Anyway, once we're out the village and onto the road, the Audi takes off like a silent rocket – *shhhhuuuushhhhhhh* – and before you know it we're purring through the streets of Moulton, into the town centre, then up and down the hilly backstreets, then pulling up at the back of a smart-looking office building. It's one of them big old white places, with bars on the windows and stone steps and pillars and stuff. There's a little car park outside the building and it's jammed up with BMWs and Mercs and Porsches, all of em clean as a pin.

Very nice.

The driver, or clerk, or whatever he is – who, by the way, ain't said a word since we left the house – he gets out the car and opens the door for us. Mum smiles at him and we both squeeze out.

'This way,' he says.

We follow him across the car park to a flight of steps that leads up to a shiny black door. A brass plaque on the wall beside the door says – *HAWKS, SPALDING – SOLICITORS*.

I nudge Mum's arm. 'Hawks, Spalding,' I tell her. 'Not Horse and Poldy.'

She shrugs and grins. 'Close enough.'

Inside the building it's all plush carpets and leather chairs and gold-framed pictures on the walls. BIG pictures, like paintings, most of em beardy old guys on horses, that kinda thing. Short-arse leads us past a reception desk, where the SEXIEST GIRL IN THE WORLD is tapping a keyboard and smiling enough to nearly KILL me . . . then the midget stops outside a big wooden door and knocks gently.

'YES?' goes a voice on the other side.

The midget guy opens the door and shows us in, then he turns around and creeps back out.

I ain't even thought about this up to now. I'm just kinda going along with it . . . enjoying the ride . . . *half*-enjoying it anyway. Riding in the Audi was OK, and I kinda like the fact that Mum's having a good time – that gives me a bit of a kick . . . but the rest of it – this, walking into an office where a guy in a million-pound suit is sitting behind a leather-topped desk . . . I ain't given this much thought . . . which is probly just as well, cos I wouldn't know where to start.

It's a pretty BIG office. A BIG window with BIG white blinds. Loads of glass cases and shelves and stuff, books all over the place, framed photos on the wall showing the guy in the suit with sexy girls and local footballers and soap stars and other guys in suits. It's the kinda place that makes you feel *uncomfortable*, if you know what I mean.

The guy in the suit stands up and smiles and comes out from behind his desk, offering his hand.

'Pleased to meet you, Mrs Nelson,' he says – shake shake shake. 'My name's JD MacDonald, I'm a senior partner here. Thanks very much for coming.'

Mum gives an embarrassed nod. She's probly wondering, like me, if he said *JD* or *Jaydee* or *Jadey* or what.

MacDonald turns to me. 'And you must be Michael?'

'Yeh.'

'It's a pleasure to meet you.' Shake shake shake. 'Please,'

he says, showing us a couple of big leather chairs, 'sit down.'

We sit down. He slopes off behind his desk.

'Can I get you anything?' he says. 'Tea, coffee . . .?'

Mum looks at me. I look back at her, like – hey, don't look at *me* . . . *I* dunno what to say.

MacDonald says, 'Have you eaten yet?'

Dumb question. I mean, do we *look* like the kinda people who ain't gonna eat before coming out? Yeh, course we've *eaten*. Sausages, bacon, fried eggs, and fried bread, thanks very much. I don't say nothing, though, cos Mum's giving me this hungry look, and I can see her thinking – *free food, free food, free food* . . .

'Listen,' MacDonald says to her, leaning forward and pulling a fat leather wallet from his pocket. 'You're more than welcome to stay while I go over a few things with Michael . . . but, to tell you the truth, it may get a little boring . . .' He smiles, like – ho ho ho, you know what us *solicitors* are like. 'If you'd rather nip out for a little shopping or a bite to eat . . .' he peels a few notes from his wallet '. . . we'd be more than happy to reimburse you for your time. It's entirely up to you, Mrs Nelson.'

Mum eyes the cash, which looks like – and I ain't joking – about 60 quid. 60 quid! Just like that.

'Well . . .' says Mum. 'I don't wanna get in your way or nothing . . .'

'Of course,' goes MacDonald. 'Of course.' He hands her the cash and picks up a phone – *click*. 'Tracy?' he says. 'Mrs Nelson is popping out for a while. Would you show her to the car, please . . . and make sure she gets everything she needs. Thank you.' *Click*. He says to Mum, 'Mr Clark will drive you wherever you want to go and pick you up later. Is that OK?'

'Very nice,' says Mum.

The office door opens and Tracy comes in, all legs and teeth and golden hair . . . AAAAAAHHH! . . . and then she takes Mum out and shuts the door, leaving me and Mr MacDonut looking at each other across the desk.

'Lovely woman,' he says.

'Yeh,' I reply, not sure if he means Mum or Tracy.

'Right,' he goes, opening a folder on the desk. 'Let's get down to business.'

He's a skinny guy, kinda tall and beaky, with milky eyes and a long chin and a long narrow face. He's got that superfine blondy hair that all the posh guys have, in fact everything about him is posh posh posh. He *oozes* posh. You could dress him up like a dosser and rub dirt in his face, and he'd *still* look posh.

'Right,' he says again, this time making a note on a piece of paper with a slim silver pen, then looking up at me with one of them awkward smiles that grown-ups put on when they ain't used to being alone with kids. 'Right – is everything OK?'

'Yeh.'

'Good . . . well, let me explain the situation here.' He clears his throat. 'We – that is my company – Hawks, Spalding – we specialise in criminal law. Do you know what that means?'

'Murder and stuff?'

He laughs – *phnur, phnur, phnur* – like his nose is blocked up with snot. 'Yes, well,' he goes, 'I dare say that's as good a definition as any – *phnur, ha-phnur, phnur* . . .' He stops laughing and clears his throat. 'Actually,' he says, 'what we do . . . well, we mainly deal with clients accused of substantial crimes, crimes *such* as murder and . . . and *stuff*, as you put it.'

'You defend em?'

'Yes,' he says. 'That's right. We're defence lawyers. In this particular case . . .' he taps the folder on his desk '. . . we're acting for Mr Vine who's been charged with the murder of Mr Burke. Are you with me?'

'Yeh.'

'Good. Now then . . .' he slips a sheet of paper from the folder '. . . in a case such as this, all the evidence and witness statements gathered by the police are passed on to us through the CPS lawyers . . . sorry, CPS – that's the Crown Prosecution Service. They have to disclose the material they plan to use in court, you see . . . and also the material they *don't* plan to use – which is where you come in, Michael.' He looks across at me – Mr Sympathetic. 'I'm sorry if this is a lot to take in all at once, but I think it helps to know the background . . . you know, it helps to understand these things.'

'Right.'

'So,' he says, 'your statement . . . the written statement you gave to . . .' he looks down at the papers on his desk, searching for the names '. . . DS Bowker and . . . ah . . . let's see . . . a DC Dorudi. Is that right?'

'Yeh – they came to my house.'

He nods, narrowing his eyes and pursing his lips, like he's REALLY listening to what I'm saying. 'Good,' he goes, 'yes . . . very good. Now . . .' He scans the papers on his desk then looks up again and smiles. 'This is all very helpful, Michael. Very helpful indeed.' He picks out some papers and slides em across the desk – photocopies of my statement. 'This is the statement you gave to the police?' he says.

I read through the first few lines.

'Yeh,' I tell him, 'that's it.'

'Would you mind reading it through to the end? Just to refresh your memory.'

'OK.'

I start reading again . . . scanning the words . . . remembering how they was copied down – I said something, Dorudi repeated it, made it sound right, then wrote it down . . . I said something else, Dorudi repeated it, made it sound right, then wrote it down – which makes it read kinda funny, like it ain't got nothing to do with me, like it's just some kinda newspaper story or something . . . but I guess it's pretty much what happened. Anyway, I get about halfway down the first page and then I start getting bored . . . I just can't be arsed to read it ALL again . . . and I can't concentrate anyway, not with MacDonut sitting there watching me like a hawk (a spoldy hawk), so I just stare at the words, moving my eyes a bit, moving my lips, turning the pages . . . dah-di-dah-di-dah . . . dah-di-dah-di-dah . . . till I reckon it's OK to pretend I finished.

'Yep,' I tell him, passing back the pages. 'That's it.'

'Good,' he says. 'Now . . . I just need to ask you a few questions, if you don't mind. Is that OK?'

'Yeh.'

'Right . . . OK. You're happy to confirm that this is the statement you originally made to the police?'

There's that *HAPPY* thing again . . . why'd they keep asking me if I'm *HAPPY*? Maybe it's some kinda LAW or something, something to do with witnesses? Like they GOTTA keep asking me if I'm HAPPY about everything, cos it's against the witness-rules NOT to . . .

'Michael?' says MacDonut.

'Yeh?'

'I need to know if this is your original statement.'

'Yeh . . . yeh, it is.'

'And you're positive that the account of the events you've given is accurate?'

'That's what happened, yeh.'

'OK . . . good. Now, is there anything you wish to add to the statement, or anything you think needs clarifying?

'Nope.'

'Excellent. So . . . you wouldn't have any problems standing by what you've said in court?'

'Court?'

'As a witness . . . under oath.'

'What – like a defence witness?'

'Indeed.'

'I'd have to stand up in one of them boxes?'

'In the witness box – yes.'

Now I'm suddenly getting this picture of me standing up in front of all these people, lawyers and judges and cops and whatever, all of em looking at me, asking me questions . . . and I can see old Callan sitting there, too, giving me his frozen stare . . . and it don't feel too good.

'Well . . .' I say. 'I dunno . . .'

MacDonut leans across the desk, serious as hell. 'Listen to me, Michael . . . this is important – *very* important. You *know* what happened that Day . . . you were there, you saw it. You *know* Mr Vine is innocent, don't you?'

'I din't see him stab no one.'

'Precisely – he's an innocent victim of . . . well, I'm not at liberty to go into the *complexities* of the case with you . . . but let's just say there are – how should I put it? – there are *ulterior* motives at work here.'

'He's been fitted up?'

MacDonut raises his eyebrows and shrugs, like Mr Mysterioso . . . you know, wink, wink, Secret City, you din't hear it from me, so keep it under your hat . . . or maybe that's just what he *wants* me to think? I dunno . . . I guess I ain't smart enough to know the difference.

'D'you know Mr Callan?' I ask him.

Bing! – his eyes light up. 'Ah, yes,' he says. 'Detective Inspector Callan, our friendly investigating officer. You've met him, I take it?'

'Yeh – he wanted me to change my story.'

'Did he, indeed?'

'Said I was confused.'

'Really? That's very interesting. Mind you, I can't say I'm altogether surprised – Mr Callan is a very determined man.'

'Why's he fitting up Vine?'

MacDonut smiles, and for the first time I realise he maybe ain't so wussy as I thought. There's a streak of nasty in his face, like a cold flash across his eyes, and I get that shivery feeling you get when you're out in the hot sun and an unexpected cloud rolls across the sky and just for a second everything goes shadowy and cold . . . and then it's gone again, and the sun starts shining . . . and MacDonut's back to normal.

'Was anyone with you when this happened?' he says.

'When what happened?'

'When DI Callan asked you to change your statement.'

'No . . . it was just me and him.'

He nods, nods again, then makes a note on a piece of paper. 'Anything else?' he asks me.

'Like what?'

'Has anyone else talked to you about the case?'

'Like who?'

He frowns at me. 'Anyone . . . other police officers . . .'

'Yeh, Bowker and Dorudi, the ones who took my statement—'

'Any problems with them?'

'Nah, not really. Bowker's a bit . . . I dunno . . . he's a bit kinda weird, I spose. But at least he ain't tried to make me change nothing.'

MacDonut nods again. 'Paul Bowker's a good officer. You won't get any trouble from him.' He looks up at me. 'You know his son, I believe?'

'I know who he is, yeh.'

Nod, nod – he's really getting into this nodding business now. 'So,' he says, 'apart from Callan . . . you've not had any problems?'

I look at him, thinking, thinking, thinking to myself, asking myself – why'd you tell him anything in the first place? he probly ain't no better than the rest of em . . . why din't you just keep your big mouth shut?

I ain't got no answers.

And anyway, I done it now, I already gabbed about Callan, I might as well tell him the rest of it . . .

So . . .

'There's this man,' I says.

And then I start telling him about the guy in the raincoat, the Volvo guy, how he's been following me about and watching the house and everything. Donut listens, makes some notes – description, car, make, model, number, times and places – and then, when I'm done, he goes *Hmmmm* for a bit, and then he says, 'OK – well, I don't think it's anything to worry about, but we'll certainly look into it for you. I expect it's just . . .' he pauses, thinking '. . . well . . . leave it with us, OK? We'll see what we can do.'

'Right.'

He smiles again. 'And don't concern yourself about appearing in court. It's really nothing to worry about. You'll have someone with you all the time . . . and if there's anything you need to know – just ask. That's what we're here for. The trial won't be for a while yet, anyway – these things usually take a good 6 months or so. In the meantime, if there's anything you need . . .' He leans across the desk and lowers his voice. 'We're not actually allowed to *reward* witnesses, as such, but it's perfectly acceptable to pay their expenses and make compensation for loss of time . . . so, you know, if anything *should* happen to crop up, anything we can help you with . . . we're only a phone call away.'

'Right.'

'And, of course, that goes for your parents, too.'

'Of course.'

'Good . . . well, I think that should do it for now. There'll doubtless be a few more details to sort out at a later date, so we'll need to contact you again . . . if that's all right with you.'

'Yeh.'

'We'll do our best to keep things as con*ven*ient as possible . . . although I don't expect you'll mind another Day or 2 off school, will you?' *Phnur, phnur*. 'Is there anything else you'd like to know.'

'Yeh – where's Mr Vine?'

He blinks. 'I'm sorry?'

'Keith Vine – where is he?'

'Where is he?'

'Yeh.'

'May I ask why you wish to know?'

'I dunno – just curious, I spose. I mean, he's the one it's all about, this whole thing, but it's kinda like he ain't got nothing to *do* with it . . . like he don't actually *exist*. D'you know what I mean? So I was just wondering where he is . . . you know, like where's he banged up?'

Donut smiles at me, but I can tell he don't like it. I can see him thinking – what's with all these *questions*? who's this FATSO kid think he is – some kinda MASTERMIND or something? No, he don't like it one bit. He's still smiling, but it looks like it's starting to hurt. And for some weird reason, I kinda like that.

'Mr Vine,' he says eventually, 'was released on bail some weeks ago. I'm afraid I'm not at liberty to divulge his present whereabouts.'

After that, Donut kinda clams up and loses the smile altogether, like he can't be bothered with it no more, it's too much trouble . . . or maybe he just don't need it no more . . . I dunno . . . his face just goes kinda blank. He makes a few notes on a notepad, stares at some papers for a while, then clears away all his files and stuff and takes me out to the reception place.

'There's tea and coffee over there,' he says. 'If you need anything else, just ask Tracy.'

Fair enough, I think, watching him go back into his office . . .

Fair enough.

I'll just hang around here then, drinking tea and eating biscuits and ogling TRACY till Mum gets back . . . and, by the way, you oughta see the look on her face when she walks through the door with a couple of bags full of stuff from Primark and Woolies and a load of PicknMix stashed in her pockets . . . it's like she's won the Lottery or something. And then – guess what? Donut only goes and gives her a brand new Ericsson mobile . . . can you *believe* it? He comes out his office – with a freshly-made smile fixed to his face – and he walks up to Mum and just GIVES her this phone.

'There you go,' he says. 'It's all paid up, just in case you need to get in touch with us . . .'

Speaking all low and whispery, like Mum's got brain damage or something, or maybe he thinks we ain't never see a phone before, what with us being so POOR and

PIG-IGNORANT and everything . . .

I dunno . . . maybe I'm being too – what's the word – *critical*? *cynical*? Is that right? You know, when you don't trust no one cos you think they're all *after* something. I mean, maybe he's just being NICE . . .

Just being nice?

Yeh, right . . . like *that's* gonna happen.

Anyway, I gotta think about it.

I gotta shake hands with Donut then get in the Audi with Mum and her STASH and drive back along the road at 190mph . . . with Mum pleased as PUNCH, going on and on about what she got at the shops . . . look at this, look at that . . . her eyes all shiny and bright . . . which I guess is OK . . . I mean, she don't get out all that much, and she likes buying stuff . . . so I guess it's kinda nice to see her happy and everything . . .

It's just . . .

I dunno.

It's just . . .

Nothing.

It's OK.

It don't matter.

Anyway, as soon as we get back, as soon as we get in the house, I gotta get out again . . . I gotta get back to the bridge . . . to MY PLACE . . . to THINK . . .

And I think.

I think . . .

You ever tried thinking about what you was thinking about 6 months ago? I'll tell you what – it ain't easy. For one thing, it's just HARD to remember. I mean, it's bad enough trying to remember what DAY it was, let alone what was going on in your head. And for another thing, even if you CAN remember what you was thinking about . . . whatever it was, it ain't the same thing no more. Cos **now** you got loads of new stuff in your head, stuff you din't have back then, so everything's all mixed up. The old stuff, the old thoughts, they're all mixed up with the new stuff. It's like . . . lemme think . . . OK – say you got a big box full of coloured chalks, right? And they're all different colours and different shapes and sizes – small bits, big bits, thin bits, fat bits, broken bits . . . OK? So you put a couple of newish bits in, maybe a red bit and a blue bit, and then you shake up the box . . . and you keep on shaking it up and adding other bits of chalk . . . and then more shaking . . . and more chalk. . . more shaking . . . more chalk . . . and then 6 months later you open up the box and start looking for them 2 newish bits you put in all that time ago – the red bit and the blue bit. OK, so if you look hard enough and long enough, you're probly gonna find em – but they ain't gonna be exactly the same as when you put em in, are they? They're gonna be all bashed around by the other chalks, all covered in dust. They're gonna have bits broken off, they're gonna be dirtier, they're gonna be all messed up with green bits and white bits and yellow bits and brown bits . . .

You see what I'm saying?

They ain't the SAME as before.

So when I say I'm thinking . . . don't forget – it's messed-up thinking.

INFORMATION is what I'm thinking. Bits of INFORMATION . . . I can see em running around in my head, like bits of a river, like the tide of traffic on the road below – *swoo-ooosh-swoo-ooosh-swoo-ooosh* . . .

Can you hear it?

Listen . . .

Swoo-ooosh – the TRUTH . . . it's like I thought . . . Vine's a bad guy and the BMW bad guys wanna take him OUT, so they rig up this road rage thing.

Swoo-ooosh – they get this guy called Burke, who looks a bit like BMW – same shape, same size, same hat – and THEY whack him, THEY stick him with a knife, and cos he looks a bit like BMW, and BMW's made out like Vine's whacked HIM, and cos it's pretty dark, and the only witnesses are zipping past in cars . . . it LOOKS like Vine done it.

Swoo-ooosh – but they din't reckon on a FAT kid watching from the bridge.

Swoo-ooosh – and Callan probly KNOWS they fixed Vine up, but he don't care cos

`on his release from prison in 1994 Vine was subsequently charged with the murder of a prosecution witness at his previous trial . . . and after his acquittal he was soon back in the crime business with his financial empire flourishing more than ever`

and Callan don't like that. I dunno if he don't like it in a GENERAL kinda way, you know, cos he's a cop, and cops don't like it when bad guys get away with stuff, or if it's something more SPEFICIC . . . like maybe Callan's one of the cops who arrested Vine all them years ago . . . I dunno . . . I don't spose it matters really. All that matters is Callan's got this thing about Vine. He wants to GET him. And he's DETERMINED. And, like he said, sometimes you gotta do what's wrong to make things right.

Swoo-ooosh – but Vine's got ASSOCIATES, and

```
amongst his associates are many respected
figures, including senior politicians,
judges, lawyers, and policemen
```

and DS Bowker's a policeman . . . a *good officer* . . . known to Donut as *PAUL* . . . and *PAUL*'s got a son who can make sure the FAT kid don't get knobbled . . .

So – *swoo-ooosh* + *swoo-ooosh* + *swoo-ooosh* + *swoo-oosh* + *swoo-ooosh* = *uuuurrrrhhhhhsshhhhmmmm* = me, Moo, the FAT kid, stuck in the middle of a hyena fight, like a manky piece of meat getting pulled and poked and yanked all over the place . . . just so's wrong can get his right and right can get his wrong . . .

And the thing is – I DON'T EVEN *CARE* what's true or right or wrong. What's it MATTER? What's it to ME if Vine gets done for something he din't do? He's BAD, ain't he? BAD's bad . . . you do it, you get it. But then if he DON'T get it . . . so what? He ain't done nothing to ME . . . what do I care?

Bad = bad = good = bad = what?

I dunno . . .

I dunno what I'm talking about.

Now I know I'm only halfway there. I got a whole lotta pulling and poking and yanking to get through yet . . . enough to take me from I DON'T CARE to *THIS* . . . and *THIS* is about as far away from I DON'T CARE as it gets. This is a million miles away. This is 3 o'clock in the morning, dark and cold and dead as a grave . . .

This is a long way from everything.

10/ Jumbo Stalloney

OK – here's a Day and a half. It's some time around the start of February, I think. One of them Days when it's too cold and dark to get outta bed in the morning, when you just wanna lie there all wrapped up, warm and sleepy as a LUMP . . . but the radioclock's going off and Mum's shouting up the stairs – COME ON, MOO, GET UP, YOU'RE LATE!

By the way, about Mum . . . I dunno what's going on with her. She ain't said much about Donut in the last few weeks, but I know she's talked to him on the mobile a couple of times, and I know she's after getting more stuff, and I know Dad don't like it. I heard em talking about it one night –

Come on, Shell (that's Mum – Michelle), *it ain't worth it . . .*

Why not?

It's too close . . .

Too close to what?

You know what I mean.

Yeh, but it ain't like it's wrong or nothing, is it? They wanna give it – where's the wrong in taking it?

I dunno . . . it just don't feel right.

Feels all right to me . . .

I think I get the drift of it, that Mum's OK with taking stuff from Donut, but Dad don't like it cos he don't like NOTHING to do with the LAW . . . right or wrong, in or out, front or back . . . he just don't LIKE it.

But, anyway, that's by the way . . .

The radioclock's going off and Mum's shouting up the stairs – COME ON MOO, GET UP, YOU'RE LATE! – and I'm groaning and moaning and rolling outta bed . . . and – *KEE-RIST!* – it's FREEEEZING! How come this house is always so COLD? I put on a hood AND a dressing gown, and then – *tumptumptump* – it's off to the bathroom, quick as you can, doing the cold shuffle, shivering and skipping and breathing hard and – oh yeh, another by the way – I'm losing weight. I'm actually LOSING WEIGHT. I dunno how much or nothing, cos we ain't got no scales in THIS house, but the face in the mirror is definitely getting thinner . . . and, yeh, all right, so it's thinner as in NOT SO FAT, which ain't saying much, I know . . . I mean I ain't no SKELETOR yet, but even so . . . there's SOMETHING there, SOMETHING missing, SOMETHING like 1% LESS roundness than before . . . and that's OK with me. In fact it's EXTRA OK cos I ain't done nothing to get it. I ain't stopped eating, I ain't on a DIET, I ain't exercising . . . I ain't doing NOTHING . . . and you can't beat THAT for losing a couple of pounds, can you?

So, anyway, I spend maybe 5 seconds more than usual looking in the mirror, admiring my THINNESS, then the cold kicks in again and it's time to do the business, get ready, get dressed, go downstairs, hit the kitchen, and EAT.

NOSH NOSH NOSH . . . the usual stuff . . .

Then it's coats and gloves and hats and scarves and out the door into the biting wind. And there he is – the Volvo guy – parked at the end of the road again, his engine running and his windscreen white with ice . . . and I don't even bother looking at him or not looking at him or crossing the road or nothing . . . cos what's the point? I'm just a monkey-boy going about my business, keeping my head down and my hood pulled tight, keeping out the cold . . . and, besides, I got other eyes now – eyes the Volvo guy dunno nothing about. Parked across the road, about 2 cars back, there's a guy in a Ford Escort van. He's been there for the last 2 Days. It's one of them scruffy white vans – all grimy and covered in dirt, with a roofrack and a tow bar – and the guy inside's pretty scruffy too. A youngish guy, with dusty hair and a check shirt, like a builder or a plumber or something. But he ain't no builder. He looks away when I walk past, but it's one of THEM *looks away*, like – yeh, I know you seen me, but pretend you din't, all right? Pretend you dunno nothing.

Yeh, all right.

Then it's off down the lane, through the grey of the village, getting wet feet and a frozen finger from a hole in the end of my glove . . . and it's kinda quiet everywhere, everyone's hunched up and hurried and all clammed up, like the miserable cold's got em all so busy with getting out of it that they ain't got the energy to do nothing else. No hanging around yakking, no arsing about, no pushing or shoving or tripping or shouting or gobbing or kicking or giving it hell . . . no nothing. It's too cold for the RAIN. And the funny thing is – I kinda miss it. The RAIN of words – *HEY MOO! LOOKING SLIM TODAY! SHAKE IT, FAT BOY! WHOO-HOO! HERE COMES THE FATSTUFF!* – the boys on bikes, the girls in short skirts, the spite and the PITY . . . I don't MISS it like I want it back . . . I just . . . I dunno . . . I guess I just miss it cos it was mine. It was MINE. My RAIN. It's what I HAD. It wasn't great, in fact it was crap, but at least it was something. Now, though . . . well, now I ain't got nothing. I'm just living in a void, living in a bubble . . . it's like I'm UNTOUCHABLE. Which is OK. I mean, don't get me wrong, I ain't complaining, it's just . . . I dunno . . .

Nothing's ever RIGHT, is it?

There's always something fogging up your head . . .

And all you can do is walk through it all with your eyes down, same as always. Down the lane, through the grey of the village, through the shut-up cold, up to the school gates . . . *tump, tump, tump* . . . here we go . . . nothing. No Bowker, no Jicky, no monkeys, no eyes, no dirty looks, no parents in cars, no girls in short skirts . . . they're all THERE, but they ain't got nothing to do with me . . . or I ain't got nothing to do with them. No smiles. No looks that DON'T hurt . . . no looks at all. No *INTEREST*.

NOTHING.

And it DOES ME IN.

It's TOO cold and TOO dry and TOO much of nothing.

But later – and this is what I'm getting at – later in the Day the weather takes a turn and things get HOT.

It's about me and Brady, which is a tough thing to think about. And I'm tempted to leave it at that . . . cos it's more than just tough, it's kinda skin-crawly . . . if you know what I mean. It's one of them FEELY kinda things you just wanna shut your mind to . . . a bit like imagining your own skull. Like if you close your eyes and try to imagine the skull beneath your skin . . . think about it . . . really concentrate . . . imagine the hard white bone, the cold black sockets, the grinning teeth . . .

Kinda shivery, ain't it?

Anyway, I ain't saying Brady's the same as my skull or nothing, I'm just saying that – thinking-wise – they're both kinda skin-crawly. Kinda shivery. I mean, it's bad enough that sorta stuff just BEING there – why make it worse by THINKING about it?

But I guess . . . I dunno . . . I guess I'm on my own here, there's only me and you and these 4 walls, so maybe it's OK to take a quick look at Brady and me . . . you know, just lift up the covers and take a peek.

Yeh . . .

Mind you, the thing is . . . thinking about it now, there ain't really THAT much to look at. There's just me and Brady, really . . . just a couple of sludges stuck together in the RAIN. One short and ugly, the other one FAT. We ain't a TEAM or nothing . . . we ain't like Ant & Dec or Vic & Bob or them old black-and-white guys you get on TV at Christmas, you know, like Laurel & Harding, or Morton & Wise. We ain't CHUMS, me and Brady. To tell you the truth – I ain't even sure we LIKE each other that much. Yeh, OK, we probly *like* each other a bit, but that ain't the same as *LIKING* each other, is it? I mean, for a start, what's there to LIKE? I spose there's gotta be something . . . something about Brady . . . else I wouldn't be thinking about him. But I ain't got a CLUE what it is. I mean, he's *all right*, I guess . . . but don't ask me why. He ain't got nothing going for him. He ain't exactly INTERESTING . . . all he likes is cars and computers . . . and he ain't got no sense of humour, neither. He's FUNNY sometimes, like when he gets his words wrong or when he tries to make out he's cool and does this little hip-hop dance that makes him look like a pygmy having an epeleptric fit . . . yeh, that's pretty FUNNY. But that's about it. Most of the time he's just a bit boring – a bit dim, a bit dull, a bit kinda STUNTED. He's also a bit whiffy, to tell you the truth, which don't make things any better. He smells like stuff in Oxfam shops – you know, that sicky-old-poor-people smell.

Anyway, that's him.

Him to me.

And me to him?

I dunno . . .

I dunno what he thinks of me. I think he probly LIKES

me . . . but I ain't sure how or why . . . and that's the skin-crawly bit . . .

Which I don't really wanna think about.

It's just a funny thing . . . like we NEED each other, but we don't wanna get too close . . . but we dunno WHY we don't wanna get too close. It's just THERE. That's HOW IT IS. I dunno much about him and he dunno much about me. He don't come round to my place and I don't go round to his. I don't even know where his place is . . . not exactly, anyway. I know he lives on the estate round the other side of the village, but that's about it. I dunno his house or nothing. I mean, we see each other sometimes, but we don't ARRANGE things, we just . . . you know . . . we just BUMP INTO each other now and then. Dinnertimes, after school, maybe a Scatterday afternoon some place . . . we both know where we go and when . . . you wanna be there, be there . . . maybe I'll see you, maybe I won't . . . ain't no BIG DEAL.

That's just HOW IT IS.

But things change, I guess. Things get under your skin and bring out stuff you din't know was there. Or maybe it's something else, something . . . I dunno . . . something DEEP or something. Don't ask me what, though . . . cos I ain't too good on DEEP. All I know is what happened.

It's dinnertime, OK? About 20 minutes before we're due back in class, and I'm in a cubicle in the toilets . . . nah, I ain't eating this time, I'm just doing what needs to be done after a BIG plate of undercooked toad-in-the-hole and too much crumble for afters. It's the toilets in the science block. I go there 1) cos it's Chemistry next, so I don't have far to walk, and 2) cos it's quieter than the toilets in the main building. Not that it's all that quiet just now, if you know what I mean . . . but that's the whole point. You need a bit of quiet if you're gonna make some noise, don't you? So, anyway, there I am, just sitting there minding my own business, doing what's gotta be done – and then I hear the door open . . . and footsteps crossing to the urinals. It's OK, cos I'm just about finished anyway . . . I mean it's OK in THAT sense . . . but toilets are dodgy places, specially for FAT kids. Stuff goes down in toilets. And a FAT kid having a shit is just ASKING for trouble. Yeh, I might be UNTOUCHABLE now, but I got years and years of having to watch out, and that don't disappear overnight. So I'm ready, I'm edgy, I'm WARY, I'm primed . . . I'm all ears and no troozies. Listening, keeping quiet . . . listening. It's probly OK . . . it sounds like there's only one of em, but you never know. It's best to play it safe – sit tight, keep quiet, wait for em to finish and go. Whoever it is, I can hear em taking a leak, humming a little tune . . . then the tune gets a bit louder . . . a bit clearer . . . half-talking/half-singing . . . *duh, duh-duh, duh, dee, duh, dah-dah, dah .. he dah-dah hooded horse* . . . and I know that voice. Tuneless, dumb, getting it wrong – it's Brady.

Now what?

Do I wanna talk to him?

We ain't seen much of each other lately, not like that anyway. I mean, we SEEN each other plenty of times, but we ain't said much. A passing nod, a mumbled *all right? . . . how's it going?* I ain't WORRIED about it, cos I know what Brady's like when he's in one of his sulks – they last for AGES. He'll come round in the end, make out like nothing ever happened . . . but still . . . I wouldn't *mind* having a chat. Just to say hello, you know . . . the trouble is, I go out now and he's gonna know I been sitting in here listening to him having a piss and singing – or *trying* to sing – *2 Little Boys* by Ralph Harris, and he ain't gonna like THAT, is he? Nah

. . . I don't think so. And, anyway, he's probly gotta get off back to the main building . . . cos he's in a different class to me . . . and I think he's probly got Engerlish next, which is in the main building . . . so . . . I think I'll just sit here for a while . . . I'll just quietly do up my troozies and sit here for a while . . . have a chat with Brady some other time . . .

Then the door outside slams open and a big bunch of monkey-boots come crashing in, the sound of bodies looking for a fight –

'Hey, Spaz,' says one, 'what you doing?'

'Uh?'

'You deaf?'

'Wha—'

'What you doing? What you looking at?'

'I think he fancies you, Jick.'

'You what?'

'Short eyes . . .'

'I'll give him short eyes . . .'

Then there's grunts and laughing and shuffling feet and nasty voices, and I KNOW what's happening out there, I seen it a hundred times before, I BEEN there. There's 3 or 4 of em, maybe 5 – Jicky Collins, Gray Jenner, a poxy kid called Darren Hollis . . . the rest I can't make out. One of em's gonna get the door, then Jicky's gonna move on Brady while the others back him up. I can SEE it . . . I can SEE right through the cubicle door. Brady's zipping himself up, looking shit-scared, backing away, knowing he ain't got nowhere to go, but looking for it anyway.

'Smell that?' says Jicky.

'Whooo . . . shit,' says Gray. 'Smells like someone *died*, man.'

For a second I think they're talking about me . . . and that brings it home – I'm IN HERE . . . d'you know what I mean?

I'm IN HERE. They're out there and I'm in here, and all that's keeping em off me is a toilet door with a half-broken lock . . . all they gotta do is give it a kick or something . . . and my heart's going *dump-dump, dump-dump, dump-dump* . . . but then I think – hold on, it ain't so bad . . . they got Brady . . . they ain't looking for no one else . . . and the cubicle's kinda tucked away down the end . . . and the door ain't shut properly cos of the half-broken lock, so it ain't TOO obvious there's someone in here . . .

Jicky laughs. 'Nah . . . that ain't it. He don't smell dead. He smells like . . .' he sniffs, a long hard snort '. . . you know what that is?'

'Midget piss?' says Hollis.

'Nah . . .' goes Jicky, 'it's the stink of a mouthy little shit, that's what it is – the stink of a grass. How come you stink like a grass, Brady?'

'Uh?' says Brady. 'What grass?'

'*What grass?*' he says, copying Brady's whine, and I hear him step forward, and I can SEE him getting in Brady's face, yapping his fingers at him. '*Grass*,' he sneers. 'You know what a *grass* is, doncha?'

Brady just whimpers.

Jicky slaps his hand against the wall over Brady's head. 'You been *gabbing*, aincha?' he spits. 'You been a *naughty* boy.'

'I ain't done nothing—'

BOOF! – like the dull smack of a pillow – then a groany breath – *UURGH!* – like someone being sick, and I can FEEL Brady's pain, the short jab in the guts, I can SEE him doubling over clutching his belly.

'Tell im, Gray,' says Jicky.

Shuffling steps, then another dull *BOOF!*, this time the harder sound of a kick in the arse or the back, and then

Gray's voice spitting out a shock of words –

'You been down the cops, aincha?' he says. 'You been down there gabbing you seen that guy got stabbed – right?' *BOOF!* 'And don't say you ain't cos you was – you *listening*?' *BOOF!* 'What d'you tell em? Eh? What d'you *tell* em?' *BOOF! BOOF!*

'Nunh . . .' says Brady. 'Nunh . . .'

Jicky butts in. 'You tell em you seen Vine stab the other guy, dincha? You tell em you was there, you seen it – Vine got a blade and stuck the other guy. That's what you told em, innit?'

'Nunh . . . theym .. they m-made me—'

'You lying little *shit.*'

BOOF!

Now I'm kinda PARALYSED here. I dunno WHAT they're talking about . . . I don't GET IT . . . I don't WANNA get it . . . and I'm whacked in the head with the shock of it all. It's too HARD, they're giving him TOO MUCH. I mean, a couple of *BOOF!*s is OK, no trouble, you just take em and go down . . . but this . . . this is WAY TOO MUCH.

'Tellya what,' Jicky's saying now. 'Hey, shit-head, look at me . . .' *BOOF!* 'That's better. Keep looking . . . you looking? Right, listen . . . hey!' *BOOF!* 'Yeh . . . OK, listen. You got a choice. You go down the cops and tell em you bolloxed up, you give it up, right? You tell em you been making up stories . . . tell em you lied, OK, and you might be all right.' He snorts and spits. 'I ain't saying you *will* be all right, but I tellya what – you *don't* do it . . .' *BOOF! BOOF!* '. . . you're dog food. Got it?'

'Yunnh . . .' says Brady.

'Say what?'

'Yunnh . . . *yuh.*'

'Yeh, right – good choice. And just so's you don't

forget . . . Daz? Gimme your lighter. Gray . . . Lukey . . . get im up—'

'Nuh-NO!' sobs Brady, 'Nonono . . .'

'Shut im up!'

'NUN!nnh . . . UNh . . . mmm . . .'

I can't stand it no more . . . I can't STAND it. Yeh, I KNOW they *probly* ain't gonna do nothing, they probly just gonna freak him out, scare him half to death . . . but that ain't the point. The point is, I ain't got no choice here. There's a mad guy inside me who's already up off the toilet and opening the cubicle door, and now he's crashing across the tiled floor towards the sinks where Gray and the kid called Lukey's got Brady held tight with a hand clamped over his mouth and Jicky Collins is yanking his head by the hair and flicking a cigarette lighter in his face . . . and they all stop dead and look at me with bugged-out eyes . . . cos I'm this BIG FAT MAD guy . . . I'm 17 stone of CRAZY FAT heading towards em at 90mph . . . and that's a whole lotta mad guy.

'Muh—' says Jicky, stepping back – but that's as far as he gets before the mad guy takes off like a flying whale and *BOOM!*s right into him, belly first, crashing him back against the sinks. It's like a 20-ton truck ramming a crash-test dummy against a wall – *KER-THUDD!!* Only it's more of a *KER-RACKKK!!* – cos Jicky kinda hits the sink with the top of his legs but the rest of him keeps going, whipping back hard over the sink and cracking his head against the mirror – *KER-RACKKK!!* There's a stunned nothing for a moment, just the sound of the impact echoing round the toilet walls and a vague scattering noise as Gray and Lukey shuffle out the way, and then a cold and scary silence . . . the tinkling of mirror glass . . . the gasp of heavy breathing. That's me, the breathing. Cos the mad guy's gone now, leaving ME to mop up his mess, and it's suddenly hit me – it's a HELL of a mess.

Jicky's staggered away from the sinks holding the back of his head, wincing and swearing, then bringing his hand round, staring at the blood, swearing harder now cos there's a LOTTA blood, all pink and runny between his fingers.

'Shit! Jesus, man! *SHIT!* . . .'

And I'm backing off, looking over at Brady who's sitting on the floor slumped against the wall holding his belly, looking up at me like I'm SUPERMAN or something . . . which maybe I *was*, 15 seconds ago, but I ain't no more. Now I'm just a dumb FAT kid . . . a dumb FAT kid who's just made a BIG mistake, and now he's gonna pay for it. Cos now the shock's worn off, and Jicky's coming on to me, his eyes on fire, and the rest of em are moving in too. Daz, Gray, Lukey, even the kid who was watching the door – a nasty little bastad called Andy Gee – they're all coming on to me now, all slit eyes and tight gobs, mad as hell, like I'm a DEAD man. I ain't got NO chance.

I been here before, about to get done, so I know how it feels . . . it feels like – OK, so I'm about to get done, and it's gonna hurt, but it ain't gonna last for ever, is it? It's only a BODY thing . . . it's only gonna HURT. It ain't gonna rip you apart or scar you for life or nothing . . . it's just a couple minutes getting whacked, that's all. 10 minutes from now it'll all be over. Finished, done, gone. A few bruises, an ache or 2, maybe a sore head . . . what's the big deal? Getting all PETRIFIED about it ain't gonna help, is it? That's just gonna make things worse. So . . . just switch off and take it . . .

OK?

Yeh . . . OK.

That's how it feels.

Usually . . .

But not this time.

This time's different.

I dunno why, but this time it feels like something else. This time it feels BIG, like it IS gonna rip me apart, it IS gonna scar me for life . . . and instead of switching off, it feels like I been switched ON. I feel ELECTRIC, like every cell in my body is wide-open and RAW, like a touch of breath is enough to kill me . . . and all I can do is stand here and take it, shaking like a leaf, wishing I din't feel this way, but knowing I do.

And when it comes, it's coming fast. Cos Jicky and the rest ain't got time for clever words or looking hard or nothing like that . . . they just wanna DO it. So they DO it. Jicky gets in first, kinda flat-handing me hard in the nose with the palm of his hand, which HURTS like a *BASTAD* and sends me back-pedalling across the floor with both hands grabbing my face, wet with blood and tears. My head's going black already, all black and crashy like a storm, and I ain't even got time to get enough breath to moan before they're all over me. Bodies, knees, heads, hands – *whack whack whack* – like a 10-armed monster playing me for drums. *Switch off and take it*, I'm going, *switch off and take it* . . . but I know I can't. It's too much. *Whack whack whack whack* . . . then I'm hitting the wall, I think, arms up, shoulder turned, trying to cover my face, getting ready to go down . . . and I can't hear nothing or see nothing, just things hitting me and black stars screaming in my head . . . but *something's* telling me something . . . something . . . I dunno . . . *whack whack whack* . . . dunno . . . can't think . . . don't care . . .

'HEY!HEY!HEY!'

It's the monster-tamer, like in a dream . . . come to take

his monster home . . .

'HEY – JICK! *JICKY!!* NO! GET OFF HIM, CHRIS-SAKE! GRAY!! DAZ!! WHAT YOU *DOING*, MAN?'

. . . and now the monster's getting weaker . . . *whack* . . . he's dying . . .

'WHAT YOU *DOING*, JICK? SHIT! NOT *HIM* . . . WHAT'S THE *MATTER* WITH YOU?'

. . . he's gone . . .

'Hey, Moo? Y'OK? Moo?'

I ain't sure if I wanna look . . . I ain't sure if I *can*. My eyes are shut too tight. One of em feels like a cannonball, the other one's wet with blood.

'Moo . . . Moo? Jick, get some water or something . . . chris*sake*! *Moo* . . .'

I open one eye, the wet one . . . slow as I can . . . half-expecting I'm blind or something . . . but it's OK. The wet's mostly tears . . . pink tears . . . but I can see all right. It's all a bit wet-and-pink-looking . . . but it's OK. I can SEE. I can SEE Dec Bowker squatting down beside me, looking into my eyes . . . I don't BELIEVE it, but I can SEE it.

'Y'all right?' he says.

'Whuh?'

'Y'all right? Nothing bust?'

'Nuh . . .'

'Here.' He passes me a damp hanky. 'Come on, y'all right . . .' and he's helping me to my feet. Dec Bowker . . . he's helping me up . . . Dec Bowker . . . HELPING me . . .

'Look,' he says. 'They dunno what they was doing . . . they din't mean nothing . . . all right?' He glances hard at Jicky. 'Tell im . . . tell im you din't mean it.'

Jicky looks annoyed. 'Ah come *on*, Dec – he jumped us . . . nearly cracked my bastad head open, look.' He turns around, showing Dec the bloody gash on his head. 'What am

I sposed to do? Kiss his arse?'

'You do what I say – OK?'

'Yeh, but—'

'Shut up. Don't get me going, just get some—'

'WHAT'S GOING ON HERE?'

8 heads whip round at the sound of the voice – and there's old Greasy Simmons standing at the door, looking just as tough as he can . . . which ain't that tough, cos he's a chemistry teacher, and you know what they're like – tweedy old jacket, all stained with acid burns, thin shirt, cord jeans, thick glasses, thin head, greasy hair . . .

'What's going *on* here?' he repeats, getting 8 mumbled *nothings* in reply. He looks around, taking it all in – me and Brady all beat up, Bowker and Jicky and the rest looking guilty as sin.

'Nelson?' he says. 'What's going on? What happened to you?'

'Nothing.'

'It doesn't *look* like nothing.'

'I fell over,' I tell him. 'They was just helping me . . .'

Simmons shakes his head and turns his attention to Brady, who's still sitting on the floor. 'And what about you?' he says to him, sarky as hell. 'Did you fall over, too?'

Brady looks at me, then at Bowker . . . who gives him back a don't-you-DARE look. Brady wipes snot from his nose. 'I was helping Moo,' he tells Simmons. 'I was trying to lift him up . . . I hurt my back.'

Lukey and Daz can't help giggling.

'Shut up!' says Simmons, his eyes fixed on Brady, trying to make him feel guilty. They do that sometimes – some of the teachers – they try to make you feel guilty about getting beaten up. They think it helps. It's like they're saying – look, here I am, *trying* to stand up for you, *trying* to put a stop to this BULLYING, and all you ever do is take my help and spit it back in my face . . . God, you make me *sick*.

'Get out,' he says, giving up. 'Go on, the lot of you – out!'

Bowker and the rest start mooching out, doing their best not to SMIRK, and I go over to Brady and give him a hand getting up.

'Y'all right?' I ask him.

'Yeh . . .' he sniffs, wincing a bit.

'Sure?'

He won't look at me. 'Yeh . . . I'm all right . . . thanks.'

Simmons is still waiting at the door. 'You 2 get cleaned up before you go anywhere. Wash the blood off your face . . . especially you, Nelson. I don't want you dripping blood all over my test-tubes.' He watches us hobble over to the sink, shaking his head and clucking his tongue. 'I don't know why I bother sometimes,' he mutters. 'I really don't . . .'

'Me neither,' I mumble.

'What was that?'

'Nothing.'

Me and Brady start running the taps, getting the blood and snot off our faces. In the mirror I can see old Simmons just standing there watching us, not knowing what to do, then he looks around, like he's making sure he's on his own, and then he turns around and walks out the door.

I look at Brady. His face don't look too bad, mostly messed up with crying, but he's standing kinda bent over and twisted, like there's something wrong in his guts.

'Y'all right?' I ask him again.

'Yeh.'

'You don't look it.'

'I'm all right.'

I give him another look. He still ain't looking at me. I

stoop to the tap and get a mouthful of water and rinse the blood from my gob. When I spit it out it's all pink and stringy.

'Shit,' I says, turning to Brady again. He's checking his face in the mirror, wiping his eyes with a damp paper towel. I says to him, 'What the hell was *that* all about?'

'What?' he goes.

'What d'you mean – *what*? All that stuff about you talking to the cops—'

The door slams open again. I turn around, expecting to see Simmons coming back in, but it ain't him – it's Bowker. He stomps up to me and Brady and without stopping he thumps Brady hard in the gut. Brady doubles over again, this time puking up, but Bowker don't care. He grabs Brady by the hair and yells in his ear, 'YOU BETTER GET DOWN THE COPS BY THE END OF THE WEEK AND TELL EM YOU DIN'T SEE NOTHING, ELSE YOU'RE DEAD – *RIGHT?*'

Brady nods, gagging.

Bowker gives his head a flick then lets him go and grabs my arm. 'And YOU,' he says, pulling me towards the door. 'I see you anywhere near him again and you'll *wish* you was dead.'

'I don't—'

'Shut up, listen . . .' He drags me through the door, glancing back at Brady as we go, then shoves me up against the corridor wall. 'Listen,' he hisses. 'All you gotta do is keep away from Brady and Callan and keep your mouth shut – OK? The stuff with Jicky was a mistake . . . just forget it. He shouldna done it. It was a *mistake* – all right? It din't happen.'

'I dunno what—'

'It din't *happen*.'

'All right, yeh . . . if you say so.'

'That's it – here,' he pulls a crumpled £50 note from his pocket and shoves it into my hand. 'Compensation,' he grins, bending my fingers so I can't let go of it. 'Blood money – OK?'

'Yeh, but—'

'*OK?*'

'Yeh.'

'Good – right. OK . . . I gotta go . . .' He gives me one of them hard, kinda *intimate* looks, then a quick wink, a don't-forget slap in the face, and he's gone.

Yeh, that was a Day and a half all right. And it ain't over yet, neither – both ways. It ain't over **now** and it ain't over then.

After school, when I get back home, the Volvo's gone – no car, no guy in a raincoat, no nothing. Just an empty space at the side of the road. It ain't *unusual* . . . cos he ain't *always* there . . . I mean, there's plenty of times when I ain't seen him for Days. But this is different . . . don't ask me why . . . cos I dunno . . . but I know he ain't coming back this time. I just KNOW it. It's the empty space, I think . . . the space where the car was. It's got something about it . . . I dunno what . . . a kinda *derelict* look, like it's done, finished, used up . . . it's like when you look at a picture of a dead guy, a photograph, and you can tell he's dead cos the picture's got that dead-eyed look about it.

Anyway, he's gone.

So I go inside and get upstairs before Mum and Dad get a look at my mashed-up face, which is a pretty dumb thing to do, seeing as how they're gonna see it at some point anyway . . . and it ain't exactly the first time it's happened neither. I mean, they seen it all before, so it's no big deal or nothing.

All I'll get is 5 minutes fussing and poking about – Dad shaking his head, telling me I gotta STAND UP for myself, Mum getting the eyedine oinkment out the cupboard, wiping it into my face, making it sting like hell – and that'll be that. So it ain't like it's nothing I gotta void like the plague, it's just that right now I wanna be on my own for a bit. I wanna get upstairs and pee and get changed . . . and I just wanna take my time, you know, my moment, my small reward . . . I wanna take my time to take a good long look at myself and say – *you made it, Moo. You got through another Day. You made it . . .*

It's still something.

But it's getting so it don't MEAN that much no more.

Downstairs the kitchen's hot . . . and we go through it all – Mum upset, *Oh, Moo! look at your poor face . . .* cotton wool, oinkment, stinging . . . Dad at the table, flexing his fat, then it's big plates of cheese on toast and beans and eggs, with extra ice-cream and cake for afters, cos I'm such a POOR beaten-up BOY . . . and then the QUESTIONS – the who-was-its? the whys? the d'you-want-us-to-talk-to-your-teachers? – and the ANSWERS – just some kid, dunno, no.

Dad hates it when I get beat up. He dunno what to do about it. He KNOWS that going-to-the-teachers ain't no good, he KNOWS it's OUTSIDE of that . . . he KNOWS there ain't nothing HE can do to make it better, cos it's OUTSIDE of that too . . . and he KNOWS it's down to ME and THEM, cos that's ALL there is – ME and THEM . . . but he also KNOWS I ain't got what it takes to do it . . . I ain't TOUGH enough to stand-up-and-fight . . .

And today I wanna tell him – I wanna tell him I DID stand-up-and-fight, at least for about 10 seconds anyway. I stood up, got up, got mad, and *BOOF!*ed the guy . . . I

*BOOF!*ed him good . . . but the thing is . . . it wasn't for ME. I din't do it for ME, I did it for someONE else . . . which makes me WHAT? Dumb? Stupid? Good? *GOOD?* Nah . . . there ain't nothing GOOD about it, cos in the end you only do stuff that makes YOU feel all right . . . even if it LOOKS like you're doing it for someone else, you ain't really. You're doing it for YOU. But, anyway, the thing I wanna tell Dad is – I DID stand-up-and-fight . . . and it din't make no difference. I STILL got whopped.

I ain't gonna tell him that, though. I ain't gonna tell him nothing, cos that's the way we do it. I tell him it's OK, he nods, looks at my face again, looking worried, and I tell him – 'You shoulda seen the *other* guy' – and he laughs . . . coughs . . . turns red . . . then wipes his mouth and pats me on the back.

'Sure you're all right?' he asks me.

'Yeh.'

'What you doing now – off to the bridge?'

'Nah . . . not tonight.'

He turns on the TV and we finish off the ice-cream and cake to the sound of Anne Robinson shouting at idiots.

It's nearly done now, this Day and a half. All that's left is a night in my room listening to SLIPKNOT and SLAYER and talking to Brady in cyberspace.

He's first:

`moo – u get out of it alright?`
`b`

`yeh –` I tell him `– hows your belly?`

hurts like a bastad – i think they done my jiblets in . . . . probly coulda been worst tho if u dint come out the bog like a rambo-elehpant! i thought u was gonna KILL im.

yeh – like jumbo stalloney! anyways b – u shoulda tole me. you know? this u & the cops thing – whats going on?

That one he don't answer for a while. I change the CD, put on *Seasons in the Abyss*, wait for it to get thumping, then mess around on the net for a bit. I ain't really bothered what I look at . . . I just think of some searchwords, stick em in Google, and see what happens. *Moo Nelson* gets a load of weird computery stuff, like this:

MUSH is another flavour of MOO, pretty kludgy from the programming point of view but lots of history. This is a good list of MUSHes . . .

Which is REALLY interesting. Then I put in *Callan* + *Vine* which brings up another bunch of useless crap. There's a thing about MOLLUSCS or something, some guy saying:

. . . at the national museum of denmark we are working on a collaction of molluscs from the late seventeenths century. do anybody have any suggestions for labelling (numbering) by means of painting materials directly on the objects?

Which I'm actually *reading* when Brady gets back to me:

ok moo – he goes – i was gonna tell u anyway. all it is i rung up the cops & told em i seen it. they was on tv asksing for iwitnesses to come fowrard so i did.

YOU WHAT? – I says – what for? u dint see NOTHING.

yeh? u dunno do u? i coulda been there & u dint know. u was on the bridge. i coulda been in the lane or in a car & seen it.

yeh but u DINT!

no? its alright for U getting drove around in audis & U getting bowker lookingout for U . . . anywy callun says your only making it up cos your scared vines gonna get u. so whats the diffrence? how much U getting?

i aint getting nothing! i just told em what i seen & thats it. i aint making up noithing & i aint scared vines gonna get me cos he aint & i aint GETTING nothing. what u tell em anyway? what u know about bowker? how much u getting?

i told em i was coming up to see u & i seen the cars by the road. callun shows me this drawin with car pix on it & he goes like – where was he & wehre was he & what happend then . . . so i just kinda make it up a bit from pix i seen in the paper & he helps out

`when i get stuck. hes alright. i told him i seen vine get the other guy but i went when the wiggies come cos i dint wanna get invloved. bowkers in dirty with vine. u know that? how much am i getting? ahhh well . . . see, i aint ALLOWED to say. some kinda legal thing . . . whats the word? witless somthing? comsomething? yeh some-thing like that. some legal word. its all signged & everything – you know – keep yor mouth shut. i aint got no choice.`
`see?`
`gotta go.`

You never know with Brady if he's the dumbest kid in the WORLD or as smart as Stephen Hawkins. I got a pretty good idea he's probly a bit of both – mostly dumb, with just a sprinkling of smart – which by my reckoning is just about the WORST possible way to be. And I should know. Cos if I was either 100% dumb or 100% smart, I probly coulda fixed things then. I coulda DONE something . . . I dunno what. But I coulda done SOMEthing. Dumb or smart . . . it don't matter which. Either way woulda done it. Then I wouldn't be sitting here **now** waiting to fix things, to do things . . . bad things.

Bad = good.
Good = bad.
TRUTH = lies.
Lies = TRUTH.
But **now** don't = then.

11/ Stuck in a Hole

I ain't sure about the months **now** – February, March, April, May . . . they all just kinda merge together in my head, just Days and weeks and Days and weeks of Days passing and stuff going on. Mind you, come to think of it, there ain't all THAT much going on. I mean, it's not like something's happening EVERY Day . . . in fact, it's kinda weird how there's so many Days when NOTHING happens at all – not to ME, anyway. Course, there's probly all kindsa other stuff going on which I dunno nothing about – cop stuff, legal stuff, *ill*egal stuff, sneaky stuff, DISCUSSIONS, DECISIONS, ACTIONS . . . you got Callan doing his stuff, DS Bowker, Dec Bowker, Donut, Vine, the BMW guys, Brady . . . they all gonna be thinking and planning and doing their stuff . . . but I dunno nothing about most of it. Far as I'm concerned, most of it don't exist. It's like it's there, I KNOW it's there, but I can't see it. Which is OK with me. Cos if I can't see it, it ain't there – and if it ain't there, it ain't gonna hurt me.

Right?

Yeh, right as RAIN.

Fact is, it's what you CAN'T see that DOES it. THAT's what does your head in. Cos when you know something's there but you dunno what it is, your brain makes it up for you, and your brain ain't got NO LIMITS, so if you're THINKING bad stuff, it ain't just bad, it's UNLIMITED bad. And that's BAD.

Like with Brady, for instance.

After that night with the emails, that's about it. We don't hardly speak for the next couple of months. He don't answer emails, I dunno his phone number, and trying to get him at school's a complete waste of time. He don't wanna be seen with me and I don't wanna be seen with him. I KNOW why I don't wanna be seen with him – ain't no point in denying it – it's cos I'm dead-scared of Bowker. I can still feel him grabbing my arm, slapping my face, telling me – *I see you anywhere near him again and you'll WISH you was dead.* And I know he ain't joking. Cos, before all this – when I was just THE FAT KID, when I din't have nothing no one NEEDED – all I was to Bowker was a piece of junk to kick about . . . a toy, a dog, a bug . . . something weak to make him strong. He din't HATE me or nothing – why should he? You don't HATE a punchbag, do you? You don't HATE bugs, you just squash em. But now it's different. Cos now he ain't got me to kick about no more, and he don't like that. He don't like it one bit. And what makes it worse, a hundred times worse, is he's actually gotta LOOK AFTER me . . . like, instead of whacking me and squashing me and kicking me about, he's gotta make sure I DON'T get whacked and squashed and kicked about. And if I do, like I did with Jicky and the boys, Bowker's gotta make it up, like giving me the 50 quid – which, by the way, I thought about tearing up, or giving to children-in-need or something . . . you know, as a MATTER-OF-PRINCIPLE . . . yeh, I thought about that for about 5 seconds, then I went out and bought a bunch of CDs. Children-in-need? I'm a children, ain't I? I *need* my CDs.

Yeh, anyway, so now Bowker's got a REASON to hate my guts, which makes him 10 times scarier than he was before, and he was pretty damn scary in the first place. So when he says keep away from Brady, I ain't arguing.

All right, so that's why I'm keeping away from Brady – but why's he keeping away from me? THAT's the bit I dunno, the bit that does my head in . . . the BAD bit. It's BAD cos it gets me thinking . . .

What's he DOING?

What's he DONE?

Has he done what Jicky and Dec told him? Has he gone down the cops and told em he bolloxed up, told em he's been making up stories, told em he lied?

Or not?

And if not, when's he gonna get it? Cos he IS gonna get it, 100% guaranteed. I just KNOW it, I can FEEL it in my blood. I dunno when or where, or who's gonna do it, and I dunno how bad it's gonna be, but if he don't give it up, he's definitely gonna get it, and it's gonna be SOME kinda BAD . . .

That's what I'm thinking.

It ain't like I'm WORRIED about it . . .

I mean, it's up to him what he does. He can do what he wants. If he wants to stick his ugly head in the fire . . . if he thinks it's worth it . . . that's up to him. I ain't gonna stop him. I ain't his MOTHER.

Nah . . . I ain't WORRIED . . .

I got my own stuff to worry about.

It's just . . . like, all I wanna do is tell him to WATCH IT, tell him about Vine. Cos I dunno if Callan's told him that Vine ain't banged up – which, by the way, I been thinking about, cos at first it don't make sense. I mean, how come Vine's out on bail? It ain't like he's charged with shoplifting or burglering or something piddly like that . . . this is BIG stuff . . . this is MURDER. You don't get bail for MURDER, do you? I dunno . . . maybe you do? Or maybe – and this is what I been thinking – maybe if you *know* people . . . you know, like `senior politicians, judges, lawyers, and policemen . . .`

maybe that makes a difference? Yeh, I reckon it probly does . . .

Not that it matters.

WHY don't matter. WHY ain't the point. The point is – Vine's OUT THERE somewhere . . . and he ain't gonna like some dwarfy little snot telling lies about him, is he? He ain't gonna like it BIG time.

But Brady won't listen.

I tried sending him the Vine stuff I got off the internet:

`LOOK` – I tell him – `LOOK!! This is stuff about Vine` – <u>`On his release from prison in 1994 he was subsequently charged with the murder of a prosecution witness at his previous trial . . .`</u>

But it comes back undelivered, cos now Brady's gone and changed his email address, which REALLY pisses me off. I mean, ignoring me at school's one thing – I can put up with that – I can even put up with him ignoring my emails . . . but CHANGING his email address so he don't even GET em . . . what's THAT all about? It's like he's turning his back on me, TOTALLY ignoring me . . . in fact, it's MORE than TOTALLY ignoring me – it's like saying I don't EXIST. So, I says to myself – why bother? If he's gonna be like that, why bother? What's it to you, anyway? I mean, what do you care? It's only Brady . . .

Forget it . . .

Forget the whole damn thing.

It ain't worth it.

So that's what I do, I just forget the whole damn thing, I DON'T bother about it. But you know how it is . . . how sometimes you CAN'T STOP thinking about stuff, no matter how hard you try? Well, that's how it is with me and this Brady stuff. I don't WANNA think about it, but it won't stop nagging at me, it won't go away, it won't leave me alone . . .

So, a couple of weeks later, I give it another shot. Only this time I do it face to face. I get Brady where he can't get away, where no one's gonna see us, where he's GOTTA listen to me – I get him in a storage room in the corridor near the basement toilets in the main building.

It's a poky little place where they keep the bog rolls and soap and cleaning stuff . . . ain't much more than a cupboard, really. But it's big enough, and it's got a door, which is the main thing. OK – so I get down there one dinnertime, wait till no one's around, then open the door (*STAFF ONLY*) and sneak in. I know Brady's gonna come down some time, cos he's ALWAYS taking a leak . . . I dunno why . . . I think he's got something wrong with his innards, like he's on anti-diabetics or bladder pills or something . . . I dunno. Anyway, whatever it is, I know he's gonna come down some time. So I just sit there and wait, peeking out through a gap in the door, watching the comings-and-goings – the kids on their own, scratching their arses . . . the kids in pairs, too scared to go to the bogs on their own . . . the kids in groups, the smokers, the jokers, the pokers, looking out for the kids on their own . . . all of em yakking and laughing and pushing and shoving . . . and I'm in here watching em . . . perched on a box full of *INDUSTRIAL DISINFECTANT* . . . watching, watching, watching . . . drifting away . . . HIPPONOTISED by the trail of steps and voices . . . moving . . . echoing . . . moving to the sound of lights . . . glimmering . . . merging into one . . .

falling away . . . fading . . . I'm watching . . . watching . . . eyes closed . . . watching . . . when – *KA-BOOOM!!* – a volcano erupts in the sky, a fountain of blue, a mushroom cloud, and my eyes jerk open and the dream of the road is gone. It's OK . . . ain't nothing . . . I was just a bit tired, that's all . . . probly all the disinfectant fumes in here or something . . . but anyway, I'm awake now . . . I'm alert again . . . and I can SEE Brady walking along the corridor – *shuffling* along the corridor – and there ain't no one else around, so I open the door, grab his arm, yank him inside, and slam the door shut.

'What the f—'

'It's all right,' I tell him. 'It's only me.'

'*MOO! SHIT!* What you *doing*?'

'*Shhh!*'

'*What?*'

'Shut up – keep your voice down.'

He looks around, all boggle-eyed, like a startled frog. 'What's going on? What you doing in *here*? What—'

'Shut up a minute – I just wanna talk, OK?'

He looks at me, his blue eyes mixed up with fear and confusion, plus a little bit of anger . . . and there's something else there, too . . . something I can't work out. It's almost embarrassment, but not quite. Like embarrassment WITHOUT the embarrassment, if that makes any sense.

He looks away and reaches for the door. 'I gotta go.'

I block his way.

'Come *on*, Moo,' he says. 'Don't mess about.'

'*Me* mess about? *I* ain't messing about. I ain't the one's changed *my* email address.'

He looks down, all mopey-eyed, like he's ASHAMED of himself . . . but I know he ain't. He's just doing that thing – trying to make me feel bad about him feeling GUILTY – and

I ain't falling for that. He don't feel GUILTY anyway . . . he don't even know what guilty MEANS.

'I been trying to email you,' I tell him. 'I been trying to send you stuff.'

'What stuff?'

'About Vine.'

'Yeh?'

'Yeh.'

'Like what?'

'Like he's out on bail, like he knows what's going on cos he's got cops in his pocket, like he *whacks* people who grass him up.'

'So what?'

THAT shuts me up for a second. I can't believe it . . . what's the matter with him? Why ain't he SCARED? He's ALWAYS scared. He's scaredier than ME . . . and you don't get much scaredier than that. So why ain't he scared? Why ain't . . .

Then I get it.

'You told em, din't you?'

'What?'

'The cops – you told em you was lying.'

He just looks at me.

'Shit,' I says. 'You DIN'T tell em, did you?'

He still don't answer, but he don't have to now – the answer's burned in his eyes. I can SEE it, plain as Day, and it does me in. It KILLS me. It gets me so mad . . . GOD. I dunno why . . . it just GETS me, and I start yelling at him.

'What's the *MATTER* with you? You got a DEATH WISH or something? You WANNA get killed? GOD . . . you KNOW what Jicky and Dec said . . . you KNOW what they're like. They ain't messing about, B . . . they gonna KILL you . . . or WORSE, probly . . . they'll probly . . .'

I'm really RAGING away at him, roaring and howling and spitting in his face, and he's just standing there looking at me, all stumpy and pathetic, like he's dead already . . . and suddenly I can't do it no more. Can't shout, can't yell, can't even speak. It's his eyes . . . the look in his eyes . . . it's like I'm looking in a mirror, looking at someone stuck in a hole . . . someone just like me. I dunno what it is, this hole of his . . . it's probly something to do with him and Callan . . . like he's got himself into something and now he can't get out of it . . . and Callan's probly gone and told him that I'm IN with Vine or something . . . so Brady thinks if he talks to me he's gonna GET it . . .

Which is probly why he's been keeping away from me . . .

Does that make sense?

I dunno . . .

I can't think.

It don't matter anyway, cos whatever it is, there ain't nothing I can do about it. Not now. It's too HARD. Too much. Too CLOSE. All I can do is look at Brady with empty eyes . . . then step to one side, open the door, and let him go.

Looking back on it **now**, I think that was some kinda – what-d'you-call-it? – some kinda TURNING POINT. I ain't sure why . . . it just feels really BAD after then. Not that it din't feel bad before, cos it did, but that was a different kinda bad. That was MY bad. Like the RAIN used to be MINE, and I knew what to do with it. I could DEAL with it. But when I seen the look on Brady's face, I knew the clouds had moved. They was something else now. SomeWHERE else. And they was bigger, too, and darker and heavier, and he din't know what to do with em, cos they weren't HIS. They was MINE.

And that felt BAD.

Yeh . . .

Really BAD . . .

But it also felt kinda GOOD, in a messed-up kinda way. You know, that messed-up kinda GOODness you feel when you're feeling bad about something and you find out that someone else is feeling bad about it too and it kinda makes you feel better? Like you know it ain't right to feel GOOD about it, cos there's twice as much badness as there was before, which oughta make you feel even worse . . . but it don't. It makes you feel BETTER. But then you start feeling BAD again, cos you know it ain't RIGHT to feel better, and the GOOD gets mixed up with the BAD, so instead of feeling *just* BAD or *just* BETTER, you end up with a mixture of BOTH, like a cross between BAD *and* BETTER . . .

BATTER, maybe . . .

Or *BEDDER*.

Or *BADDER* . . .

Yeh, BADDER.

I dunno . . .

Course, there's the other thing, too . . . the WHOSE-FAULT-IS-IT-ANYWAY? thing . . . but that ain't worth thinking about. Cos, in the first place, it don't matter, and in the second place –

It ain't MY fault.

It's Brady's fault.

He shouldna poked his ugly nose in, he shouldna been such a MONG . . . he shouldna got INVOLVED . . .

But he did.

Chrissake.

Now look at him . . .

Now see where he's got me . . . sitting here, feeling BAD, feeling GOOD, with the clock crawling round to 4 o'clock in the morning . . .

Tick tock . . .
Tick tock . . .
It don't get much BADDER than this.
Yeh, good one, B, thanks a lot.
Thanks a million.

12/ Getting Difficult with Donut

A week or so after grabbing Brady in the store room, I get another call from Donut. Mum gets the call, actually, cos I'm at school when he rings. And it ain't Donut himself, it's the Clark guy . . . the midget man . . . Mr Clark the solicitor's clerk. Anyway, the thing is, I gotta go see Donut again.

'Ain't nothing to worry about,' Mum tells me when I get back from school. 'It's just a few bits and bobs . . .'

'Bits and bobs?'

'That's what he said – bits and bobs . . . Ps and Qs . . . dotty Is and Ts . . . you know, *details* . . .'

'*What* details?'

'*I* dunno, do I? Just legal stuff, I spose . . . he din't say *exactly*.' She's standing in the kitchen doorway beating up eggs in a bowl. She stops for a minute and gives me a squinty look.

'You all right, love?' she says. 'You look a bit peaky.'

By PEAKY, I guess she means NOT-AS-FAT-AS-USUAL. Cos, magically, I still been losing TINY bits of weight. It ain't a lot – maybe half a milli-killigramme per week – but it's something. In the last 3 months I reckon I lost about half a centimetre off the circumference of my head. Gimme another 100 years and I'll be a dead ringer for Johnny Depp.

Anyway . . .

'Yeh,' I tell Mum. 'I'm all right.'

'Sure?'

'Yeh.'

She carries on squinting at me for a couple of seconds, then starts beating the eggs again.

'Go on, then,' she says. 'Go and get yourself changed. Dad'll be back soon. Pancakes all right for tea?'

'Yeh.'

Yeh . . .

Yeh . . .

Yeh . . .

Next morning then, about 9 o'clock, the Audi Quattro comes rolling down the street again and stops outside our house. The midget guy gets out and rings the bell, and Mum gets the door.

'Good morning, Mr Clark,' she says, like they're good old buddies or something.

'Yeh,' the little guy grunts. 'You ready?'

And off we go, same as before – me and Mum in the back, the midget guy lost in the driver's seat. Out through the village, onto the road – *shhhhuuuushhhhhhhh* – and before you know it we're purring through the streets of Moulton, into the town centre, then up and down the hilly backstreets, then pulling up at the back of the smart-looking office building . . . parking with the BMWs and the Mercs and the Porsches . . . getting out . . . crossing the car park . . . shiny black door . . . plush carpets and leather chairs and gold-framed pictures on the walls . . . past the reception desk . . . past TraAAAAAAHHH!cy in a KILLER dress . . . knock, knock, knock . . . open the door . . .

Donut's in a cream-coloured suit today, standing by the desk, looking like a gameshow host.

'Mi*chelle*!' he beams. 'Good to see you . . . and Michael – you're both looking well.'

'Thanks,' says Mum, flicking at her hair.

'So,' he goes. 'How *are* things?'

'Well . . .' Mum starts to say.

'Good, good,' says Donut, flashing her a quick grin. 'I'm *so* sorry we had to call you in at such short notice . . . I hope it's not too inconvenient for you.'

Mum starts to open her mouth, but Donut cuts her off again.

'I'm afraid we're a *little* pushed for time this morning,' he says, stepping up to her. 'So if you wouldn't mind . . .' He puts his arm round her shoulder and walks her to the door. Mum looks back at me, looking a bit worried. 'Don't worry,' Donut tells her, 'we won't keep him long. You go and enjoy yourself.' He gives her a crappy little smile, then opens the door. 'Tracy? Look after Mrs Nelson, would you?'

I see a flash of long legs and a snow-white smile, then Mum's led away and Donut shuts the door.

'Lovely woman,' he says, like he's never said it before. Like he REALLY means it. Like I ain't got no memory at all. 'Right,' he goes, walking past me to his desk, 'let's get down to business.' He sits down, flaps through some papers, gets a pen from his pocket, squints at something, slicks back his blondy hair, then looks up at me. I ain't moved. I'm still standing in the middle of the room. And I get the feeling he don't like that.

'You can sit *down* if you want,' he says.

I sit down.

He gives me a funny look, then goes back to his papers. He's got this zippy-quick way of flipping through things, all jerky with his eyes and hands, like he's really pissed off with what he's looking at. And he blinks really fast, too – *blinkblinkblink* – like his eyes are little spy cameras and he's taking zippy-quick pictures of secret files.

'OK,' he says – *blinkblinkblink* – 'right . . . yes.' He puts down his pen and looks at me – Mr Smiley. 'Now . . . first things first. The chap who was following you – that's been rectified, I believe?'

'What?'

He sighs. 'Last time we met you expressed some concern about a man who may have been following you. Is that right?'

'Yeh, the guy in the Volvo.'

'Right – well, I'm given to understand that this situation has now been rectified.' He looks at me. 'Rectified . . . *fixed.* He's not following you any more.'

'Oh – right.'

'No – I'm *asking* you, Michael. Is that right?'

'Yeh – I spose. I ain't seen him for a while.'

'Good.'

'Who was he?' I says.

'Hmm?'

'Who was he?'

He shrugs. 'I shouldn't worry about it.'

'I *ain't* worried about it – I just wanna know.'

He gives me a dirty look, like I'm a real pain in the arse. 'You *don't* want to know, believe me.'

'Was he a cop?'

'Very possibly . . . anyway, the main thing is that he's gone.'

'What happened to him?'

'Does it *matter*?'

The sudden snap of his voice makes me jump. It ain't like it's SCARY or nothing, it's just a bit of a shock.

'Look, Michael,' he says, suddenly all smiles again, 'we really *don't* have a lot of time this morning.'

'I was only asking.'

'Yes, well . . . perhaps some other time . . . all right?'

'Yeh . . . whatever.'

'OK, well . . . if it's all right with you, I'd like to go over your statement again.' He picks out the photocopied pages and looks at em. 'Have you had any more trouble from Mr Callan, by the way?'

I shake my head.

'No problems at all?'

I shrug.

'Is that a *yes* or a *no*?'

'No – no problems.'

'And how's it going at school?'

'What d'you mean?'

Now it's his turn to shrug. 'Nothing – I was only asking.'

'Yeh, well,' I says. 'Perhaps some other time . . .'

That gets me another dirty look, this time with a hint of – *Watch it, you fat bastad. Don't get smart with ME.* I smile at him, thinking – Yeh? Well if you can't take it, mister, don't dish it out. And he smiles back. And we're all nice and cosy again.

'OK, Michael,' he says. 'What I'd like you to do is tell me in your own words what happened in the early evening of November 2nd last year.'

'When?'

He sighs. 'When you saw the 2 cars . . . from the bridge.'

'You want me to tell you what happened?'

'Yes, please.'

'Why? You got it all down there in my statement. You *know* what happened.'

He stares at me, his mouth getting all tight and nasty, and I think he's about to lose it . . . but then he looks down at his desk and takes a couple of deep breaths, and when he looks up he's just about smiling again. 'Look,' he says slowly, trying to stay calm, 'look – we need to prepare you for the trial – OK? When you go to court you'll be asked by the prosecution barrister to describe what happened. I just want to make sure that you've got things straight in your mind – do you understand?'

'Yeh.'

'Go on, then.'

'What?'

He grits his teeth. 'Tell me what happened.'

So I tell him. From the moment I left the house . . . to the moment Laser Cop told me to go home. I tell him the story. As I'm telling it, he keeps interrupting me – asking me to clarify this, explain that, confirm this, repeat that . . . I KNOW what he's doing, I ain't dumb. I seen my share of courtroom stuff on TV. He's trying to trip me up, catch me out . . . he's testing me, making sure I ain't gonna start blubbing in court . . . or I ain't gonna go mental or nothing . . . which I KNOW I ain't, cos there ain't nothing to go mental about, cos it's the TRUTH, and the TRUTH's dead easy. It ain't like lying. You ain't gotta work nothing out, you ain't even gotta THINK of nothing – all you gotta do is say what happened.

This, this, this . . .

It ain't exactly *difficult*.

Unlike me.

Cos when Donut's finished testing me, when he's satisfied I ain't no blubbery moron, when a big fat £££ smile spreads across his face, that's when I decide it's time to get difficult. Just for the hell of it.

'I ain't sure I can do it,' I tell him.

'What?' he says, his smile turning sour. 'You can't do what?'

'This – what-d'you-call-it – giving evidence. I ain't sure I can do it.'

'Don't be *stupid*. Of *course* you can do it. You just *did* it, for God's sake.'

'That's different.'

'No, it's not. It's *exactly* the same. You explain what you saw, you answer a few simple questions, and that's it. You can do that.'

'I dunno . . .'

'We're looking after you, aren't we?'

'What?'

'We're looking after you – we're treating you well.'

'Yeh, I guess.'

'So what's your problem?'

'I dunno . . .'

'Is it Callan?'

'No.'

'*What* then?' he whines, his cool blondy head getting hotter by the second. 'Now look, Michael,' he says, trying to control himself, 'we've spent a lot of time and money here . . .'

'Yeh, but—'

And that's when he cracks, slamming his hand on the desk. 'No BUTS. You're DOING it. End of story.'

'You can't *make* me.'

'No?'

'I ain't done nothing wrong.'

He leans back in his chair. 'I'm not sure Mr Vine would see it like that.'

'What d'you mean?'

'Well, put yourself in his place. How would you feel if *you* were wrongly accused of murder, and the only person who knew the truth refused to testify on your behalf? How would you feel about that?'

'I dunno . . . not too good, I spose.'

'No, not too good . . . I don't expect Mr Vine would feel too good, either.' He leans forward and lowers his voice. 'Mr Vine's not a pretty sight when he's not feeling good.' He gives me a wise-arse look, then leans back again, adjusts his tie, and stares at me.

I spose I could try telling him the truth – look, Donut, I was only *joking*, I was only having a *larf* . . . but I don't reckon he'd take it too well. No . . . I reckon I bolloxed things up a bit there. I reckon I shoulda give the whole *being-difficult-just-for-the-hell-of-it* thing a bit more thought. Yeh, I guess I got a bit too cocky for my own good, din't I? A bit too full of it. And now it's time to pay up.

'I din't say I *wouldn't* do it,' I tell him.

He frowns at me, lowering his head, tucking his chin into his neck. 'Really?'

'No,' I tell him. 'It's just . . . you know . . . I get a bit nervous sometimes . . .'

'So what are you saying, Michael?' he goes. 'You've changed your mind now? Is that it? Are you saying you *are* quite happy to appear as a witness for the defence?'

'Yeh . . . I'm happy.'

'You're quite sure about that?'

'Yeh.'

'You're not going to change your mind again?'

'No.'

'Are you absolutely sure? Because I don't want to have to tell Mr Vine he can rely on you, only to find out at the very last moment that he can't. That would cause all *sorts* of nasty problems for all *sorts* of people. Do you understand what I'm saying?'

'Yeh, I think so.'

'You'd better.'

The phone rings. Donut picks it up, goes – *yeh, yeh, I know, yeh* . . . then he starts talking about reasonable 4s or something, legal-lingo, *longius wordius*, and I get up and wander around for a bit, looking out the window, looking at the pictures on the wall, looking at the sweaty-bum mark I left on the chair . . . trying to work out how the hell I got myself into all this . . . then Donut gets off the phone and TELLS me to sit down, which I'm glad to, thanks very much. And now there ain't no pretending no more. He TELLS me what I'm gonna do. TELLS me to keep my mouth shut, don't worry about nothing, do as I'm told, and I'll be all right. TELLS me he'll let me know when and where the trial's gonna be, and I'd better be there, or else.

I'm tempted to ask – or else what? But I reckon I said enough dumb things for today, so I leave it. Then Donut starts going over some detaily things, like what happens in court, what to wear, where to go, how it all works, who's gonna be there . . . and I sit there looking at him with INTERESTED eyes, but behind em I'm nowhere, just drifting away . . .

This time, on the way back – sitting in the Audi, zipping along at 190mph – Mum's pretty quiet. I dunno what it is, but she ain't so pleased as PUNCH as she was before, she ain't going on and on about what she got at the shops . . . she ain't showing me this or showing me that . . . and her eyes ain't shiny and bright like they was the last time, they're just kinda tired and dull, like someone's switched em off.

'You all right?' she goes, after a while.

'Yeh.'

'Sure?'

'Yeh.'

She looks out the window, scratching her neck. 'You gotta

go there again?'

'I don't think so.'

'Good.'

She smiles at me, looking kinda lost, then turns her head and carries on looking out the window.

'Mum?' I says.

'Hmm?'

I look at her.

She smiles again . . . doing her best.

'Nothing,' I says. 'It don't matter.'

'Sure?'

'Yeh, it's OK.'

As soon as we get back, as soon as we get in the house, I gotta get out again . . . I gotta get back to the bridge . . . to MY PLACE . . . to THINK . . .

And I think.

I think . . .

It ain't so bad. OK, so Donut's getting hard, giving me all this OR ELSE stuff, putting me in the picture, laying it on the line – YOU BETTER DO THIS COS VINE'S A CRAZY GOON AND HE'S LIKELY TO CUT YOU UP IF YOU DON'T . . . or something like that. Could be he's just trying to scare me, but he probly ain't. Well, he IS . . . but it ain't like a gutless scare, it ain't like Vine probly WOULDN'T go crazy, cos I think he probly would. So, OK, that ain't too GREAT . . . but if you think about it, it don't mean much. It only means something if I DON'T do it, and I ain't got no intention of DON'T doing it. And even if I did, which I don't, I'd have to be dumber than the dumbest kid in the world not to change my mind, wouldn't I?

Nah . . . it ain't so bad.

I mean, if you think about it, it ain't no different to crossing the road. Say you're standing on the pavement, right? And there's a 20-ton truck coming down the road. If you step out in front of it, it's gonna squash you dead. Guaranteed. Now that ain't a nice thing to think about, is it? But it don't matter – it don't matter one bit. Cos you AIN'T gonna step out in front of it, so you AIN'T gonna get squashed to death.

Stands to reason, don't it?

THAT's what I'm thinking.

It stands to reason . . .

And that's what keeps me going . . . Day after Day, hour after hour . . . *not* thinking about it . . . cos up here on the bridge you DON'T think about nothing. *Swoo-ooosh-swoo-ooosh-swoo-ooosh* . . . cars, vans, lorries, bikes, 20-ton trucks . . . heading north, heading south, rumbling, racing, roaring, screaming, silent as nothing . . .

It takes me away.

Then, maybe a month later, it brings me back.

13/ Slices of Night

Like I said, I ain't too sure about the months **now** – February, March, April, May . . . they all just kinda merge together in my head. But I reckon what happened next musta been around April some time, cos I'm thinking about it **now**, kinda PICTURING it in my head, and I'm pretty sure the skies are blue and Aprilly, kinda warmish but not too hot, and the birds are singing and there's bits of green on the trees . . . and I ain't wearing a coat or nothing, just a hood and a T-shirt . . .

So, yeh, I reckon it's around April some time . . .

Not that it makes any difference.

I'm just on the bridge, watching the traffic – THAT's what time it is. The time when time don't matter. When I been up here for hours, just doing my thing – up here, down there . . . watching, watching, watching . . . maybe flicking at bits of peeled-off bridge-paint, watching em flitter down into the river, dancing round the wheels . . . watching em fly . . . watching em flutter . . . watching em die . . . dead-eyed and blind . . . drifting away . . . losing my mind . . .

THAT's where I'm at when it all comes back.

Nowhere . . .

One minute I'm all alone, the only thing in the world . . . and then – *PHSSHHHTT!!* – the sound of NOTHING, like a SLICE of NIGHT, and I'm suddenly aware of this darkness beside me. A shadow, the smell of wax-cloth and skin . . .

'Hello, Michael.'

. . . and just for a second my bones go rigid and my belly jumps into my throat.

'Sorry,' says Callan. 'Did I frighten you?'

All I can do is stare at him, all white-eyed and shaky, thinking – frighten me? Did you FRIGHTEN ME? Jesus CHRIST! . . . I nearly filled me *PANTS*.

'You all right?' he says.

'Yeh – great.'

Breathing deeply, I look around, looking for his car, but he musta walked or got dropped off or something, cos there ain't no parked cars in sight.

'You like coming up here?' he says.

'Uh?'

'You like it up here?'

I look at him, leaning on the railings beside me, looking down. He don't look too great. His skin's kinda dry, and less white than it was, like a bit of old paper you find at the back of a drawer. And his hair ain't so neat no more. It's getting a bit long, a bit scruffy. His eyes ain't changed, though – grey as the bridge – and his mouth's still got that steely look, the look that says – Don't Mess With Me.

'Yeh,' I tell him. 'I like it up here.'

He nods, looking around. 'Gets you away from it all, I expect . . .'

'Away from all what?'

'Oh yeh,' he goes, 'I forgot – you don't get any trouble at school these Days, do you? You're a protected species now.' He gives me a snidey look. 'That must be nice.'

'I din't ask for it.'

'Posh cars, bodyguards, treats for your mum – makes you feel big, does it?'

'Like I said, I din't ask for it.'

He don't say nothing for a minute, just stares into the distance, chewing on his cheek. I'm kinda tempted to ask him about Brady, like – what you got on him? what you giving him? and, what the hell d'you think you're DOING? – but I ain't sure that's a good idea. And he probly wouldn't tell me nothing anyway. So I don't say nothing, just act dumb.

After a bit he looks at me and says, 'I'm giving you one more chance.'

'For what?'

He looks away. 'Last chance. After this – that's it.' He looks at me again. 'It's up to you – understand?'

'No.'

'Oh, I think you do, Michael. I think you understand a lot more than you let on. But OK . . . listen, here's how it is. Black-and-white.' He pauses for a moment, gazing off into the distance, then starts talking. 'Keith Vine,' he says, 'is what we call a career criminal. He makes a living from crime. He steals, he robs, he cheats, he hurts people . . . he kills people. That's a fact, Michael – he *kills* people. And whatever you think of me, whatever you think of what I'm doing, whatever you *believe* – don't ever doubt that one simple fact. Keith Vine is a killer. He's killed before and he'll kill again. Fact – he places no value on human life. Fact – if he has to kill someone to get what he wants, he'll do it.' Callan snaps his fingers. 'Just like that.' He looks at me. '*That's* the kind of man we're dealing with here. *That's* what I'm trying to stop. Do you understand me? That's my job – it's what I do.' His eyes fix on mine for a moment, freezing me to death, then he looks away again.

'Now,' he says, 'there's all sorts of things going on here, some of which I expect you know, and others you'd never even dream of. It's a complex situation. But – and this is what's important – when you clear away all the mess and the stupid little games, you're left with something incredibly simple. And that's this: Keith Vine is an evil man, a man who hurts and maims and kills, and the world's a better place without him. That's it, Michael – that's all there is to it. You help me put him away and you'll be doing something for the greater good. You'll be saving lives, Michael . . . saving *lives*. Think about it.' He looks at me. 'Are you thinking about it?'

'Yeh.'

'How does it feel?'

'I dunno . . .'

He shakes his head, VERY unhappy. 'Maybe you ought to think about it some more . . . have a good long think. Use your imagination. Imagine how you're going to feel a year from now when I come knocking on your door and show you a photograph of Keith Vine's latest victim. Think about that. Then imagine how you're going to feel when I show you a photograph of the victim's wife, or mother, or child. You think about that. Now imagine how *you'd* feel if someone *you* loved was taken away from you. D'you think you can do that? Eh?'

'I dunno . . .'

'All right,' he says, his voice cold as hell, 'you want to play stupid? Let's play stupid. Let me make it a bit *easier* for you.' He sniffs hard, like he don't REALLY wanna do this, but he ain't got no choice. '5 years ago,' he says, 'your father was summoned to appear in court on a charge of fraudulently claiming invalidity benefit. The charge is still outstanding, as is a civil claim for unpaid rent. For the last 4 years your father has again been claiming invalidity benefit, not only under false pretences, but this time under an assumed name as well. He's also been observed dealing in stolen goods.'

'He ain't got nothing—'

'Shut up – listen to me. Just listen. I don't give a toss

about your dad – OK? I don't care what he's done or what he's doing. But I've got enough evidence to send him down for a couple of years, and if I have to use that to make you see sense, I'll do it. D'you understand what I'm saying? You help me and I'll help you. But if you carry on pissing me about, that's it – you can wave goodbye to your dad. And that's not a threat, Michael, it's a stone-cold promise. Believe me, I'll do it.'

I dunno what to say . . .

Bastad is all I can think of – dirty bastad, sneaky bastad, clever bastad . . .

'It ain't right,' I tell him. 'You ain't allowed to do that—'

'Do what?' he says innocently.

'Threaten me.'

'*Threaten* you? When did I threaten you?'

'Just *now* . . .'

He shakes his head. 'I never said a word.'

'You said—'

'I was never here, Michael. I never met you. Never spoke to you.' He looks at his watch. 'For the last half hour I've been interviewing a suspect in an unrelated case – a young man called Danny Anderson. He'll be more than happy to confirm my whereabouts. So, you see, I *couldn't* have been here. I think you must be imagining things.'

Clever bastad.

He steps away from the railings and stretches his back, then reaches into his pocket and pulls out a business card. 'When you've finished thinking,' he says, 'give me a call.' He slips the card into my hood pocket and pats me hard on the belly. 'And, if I were you, I wouldn't leave it too long – OK?'

'Yeh.'

'Good lad.' He buttons his coat. 'Right, well, I'll leave

you to it then . . .' and he does, striding off across the bridge like he's the dog's bollox, which I guess he probly is.

I watch him for a while . . . I watch him go down the steps – zag, zig, zag – down the lane, and then he disappears around the corner. I dunno where he goes, I don't care – I ain't got the energy to care. I ain't got nothing left. All I can do is stand there staring at the traffic, watching the river, thinking . . .

Thinking . . .

I can't think no more.

But you know how it goes, how when something's happening you dunno what to say, you can't think of nothing, but then afterwards you can't think of nothing else? Yeh, well, that's how it goes that night, lying in bed, thinking of all the stuff I coulda told Callan. Like when he said that stuff about school, about me being a *protected species*, like THAT's the reason I ain't changing my statement – cos I don't wanna get no trouble, cos I'm scared, cos I LIKE being a protected species, cos it *makes me feel big* . . . I coulda said stuff to him then . . . I coulda said – Oh yeh, what do *you* know? You ever been fat? You ever had 50 kids laughing at your belly? D'you know how it FEELS to be 17-stone FAT? D'you know how it *FEELS*? FAT FAT FAT . . . no, you dunno how it feels. You dunno NOTHING. So don't talk to me about *getting away from it all*. Don't talk to me about *trouble*. Don't talk to me about feeling *BIG*. All right? And then I coulda told him stuff about right and wrong, about JUSTICE, and I coulda said – You talk about right and wrong, you make out like you're a SAINT, but you ain't no better than the rest of em. Yeh, I coulda said that. I coulda said – Doing your JOB? You ain't doing your JOB, all you're doing is trying to get even with Vine cos he got away with whacking some guy before, and you don't like that cos it makes you look stupid. So don't go giving me all this GREATER GOOD + SAVING LIVES crap, cos it's all BOLLOX. Yeh . . . I coulda told him that. And then I coulda said – Hey, you wanna do my dad for fiddling the social? Yeh, all right, go on then, see if I care. But don't come moaning to me when I give out the goodies on YOU, and YOU end up inside, and then all the crazies you ever banged up gonna come knocking on your door in the middle of the night, just DYING to meet you . . .

Yeh . . .

I COULDA said all that, plus a bit more for afters . . . but it wouldna made no difference. Cos, let's face it, Callan's at least 10 times smarter than me. Whatever I said, he woulda got me. I mean, it's all right me lying here in bed being a smart-arse, running rings round him, tying him up in knots . . . but he ain't HERE, is he? So it don't mean diddly. Like, I could beat Tiger Woods at golf if he WASN'T HERE . . . but that don't make me no golfer, does it? Nah . . . if I'd said them things to Callan, all I woulda done is wind him up, get him even madder, and he's probly the kinda guy who, the MADDER he gets, the SMARTER he gets . . . so maybe it's best I DIN'T say much.

Yeh, I guess I did all right.

I probly did the best I could . . .

There's one thing, I spose . . . one thing I coulda done.

I coulda thrown him off the bridge.

Yeh, see how *SMART* he is then . . . see how smart he is with a 20-ton truck on his head – *BOOF!! AAAHHH!! HOONKKK!! KER-SPPLATT!!* How's THAT feel, Mr Clever Bastad? D'YOU UNDERSTAND WHAT I'M SAYING? EH? HOW D'YOU FEEL *NOW*?

Yeh, I coulda done THAT.

14/ Mr Keith Vine

Looking at it **now**, it's pretty clear what's going on and where it's gonna end. It's obvious, innit? Yeh . . . and maybe . . . I dunno . . . but maybe if I'd done this before . . . then maybe I coulda seen the end before. If I'd done what I'm doing **now**, if I'd sat up all night, just talking it through, bit by bit, picking out the big stuff and chucking out the rest . . . if I'd done THAT in March or April or May, then maybe I coulda seen the end BEFORE it got too late.

Yeh . . .

Then . . .

Maybe . . .

But . . .

Nah . . . it wouldna made no difference. Cos it's one of them things . . . like a guided missile – it don't matter WHAT you do, it's ALWAYS gonna get there in the end. THAT's where it's going – the place it's ALWAYS gonna get to. That's the WHOLE POINT. It's always gonna get to the place you can't get away from, a place that says –

DO THIS or DO THAT.

No ifs, no buts, no turning back. You got ONE THING or THE OTHER. That's ALL you got –

THIS or THAT.

No way out.

THIS or THAT.

Which is OK if one of em's OK. I mean, if you gotta do THIS or THAT, and you don't *mind* doing THIS, or you don't *mind* doing THAT, you ain't got a problem. And you ain't *really* got a problem if THIS and THAT are BOTH pretty crappy and you don't really wanna do neither. All you gotta do is pick the least crappiest one. But the thing about *this* THIS or THAT – the THIS or THAT I'm at then, the THIS or THAT where it's always been going . . . the thing about it is –

I CAN'T DO IT.

I *can't* do THIS and I *can't* do THAT.

That's it.

That's where I'm at.

Cos I gotta go to court, right?

The letter came in the morning. Recorded Delivery. The postman – a stubby little guy called Roy – he rang the bell and Mum got the door, chewing on a piece of toast, still dressed in her big baggy jimjams.

'Sign and print,' goes Roy.

'Print what?'

'There – your name.'

She brings the letter into the kitchen and opens it up, getting buttery fingerprints all over the place. She reads the letter, then passes it to Dad. He reads it, grunts, and passes it to me. I wipe it clean and read it. It's from Donut, telling me the trial's set for June 3rd, which is about 2 or 3 weeks away. Monday June 3rd, at Wickham Crown Court. There's a little map showing me how to get there. There's also a little leaflet telling me all sorts of stuff about being a witness, like what happens in court and what I gotta do and who's gonna be there . . . there's even little drawings of the courtroom, with all these guys in wigs and suits, and little labels saying who they are – JUDGE, LAWYERS, USHER, CLERK . . . which is pretty good. In the letter, Donut says he can't say *exactly* when I gotta be there, cos there might be delays or something, and the defence stuff don't start till after the prosecution stuff's finished, so I probly won't be needed till the following week . . . but he'll get in touch closer to the date and let me know.

'Expenses,' say Dad.

'What?'

He's looking at the witness information leaflet. He's also dipping toast into a boiled egg and dripping eggy goo all over the pages.

'It says you can claim expenses,' he goes. 'Meals, travel . . .' He looks up. 'How you gonna get there?'

'I dunno.'

'Get a plane,' he grins. 'Hire Concorde or something . . . if they're paying . . .'

'Yeh,' I says.

Good one, Dad. HIGHLY amusing.

So . . . I gotta go to court, right? I got the letter. It's all official. Signed, sealed, written in black-and-white. Yeh, I KNOW it don't mean nothing. I KNOW it's just a piece of paper. But that ain't REALLY what it is. What it is REALLY – it's a dirty great smack in the face. Like, Hey – *SMACK!!* – wake up, Moo! It's HAPPENING!! It's HERE!! It ain't gonna go away if you close your eyes. It ain't no good pretending it ain't gonna happen no more, cos – *SMACK!!* – it's HAPPENING RIGHT NOW.

Yeh . . . it's happening.

In 2 or 3 weeks time I gotta tell some kinda truth.

THIS or THAT?

And that's the thing.

Cos if I tell it like it is, the TRUTH truth, Callan's gonna get Dad for fiddling the benefit. It ain't no good thinking he won't, cos he ain't that kinda guy. I mean, I dunno much – but I know cold blood when I see it. I know the difference between a threat and a promise. Callan ain't gonna waste his time getting guys in Volvos to get the dirty on Dad if he ain't gonna use it. Nah . . . no chance. He'll do it all right. So that's that. Telling the TRUTH is OUT. Cos I ain't letting NO ONE take Dad away. Not in a billion years.

But if I tell it like Callan wants, the WRONG TRUTH, then Vine's gonna get done for murder and I'm gonna wish I was dead.

THIS or THAT?

Take your pick.

What you gonna do?

I dunno . . .

Not much, I guess – just go to school and think about it, spend all Day weighing things up. That's all I can do all Day – think think think. And I keep getting this picture in my head, the picture from the cover of the witness information leaflet. It shows this woman in a long white dress and a spiky hat, standing on top of some kinda ball, like a big metal sphere thing. She's just standing there with her arms stretched out, like Jesus on the cross, with a sword in one hand and a pair of scales in the other . . . you know, them balancing scales, the ones you use for weighing stuff. It's the scales I keep seeing. The way I seem em, right, inside my head, they got THIS written on one side and THAT on the other, and they keep moving up and down. Like, I'm looking at THIS, and it's saying – *yeh, you gotta pick ME, I'M your only way out*. And I'm thinking – yeh, you're right . . . but then the scales start moving again, and the other side starts yelling out – *nah, don't be STUPID, you can't do <u>THAT</u> THIS, you gotta do <u>THIS</u> THIS – you gotta pick ME, I'M your only way out*. And it goes on like that all Day – THIS . . .

THAT . . . THIS . . . THAT . . . THIS . . . THAT . . .

It's driving me MAD.

In the end – and funnily enough, I get to the end when I'm in the toilet – I realise I gotta get rid of em. The scales, I mean. I gotta block em outta my head. So that's what I do – I block em out. And then I says to myself –

Look, it's simple. Callan's gonna get Dad if you tell the truth, right?

Right.

And you ain't having that.

No.

Definite?

100%.

Don't matter what else happens?

No.

OK – there you go then. That's it. You gotta do what Callan wants. You gotta lie. End of story.

Yeh, but what about Vine?

End of story.

Yeh, but—

END OF STORY.

It's afternoon by then, last break. I got Art next. We're doing Collage & Society, which basically means sitting around cutting pictures outta magazines and gluing em on to bits of card while Weedy Pete the art teacher sneaks off for a fag. And I don't reckon I'm gonna DIE if I miss that. So I wait in the toilets till classes start again, then I creep along the corridor, through a side door, out round the back, through a little gate in the teachers' car park, and I'm outta there. I'm gone. Walking the afternoon streets. I ain't really bothered if anyone sees me, but it's probly best if they don't, so I keep to the backstreets, heading up around the shop and down across the little park towards the phone box at the end of the bank.

There's a little woody place down there. It ain't exactly a *wood*, just a scrappy kinda place between the park and the estate (where Brady lives), but everyone calls it The Woods. There's a few trees and bushes and stuff, and a bit of a track where kids mess around on trail bikes, but it's mostly just one of them places where people go when they wanna do stuff they ain't sposed to do. You know the kinda place – beer cans, bottles, ripped-up porn mags and rubbers all over the place, that kinda thing.

Anyway, there's a phone box there, between the park and the woods, and that's all I want.

I get inside, get out the card that Callan gave me, and ring his number.

Some woman answers.

'Moulton CID,' she goes. 'Penny James.'

'Who's that?' I says.

'DC James, Moulton CID. Can I help you?'

'Is Mr Callan there?'

'Who's speaking, please?'

'Michael Nelson.'

'What's it concerning?'

'Keith Vine.'

'One moment.'

There's a load of noise in the background – beeping, talking, coughing, laughing, keyboards tapping . . .

'Who's calling, please?'

Same woman.

'What?' I says.

'Who is it? What's your name?'

'Michael Nelson. I just told you—'

'One moment.'

This time she's gone for a lot longer. I listen to the phone for a while, but there ain't nothing there no more – no background noise, no beeping, no talking . . . it's all gone dead, just a hollow kinda hissing noise and a faint *click-click*ing, like the sound of insects in outer space. I look out through the phone box windows, looking for something to look at. There ain't much – a big bushy tree with carrier-bags flapping in the branches . . . a mesh fence . . . a plastic bollard stuck on a pole . . . and I start to wonder – maybe I oughta put the phone down? maybe I shoulda given this a bit more thought? maybe it's dumb? maybe I could—

'Michael?'

It's Callan.

'Michael? Can you hear me?'

'Yeh.'

'Where are you?'

'I wanna see you.'

'OK, that's good . . . good lad. Where are you?'

'I ain't doing it for nothing.'

'Sorry?'

'You gotta look after me.'

'Michael, listen—'

'You gotta keep Vine away and you gotta promise me about Dad. You gotta gimme a signed letter or something, else I ain't doing it.'

'OK – just tell me where you are, Michael, and we'll talk about that when I see you.'

'You gotta promise.'

'Everything will be all right, trust me. But I need to know where you are – the sooner we meet, the sooner we can sort things out.'

I stick another 20p in the phone and tell him where I am.

'Right,' he goes. 'That's the little park where we met before?'

'Yeh.'

'OK – stay where you are and I'll be there in 20 minutes. All right?'

'Yeh.'

'And don't worry – you're doing the right thing.'

'Yeh.'

'20 minutes.'

Click.

You're doing the right thing, he says . . . *you're doing the right thing*. Yeh, like hell I am. I know I AIN'T doing the right thing, cos there AIN'T no right thing to DO. There's just 2 wrong things. And, like they say, 2 wrongs don't make a right. All they make is a pain in the arse.

Anyway, it don't matter – I done it now.

I get out the phone box and go and wait on a bench by the carrier-bag-tree. It ain't too comfortable, cos the back of the bench's been smashed off, but it's better than nothing. I can see the grass bank that leads down to Brady's estate, and I can see the road down below, the mini-roundabout up the other end. It's something to look at. Traffic's starting to build up now, so I guess it's getting on for end-of-school time. The traffic . . . *swoo-ooosh-swoo-ooosh-swoo-ooosh* . . . cars, trucks, vans, lorries, bikes . . . it ain't as good as MY traffic, nowhere NEAR as good, but it'll do for now. At least it stops me looking at the gap in the hedge where I talked with Brady that time. It stops me remembering –

Him saying, 'So is that right what you said?'

Me saying, 'What?'

'You know – about the bridge thing . . . not saying nothing. . . you said the cops told you not to say nothing . . . is that right?'

'Yeh . . .' (like I'm *really* sorry) 'it's some kinda legal thing. Something to do with witness . . .' (what's the word?) '. . . witness . . . I dunno . . . witness something. *Com*-something . . .'

'Witless *com*-something?'

'Yeh . . . something like that. Some legal word. It's all signed and everything – I gotta keep my mouth shut. I ain't got no choice.'

And him saying, 'Right,' and tilting his strange head and lowering his eyes, knowing I'm lying, but also knowing there ain't much he can do about it. Then, sniffing again and pinching his nose, 'Yeh, well . . . maybe later?'

'Yeh.'

'OK.'

And off he went along the bank. Dragging his feet, head down, stuffed full of ugliness . . . thinking bad stuff about me, no doubt.

Yeh . . . I reckoned I could live with that.

And I guess I am.

Sitting here, waiting, trying not to think if I'm right or wrong, smart or dumb . . . just living with it.

I ain't got a watch, so I dunno what time it is when I start to think that Callan's late, but it's been more than 20 minutes, easy. It's time he was here – that's what time it is. School's out now. There's kids crossing the park, some of em coming along the bank, a couple going into the woods . . . and it don't look good, me sitting here on my own. It makes me look like a perv. You know, some fat weirdo hanging round the woods on his own . . .

So I'm thinking to myself – maybe you oughta go? And I start to get up off the bench . . . but then I think – yeh, but what if Callan shows up and you ain't here? He ain't gonna like that, is he? So I sit down again. Then a couple of first-year girls walk past, looking at me with monsters in their eyes, like I got a blood-soaked chainsaw in my hand or something . . . so I wait for em to go by, then I start getting up off the bench again . . . but I still ain't sure what to do . . . so I stop getting up, but I don't sit down, I just kinda crouch there, half-hovering over the bench with my bum in the air, trying to work out what to do – should I hang around for Callan a bit more? . . . ring him again? . . . go home? . . .

Then a voice booms out behind me.

'Yo Fats,' it goes. 'What you doing?'

The air goes dead and my heart stops beating. It's a killing voice. Cold and empty. A paralyser. It chokes me. I can't move for a second . . . I'm stuck there, crouched over the bench, frozen stiff, waving my bum in the air, not breathing . . . then a stick snaps – *crack* – breaking the silence, and my body starts working again. I straighten up, take a deep breath, and slowly turn around, WANTING it to be Callan – PLEASE PLEASE PLEASE – but KNOWING all along that it ain't – and it ain't. It's a hard-looking mug with wiry black hair, his skin all tanned and orangey, like he's dried up in the sun . . .

Keith Vine.

'All right?' he says.

He's coming out the woods – tall, stooping under a branch – wearing a black Armani sweatshirt and white chinos with a mobile phone clipped on the belt. He's got a rock-hard grin on his face.

'What's up, Moo?' he says. 'You look surprised.'

I can't speak.

He walks up to me, digging a packet of fags from his pocket. He stops in front of me, sticks a cigarette in his mouth, and lights it. He stares at me. He blows smoke out the side of his mouth.

'Waiting for someone?' he says.

'Sort of . . .'

'Yeh? Who you waiting for?'

My mouth's gone dry.

'Girlfriend?' he grins, looking me up and down. 'Nah . . . I don't think so. Boyfriend, maybe? You waiting for your boyfriend, Moo? Waiting for Brady?'

I shake my head.

He takes a long puff on his cigarette, still staring at me, still grinning. He's got the whitest teeth I ever seen.

'If you're waiting for Callan,' he says, 'he ain't coming. Got an urgent call at the last minute, apparently. Something to do with his wife.' He flicks ash from his cigarette. 'So . . . if you wanna talk, talk to me.'

'I don't wanna—'

'Course you do. Come on . . .' He steps up to me and puts his arm round my shoulders. My whole body goes stiff. 'Relax,' he says, breathing sour breath in my face. 'I just wanna chat, that's all. Sort a few things out. Won't take a minute.' His arm drops, he takes a quick look around, then he grabs hold of my elbow, and before I know it, he's leading me into the woods.

Like I said, it ain't really a *woods*, exactly, just a few trees and bushes and that, but right now, as Vine's leading me into it, with his clawy fingers gripping my arm, it looks like one HELL of a woods . . . it looks like one of them woods you get murdered in.

Christ, I'm SCARED.

I never been so SCARED in all my LIFE.

And you know what happens when you get THAT scared?

YOU CAN'T DO NOTHING, that's what happens.

YOU CAN'T DO *NOTHING*.

And when you can't do nothing, you get stupid. You get zombied. You do exactly what you're told. Walk? Yeh, I'll walk . . . where d'you want me to go? Into the woods? Yeh, OK, sure . . . why not? I mean, it ain't like you're gonna hit me over the head with a shovel or nothing, is it? HA HA HA HA . . .

We walk.

In silence.

Along a scrubby little path . . .

Around the remains of a fire . . .

Through burnt beer cans, chicken bones, more carrier-bags . . .

Finally, after the longest 2 minutes in the world, we get to a place near the other end of the woods, a place I never seen before. It's like a tunnel of trees, all dark and shady and cold, and under the trees there's a scummy little track that leads down to the back of the estate. There's a gateway at the end of the track, but there ain't no gate, just 2 mouldy gateposts with the tops broke off. A black Range Rover is parked under the trees near the gateway – a Vogue SE, 4.6, V8. Brand new. Shiny black. All the trimmings. I dunno if it's the same one as before . . . it *looks* like it . . .

But who cares?

'Get in,' Vine says.

He lets go my arm and walks round to the driver's side. I open the passenger door, climb up, and get in. Vine gets in and slams the door and lights another cigarette, sucking the smoke through his teeth. He looks at me.

'Y'all right?' he says. 'You look a bit pale. What's the matter?' He grins. 'You think you was gonna get popped in the woods?'

I still can't say nothing.

He grins again. 'Don't worry, kid – you ain't getting

popped. Shit – look at you. What d'you weigh? 20-odd stone? Christ – I ain't burying *that*. I'd be digging for Days.' He hits a button and the window winds down. He flicks ash into the wind. 'Right,' he says. 'I got some questions. You tell me what I want, you go home. Simple as that – all right?'

'Yuh . . . yeh.'

'OK. What d'you want with Callan?'

I look at him, which is a pretty scary thing to do, cos he's got the kinda eyes that suck you in and take you down.

'I ain't got all Day,' he says. 'What d'you want with Callan?'

I cough, clearing the snakes out my throat. 'He wants me to say you stabbed that guy.'

'I din't ask you what *he* wants, I asked you what *you* want with *him*. I asked you 3 times now. Don't make me ask again.'

'I was gonna tell him I couldn't do it.'

'Do what?'

'What I just said, about you stabbing that guy.'

'You wanted to see him to tell him you ain't gonna testify against me?'

'Yeh.'

'Why?'

'Cos he said if I din't, he's gonna lock up my dad.'

Vine laughs. 'What for – being a fat slob?'

'No, he said—'

'Yeh, yeh . . . I know what he said – fiddling the benefit and handling stolen goods.' He sniffs. 'Don't worry about it. It's nothing. Most he'll get with a decent brief is a fine – if that.'

'He can't afford a lawyer—'

'I said don't worry about it – it's covered. Your old man ain't going nowhere. No one's getting locked up. It won't even get to court. Trust me. Callan ain't got nothing. He's just flapping around, stirring up shit. What you gotta worry about is me, not Callan. Cos it's me you gonna be looking at in court, and I ain't gonna like it if I see you lying. Know what I mean?'

'Yeh.'

He looks at the end of his cigarette, blows on it, gets it glowing, then slowly pinches it out between his thumb and finger. There's a dull hissing sound, and then a smell of burnt meat.

'You was there, right?' he says, flicking the cigarette out the window. 'On the bridge?'

'Yeh.'

'You seen what they done?'

'Most of it.'

He shakes his head. 'Bastads . . .' Then he grins and looks at me. 'Gotta give em credit though, cos it probly woulda worked if you wasn't there. They had it all worked out pretty good – Burke, the hat, the cops – yeh . . . they had it all worked out – but they din't reckon on some fat kid watching from the bridge, did they? They din't reckon on *that*.' He laughs – a deep hacking sound – then coughs into his hand. 'So,' he goes, 'I guess I owe you one, right?'

'I din't . . . I dunno . . .'

He laughs again, making me feel like a dumb dog falling for a dumb trick.

'Tell you what,' he says. 'I'll lay it all out for you, nice and easy . . . plain and simple.' He looks at me, wide-eyed, like – you listening? I look back at him and do something with my head . . . I ain't sure what, exactly, cos it don't feel like it's mine any more . . . but I probly nod or something. 'OK,' says Vine, grinning. 'Listen – Callan's stuffed. All right? He ain't got nothing and he ain't going nowhere. All he's got is my fingerprints on the knife and them 3 bastads what stitched me up. You saw em putting the knife in my hand, right?'

'I spose . . .'

'You what?'

'Yeh . . . yeh, I saw it.'

'Right – *and* you saw the rest of it, and them 3's gonna get ripped apart by my brief anyway, and that's all they got.'

'What about—'

'What about what?'

'Nothing.'

'What about *what*?'

'I dunno . . . other witnesses . . .'

'What other witnesses?'

'People in cars, stuff like that.'

He stares at me. 'Funny thing,' he says. 'They all changed their minds.'

'All of em?'

'Just about – and if they ain't changed em yet, they soon will. So, like I said, Callan's got nothing. No witnesses, no evidence . . .' he shakes his head '. . . if he wasn't so hung up about what happened last time . . .' He looks at me. 'You know about that?'

'What?'

'You know why Callan's sticking with this when he knows I ain't done nothing?'

I shake my head.

Vine grins. 'Cos it was him that bolloxed up last time, when they had me down for stabbing that witness guy.' He picks at his teeth with his thumbnail. 'They got me on this murder charge, right? They got me tied to the knife, they got my prints on it . . . I ain't got a chance . . . but then it gets to court, and it turns out Callan dicked up on the search warrant, din't follow procedures or something, so they can't use the knife as evidence . . . it's all thrown out . . . illegal search . . . inadmissible evidence . . . it's all over.' His grin widens and he thumps his fist on the dashboard – *bash bash* – like a judge banging his hammer. *'Not guilty!'* he booms, laughing. '*You're free to go Mr Vine* . . .' He looks at me. 'All cos of Callan . . .' And he starts laughing again, cackling like a madman, like it's the funniest thing he ever heard . . .

I just sit there.

Waiting.

Looking . . .

In the shady light, I can see my face reflected in the windscreen.

It don't look too good.

After a while, Vine stops laughing. He lights another cigarette, sucks the smoke deep into his lungs, and looks at me.

'How old are you?' he says.

'15'

He nods. 'You ever killed a man?'

'What?'

His eyes bore into mine. 'Simple question – Have. You. Ever. Killed. A. Man?'

I shake my head.

He grins at me. 'I killed a guy when I was just 15. Bang – shot him dead. Just like that. Shoot him again, too, I ever see the bastad.'

I dunno what to say.

He says, 'It don't mean nothing.'

I look at him, drawn to the emptiness of his voice.

'Nah,' he says. 'Don't mean a damn thing.' He smiles at me, dead-faced, like a grinning skull. 'We're all just little things, Moo. Remember that. Ain't none of us mean nothing.'

I look away again, looking through the window, through my reflection, at the evening sky . . . the clouds dimmed with grey and pink, the dark trees, the silence spiked with the cackle of birds, black shapes flickering in the gloom . . .

'OK,' says Vine. 'You think you're ready?'

'For what?'

'For court – the witness box. Old MacDonald thinks you're gonna be all right. Yeh, Fat Boy Nelson – the boy with the golden eyes. The star witness.' He grins in my face. 'How about that?'

I nod blankly, still looking out the window, looking for something to help me . . . anything . . . to help me think . . . to think about . . . about . . . I dunno . . . I dunno what to think. I wanna get outta this car and go home, that's all I can think. I wanna go home.

'You listening to me or what?' says Vine.

My mouth opens, but nothing comes out.

'All right,' he says, reaching into his pocket. 'Here's how it is – you don't say nothing to Callan, right? You don't phone him, you don't meet him, you don't go nowhere near him. You got that? Good. And don't worry about *him* cos he won't be bothering you, I seen to that. All right?'

'Yeh.'

'Right, this is for you.' He lobs an envelope into my lap. It don't weigh much, but it gets me right in the googlies . . . which makes me GASP a bit. Vine snorts a laugh. I take a deep breath and pick up the envelope. It's one of them brown ones, unsealed, folded shut.

'Go on,' Vine says. 'Open it.'

I open it. There's a wad of cash inside.

'3 grand,' says Vine. 'Call it expenses.'

I take out the cash and flick through it. It don't look like much.

'Get yourself some more CDs,' he says. 'Computer games . . . whatever.'

I look at him.

'What?' he says. 'You got a problem?'

'No . . . no problem.'

'Don't you want it?'

'Yeh . . . I guess.'

'Well don't just sit there flashing it about – put it away, for chrissake.'

I fold the envelope into my pocket.

'That's better,' says Vine. 'OK – you get another 3 grand after the trial. All you gotta do is turn up and tell the truth. That ain't too much to ask, is it? I mean, 6 grand for telling the truth . . . that can't be bad. What d'you reckon, Moo? You think that's fair?'

'Yeh . . .'

'You sure?'

'Yeh.'

'Good – cos I'd hate to think you was *disappointed* about it, you know what I mean? That'd really bother me. You ain't *disappointed* about it, are you?'

'No . . . it's OK. It's fine.'

'Yeh, right – that's *exactly* what it is. It's just *fine.*' He flicks his cigarette out the window, then hits a button and the window winds up. 'OK,' he says. 'I'm glad we got that sorted out. Now, one last thing before you go.' He looks at me, cold eyes and a tight-lipped smile. 'I'm a reasonable man, Moo. I got values – you know what I mean? Someone does me a favour, I pay em back. Someone gets shafted cos of me, I make it up to em. That's values, see? But you gotta play it straight – you gotta get as good as you give. You know why? I'll tell you why – respect. You gotta get respect for your values. Cos if you don't, they ain't worth nothing. Y'understand?'

I nod.

His smile tightens. 'OK – there's 2 ways it can go, Moo. I already told you the good way – you give me something, I give you something. We both got what we want. We both got respect. That's the good way. The other way ain't so good.' He moves closer, looking into my face, and his voice lowers to a hard whisper. 'The other way's gonna hurt,' he says. 'Cos if you go against me on this – if you go with Callan, or if you don't show up in court . . . you do *anything* that gets me sent down . . .' he moves even closer '. . . you're gonna get *hurt*, fat boy. That's a stone-cold fact. You're gonna get hurt. See, I got me some boys who like doing stuff you wouldn't *believe*. And they don't ask questions. I go down, they're gonna find you. Don't matter where you are, they'll find you. And when they do, you're gonna hurt so bad you'll end up begging em to cut your throat. And that's just for starters. You wanna know what else is gonna happen? Cos I can do anything, Moo. You know that, don't you? I can do *anything*. I can keep your old man out the nick, I can put him away . . . I can even get him in a cell with some old mates of mine—'

'No—'

'Then there's your dear old mum—'

'*NO!*'

He glares at me for a second, breathing violence, then – *click* – he blinks once, and the violence is gone. The smile's back. 'Hey,' he says, NICE as hell, 'don't take it *personal*, Moo. It's just business.'

'My mum and dad ain't none of your *business*. You better not—'

'What?' he grins. 'I better not *what*?'

'They ain't done nothing . . .'

He don't speak, just sits there grinning at me. I'm sweating. I'm shaking inside. My chest's all tight and tingly, like there's a tiny black planet spinning around inside my ribs, spitting out bolts of lightning . . .

'Y'all right?' goes Vine.

'Yeh, great.'

He smiles again, then leans forward and puts his hand on my shoulder. It feels like a red-hot vice. 'Look, Moo,' he says, all soft and sweet, 'There ain't nothing to worry about. Just do it right and everything'll be OK. I promise. It'll be OK. All right?'

'No, it AIN'T *all right*. Get your hand off—'

Which is a BIG mistake, cos the next thing I know he's grabbed my hair and yanked my head back across the seat, then – *BOOM!!* – he hits me so hard in the belly I think I'm gonna EXPLODE . . . *GOD!!* . . . it HURTS so MUCH . . . my gut's bursting, my bollox, my heart . . . I can't breathe . . . *JESUS!!* . . . there ain't no AIR . . . ain't nothing but killing pain and the taste of puke . . . I ain't NEVER felt nothing LIKE it . . .

GOD . . .

'Go on, you fat bastad,' a distant voice says. 'Get outta here before you throw up.'

A steel hand grabs my arm. I hear the muzzied clack of a door latch, there's a sudden breeze of air, then a hard shove sends me toppling out the car and I'm sprawling on my hands and knees in the dirt, sucking down oxygen . . . gulping fresh air . . . sucking it down in bubbles . . . snot and tears stringing down my face . . . and somewhere above me a car door slams . . . the engine roars . . . tyres crunch . . . and I'm split open inside . . . choking on the heat of exhaust fumes, spitting muck and puke to the ground . . .

The roar of the car fades into the distance.

He's gone.

Left me here.
Crawling in the dirt.
Hurting like a bastad.

Hours later . . . I'm lying in bed, fully dressed, clutching a pillow to my still-aching belly, listening to the silence. The door's shut, the window's shut, I got the duvet wrapped around my head. It's dark outside, dark inside. I dunno what time it is. I don't care. It's dark. I never wanna leave this house again. Never. I wanna stay here for ever, wrapped up in bed in the dark.

15/ Pictures of Brady

I read something in a book once, something about remembering stuff. I can't remember what the book was called or who wrote it or nothing, it was just this dumb story about a kid with a stupid name who kills his dad or something . . . something like that . . . I dunno. Anyway, the bit I remember is when this kid's talking about remembering stuff, stuff like cold and pain and fear, and he says you don't really remember that kinda stuff, you don't REMEMBER the actual cold, or pain, or fear, but just the IDEA of it. Like you can remember you *were* cold, you *were* in pain, you *were* afraid, but you can't actually remember the FEELING of it.

I always thought that was pretty smart, you know, a pretty good idea . . .

Till **now**.

Now I think it's a pile of CRAP. Cos **now** I'm sitting here, at 5 past 5 in the morning, a month after getting hit in the belly, and I can REMEMBER every stinking little bit of it. The pain, the puke, the agony – I remember *EXACTLY* how it felt. It felt like getting punched by GOD.

And that's something you DON'T forget in a hurry.

Which, I guess, is why I'm here.

Here, sitting by the window, looking out at the morning light . . . which, by the way, is kinda surprising . . . the light, I mean. I never knew it got light THIS early in the morning. I din't think Daytime started till at least 7 or something. But here it is – blue skies, morning colours, a bright yellow sun

. . . and it's only just gone *5* . . . how about that? Mind you, it ain't *really* Daytime. I mean, it's LIGHT outside, and the birds are singing and everything, but that's about it. There ain't nothing else going on. No cars, no people, nothing moving. The street's still asleep. It's kinda like the night's still here, it just ain't dark no more. And even the light ain't *really* Daylight yet . . . yeh, it's LIGHT, but it don't *sound* like LIGHT. It sounds like DARK. It's got that night hush to it – that flat sound . . . the blackness . . . the sound of whispering . . . the sound of the road in the distance . . . the sound of the traffic . . . the sound of the bridge. It sounds a long way away . . . but I know it ain't. It ain't far away at all . . . and it's getting closer all the time . . .

Less than 2 hours away **now**.

2 hours and I'll be there.

We'll be there.

Fixing things.

Fixing THIS *and* THAT . . .

OK – first thing. You wanna know what I did with the money? The 3 grand Vine give me? Nothing – I din't do nothing with it. Din't even look at it. Just stuck it under the carpet under the bed and wiped it outta my head. I mean, it's 3 GRAND, for chrissake – 3 thousand quid. What the hell am I gonna do with THAT? What am *I* gonna get with 3 grand? 200 CDs? 100 computer games? 10 thousand Mars Bars? Yeh, right. HIGHLY unsuspicious. Ain't no one gonna notice *that*, are they? So, yeh, I can't spend it on nothing, but I ain't gonna just chuck it away, am I? It's 3 GRAND – I ain't chucking away 3 grand. And I ain't it giving back, neither. Firstly, cos I dunno where Vine is, and if I dunno where he is, how am I sposed to give it back? And secondly, even if I did know where he was, you think I'm going anywhere

NEAR that psycho again? NO CHANCE. I'd rather stick my hand in a starving pitbull's gob. All right, so I'd get my hand bitten off, but at least I'd know where I stood. I wouldn't get none of that tough-one-second-nice-the-next crap. All I'd get is – *CHOMP!! AAAHHH!!!* – and then it's all over. No threats, no nightmares, no confusion, no one else involved . . .

Yeh, if I had the choice, I'd take the pitbull over Vine any Day.

But I AIN'T got the choice, so it's a waste of time talking about it.

No, what I'm talking about – first thing – is the money. And I already said all there is to say about that – I stuck it under the carpet under the bed and wiped it outta my head.

OK – second thing. After getting nightmared by Vine, the world goes kinda blank for a bit. I get over the wrapped-up-in-bed-in-the-dark-for-ever stuff . . . I ain't got no choice BUT to get over it. Cos if I DO stay there for ever, I'm stuffed. I gotta EXPLAIN things, I gotta EXPLAIN what's-the-matter, I gotta tell the TRUTH . . . and I ain't getting into THAT. NO WAY. The TRUTH? You gotta be joking. Nah . . . I ain't got time for that no more. And another thing, if I don't get outta bed, I'm gonna STARVE. I mean, OK – I got hammered in the belly and it hurts like hell, and I'm all shook up and scared like a baby . . . but still, you gotta EAT, doncha? Yeh, all right, so you lose your appetite for a bit, you just lie there shaking like a headcase and you don't even wanna THINK about food, but it don't last for ever. Sooner or later you get that feeling again, the feeling that starts in your belly, works its way up your throat, and ends up screaming inside your head – FOOOD!! FOOOD!! I'M *STARVING*, GUY, GIMME SOME *FOOOODDD!!*

So, you know . . . you might as well get up.

You might as well EAT.

It ain't gonna make things any WORSE, is it?

If anything, it's gonna make you feel better.

And it does.

CHEESE, CAKE, CHIPS, KFC, MARS BARS, EGGS & BEANS, MCMUFFINS, PIES, TWIXES, PIZZA, PORK CHOPS, ROLLS, KING CONES, TOAST, diet coke, SQUIRTY CREAM, BURGERS, CHEESECAKE, CHIPS . . . Day after Day after Day . . . blanking out the bad stuff . . .

But the world's still kinda WRONG. It's like there's something coming, something on the horizon, something big and bad, and it's getting closer every Day. And you know it's coming for YOU, but you also know it's gonna do some damage on the way. There's someone else out there, someone who DON'T know this bad thing's coming, and if you don't do something about it, this someone out there's gonna get got. But there ain't much you CAN do about it, cos this someone else don't wanna KNOW you. They're hiding from you. And if you go looking for em, the bad thing's gonna get worse . . . but if you DON'T go looking for em, you're gonna feel so bad you're gonna . . .

Gonna what?

You're gonna feel so bad you're gonna what?

Wish you was dead?

Yeh . . .

Takes you right back where you started, don't it?

It goes on like this for a couple of weeks – Days, circles, round and round, THIS and THAT, Day after Day . . . and the bad thing's getting closer all the time. Closer and bigger and REALer. I see Brady most Days, scuttling round school, keeping in close to the walls like he's scared of his own shadow. I wanna get hold of him and yell in his face – *WHATEVER YOU'RE GETTING, IT AIN'T WORTH IT!!!* –

but I can't even get close to him. He's like a wild animal now, he can smell me a mile away. The closest I get is the Day it happens.

The Day . . .

It happens.

The Day – French, Maths, break, Lion Bar, Physics, molecules, yawns . . . dinnertime . . . salad, ham, pie for afters . . . and you're still sitting on your own, but now you ain't getting watched no more. The word's out – don't look at him, he's CONNECTED . . . he's mixing with the bad stuff. I ain't gotta SEE em to know they ain't watching me . . . I can FEEL em . . . but what do I care? Eh? What do I care? Let em NOT look. I ain't WORRIED. I ain't ASHAMED. I ain't done NOTHING. Yeh, all right, so I got Bowker watching out for me and Donut on my case and Vine giving me 3 grand and punching holes in me . . . but so what? Who cares? What's it to you? What you gonna do? KILL ME?

Anyway, the Day goes on – Eng Lit, Chemistry, break, double Twix, double Art, more collaging – and the afternoon gets hotter, the Day heats up, your clothes stick to your skin, and then it's time to go home. I ain't smiling no more. I ain't going to the bridge. I ain't got the energy. I'm just walking home . . . out through the gates, down the school road, sweating like a pig, looking out for Brady, not really *expecting* to see him, but – there he is, look, at the end of the road, walking towards me. Mind you, he ain't walking towards me cos he WANTS to, he's walking towards me cos Dec Bowker and the rest of em are standing at the other end of the road waiting for him. Nah, he ain't walking TOWARDS ME, he's walking AWAY FROM THEM. In fact, I don't reckon he's even seen me. And I don't reckon the others have, neither. Cos they only got eyes for Brady.

So I think to myself – why not turn around and walk back the other way today? Around the back of the shop and through the park. Yeh . . . why not?

So I turn around, bumping into a bunch of kids behind me –

('Sorry, Moo!'

'Uh?'

'Sorry.')

– and head for the park.

See, the way I see it, Dec Bowker ain't coming after Brady, he's just showing his face, keeping Brady jittery, letting him know the bad thing's coming. And I'm pretty sure that if Brady gets done, he ain't gonna get done by Bowker, cos Bowker ain't BAD enough for that. Bowker's OK if you just want someone beat up, maybe scared half to death, but he ain't got what it takes to scare someone COMPLETELY to DEATH. Plus, he's too close to things. Dec Bowker → DS Bowker → Donut → Vine . . . it's too obvious. TOO connected. Nah . . . if Brady gets done, he's gonna get done by someone who ain't got nothing to do with nothing.

That's what I reckon, anyway. Which is why I reckon it's safe for me to wait for Brady round the back of the shop. Which is where I am now. Waiting, waiting, my heart beating hard . . . and here he comes, scuttling round the corner, looking over his shoulder, nervous as ever, *more* nervous than ever . . .

'Hey, Brady.'

He stops dead, staring at me.

'They following you?' I ask him.

'Nah . . . don't think so – what you doing here?'

'We gotta talk, B. There's bad stuff going on—'

'No,' he goes. 'I can't—'

'You gotta listen – just gimme a minute.'

He looks over his shoulder again, then back at me. I think he's trying to work out if he can get past me. The path round the back of the shop ain't that wide – maybe a metre or 2 between the shop wall and a mesh fence – so all I gotta do is move to the middle of the path and it's blocked. Brady steps back. I step forward.

'Vine beat me up,' I tell him. 'Got me in his car and whacked me so hard I puked up.'

'When?'

'Couple of weeks ago – but that ain't it. That's just a warning. I mean, he's a *really* heavy guy – he told me all this stuff he's gonna do . . .'

'Like what?'

'Stuff . . .' My voice chokes at the memory of it. 'Shit stuff . . . you don't wanna know. But that's just for ME – you know what I'm saying?'

'Yeh . . . but you're on his side, ain't you?'

'I ain't on *nobody's* side – that's what I'm trying to tell you. All right, he *thinks* I'm on his side . . . but that's what I mean. He does that to ME, what you think he's gonna do to YOU?'

Brady shakes his head. 'Nah .. he won't do nothing . . . it's all just an act. Callan told me—'

'An *act*?'

'Yeh – Vine just likes to scare people.'

'What – like he *scared* that other guy?'

'What guy?'

'The witness guy at Vine's trial – you know, the one he *killed*?'

Brady shrugs, like he really don't care. 'I got protection.'

'Yeh?'

'Yeh. I got people watching me.'

I make a big show of looking around. 'Where? I don't see

no one. They all on a tea-break or something?'

'You always gotta take the piss, doncha?'

'I ain't taking the piss—'

'Yeh, you are. Just like the rest of em.'

'*What?* I ain't nothing like – GOD, what's the *matter* with you? I'm just trying to HELP you—'

'No you ain't – you're just pissed off cos you ain't got all the attention no more.'

'*What?*'

'You don't like it, do you?' he sneers. 'That's why you keep bugging me – following me around all over the place. You don't wanna *know* me when *YOU* got all the attention, but now *I* got some, you wanna be all PALLY again.'

'I don't wanna be—'

'Or maybe you're just pissed off cos you ain't got me running round after you all the time . . .'

I just stare at him, speechless.

'Yeh,' he says, curling his lip and nodding his head. 'Yeh, that's right . . . see how *you* like it . . .'

I ain't used to helping people, so I dunno what to do with this feeling I got inside me right now. I dunno if it's normal or not. I guess it's the kinda feeling you'd get if you liked someone a lot, and you knew they liked pies, so you gave em the last piece of this really nice pie, even though you was really hungry and you really wanted it yourself, and then this person just takes the piece of pie and chucks it on the ground and stomps on it.

I mean, what the hell are you sposed to do with a feeling like that?

I dunno . . .

I ain't got a CLUE.

Not that it matters, anyway . . . cos Brady's gone now. He's gone . . . got himself good and mad, stepped up, pushed past me, and stomped off down the path – *scuffle-stomp, scuffle-stomp, scuffle-stomp, scuffle . . .*

Gone.

Bastad.

I ain't gonna WORRY about it no more. What's the point? What's it to me? Brady wants it, let him have it. He knows the score – and even if he don't . . . well, I tried, din't I? I done what I could. Nah, I ain't WORRIED about it . . . I ain't ASHAMED or nothing . . .

Better him than me.

Better him than me.

Better him than me.

Better him than me.

That's the way it goes.

See you later, Brady.

I'm going home.

I get the story next morning at school.

I don't get it at first. I know SOMETHING's going on, cos there's a buzz going round the place. At the gates, in the playground, along the corridors . . . kids talking in whispers, looking excited, waving their hands about. I dunno what it is . . . probly some fight or something, or some boyfriend/girlfriend thing . . . something like that. I don't really care. I got other stuff to think about – like TRIAL stuff. Cos when I got back last night, Mum told me that Donut called to confirm the date of the trial – 10 o'clock in the morning, June 3rd, Wickham Crown Court. Less than 2 weeks away.

'He reckons you'll probly get called the week after it starts,' Mum told me. 'On the Monday. He's gonna send a car. Pick us up at 9 o'clock, so we got plenty of time to get there.'

'Us?'

'You're a minor,' she said. 'I gotta go with you.'

'A miner?'

'Yeh.'

That's what I'm thinking about when I walk into the classroom – about Donut and the trial and everything. I'm thinking – it's kinda embarrassing, Mum coming along with me, like when you gotta go shopping for pants or something . . . but it's also kinda OK too . . . kinda comforting . . . and at least I won't be stuck on my own with Donut . . . and another thing – the thing about him picking us up at 9 o'clock so we got plenty of time to get there . . . oh yeh? Plenty of time for him to keep an eye on me, more like. Make sure I don't go mad and run off . . .

Yeh, that's what I'm thinking about when I walk into the classroom, sit down, and wait for the lesson to start. That and some other things . . .

But then, just as I'm getting my stuff out my bag, this girl comes up to me and says, 'You seen him yet, Moo?'

Her name's Kimmy. She's sort of OK. One of them girls who don't *really* fit in, but don't get RAINed on neither . . . they just kinda float around in the middle somewhere. Not too fat, not too thin. Not too pretty, not too ugly. Not too bad, not too good . . . you know?

'Seen who?' I says, looking at her.

'Brady – you seen him?'

'When? What you talking about?'

She glances over her shoulder, like she's worried someone might see her talking to me.

'Din't you hear what happened?' she says.

'When? What happened?'

'Brady's in hospital – din't you hear about it? I thought everyone knew—'

'Hospital? Why? What happened?'

'That's what everyone's talking about—'

'Just tell me what *happened*, for chrissake.'

She gives me a dirty look, like – excuse *me* for trying to be nice.

'Sorry,' I tell her. 'I din't mean nothing . . . Is he all right? Is Brady all right?'

'I dunno . . . no one knows much about it. That's why I was asking you. I thought you mighta been in to see him.'

'No . . . I dunno nothing about it. What happened?'

'He got beat up in them little woods by the estate . . . pretty bad, they reckon. Someone said he got his legs broke.'

'*What?*'

'Yeh, I know . . . it's terrible.'

'When was this?'

'I dunno . . . last night some time, I spose. They think it might be—'

'Where is he?'

'Uh?'

'Where *is* he – which hospital?'

'Moulton General, I think. They took him – hey, where you going, Moo? Lesson's about to start. Where you going?'

Along the corridor, through a side door, out round the back, through a little gate in the teachers' car park, and I'm outta there. This time I REALLY ain't bothered if anyone sees me. I don't give a flying shit. I head straight for the phone box at the end of the school road. There ain't no phone book, so I call 192 and get the number for Donut's office. Stick 20p in the slot, dial the number.

Tracy answers. 'Hawks, Spalding, can I help you?'

'Yeh, it's Mike Nelson. I gotta see MacDonald – it's really important. Can you send a car and pick me up?'

'I'm sorry?'

'Mike NELSON! You know – the Keith Vine case? I'm a witness—'

'Oh, yes,' she says. 'Of *course*. I'm sorry – would you like to speak to JD now?'

'No, I need to see him. I need a car – right now.'

'Just a moment.'

'I need – hello?'

She's put me on hold. GOD . . . I don't wanna be put on hold . . . I don't want time to THINK . . . I just wanna MOVE . . . cos if I ain't moving, if I ain't moving . . .

'Mike?'

'Yeh, who's that?'

'JD MacDonald. Are you all right? Tracy said—'

'I gotta see you right now.'

'What's the matter?'

'I can't talk on the phone – I gotta *see* you.'

'All right – where are you? At home?'

'No I'm outside school.'

'Where's that – Cox's Lane?'

'Yeh.'

'Wait there – I'll call a local taxi, get you picked up in 2 minutes.'

'I ain't got no money.'

'Don't worry about it – just wait there. 2 minutes – OK?'

'Yeh.'

Click.

See? Even when I'm thinking smart, old Donut's 100 times smarter than me.

The taxi's a Mondeo 1.8, which ain't the worst car in the world, but it ain't no Audi Quattro, so it takes a bit longer than usual to get to Moulton. But that's OK, cos I got some stuff to think about now anyway. Like the taxi driver, for instance. I gotta work out what he is. Is he just a taxi driver? Or is he in with Donut and Vine? He LOOKS pretty much the same as any other taxi driver – kinda grey and tired and grouchy and bored, like he's been sitting in a car all his life. He don't look like the *dimmest* guy in the world, but I don't reckon he's *that* smart else he wouldn't be driving people around in a Ford Mondeo all Day, would he?

So . . .?

What the hell.

As we're moving into the outskirts of Moulton, I says to him, 'You know where you're going?'

He looks at me in his mirror. 'Wyre Street, yeh? Hawks and Spalding.'

'Right,' I says. 'And they're gonna pay when we get there?'

'On account,' he says.

I ain't sure what that means, but it don't sound too bad. I sit back and watch the streets of Moulton pass by – the cars, the buses, the people, the shops – then the taxi takes a couple of turnings and we're winding up and down the hilly back-streets, heading for Donut's place . . .

I lean forward and say, 'This'll do, thanks. Just here.'

'It's the next street,' he goes.

'Yeh, I know. I wanna get some air. Just drop me off here.'

He nods to himself, flicks the indicator, and pulls in at the side of the road.

'You going back?' he says.

'I dunno . . . not for a while. I'll probly get a lift anyway.'

'OK.'

I get out the car, wait for him to drive off, then head across town towards the hospital.

I dunno Moulton too well, but I been there a few times before and I know where the hospital is. It ain't far. Across town, over a footbridge (looking down at the traffic – *swoo-ooosh-swoo-ooosh-swoo-ooosh*), through a multistorey car park, and there you are – Moulton General. A tall grey building stuck in the middle of a big green field. There's a long driveway through the field that takes me up to a car park and loads of little pathways and buildings and stuff, then I'm walking past the ambulance bay and up a ramp into the main hospital building. It's pretty busy inside – people sitting around the reception area, doctors and nurses and guys in green uniforms scuttling around all over the place, sick people in wheelchairs . . . and there's hundreds of corridors and doors and signs all over the place. I ain't got a clue where to go. I stand there for a bit just looking around at everything, then I go up to the reception desk, where a speccy old woman is tapping a keyboard and staring at a computer screen.

'Excuse me,' I says.

She don't look up from the screen.

'Excuse me,' I says again.

Her face twitches and she looks up from the screen. 'Yes?'

'I wanna visit someone.'

'Sorry?'

'Visit . . . you know, like a patient. I wanna visit a patient.'

'Where?'

'What?'

'Which ward?'

'I dunno . . . he come in last night.'

'Who?'

'The guy I wanna visit.'

'What's the name?'

'What – mine?'

Her face twitches again. 'No . . . the patient. What's the *patient's* name?'

'Oh, right. It's Brady.'

She taps her keyboard. 'First name?'

I look at her, looking blank, trying to remember Brady's first name . . . I know he's *got* one, I just can't think of it . . .

The receptionist sighs. 'Is there a problem?'

'No, sorry . . . I was .. umm . . .' *Click.* 'It's Pete. Peter. Peter Brady.'

'Thank you.'

She starts tapping away on the keyboard again. I wipe sweat from my face, watching her fingers skip across the keys. Without looking up, she says, 'Are you family?'

'Yeh,' I hear myself say. 'He's my brother.'

I got NO idea why I said that. It's so dumb it's unbelievable. I mean, me and Brady's the least likely-looking brothers in the whole WORLD . . . why did I SAY that? I dunno . . . but it don't seem to matter, cos the receptionist don't even blink. She just goes, 'Stanton Ward, 4th Floor. There's a lift at the end of the corridor.' She looks up, almost smiling. 'OK?'

'Yeh, thanks.'

On the 4th floor there's a waiting area with seats and coffee machines and stuff, then a pair of swing doors with a sign saying STANTON WARD. I go up to the doors and take a peek through the little windows. It's a long white room with a row of beds on each side, all of em full of sick people. Brady's in the second bed from the door on the right. I can't see much of him just yet cos there's 2 people standing beside his bed, a man and a woman. I ain't seen neither of em before, but they gotta be his mum and dad cos they look just like him – both of em short, ugly, kinda stunted. It looks like they're just leaving. The mum's leaning over and kissing Brady's head, and the dad's fiddling around with a chair, trying to find somewhere to put it. I step back from the door and go over to the coffee machine. It's a big one, with loads of lights and loads of buttons, and I'm just standing there staring at the buttons, making out like I'm deciding what to get, when the doors swing open and Brady's mum and dad come out. I can hear em talking.

'. . . not telling us everything,' the mum says. 'I know he's not.'

'Give it time, love. You know what the doctor said . . .'

'I don't understand it . . . I just don't *understand* it . . . how could anyone *do* such a thing . . .'

'I know, I know . . . but he's going to be all right . . . that's the main thing . . .'

Their voices fade as they pass behind me and walk off down the corridor. I give it another minute or so – going over what they was saying in my head – then I turn around, walk back to the doors, and go inside.

Now I can see him properly . . . and it don't look good. His legs ain't in plaster or nothing, so I guess they ain't bust after all, but the rest of him looks pretty mashed up. He's lying on his back, with his arms at his sides, staring at the ceiling. There's tubes all over the place – stuck in his hands, coming outta his nose . . . his nose is busted . . . his face is all puffed up and beat to hell – black eyes, cuts, broken teeth, stitches, bandages . . . he's even had some of his hair shaved off. Christ . . . he's in a BAD way.

I walk up to the bed.

'Hey, Brady . . .'

His head turns and he squints at me through swollen eyes.

'Moo?' His voice is all thick and slurred.

'Yeh . . . how you doing?'

He tries to smile, but his lips ain't working too well. They're all split and puffy.

I pull up a chair and sit down.

'You look like shit,' I tell him.

He grins. 'Yeh . . .'

'Can you talk?'

He nods, wincing at the pain.

'You all right?'

'Hurts,' he says.

'Where?'

'Everywhere . . . they done me all over . . .'

There's tears in his eyes . . . and I dunno what to say. I dunno how to deal with this. I'm feeling stuff I don't understand.

'What happened?' I ask him. 'Who did it?'

'Drink,' he says.

'What?'

'Gimme drink.'

I pour him a glass of water from a jug on the bedside cabinet, then I help him to sit up and drink. His gob's such a mess he's gotta drink through a straw. About half the glass spills down his chin.

'All right?' I says.

'Yeh . . . thanks.'

Then he tells me what happened. It takes a long time, cos he keeps stopping to cough or groan or drink more water, and he can't talk too loud cos there's people in the beds either side – a spluttery old guy with a sick-yellow face on the right, and a tattooed guy who looks like he's dead on the left. So Brady's gotta whisper, and it's hard to get what he's saying even when he ain't whispering, so he has to keep repeating stuff. But, basically, what happened is this –

After I left him yesterday, he started walking home along the path on the bank above the road. He's about halfway along when he sees Jicky Collins at the estate end of the path, waiting for him. So he turns back, but then he sees Dec Bowker standing at the other end. Neither of em's doing nothing, they're just waiting there, blocking both ends of the path. So Brady ain't got no choice – he's gotta go through the woods to get home. He don't WANNA go through the woods – cos if you're the kinda kid who gets beat up a lot, you KNOW you gotta stay outta places like that – but he ain't *too* bothered, cos he's done it before, and it ain't too far, just a couple minutes walk . . . so off he goes. Into the woods, along the scrubby little path, around the remains of a fire, through burnt beer cans, chicken bones, carrier bags . . . walking fast, checking over his shoulder all the time, trying to stay calm . . . then suddenly these 2 guys appear outta nowhere, grab him by the arms, and drag him off into a little dip behind a hedge.

Brady stops talking then. His face is all pale and his eyes are staring at nothing. I can't look at him. I just look at the floor, waiting for him to go on.

When he does, his voice is really strange – kinda dead and cold, like he's in a trance or something.

'They din't say nothing,' he says. 'They just grab me . . . pick me up like I'm nothing . . . bundle me off the path . . . down into this dirty little place . . . I dunno what's going on . . . it's all really quick . . . but kinda slow, too . . .' He closes his eyes, takes a shaky breath, then carries on talking. 'One of em grabs my head and cracks it into a tree . . .' His hand reaches up and brushes the bandage on his forehead. '. . . funny thing is, it din't really hurt. I just get this dull kinda lump in my head . . . but my legs go all wobbly . . . then they both start pushing me around, shoving me all over the place . . . then one of em grabs me again, gets my arms up behind my back, and the other one whacks me in the face . . . then he does it again . . . and again . . .' His eyes open, looking right at me. They're filled with tears. 'They just keep whacking me, Moo . . . these big heavy hands – *boom, boom, boom* . . . mashing my face up . . . and they're laughing . . . the bastads is laughing at me.' He stops for a moment and looks away, ashamed of his tears.

'D'you know em?' I ask quietly.

'Nah . . . never seen em before. Really big guys . . . one of em thumped me in the belly . . . GOD it hurt so much . . . and then I'm down on the ground . . . and they're kicking me around . . . stomping my legs and stuff . . .' He shudders, wipes his face, then looks at me. 'I ain't told no one nothing, OK? I just said they was a couple of guys.'

'Yeh . . .'

'So if anyone asks . . .'

'What?'

'I din't tell em, Moo. I din't tell em what it's about . . .'

I dunno what to say. His face is white as death, his black eyes sunk into his skull.

'The cops,' he says. 'Cops, doctors, Mum and Dad . . . I din't tell em nothing . . .' He goes quiet then . . . dead eyes staring into space. I look at him, then look up as a nurse walks past at the end of the ward. She gives me a look, like – who are you? I smile at her. She don't smile back, just gives me a bit more eyeball, then walks off. I look back at Brady. He's all tensed up, like his skin's too tight. His face, his staring eyes . . . GOD, he looks BAD . . . I ain't ever seen nothing like it. It's scary.

'Brady?' I says.

'Uh?'

'You OK?'

'Hurt me,' he says, his voice so quiet I can hardly hear it. 'They hurt me bad . . .' He blinks his eyes and looks at me. 'I ain't gonna say nothing, Moo. You tell him – I ain't saying *nothing*.'

'Tell who?'

'Vine – tell him I'll do whatever he wants, OK? Just don't . . . I don't wanna get hurt no more—'

'Excuse me,' a voice interrupts. It's the nurse, the one I saw earlier. She's standing by the bed looking at me.

'Yeh?' I says.

'Who are you? What are you doing here?'

'I'm his brother. I'm visiting.'

She looks at Brady. He's gone back to his staring again . . . he don't even know she's there. She goes over to the bed and starts fiddling around with him, making him comfortable, checking his tubes and stuff.

Without looking round, she says to me, 'Do you know what happened here?'

'No,' I says.

'Do you know who did this?'

'No.'

She smiles at Brady, wipes something from his face, then turns around and looks at me, the smile gone.

'Who are you?' she says.

'I already told you . . . I'm his brother.'

'He doesn't have a brother. Who are you?'

'All right . . . I'm just a friend. I din't—'

'You're not his friend. If you were his friend, you'd tell me who did this to him.'

'I *dunno* who did it. I dunno what happened . . .'

She stares at me.

I gotta look away.

'Get out,' she says, like she's sick of me.

'I *am* his friend—'

'Go on, get out of here, before I call the police.'

I look at her. Her face is cold as stone, like it's all MY fault . . . and I wanna tell her . . . I wanna tell her it AIN'T my fault . . . but she ain't gonna listen . . . she ain't got time for me. She hates my guts.

I get up out the chair. I look at Brady. His eyes are shut, his lips are moving, kinda fluttering, like he's dreaming.

'Is he gonna be OK?' I ask the nurse.

She looks at me. 'What do you care?'

I don't say nothing.

She shakes her head. 'His body will heal eventually. But the rest of it . . . who knows? He's going to need a lot of help.'

'Right,' I says, like I know what she's talking about. 'Thanks.'

She gives me another nasty look, then turns her back on me.

On the way out the hospital, I got this strange kinda coldness inside me. It ain't anger, exactly . . . and it ain't pity or nothing . . . in fact, it ain't really any kinda emotion at all. It's just a coldness, like a streak of ice running all the way through me. There's all kindsa stuff whirling round it, all sortsa mad feelings, but I can't hardly feel em, cos the coldness is so BIG it blanks em all out. It's so BIG it blanks out EVERYTHING, and all I got left is this weird kinda COOLness . . . like an icy-black HARDness . . . which I ain't sure I like, cos it makes me feel like I'm in some kinda control, and I don't *wanna* be in control. But there ain't nothing I can do about it.

I got it . . . and that's that.

In the reception area downstairs I find a payphone and

call Donut's number.

Tracy answers. 'Hawks, Spalding, can I—'

'Mike Nelson,' I says.

'Sorry?'

'Mike Nelson.'

'Oh, right – did you want Mr MacDonald?'

'Yeh.'

'One moment.'

Click, click, whirr, whirr . . . click.

'Michael?'

'Yeh.'

'Where are you? I thought you were coming in. You wanted to see me—'

'I changed my mind.'

His voice gets worried. 'You changed your mind?'

'About seeing you. It's all right, there ain't a problem. I thought there was, but there ain't. Everything's all right.'

'You sure?'

'Positive.'

'Good . . . so you're all set for the trial?'

'Yeh.'

'No problems?'

'No.'

'Anything you want to ask? Anything you need to know?'

'No.'

'Great . . . that's great. Just a moment . . .' The phone gets muffled, like he's put his hand over the mouthpiece, and I can hear him talking to someone, kinda – *oomf, laroomf, faroomf* . . . then there's a bit more muffling, then another voice comes on the line, a voice I ain't expecting.

'Hey, Moo,' it goes. 'How you doing?' It's Vine. 'How's your belly?' he says. 'Got your appetite back yet?'

I don't say nothing.

He says, 'Where you been, Moo? I been waiting for you. Where you been?'

'Nowhere,' I says.

'Really? I guess it musta been some other fat kid up the hospital just now . . . you ain't got a twin brother, have you?'

'How d'you—'

'How's the boyfriend?' he laughs. 'I heard he bumped into a tree or something . . .'

My breath turns to stone. Hard and tight. My hand grips the phone, sweating on the black plastic.

Vine sniffs loudly. 'Hey, don't worry about it, OK? It's in the bag. Couple of weeks and it's done. All you gotta do is take it easy and you'll be all right. Y'hear me?'

'Yeh, I hear you.'

'And next time you wanna go somewhere, Moo, lemme know first, OK? You wanna go to the hospital? That's OK, no problem – I can get you to the hospital. You with me?'

'Yeh.'

'OK – you get on home now. There's a car waiting outside the hospital for you – a red Saab. Get in it, go home, and keep your fat mouth shut. I don't wanna hear another squeak outta you for the next 2 weeks – all right?'

'Yeh.'

'Good.'

Click.

And he's gone.

So, that's it then. That's where it's got to . . . THIS and THAT . . . that's it. It's gone from a Day on the bridge, watching the river, to a Day going home in a red Saab 900, my head full of pictures of Brady. I can't stop seeing him – his beat-up face, his sunken eyes, his fluttering lips . . . the way he lay there staring at nothing . . . and I keep getting this picture of him in the woods with them 2 guys . . . I can see him getting whacked about, then lying on the ground surrounded by bones and beer cans and carrier bags . . . and I got Vine's voice in my head . . . *I got me some boys who like doing stuff you wouldn't BELIEVE* . . . and then it goes blank. My brain cuts out. I ain't got the GUTS to think about it . . .

It's too BAD . . .

But what you gonna do? It's happened, it's done. Ain't nothing you can do. Yeh, it's tough shit . . . but that's the way it goes . . . shit happens. Feeling bad ain't gonna fix nothing, is it? It's just one of them things . . . yeh, and if you think of it like that, it ain't so bad . . .

So – thinking of it like that – I empty my head and stare out the window of the red Saab 900 and watch the roads pass by . . . I *think* I do, anyway. I dunno, I'm kinda dead . . . blank . . . unsensified. Just letting things happen. I let the driver – a dumb-looking mug in a football shirt – drive up my street and park outside my house, then I let myself out and walk round the back and let myself into the kitchen, where Mum's at the sink doing the washing up.

'Moo!' she says, all surprised, looking at the clock. 'What're you doing home?'

'Uh?'

'It's only just gone one. Why ain't you at school? You all right, love? You don't look so good.'

'I feel a bit sick,' I tell her.

She dries her hands on a towel, sits me down, then starts fussing all over me, asking me questions, taking my temperature, stuff like that . . .

'God, you're burning up,' she says, feeling my forehead. 'You're drenched in sweat . . . come on, let's get you to bed.'

And that's how the Day ends – with me lying in bed, all hot

and sweaty, still trying to kid myself that it ain't so bad . . . it's just one of them things . . .

Ain't nothing you can do . . .

Ain't nothing you can do . . .

Ain't nothing you can do . . .

There AIN'T nothing I can do.

16/ ANSWER ME U BASTAD!!!! I *NEED* YOU

It's getting pretty close **now**. It's getting on for 6 in the morning and the Day's starting to look like a Day. It's still quiet outside, but now it's a different kinda quiet . . . it don't sound like the night no more. It's sounds like a Scatterday, which ain't surprising – cos it is. The Day's got that Scatterday sound to it – the sound of no one going to work or school – and it looks like a Scatterday too. Blue-grey skies, bits of white cloud, a weekend wind . . . just enough to make things moody. Or maybe that's just me . . .

Probly.

Cos I'll tell you what – moody ain't the HALF of it. I'm strung-out, tired, wired . . . I'm shot to HELL. I dunno if I can do this . . . I dunno if I got what it takes. I dunno . . .

I just dunno.

We'll see.

Anyway, it's getting close now, and the stuff I'm talking about is getting close, too. This is last week . . . this week . . . a few Days ago. It don't seem like it – it seems like a thousand years ago, but it ain't . . .

It's Dumbday, June 9th – the Day before I gotta go to court. Donut rang last week and told me it's gonna be tomorrow.

'The prosecution's nearly finished,' he said. 'Now it's our turn. Vine's up on Friday, then it's you. Do you think you're ready?'

'Yeh,' I said.

Ready as hell.

So, anyway, it's 11 o'clock Dumbday morning, and I'm doing the same old morning stuff – getting up, going to the bathroom, getting dressed, going downstairs – and everything's pretty much the same as it always is. The kitchen's hot . . . coffee and eggs . . . Dad's at the table reading the *News of the World* . . . Mum's cooking omelettes and toast . . .

'All right?' she goes.

'Yeh.'

'Remind me to get your suit out later. I'll give it a brushing for tomorrow. There's plenty of clean shirts in the airing cupboard.'

'OK.'

Dad looks up from his paper. 'Fancy a walk later on?'

'A what?'

'A *walk* . . . you know. With your legs. I thought we could take a stroll over the park . . . watch a bit of football or something.'

'It's June, Dad . . . football finished ages ago.'

He shrugs. 'Just a thought.'

Yeh, a pretty *weird* thought . . . cos Dad don't go for no *strolls* in the park, and the only time he ever watches football is when there ain't nothing else on TV. So . . . I dunno . . . I guess there's something he wants to talk about . . . something he don't want Mum to hear . . . something he KNOWS about something . . .

Which kinda DOES ME IN. Conflicts me. Stirs me up and splits me right down the middle. Cos part of me WANTS to know what he KNOWS, WANTS to know what he WANTS, WANTS to know what he THINKS, WANTS to take a stroll round the park with him, tell him what's going on, WANTS to say – HELP ME DAD, I DUNNO WHAT TO DO . . .

But the other part KNOWS I can't.

Cos if I do, it's only gonna make things worse. It's BOUND to . . . whatever happens . . . whatever I tell him, or he tells me . . . whatever it is . . . it's just gonna make things worse. Worse for him, worse for Mum, worse for everyone . . .

So . . . you know . . .

What's the point?

Forget it.

Let's EAT.

Omelettes, toast . . . NOSH NOSH NOSH . . . get it all down . . . then a big mug of coffee, another trip to the bathroom . . . then a few hours sitting around watching Dumbday TV, then a few hours doing nothing, then a big old roast dinner . . . chicken, spuds, stuffing, cabbage, gravy . . . NOSH NOSH NOSH . . . then a few hours lying on my bed, stuffed RIGHT up, KILLING JOKE playing loud as hell . . . *DEEDAHDAHDAHDUHDAHDAHDAHDAHDAH* . . .

'TURN IT *DOWN!*'

Get up, turn it down, sit down . . . doing nothing . . . watching the night come down . . . staring into the darkness . . . turning on the PC . . .

Click.

Tickitty-tickitty-durr-tick-tick-teck . . . *dung-dung-dung* . . . *DURRR-DURRR-DURRR* . . . *DEEDAHDAHDAHDUH-DAHDAHDAHDAHDAH* . . . *dee-doo-dee-doo-di-di-di-da-da-du-di* . . . *eeeeee-iicchhhh-eeeee-AAAHaaah-eeee* . . . '*Wel*come to AOL . . . you have *e*mail.'

Well I'll be . . .

It's from Brady:

```
hey moo – just leting u know im home. got back a few days ago. i aint doing 2 bad but im gonna be of school til i get some stuff sorted out . . . probly go back after summer. listen moo – u dint say nothing did u? you aint gonna? i know u got court tomorow – u know i dint go? i couldnt do it. not after . . . u know. i guess you gotta go but dont say nothing about me – ok? please?
b
```

A sick feeling crawls in my belly as I click on *REPLY*:

```
yeh b – whats up guy? hows it going? u really ok? i mean REALLY? its ok . . . i aint said nothing & i aint gonna. its cool – no probs. yeh i gotta goto court . . . but its ok. im a moron, innit? duuh uuh . . . i aint gonna get no shit – u c. mebbe after u wanna meet up or something? if u aint 2 good i could praps come round . . . bring u some flowers!! lemme know, ok?
```

He don't answer for a couple of minutes. I sit there staring at the screen, checking out his new email address, staring at the email thing, waiting for it to turn red . . . the CD stops . . . the room fills with silence . . . it's dark outside. In the distance I can hear the Dumbday *swoo-oosh* of lonely trucks rumbling through the summer night . . . and I'm SO wishing none of this ever happened. Cos I could do with being there right now . . . standing on the bridge, in MY PLACE, looking down at the road, with the updraught of traffic ruffling my hair, the pulse of the bridge buzzing in my feet, sinking down into my position . . . arms crossed . . . leaning over . . . looking down . . . listening . . . watching . . . doing my thing . . . not thinking . . . no time . . . just the flow of traffic beneath me . . . never-ending, always there . . . rumbling, racing, roaring, screaming, silent as nothing . . .

Then the PC pipes up and the email thing goes red.

I click on *READ*:

yeh . . . i dunno moo – i get tired alot. theres stuff . . . i dunno. cant say it. its done me in. its like . . . u know what i want? that bastad vine . . . shit. u gotta fix him moo. i know u cant. i wish u coud. GOD hes a 100% SHITBASTAD. & them 2 guys . . . i get really bad dreams ALL the time. i gotta go . . . i aint feeling good. write me tomorow when u get back . . . mebbe c u later

That gets me pretty bad . . . makes me feel kinda twisty inside, like I dunno what I'm feeling. All BLACK and RED and STORMY. I guess it's some kinda something . . . but I dunno what. And I ain't sure I WANNA know, neither.

Yeh, I do . . .

No, I don't . . .

I do . . .

Don't . . .

Do . . .

Don't . . .

I dunno . . .

Right now, all I wanna do is sleep.

It's a long night, lots of tossing and turning, tangled sheets, whacking the pillow, trying to think of stuff that ain't got nothing to do with nothing . . . anything – secret things, games, places, dreams, counting cars . . . the bridge . . . the road . . . the bridge . . . the road . . . the bridge . . .

Yeh, yeh . . .

The bridge.

Now THERE's an idea . . .

The bridge.

Yeh . . .

YEH . . .

All right, so it's too late now, but it's something to think about . . . like one of them whatsit things – *hypo*-something . . . hypo-theoretical? – one of them things that probly ain't gonna happen but what-if-they-do? The kinda thing that's really hard to work out, which is good, cos it gets you all sleepy . . .

Yeh . . . the bridge.

I can think about THAT.

Only it don't get me all sleepy, it gets me all *UN*sleepy, cos the more I think about it the more it makes sense. This idea I got . . . about the bridge . . . yeh, it's a pretty good idea. You know how it goes, lying in bed, thinking of all the stuff you coulda done, if only you had the time . . . yeh, if only I had the time – it coulda worked. This bridge thing – it coulda WORKED. Yeh, I know it's only one of them ideas you get in the dark, one of them ideas you think is brilliant, but when you wake up in the morning you realise it ain't . . . yeh, I KNOW that. But even so . . . I can't stop thinking about it. Thinking about Vine and Callan and the rest of em, and what they done to me and Brady . . . and the things they said . . . and the way they said em . . . and how it makes you

FEEL . . . and how it AIN'T RIGHT . . . and that gets me thinking back to all the other stuff, the FAT stuff, the kids at school, the teachers, the RAIN, the girls in the playground –

What d'you rather do? Kiss Moo or eat dog poo?

Yeh – kiss Moo or die?

I'd kill him, then I wouldn't have to do neither.

YA YA YA YA YA YA YA YA YA YA . . .

– and then I get that coldness back, that streak of ice running all the way through me, and it says to me: *KISS IT, MOO. KISS IT, KISS IT, KISS IT!*

Kiss what?

The RAIN. Get out there and KISS THE RAIN.

So then I'm lying there in the dark for the next 3 hours trying to work out what the hell it means – *KISS THE RAIN? KISS THE RAIN? KISS THE RAIN?????* What? Why? What for? When? How? GOD, it's really bugging me, zipping around in my head ALL night . . . which is why, when the alarm goes off at 7 O'BLOODYCLOCK in the morning, I'm EXHAUSTED. Tired as anything. I'm so tired I can't hardly move. My head's like a beehive, buzzing with words – *KISS THE RAIN, KISS THE RAIN, KISS THE RAIN* . . . and I STILL dunno what it means . . . and even if I did (which – come to think of it – I probly do), it don't make no odds. Cos it's too late now. It's Oneday morning, June 10th. I gotta be in court in 3 hours . . .

Shit.

About 8 o'clock, then, I'm getting dressed, getting into my one-and-only suit – cos Donut said I gotta look smart for court – and I'm feeling all gritchy cos I ain't got no sleep, and I can't stop thinking – if only I'd thought about what I been thinking about EARLIER, if only, if only, if only – and THAT's really pissing me off, and then I can't get the damn suit on cos it AIN'T BIG ENOUGH. The troozies don't fit, the jacket's too tight . . . damn thing musta shrunk HA HA HA. I guess I ain't worn it for a couple of years, not since Uncle Dave got remarried. I guess I shoulda tried it on before . . . yeh, I guess . . . maybe if I wore it with a REALLY thin shirt and sucked my belly in . . .?

Yeh, right, and what you gonna do about the troozies? You gonna suck your LEGS in, too?

'Mum!' I shout. 'MUM!'

'PHONE!' she shouts back.

Uh? What?

I go to the door and shout downstairs. 'WHAT?'

She pops her head round the banister, holding the mobile phone. 'It's Mr MacDonald – for you. Here . . .' She chucks the phone up the stairs. I catch it, cool as you like (considering I ain't got no troozies on), and take it into my room. I go over to the window and put the phone to my ear.

'Yeh?'

'Michael – it's JD. There's been a delay, I'm afraid. The prosecution's taking longer than we thought, so we won't be starting until Wednesday.'

'Wednesday?'

'Same time, 10 o'clock. I'll pick you up at 9.'

'What about today?'

'What about it?'

'I dunno . . . what am I sposed to do?'

He laughs. 'You can do what you like . . . within reason. Just make sure you're ready on Wednesday.'

'Wednesday?'

'Yes, *Wednesday* – the Day after tomorrow. Look, I have to go . . . just remember what I told you, and I'll see you on Wednesday – 9 o'clock.'

'Yeh, but . . . hello? Hello?'

He's gone. Bastad. I switch off the phone and sit down on the bed, staring at my flabby white legs, thinking about what he just said – *Remember what I told you?*

Well . . . no, actually, I don't. You told me tons of things . . . how'm I sposed to know which one you're talking about? What d'you think I am – a mindreader? And anyway, *why's* the prosecution taking longer than you thought? What's that sposed to mean? Oh yeh, and thanks for keeping me bang up to date, by the way, thanks for leaving it till the very last minute. . .

Yeh, *very* thoughtful.

Ah, forget it . . .

It don't matter.

It gives me time to get a new suit, I spose.

AND – more to the point – I got my IF ONLY . . .

I got my TIME . . .

Now, if only I can find me some guts to use it . . .

See, what it is, this kissing the RAIN thing . . . well, I still ain't sure EXACTLY what it is. I THINK it's got something to do with turning stuff around . . . turning the BAD stuff around . . . like getting hold of it . . . taking its POWER, its STRENGTH, its ANIMALness, and making it work for ME . . . but, like I said, I ain't EXACTLY sure. I mean, I dunno . . . I think it's probly one of them beasty-brain things, one of them things you know you KNOW, but you ain't sure how or why you KNOW . . .

Kissing the RAIN . . .?

Nah, I ain't sure what it means . . .

But I know what it needs.

It needs ME. It needs GUTS. It needs BRADY. And, the thing is, I ain't sure I got any of em. Take ME, for example. I got *a* ME, I got the *Moo Nelson* ME, but I dunno if he's enough. I dunno if he's got what it takes. I dunno if he can shrug off his don't-cariness and actually DO something for once in his life. I know he WANTS to, but I ain't sure he can . . . which brings us nicely to GUTS. This Moo – has he got the GUTS? can he cut it? can he hack it? can he DO it?

I dunno . . .

Which is why I need Brady . . . cos if I got Brady, I'm all right. I dunno why, and I don't really WANNA know why, cos it's scary stuff – NEEDing someone. It's a scary feeling. Specially when the someone you NEED is someone like Brady.

But the TRUTH is – if I got Brady, I'm all right. Cos, if I got Brady, stuff don't seem to MATTER so much. There ain't no ifs or buts about nothing, there AIN'T no dunnos, there's just – right, let's do it, and who cares what happens. That's it, really.

That's the TRUTH.

I guess it's probly some kinda sharing thing, you know, like if there's 2 of you doing something, you always got someone else to share the blame, or the fear, or the guilt . . . or whatever.

Or maybe it's something else . . .

I dunno . . .

All I know is I gotta find Brady.

So that's what I do for the rest of the Day . . . starting with emails:

```
b – i aint gotta be in court til Day after
tomorow – i gotta c u – gotta talk – urgent
moo
```

Nothing. No reply. I give it an hour, 2 hours, 3 hours . . . still nothing . . . then I send it again, just in case . . . I dunno . . .

just in case it got lost in cyberspace or something, but I still don't get nothing back. I sit there staring at the screen for GOD-knows how long, trying to work out if I'm crazy or just REALLY STUPID . . . but I don't guess I'd know either way, would I? Cos if I'm crazy I wouldn't know nothing about it, and if I'm really stupid I wouldn't know nothing about it neither. But it AIN'T like I dunno nothing about it . . . which leaves me wondering – what does that make me? So then I get lost thinking about that for a while, and then, before I know it, it's getting on for the afternoon and I gotta go out and get a new suit.

See, after I showed Mum how tight the old one was, she called Donut and told him about it, and now he's sending a taxi to take us to this place in Moulton where he's got an account . . . a suit place, I guess. All I gotta do is pick one out, he says. It's all paid for and everything . . . yeh, yeh, yeh. GOD's sake . . . I don't WANNA go . . . I don't WANT him buying me clothes . . . it makes me feel like some kinda penniless scumbag. But it's either that or going to school . . . and I ain't going to school . . . so I guess I'll just have to put up with feeling like a penniless scumbag.

Later, when we get back – with a 200-quid suit *and* a new pair of shoes ('Go on, says Mum, 'make the most of it – he won't mind.') – I try Brady again:

```
b – u there? – i REALLY gotta c u – its
about youknwowhat – nothing bad honest –
its REALLY urgent
moo
```

Still nothing.

Shit.

Where the hell is he? Where's he GONE? Maybe he's gone back to hospital? Maybe he's cracked up and killed himself? Maybe he's dead? Or maybe he just don't wanna talk to me? Yeh, well . . . he would if he knew what I wanted to talk about. But I guess that don't help much. GOD . . . where the HELL is he? The REALLY annoying thing is, the little bastad only lives about 10 minutes away . . . somewhere on the estate . . . but I dunno what street or nothing. And he's gotta have a phone – *everyone's* got a phone – but he ain't in the book . . . I looked. And 192 ain't got nothing, neither . . .

I dunno what to do.

Sit there, staring at the screen . . .

Go downstairs, eat . . .

Watch TV . . .

Eat some more . . .

Watch TV . . .

Say goodnight . . .

Go upstairs . . .

Sit there, staring at the screen . . .

I'll try emailing him one more time, then I'm going to bed:

```
for chrissake brady this is REAALY IMPOR-
TANT – PLEASE PLEASE PLEASE – just gimme 5
minutes ok? i got something u WANT – no
joke
moo
```

Nothing.

I'm going to bed.

Next morning – still nothing from Brady. This KISSING THE RAIN thing has really got a hold of me now. I know it's up in the clouds, cos it ain't gonna happen, but I can't get it outta my head. It just won't go away. And even if it AIN'T gonna happen, which it ain't, I still gotta get rid of it, and the only way I'm gonna get rid of it is by telling Brady. I GOTTA find him. I know he ain't at school, cos I rung up anomynously (on Donut's mobile) and asked. I made out like I was a reporter, you know, investigating street crime or something . . . spoke like this: ah, y'ello . . . ah was wonderin if you could help me . . . ma name's Dick Durdly from the Moulton Evenin Star . . .

Pretty sad, I spose . . . but it worked.

He ain't at school.

And neither am I, cos what with me going to court tomorrow and everything, it ain't worth it. So . . . last resorts, Brady-wise . . . I tell Mum I'm going out for a walk and I head off towards the estate. I ain't sure what I'm gonna do when I get there, probly just walk around and ask people if they know where the Bradys live . . . but it don't really matter cos I never get there anyway. I get as far as the edge of the village, far enough to see the shop and the park and the tops of estate houses on the other side of woods . . . but that's it – the woods. No way – I ain't going nowhere NEAR em. I can't – they got me all mushed up inside like a jelly. I'm nearly puking with fear.

So I turn around and go home.

Go to my room . . .

Look out the window . . .

Play some FEAR FACTORY . . .

Arse around on the internet . . .

Think about emailing Brady again . . . nah, ain't no point, it's too late now . . .

Then the door opens and Mum comes in.

'It's been put off again,' she says.

'What?'

'Going to court – Mr MacDonald just rang. It's not till Friday now.'

'Friday?'

'Yeh.'

'Why?'

'Dunno,' she shrugs. 'Something about . . . I dunno. Delays or something . . . I can't remember. Anyway, he said he'll pick us up—'

'At 9.'

'Yeh.' She smiles, leaning in the doorway, looking at me. 'How you doing, anyway?' she says. 'All this messing about and stuff – phone calls, going places, getting dressed up . . . all the rest of it. I bet you're getting tired of it.'

'Yeh.'

'Just think – if you wasn't at the bridge that Day . . . I bet you wish you was never there.'

'It's crossed my mind.'

'Ah, well,' she goes. 'It won't be long now. Soon be over. And at least you got a nice new suit and a pair of shoes out of it . . .'

Yeh, I think, plus a mobile phone, a ton of cash, a lost bridge, a mashed-up head, a pulverised belly, a busted friend . . . and LOTS LOTS MORE . . .

Mum smiles again. 'You gonna be all right?'

'Yeh.'

'You ain't worried about nothing?'

'Nah . . . no problem.'

'Sure?'

'Yeh.'

She nods her head, looking at the floor, like there's something bothering her, something on her mind, but she dunno if she oughta say it or not. I know how she feels – I dunno if I want her to say it or not, neither.

'Well . . .' she says eventually, looking up at me with a smile. 'I'll see you later then, OK?'

'Yeh.'

'G'night.'

'Night.'

And she goes out and shuts the door.

I stare after her for a while, thinking about stuff . . . I dunno what . . . just what she means to me . . . and how come we never TALK about nothing . . . and what she knows . . . and what she thinks about me . . . stuff like that . . . then I blow it all outta my head and get on the keyboard to Brady again, cos now it AIN'T too late no more, we got another 2 Days:

```
look b – i know ur there. i GOTTA see u b4 i go to court – it aint til 5day now – we gotta TALK – if i could tell u what its about i would. but i cant – not here. it aint safe. but listen – its about fixing what u want. ok? think about it . . . but be quik.
moo
```

No reply.

That's it, I reckon. There ain't nothing else to do . . .

So I go to bed.

Think about it, sleep.

Wake up.

Next Day . . .

Threeday . . .

Email him. Wait. No reply. Nothing.

Email him. Wait. No reply. Nothing.

Wait.
Go to bed.
Think some more, sleep some more.
Wake up.
Next Day . . .
Fourday . . .
Email him. Wait. No reply. Nothing.
Email him. Wait. No reply. Nothing.
Email him. Wait. No reply. Nothing.
Nothing.
OK – one more time, last time:

`ANSWER ME U BASTAD!!!! I` *`NEED`* `YOU.`

Nothing.

And the Day goes on and nothing happens, and then it's nearly midnight, the Day before the end of the world, and Donut called again saying this time it's DEFINITELY on . . . and my new suit's hanging on a hanger, and my new shoes are shiny and clean . . . and the clock's tick-ticking . . . tomorrow's nearly here . . . and so I guess it's FINALLY REALLY too late to do anything about it.

Finally.
Really.
Too late.

17/ Sweating by Almighty GOD

Next morning, then, just before 9 o'clock . . . it's one of them Days when the sun ain't shining but the air's hot enough to melt your head, which is JUST what I need. First hot Day of the year and I gotta get all ragged up in a sweaty new suit – suit, shirt, tie, shoes, the works . . . nice and sweaty – yeh, great, JUST what I need. Anyway, it's nearly 9 o'clock. I got my suit on, Mum's wearing a dress, and we're both standing around getting boiled up like lobsters, waiting for Donut, looking out the window, pacing around, pacing around . . . then stopping at the sound of a car rolling down the street. I go over to the window. It ain't the Audi this time, it's a long black Jaguar XJR, 4-litre . . .

'OK, Moo?' says Mum. 'You ready?'

'Yeh.'

'Got everything?'

'Yeh.'

'Hanky, deodorant—'

'*Yeh* – I got everything, Mum.'

'You need a wee?'

'No – come on, let's go.'

Get it over with.

Mum turns to Dad, who's sitting in his chair with a local newspaper and a mug of tea.

'Sure you don't wanna come?' she says.

He looks at her, then at me. 'Do you want me to come?'

'No,' I says. 'You're all right.'

'Sure?'

'Yeh.'

'It's just—'

'Yeh, I know, Dad – it's OK, really.'

He smiles sadly and nods.

The doorbell rings.

Ding dong.

Mum picks up her handbag. 'OK,' she says. 'Let's go.'

The Jag's ENORMOUS, it's bigger than our front room. Better seats, too. Better windows, come to that. Me and Mum sit in the back, Donut's in the passenger seat, and the midget guy's driving. He's going pretty fast, as usual, and it don't take long to leave the village behind and roar up the road towards Wickham. Donut and Midget are both dressed in dark suits, and one of em smells like he's dipped his head in a bucket of aftershave. It's Donut, I reckon. The midget guy ain't gonna bother with aftershave, is he? I mean, why bother smelling nice when you're short and bald and ugly – what's the point?

Donut turns around and smiles at us. 'Everything all right?' he says.

'Yeh,' I tell him.

Mum just nods.

'Good,' goes Donut, looking at Mum. 'Do you know Wickham, Mrs Nelson?'

'Not really.'

'How about you?' he says to me.

'Nope.'

'Well, it's not far. We'll be there in about 10 minutes. You're looking very smart, by the way. Well done.'

'Thanks.'

He smiles, curling his lip, like he don't like the tone of my voice – but what's he gonna do about it?

'Hopefully there shouldn't be too much waiting around when we get there,' he says. 'Mr Vine's finished on the stand – you're the next witness. So once we get going, you'll be called almost immediately . . . Michael, are you listening?'

'Yeh, I was just opening the window—'

'Listen to me – this is important.'

'I'm hot—'

'We're all hot—'

'Let him open the window,' Mum says. 'You don't want him all sweaty in court, do you?'

Donut looks at her, like he's surprised she's got the nerve to say *anything*. He gives her one of his crappy little smiles, then looks back at me. I give him one of *my* crappy little smiles, like – *nyah nyah nyah* . . .

And he says, 'Your father decided not to come, then?'

And I stop smiling.

He stares at me for a bit longer, just to make sure I got the message, then he looks out the window to see where we are. We're going down this long curvy hill. There's a railway track down below on the left, and on the other side there's one of them ski slope things – like a long grey carpet rolling down the hill, with a chair-lift and everything . . . yeh, everything except skiers. The place is empty. Up ahead I can see distant streets, houses, office blocks, smoking chimneys . . . Wickham, I guess. It looks OK. Nothing special, just a place . . . 10 miles up the road . . . just like I thought. But . . . I dunno . . . I guess it's different now. Now it's a place I'm GOING to . . . but back then . . . before all this . . . back then I wasn't looking at PLACES . . . I wasn't LOOKING looking, I wasn't looking AT nothing . . . I was just looking down, dead-eyed and blind – just losing the RAIN in the river.

But now I'm in it – I'm IN the bloody river . . .

'OK, listen,' says Donut, turning back to me. 'The defence barrister's a fellow called William Cole – he'll be examining you first. All he's going to do is ask you some questions about what happened on the evening of November 2nd. Bill's a nice chap – he'll look after you. There's nothing to worry about. All you have to do is tell the truth. Just take your time, listen to the questions, and think about what you're saying. When you answer, look at the jury, not the judge or the barrister, and speak as slowly and as clearly as you can – OK?'

'I thought *you* was gonna be asking the questions.'

'No – I'll be there, but I won't be asking any questions. The barristers ask the questions. After Bill Cole's finished, you'll be cross-examined by the prosecution barrister. Now *he* might get a bit funny with you – he might try to confuse you, make out you're a liar . . . that kind of thing. But don't let it worry you – don't take it personally. That's just his job. All you have to do is stay calm, stick to the truth, and everything will be all right.' He looks at his watch, then looks out the window again. We're in the middle of town now, driving through a maze of roundabouts and traffic lights. The streets are pretty busy – lots of traffic, lots of cars, trucks, vans, lorries . . .

'Here we are,' Donut says after a while. 'This is it.'

I look out the window at a browny-grey building at the side of the road. It's kinda boxy-looking, like 2 or 3 shoeboxes stuck on top of each other, with brick walls and loads of windows and a flat grey roof . . . and that's about it, really. A browny-grey box made of bricks and glass.

'OK,' Donut says to the midget guy. 'Drop us off here and

then park round the back.'

The midget guy don't say nothing, just puts his flashers on and pulls up at the side of the road. We get out the car and Donut leads us up a ramp to some glass doors at the front of the building. There's a bunch of guys hanging around smoking fags outside the doors – a couple of nutjobs in tracksuits, and a posh-looking guy in a suit with a funny-looking tie . . . some kinda flappy white silky thing . . . looks like an albino vampire bat hanging round his neck.

'Come on,' says Donut, holding the door for me.

I follow him and Mum inside. We go through some more glass doors then stop in front of some kinda gate, like a doorway without a door. 2 old guys in manky blue uniforms are standing behind a desk. One of em's got white hair and the other one's got a beard.

'Morning, JD,' the beardy one says.

Donut nods his head and gives the guy his briefcase. Beardy opens it up and peeks inside, then smiles and puts it on the desk.

Donut says to Mum, 'They need to check your bag.'

'What for?' she says.

'Security.'

She looks at me. I shrug. She looks at the white-haired guy. He smiles.

Donut says, 'Just give him your bag, please, Mrs Nelson.'

She ain't too sure about it, but she hands it over anyway. The beardy guy pokes around inside it, checking this and that – bags of sweets, mints, a purse, 2 apples, a pork pie, a packet of tissues, a cooking magazine . . . she's got TONS of stuff in there – then the beardy guy puts all the stuff back in the bag and puts the bag on the desk. Then we gotta go through this doorway thing, which turns out to be a metal detector, so we all gotta get rid of our keys and stuff . . . well, Mum and

Donut do, I ain't got nothing to get rid of . . . then, when we're through the metal detector, Mum and Donut gotta get all their stuff back and pick up their bags, and then we gotta check in, or sign in, whatever it's called, writing our names and stuff in this book, and THEN we're ready to go.

Donut walks off across the hall, and we follow him. There's loads of people milling around all over the place. Some of em's just ordinary-looking people, sitting around on benches, reading books and magazines . . . some of em's got uniforms and name badges . . . and others are all dressed up in black cloaks and vampire-bat ties. The floor's all shiny and hard, and the corridor walls are made of brick.

'All right?' Donut asks me.

'Yeh – where we going?'

He stops by a black door. 'This is the Witness Service Office. You can wait in here until you're called.' He opens the door and shows us inside. It's like a little office room. There's 4 or 5 seats, posters and leaflet racks on the walls, radiators, a desk, bookshelves and stuff. The windows got bars on em. There's an Asian lady sitting behind the desk. She's got long brown hair and she's wearing a shapeless brown dress with a blue name badge pinned on it. She's kinda chubby, kinda pear-shaped, one of them ladies who's thinnish from the waist up but fat down below. She looks OK.

She stands up when we come in.

'Morning, Anisha,' Donut says. 'This is Michael Nelson and his mum. Michael's testifying in the Vine case.'

Anisha smiles at us, says hello, shakes our hands, sits us down, starts talking about stuff . . . I dunno what . . . I'm too hot and bothered to listen. I'm burning up. There's a fan blowing on top of a cupboard, but it ain't doing no good. It's just blowing all the hot air around. I can feel the sweat running down my back . . . cold sweat, like freezing blood, sticking to my shirt . . .

Anisha's still talking. '. . . so if you're worried about anything, anything at all, just ask. That's what we're here for – to support and reassure you. OK?'

'Yeh,' I tell her.

'Right,' says Donut. 'I have to go.' He looks at me. 'All right?'

'Yeh, great.'

He sniffs, then turns the sniff into a smile. 'Right – well, it won't be long now. It'll soon be over. Just relax, OK? I'll see you in court.'

And off he goes.

No sweat.

Not a drop.

Cool bastad.

The next half hour is mostly just sitting around doing nothing. Anisha gets out a copy of my written statement and asks me if I wanna read it through, to *refresh* my memory.

'Not really,' I tell her.

'You sure?'

'Yeh . . . thanks.'

'OK.'

She pulls up a chair and starts going through what's gonna happen when I get called to the witness box, which is basically the same stuff I already seen in the information leaflet . . . so I don't really listen to what she's saying, I just kinda sit there, drifting away, looking at the stuff on the walls, the bracelets on her wrist, the stuff on her desk . . . listening to the noises outside . . . passing voices, footsteps in the corridor . . . then Mum gets up and says she needs to use the toilet. Anisha explains where it is. Mum gets her bag and shuffles out the door. And then I'm thinking *I* gotta go to the toilet too, and I'm wondering if I oughta go now, or if I should wait for Mum to come back and *then* go . . .

And then the door opens and this big guy in a long black coat comes in. He looks like some kinda GANGSTA.

'Michael Nelson?' he goes.

'Uh?'

Anisha says, 'You're being called, Michael. It's time for you to give evidence. The usher will show you where to go.'

This guy's an *usher*?

He's standing there, staring at me, waving his hand at the door . . . and suddenly it hits me – this is it . . . THIS IS IT . . . THIS or THAT . . . THIS IS *IT* . . . and I can feel some kinda liquidy burbling deep down in my belly, like I got the screaming shits or something . . . and I can't get up off the chair . . . I can't move.

'This way, please,' grunts the usher guy.

I look at Anisha. 'What about my mum?'

'Don't worry,' she smiles. 'I'll tell her where you've gone. She can either wait in here for you or watch from the gallery. Go on, off you go now. They're waiting for you.' She smiles. 'And don't *worry* – it'll be all right.'

That's what I keep telling myself as I follow the usher along a trail of corridors, up some stairs, then along more corridors . . .

Don't worry – it'll be all right . . .

Don't worry – it'll be all right . . .

Don't worry – it'll be all right . . .

Don't worry – it'll be all right . . .

Like if I say it enough, it's gonna come TRUE.

Now . . . I'm feeling it **now**. Walking along the courtroom corridors . . . all squitty and hot and sweaty and numb . . .

and GOD . . . I never felt so crazy-bad in my LIFE. My heart's thumping like a jungle drum . . . my skin's on fire . . . I got cramps in my belly and red-hot knives in my head . . . what the HELL am I gonna do? what am I gonna SAY? how am I gonna SPEAK? I can't *SPEAK* . . . I can't even *WALK* . . . WHAT AM I GONNA *DO*?

Yeh, I'm feeling it **now** . . .

I GOTTA feel it . . .

Remember it . . .

Keep it in mind . . .

In body.

When the usher guy takes me into the courtroom, I just kinda zonk out. I dunno what I'm doing or where I'm going, I'm just following this big guy in a long black coat . . . following him across a big room filled with people . . . all of em looking at me . . . all of em mumbling . . . whispering . . . and all I can do is what I do – walk through it all with my eyes down. Umbrellarise it. It's the only way. Across the room, through the mumbling voices, the watching eyes, the whispering RAIN, then up a couple of steps and I'm standing there – in the witness box. I can't believe it – I'm actually IN the witness box. There's a microphone pointing at me, and a glass of water on a little shelf – and there's me, not daring to look up, cos I know they're all staring at me, but I know I gotta . . . I gotta look at em . . . so I take a deep breath and I says to myself – what do you care? let em stare. YOU'RE FAT, OK? FAT AND SCARED AND SWEATY . . . so what? what's it to them? what they gonna do? KILL YOU?

And I look up.

It's a big white room with a high ceiling. It's got a wooden floor, loads of wood panelling, and tables and desks all over the place. On my left there's a platform thing, like a raised stand with a wood-panelled front. That's where the judge is sitting. I think it's the judge, anyway – a wrinkly old guy in a black cloak and a wig, sitting in a big white chair, staring at me over his glasses. In front of him there's a couple of guys sitting at a long table, one in a black cloak and one in a white shirt. They're both fiddling around with bits of paper or something . . . I dunno what they're doing. Then opposite me, across the other side of the room, there's the jury – 12 people sitting in a box, all of em looking at me like I'm something in a zoo.

On my right, facing the judge, there's some more long tables, with more guys in cloaks and wigs, guys in suits, a woman in a suit, and there's old Donut, sitting behind one of the cloaky guys, *not* looking at me . . . he's gotta be the only one here who AIN'T looking at me. Cos I'm looking around, and all I can see is eyes . . . EYES EYES EYES . . . all of em stuck on me . . . LOOKING LOOKING LOOKING . . . and that's when I feel the REAL eyes . . . the LOOK . . . the stare that burns your skin, like a laser. I can FEEL it. And I know where it's coming from, I know who it is, and I don't WANNA look, but I can't help it . . . I gotta turn to the heat . . . and there he is, standing in the dock at the far end of the room, his laser eyes fixed on me – Keith Vine. Looking hard, dressed in a suit, his tanned face cold and blank in the courtroom light. And, just for a second, I see what he sees. I see a fat kid standing in a box, his fat face terrified, glowing red and shiny with sweat . . . and you know what? It's the WORST thing I ever seen. But that's to me. To him, to Vine . . . I dunno . . . he's got me in his sights, I guess, he's just GOT me . . . and cos of that I can't see nothing BUT him. I see him raise his eyes and look up at the ceiling. There's a balcony up there, a balcony full of people, all of em sitting there, looking down, watching what's going on. There's Callan, looking down at Vine. There's Bowker and Dorudi, sitting at the other end, away from Callan, looking down at me. There's the midget guy, his head just poking over the railings. There's a bunch of people with notepads and pens. And there's a couple of mugs who look like they just got outta prison . . . big guys with tattooed arms and psycho eyes . . . the kinda guys who like doing stuff you wouldn't *believe* . . .

All this looking, all this taking it in – it takes about 2 seconds.

Then the usher guy's standing in front of me, passing me a little black bible and a piece of card . . . and he's telling me something . . . I dunno what . . . my ears ain't working right . . . but I know what I gotta do. I gotta put my right hand on the bible and read from the card . . . I gotta SPEAK . . . *GOD!!* . . . I gotta *SPEAK* . . .

I look at the card, clear my throat, wipe the sweat from my face, open my mouth, and begin to read: 'I sweat . . . I *swear* by Almighty GOD that the . . . that the evident . . . evid*ence* I'll give . . . shall . . . evidence I shall give is . . . is . . . the truth . . . *shall be* the truth, the whole toot . . . *truth*, and nut . . . nothing but the truth.'

The usher guy looks at me like he can't believe his ears, then he shakes his head, takes the bible and the card from me, and sits down in a box to my right. I get a hanky outta my pocket and wipe my face. There's a lotta murmuring going on, people shuffling papers about, people coughing, then the judge looks down at me and says, 'Are you all right? You look a bit hot. Would you like to sit down?'

I look at him. 'What?'

'Would you like to sit down?'

'No . . . I'm OK – thanks.'

He smiles at me . . . at least, I *think* it's a smile – it's hard to tell with all them wrinkles. Then he looks at the guy in the wig who's sitting in front of Donut, and he says, 'Mr Cole?'

The guy in the wig stands up and looks at me. William Cole, I guess, the defence guy, the one Donut told me about – the *nice* guy. He don't look that nice to me. He looks kinda bored and sniffy . . . a bit twitchy, too, like he's got something pointy stuck up his arse. He walks towards me across the room and stops about 2 metres away, looking down at his shoes.

'Would you tell the ladies and gentlemen of the jury your full name, please?'

I look at him, wondering why he's talking to his *shoes* . . .

He looks up at me. 'Your full *name*, please?'

'Oh, right,' I says. 'It's Michael Moopert . . . sorry . . . *Rup*ert . . . Nichael . . . sorry . . .' I clear my throat and try again. 'Michael . . . Rupert . . . Nelson.'

'Thank you,' says Cole.

He's got some bits of paper in his hand. He looks through em, then looks up at me again.

'Now then, Michael,' he says. 'Would you please tell the court where you were at approximately 6 o'clock on the evening of November 2nd last year.'

'I was on the bridge.'

There's a quiet snort of laughter from someone up on the balcony. Old Coley ignores it, and looks at me.

'And which bridge would this be?' he says.

'The bridge over the road – near where I live.'

'The A12?'

'Yeh.'

My voice is all trembly and shaky, the shakiness amplified by the microphone. It's really weird – it don't *sound* like my voice at all. It sounds like a croaky idiot is what it sounds like. Anyway, Coley goes back to his table and picks up a TV remote and points it at a TV screen mounted on the wall.

A picture comes up, like a map, showing the village and the lane and the road and the bridge and everything. Coley goes over and points out the bridge.

'Is this the bridge?' he says.

'Yeh.'

'And you were standing here at approximately 6 o'clock?'

'Yeh.'

'Which way were you facing?'

'North, towards Wickham . . . here. Towards here. North.'

'How was your view of the road?'

'Uh?'

'How *well* could you see the road?'

'Pretty well.'

'It's a good view from the bridge?'

'Yeh.'

'Could you describe it, please?'

'What?'

'The view – describe what you could see from the bridge.'

I look across at the jury – 12 people sitting in a box, all of em looking at me – and I give em a quick look back. There's a long-faced black lady, an old woman with rabbity teeth, a pretty Indian girl with shiny hair and really nice eyes, a young guy in a button-down Ben Sherman shirt . . .

'Michael?'

I look at Coley. 'What?'

'The view from the bridge,' he says.

'Oh yeh, sorry . . . it's . . . uh . . .' I close my eyes and picture it. 'Right, well . . . you got 2 lanes north and 2 lanes south and you can see the road for about a mile. It goes straight for about half a mile and then it curves off to the right and disappears round a hill.'

Coley smiles at me, looks at his papers, then looks at me

again. 'So,' he says, 'you're standing on the footbridge, facing north, and you've got a clear view of the A12 ahead of you. Now, at approximately 6 o'clock, did anything unusual happen? Did you see anything unusual?'

'Yeh.'

'Would you please tell the court what you saw?'

I wipe some more sweat from my face, loosen my tie, and give my arse a quick scratch. It's really hot in here – my pants are sticking to my skin . . . it's getting hard to breathe . . . and GODSAKE – this is it . . .

This is it.

I give Callan a quick look – he's leaning forward in the balcony, staring hard at me. Below him, in the dock, Vine's got a smug grin on his face. I look up at the balcony again, wondering where Mum is, wishing she was up there, looking down at me . . . but she ain't. And my head's going – Yeh . . . right . . . well, this is it, I guess . . . the FINAL final start of it . . . the TRUTH . . . here it is . . . here we go . . .

OK . . .

'Well . . .' I says – and I'm back there, on the bridge, watching the tail-lights streaming past the pylon and disappearing down the hill . . . watching, watching, watching . . . drifting away . . .

'OK,' I goes. 'Well there was these 2 cars speeding up the south lane . . .'

And I tell it, just like I told it before. I tell em what happened . . . the cars, the BMW, the Range Rover, Vine, the BMW guy, the others, the fight, the crash cops . . . the TRUTH. And as I'm telling it, I'm kinda looking around, looking at all the cloaks and wigs and suits and faces and staring eyes . . . Callan, Vine, Coley, Donut, Bowker, the judge, the jury, the tough mugs in the balcony . . . all of em stuck on me . . . and I'm getting hotter and sweatier and stickier and shakier . . . and the funny thing is, as I'm speaking, telling what happened, my voice gets more and more *detached*, if you know what I mean, and I start drifting away and thinking about other stuff. Pretty weird stuff. Like I start thinking about the *sound* of my voice, the actual words coming outta my mouth, the sounds I'm making . . . and how they're gonna change everything. These sounds . . . they're flying through the air and zipping into people's ears and changing stuff inside their brains, and then stuff's gonna happen *cos* of them changes . . . like with Callan, say. The sounds coming outta my gob right now, they're flying across the room and zipping into his ears, then down some tubes into his brain, and his brain's, like, translating the sounds, turning em into stuff that means something, and cos it means something, it means it's gonna change things . . . it means he's gonna go after my dad and lock him up, and that's gonna change everything – for me, for Dad, for Mum . . . everything. EVERYTHING. It's all gonna change . . .

And then I realise the room's gone quiet and everyone's looking at me. I dunno what's going on. I dunno how long it's been quiet, but I guess I musta stopped talking . . . I musta finished the story . . .

'Mr Nelson?' the judge says.

I look around, looking for my dad . . .

'Mr Nelson?'

. . . and then I realise the judge means me – Mr Nelson . . . that's me.

'Yeh?' I says.

'Would you answer the question, please?'

'What question?'

Coley steps up. 'I was asking you about the altercation between the 2 drivers, Michael.'

'The what?'

'Altercation . . . the scuffle . . . the fight.'

'Oh, right.'

'The driver of the Range Rover – would you recognise him if you saw him again?'

'Yeh . . .' I point at Vine '. . . that's him over there.'

Vine winks at me.

Coley says, 'For the record, Mr Nelson is indicating the defendant. Now, Michael, you've told us that Mr Vine only struck out *after* the initial attack from the other driver – is that correct?'

'Yeh.'

'He struck out in self-defence.'

'I spose so – yeh.'

'With his bare hands?'

'Yeh.'

'There was no weapon involved?'

'No.'

'Mr Vine did *not* have a knife.'

'No – he just whacked the other guy in the face.'

Someone laughs again. Coley smiles to himself, but the judge looks around with a scowl on his face, and the room goes quiet. Then Coley starts on about the fight again . . . asking me this, asking me that, this and that, this and that . . . basically going over and over what I already told em – or what I guess I already told em . . . and all I gotta do is go *yeh, yeh, that's right, no, yeh, no, yeh* . . . and this goes on for AGES . . . *yeh yeh yeh yeh yeh yeh yeh yeh YEH YEH YEH* . . . and after a while I'm starting to get tired from standing up so long . . . my legs are aching and I'm wilting in the heat, and I REALLY need to go to the bog, and I'm wondering if I oughta say something, like is it OK to ask if I can go to the toilet, but then Coley – after he's asked me another question – takes a long look at his papers and a quick look at

Donut, then he gives the judge a look, and says, 'I have no further questions, thank you.'

The judge nods, looks at his watch, and says, 'Very well, we'll resume again at half past one.'

And then everyone's standing up and shuffling about, and the usher guy's telling me to follow him, and I follow him out the courtroom and along the corridors, where we bump into Donut and Coley.

'Well done, Michael,' Donut says, hardly even looking at me. 'You're doing very well. It's not so bad, is it?'

'I dunno . . . I guess not.'

'No . . . well, keep up the good work. You'll have to excuse me – I have to . . . um . . . yes . . . well, I have to be somewhere. Make sure you're back by 1.30, won't you? The judge doesn't like being held up.' He turns to Coley and laughs – *phnur, phnur, phnur* – then he puts his hand on my shoulder, gives me a gentle shove, and just kinda walks off, yapping away to Old King Coley. The usher guy grunts, then *he* walks off, and I follow him back to the whatsit place, the witness room. He opens the door and *ushers* me in. Anisha's sitting at her desk tapping at a keyboard . . . there's a couple of guys sitting in the chairs round the wall . . . and Mum's sitting in the corner, reading her TV magazine and eating a pork pie.

'Oh, there you are,' she says. 'How's it going?'

'All right.'

'You hungry? I got some sandwiches, or we can go out if you want – find a McDonald's or something.'

'Yeh, OK . . . I gotta go to the toilet first.'

So far, like Donut said, it ain't so bad. I mean, yeh, it's BAD – all them people, all them questions, the heat, the sweat, the fear of what's gonna happen later with Dad and everything, and then Mum not showing her face . . . yeh, it ain't exactly GREAT, but I ain't dying or nothing. Not yet, anyway.

Right now, all I'm dying for is a wee.

So I shoot off down to the end of the corridor and hurry into the toilet, where the first thing I see is Keith Vine standing at the urinal taking a leak. It's one hell of a shock. I dunno *why* . . . I spose I thought he'd be locked up somewhere, like caged up in the basement or something, guarded by Robocops . . . but I guess there ain't no reason why he should be, and it don't matter anyway, cos he ain't. He's standing right there, large as life, whistling and peeing like he ain't got a care in the world. I'm tempted to turn around and get the hell out before he sees me, but I'm nearly bursting now, I mean I REALLY gotta go, so I start sneaking over to one of the cubicles, trying to get in before he sees me, but I reckon he's got eyes in the back of his head, cos I ain't got no more than a couple of steps when his voice rings out like a foghorn.

'Yo Fats,' he says. 'What you doing?'

I stop in the middle of the floor. Vine turns around and zips himself up, grinning at me like a madman.

'All right, Moo?' he goes.

'Yeh . . . I need to—'

'Hey, you're doing pretty good,' he says. 'Yeh, I like it . . . playing dumb. Nice touch. Very *convincing*. So – what d'you think? You ready for this afternoon then? Ready for the big stuff?'

'Uh . . .'

'Tell you what – you keep it up like this and we'll be done by the end of the Day. Might even earn yourself a bonus. How bout that?'

'I don't really want—'

'Here,' he says, pulling a business card from his pocket

and shoving it into my hand. 'Just for you.' He winks. I look at the card. It ain't got no name or address or nothing, just a mobile number. Vine says, 'Gimme a ring when it's over. We'll sort something out – OK?'

'I gotta go—'

'Yeh,' he grins. 'I can see that.'

Then the door opens and Callan walks in, stopping dead at the sight of us. I stand there staring at him, my gob hanging open and my eyes on stalks . . . cos I can SEE what he's seeing – me and Vine . . . all cosy and shifty and secret and WRONG . . .

'Well, well,' grins Vine, 'look who's here. It's big Johnny C. Hey, John – long time no see . . . how's the wife?'

Callan don't answer, just stares at me.

Vine nudges my arm. 'Hey, Moo – ask him if he's got a search warrant.'

Callan flicks a glance at Vine, then turns his eyes back to me, giving me the LOOK. I pocket Vine's card, feeling guilty as HELL, then I hang my head and stare at the floor. It don't matter, I tell myself, you ain't done nothing . . . and anyway, and anyway, and anyway . . . it just DON'T MATTER. None of it. It's done now – TRUTH, LIES, MONEY, GUILT, BLOOD, SWEAT, BRADY . . . it's over. It was over the second you opened your mouth in the courtroom. Ain't nothing you can do about it now.

'I gotta pee,' I hear myself say.

'Yeh,' says Vine, grinning at Callan. 'And I gotta go – got things to sort out for the weekend.' He winks again, whacks me on the shoulder – 'See you later, Moo' – then walks past Callan – 'Keep it real, John' – and goes out the door.

Before Callan's got a chance to say anything, I scuttle into the cubicle and lock the door.

It's dead quiet for a minute. No footsteps, no breathing . . .

no nothing. I know Callan's still there, though – I can FEEL him staring at the door. And I wish he'd just go, cos he's making me nervous, and I can't pee when I'm nervous. Then I hear him sigh, a long heavy sigh, and his voice calls softly through the door.

'I meant what I said about your dad, Michael,' he goes. 'I'm a man of my word. I don't break promises.'

'Go away,' I tell him. 'Please – just leave me alone.'

'It's not too late, you know.'

'Yeh, it is. Go away.'

'OK . . . but don't say you haven't been warned.'

I don't say nothing. He sighs again, and I think he's gonna say something else, but he don't. I hear him turn around, open the door, and then his footsteps fade and the door slams shut.

Thank GOD.

My bladder's close to exploding.

That's just about it for the *ain't-so-bad* bit, except for dinner with Mum in a Burger King just down the road. The dinner's OK – I get one of them double cheesy bacon burger things – but Mum ain't doing too good. I dunno what it is, but she's acting really funny, like she's talking ALL the time, yak yak yak, yakking away about nothing, so even if I WANTED to tell her about stuff, like what's going on and how I feel about it – which I dunno if I do or I don't – but even if I did, it wouldn't make much difference, cos I'd never get a word in edgeways. Not with her yakking on like she is. I dunno what it is . . . I guess she's probly a bit nervous or something, you know, a bit jittery about being in the courthouse and everything, plus she probly WANTS to help me, like she WANTS to talk to me, she WANTS to ask me about stuff, but she ain't sure how to do it. D'you know what I mean? She just ain't got it in her. And the worst thing is, I ain't got the heart or the energy to do much about it, neither. I just can't be bothered. I can't even make myself ask her why she din't come into the courtroom this morning . . . mostly, probly, cos I'm pretty sure she don't feel that great about it herself . . . and why should I make it any worse?

What's the point?

So . . . we just eat, and she yaks, and I sit there nodding, and we eat some more, and that's about it.

Dinnertime's over.

It's time to go back.

Time to start dying.

18/ A Wall of Tears

Back in the courtroom, back in the witness box, everything's pretty much the same. Same room, same heat, same people, same eyes, same waiting around, same people shuffling papers and stuff . . . then the judge leans forward and says something to the guy at the table in front of him, the one in the white shirt, and White Shirt nods and passes him a bit of paper. The judge reads it, puts it down, then looks over at me and says, 'Refreshed, Mr Nelson?'

'Yeh,' I tell him.

He smiles. 'Good.' He adjusts his wig and speaks to another guy in a cloak and wig who's sitting at the far end of Coley's table. 'Are we ready, Mr Henry?'

Mr Henry, who I guess is the prosecution guy, nods at the judge, then stands up and walks towards me. I watch him, trying to work out what he's like, but it's hard to tell. I mean, these guys in wigs . . . I dunno . . . they all look the same to me. All they look like is guys in wigs. About the only thing I can tell about Henry is that he's a bit younger than Coley, and he's got one of them faces that's soft and flabby, but *thin* soft and flabby, if you know what I mean. Like it ain't fat, but it looks like it oughta be. Oh yeh, and his eyes, they're kinda small and pale, too small for the rest of his face . . . sneaky eyes.

'Good afternoon, Mr Nelson,' he says pleasantly. 'I'd like to remind you that you're still under oath.'

'Right.'

'Do you understand what that means?'

'Yeh.'

'Good.' He smiles at me. 'Now, I'd like to ask you a few questions about your written statement and the testimony you gave to the court this morning, if I may.' He gives me another *pleasant* look, like he's waiting for me to say something . . . something like – Yeh, of *course* you *may*. GOD . . . I'm already starting to hate his guts. I mean, why's he asking me if it's all right to ask questions? I ain't gonna say NO, am I? And even if I did, he's still gonna ask em.

'Now then,' he says. 'What time did you leave your house on the evening of November 2nd last year?'

'I dunno . . . it was just after tea – about 5, probly.'

'So you left your house about 5 and headed off towards the footbridge over the A12?'

'Yeh.'

'On foot?'

'No – on a bike.'

'I see . . . and you were definitely heading for the bridge?'

'Yeh.'

'You weren't just cycling around, getting some exercise . . .' He stops for a second, waits for the laughter to die down, then carries on. 'The bridge was your intended destination?'

'Yeh.'

'You were *going* there?'

'Yeh.'

'Why?'

'*Why?*'

'Yes, why? Why were you going to the bridge? Were you meeting someone?'

'No.'

'Then why were you going there?'

'I dunno . . . no reason. It's just somewhere to go, I spose.'

'Somewhere to go . . .'

I don't say nothing, I just look at him. He ain't asked me a question. If he ain't asked me a question, I ain't gotta say nothing. He looks back at me for a while, then turns around and starts walking across towards the jury.

'Was this the first time you'd visited this particular bridge?' he says, with his back to me.

'No.'

He stops, pauses, then turns around to face me. 'So, you'd been there before?'

'Yeh.'

'How many times?'

'I dunno – lots . . .'

'Could you be a little more specific?'

'Not really.'

'All right – let's try to narrow it down a little. Would you say you'd been to the bridge on more than, say, 10 occasions?'

'Yeh.'

'More than a hundred?'

'Yeh.'

He raises his eyebrows. 'A thousand?'

'Probly . . . I dunno. I don't keep count.'

'But it would be fair to say that you visited the bridge on a fairly regular basis?'

'Yeh.'

'How often?'

'Every Day.'

'Every *Day*?'

'Yeh – just about.'

'Why?'

I can't think what to say. I mean, I DUNNO why I go there . . . I just go there . . . it's my release . . . my PLACE . . . my shelter from the RAIN . . . but I ain't saying THAT, am I?

As I'm standing there staring at Henry, trying to think what to say, old Coley gets up and says to the judge, 'Your Honour, I fail to see the relevance of these questions.'

The judge looks at Henry. 'Mr Henry?'

Henry looks back at him. 'Your Honour, I'm simply trying to establish the reason behind the witness's presence at the scene of the crime—'

'Alleged crime,' says Coley.

Henry nods. '*Alleged* crime.'

The judge sniffs. 'You may continue, Mr Henry, but let's not dwell on this matter too long.'

'Thank you, Your Honour.' Henry turns back to me. 'Would you answer the question, please?'

'What was it?'

'You stated that you visited the bridge almost every Day – and I asked you why.'

'Right.'

'And I'm still waiting for the answer.'

'Well . . . I just go there cos . . . I dunno . . . cos it's peaceful, I spose.'

'Peaceful? A footbridge over the A12 – peaceful?'

'Yeh.'

'I find that hard to believe.'

'You ever been there?'

'I'm sorry?'

'Have you ever been there?'

His mouth turns nasty. 'Well, no . . . but—'

'How d'you know what it's like, then?'

He looks at the judge. 'Your Honour . . .'

The judge – smiling a bit – says to me, 'You're not here to ask questions, Mr Nelson. You're here to answer them.'

'I know . . . but he din't ask—'

'Please, Mr Nelson.'

'OK.'

He nods. 'Continue, Mr Henry.'

Now Henry's looking at me with nastiness in his eyes, like – OK, you wanna play it like that? Let's play.

He says, 'How much do you weigh, Mr Nelson?'

'Objection!' shouts Coley.

'Is this really necessary?' the judge asks Henry.

'Yes, Your Honour. If you'll just bear with me a moment . . .' The judge gives him a watch-it look, then nods. Henry grins, looking at me. 'Your weight, please?'

I look around the room, looking at all the hungry eyes, all the beaky faces, all of em waiting for an answer. Yeh, they want an answer all right . . . it's the kinda stuff they wanna know. THEY ain't got the guts to ask, but they're happy enough to let Henry do their dirty work for em.

'17 stone,' I says. 'Give or take.'

Henry nods. 'That's quite *large*, if you don't mind me saying.'

'You can say what you like.'

'Do you get bullied because of your size?'

'Why?'

'Please answer the question. Do you get bullied?'

'Sometimes . . . yeh.'

'At school?'

'Yeh.'

'That must be very unpleasant.'

'What d'you think?'

He smiles – the PITY smile . . . and he shows it to the jury. Like – look at me, I don't WANNA put the poor kid through this, but . . . you know . . . it's my job . . . *some*one's gotta do it. And I'm looking at my feet now, I'm thinking – yeh, it's unpleasant, getting bullied, but it ain't half as unpleasant as THIS. Cos the bullying stuff's private, it's mine – I can HANDLE it. But this . . .? This is something else. This is taking your private stuff and making it public. It's like when you got a boil on your arse or something – it ain't *nice*, but it ain't half as bad as pulling your pants down and showing it to everyone.

Henry turns back to me again. 'Do you have many friends, Mr Nelson?'

'What?'

'Do you have many friends?'

I look across at Coley, hoping he's gonna stand up and shout *Objection!* again, but he's too busy writing stuff on a piece of paper. I take a deep breath, wipe my face, clear my throat . . .

'No,' I say. 'I ain't got many friends.'

'School friends?'

'Not really.'

'A girlfriend, perhaps?'

I can hear em laughing, them snorty little back-of-the-throat laughs . . .

'Mr Nelson?'

'No – no girlfriend.'

Henry pauses to let it all sink in . . . ie, this kid's fat, he gets beat up, he ain't got no friends, he ain't getting his naughties . . . know what I mean? He's just DYING for attention. You gonna trust what *he* says? Yeh, he lets all THAT sink in . . . then he wanders over to the jury and starts talking again.

'I wonder, Mr Nelson,' he says, 'I wonder if your regular visits to the bridge – your *Daily* visits to the bridge – may be, to some extent, symptomatic of your – how shall I put it? – your *disaffection*?' He turns around and looks at me – smug git.

'You asking me something?' I says.

'Yes – is it true?'

'Is what true?'

'What I just said.'

'I dunno – I dunno what it means.'

Someone laughs – Vine probly – and Henry's face reddens. He says to me, 'You go to the bridge because you're unhappy, because you're lonely, because you're bullied—'

'Cos I'm fat. Yeh . . . so what?'

His face is all tensed up now, like someone's grabbed the skin at the back of his head and yanked it tight. And his eyes are burning up, too. If we weren't in court, I reckon he'd take a swing at me . . . yeh, I *reckon*. If we weren't in court . . . if I had a gun . . . I'd shoot the bastad.

The judge coughs. 'Perhaps you ought to move on, Mr Henry?'

Henry nods his head, looks at the floor, then goes over to his table and drinks from a glass of water. I take a drink from mine, too. I'm PARCHED. I'm baking, boiled, dried up, sweaty . . . GOD, I'm sweaty . . . even my *eyes* are sweating. I gulp down some water . . . and spill half of it down my shirt.

GOD.

GOD.

GOD!!!

I dunno if I'm telling this right. I dunno if I'm telling it BAD enough. I dunno . . . I guess maybe it's different **now**. I mean, it din't happen *that* long ago, less than 24 hours in fact, but it seems like a different LIFE, and I guess I'm looking back on it with different eyes. Yeh, my eyes . . . they ain't got no tears in em **now**. They just got ice. So maybe I'm freezing things out a bit, telling things a bit too cold . . .?

I dunno.

It WAS bad, though . . . bigger than bad. Believe me – it was BAAD.

Anyway, Henry moves on. He leaves off the fat-and-lonely stuff and starts going through my written statement, asking about the cars, the Range Rover, the BMW, where they were, what speed they were doing, that kinda stuff. They're pretty easy questions, and as I'm answering em I start drifting off again, looking around the courtroom, looking at all the faces, wondering what they're thinking about . . . cos another weird thing is, I dunno what's been going on in here for the last week or so, do I? So I dunno what no one knows about nothing. They been hearing all kindsa stuff, probly, but all kindsa the *same* stuff . . . the same story, over and over again, only different versions. Different voices, different bits, different ideas . . . different INFORMATION. So, like the jury, for instance – what do they know? More than me? Less than me? And what are they thinking? Are they listening? Dreaming? Drifting? Have they made up their minds already? Are they bored? They *look* pretty bored. The old woman – the one with the rabbity teeth – she's got her eyes closed . . . the young guy's hiding a yawn . . . and there's a guy at the end, a suit-and-tie kinda guy, and he's just sitting there staring into space . . .

'. . . and you're positive it was a BMW?' Henry is saying.

'Yeh – a 328ci.'

'And the Range Rover?'

'Vogue SE, 4.6, V8.'

He smirks at me. 'I see you know your cars. Is that how

you spend your time on the bridge . . . *car*-spotting?'

'Not specially.'

'But you do have an impressive knowledge of cars?'

'I spose.'

He pauses again, like he's thinking about that, or he wants the JURY to think he's thinking about it – cos he wants em to know how SAD I am . . . standing on a bridge, all alone, watching cars . . .

Get it?

Watching cars = SAD = unreliable.

Next thing, he flaps through the pages of my statement, then looks up and says, 'You claim that Mr Vine appeared angry when he stepped out of his car?'

'Do I?'

He reads from the statement. '"The driver of the Range Rover stopped in front of him and began shouting and shaking his fist."' He stops reading and looks up at me. 'Is that right?'

'Yeh.'

'He sounds fairly angry to me.'

No question – no need to answer.

Henry says, 'Do you think he was angry?'

'Yeh.'

He looks at the statement again. 'And you go on to say – "He stepped up and punched him in the face."' He looks up at me. 'Who punched who in the face?'

'Vine hit the guy in the BMW. The driver.'

'Mr Vine punched the BMW driver?'

'Yeh.'

'What happened then?'

'The BMW guy kinda staggered back, then he jumped at Vine.'

'He grabbed Mr Vine?'

'Yeh.'

'Just grabbed him? Nothing else?'

'Like what?'

'Did he hit him?'

'No, he shoved him earlier—'

'I'm not talking about earlier. This man, the BMW driver, grabbed Mr Vine – then what?'

'He just kinda jerked back . . .'

'Who?'

'The BMW guy.'

'Jerked back?'

'Yeh.'

'As if he'd been stabbed?'

'Your Honour!' says Coley, standing up.

The judge holds up his hand to him, like – Yeh, OK, don't wet your pants, I got it. 'Mr Henry,' he says, 'please modify that question.'

Henry nods at the judge, then turns back to me. 'You saw the BMW driver recoil from Mr Vine?'

'Recoil?'

'Jerk away.'

'Yeh.'

'What did he do then?'

'He went down – fell over. Grabbed his belly and screamed.'

'So, this man, the BMW driver, he grabbed Mr Vine, then all at once he jerked backwards, grabbed his stomach, and fell to the ground, screaming. Is that what happened?'

'Yeh, but—'

'Is that what happened – yes or no?'

'Yeh.'

'Thank you.'

He turns to the judge. 'Your Honour, perhaps now would

be a convenient time for a short break?'

The judge gives him a dirty look – dirty, but kinda respectful, too. 'Very well,' he goes. 'We'll resume in 10 minutes.'

Everyone starts moving out. I don't really wanna go nowhere. I'd be all right just staying where I am, slumped in this box for the next 10 minutes, staring at an empty room. But the usher guy says I ain't allowed to. So . . . I don't really wanna go back to the witness room . . . it's too far, for a start, I only got 10 minutes – by the time I got there I'd have to turn round and come back. And I don't really wanna see Mum or Anisha anyway, so I just slope off into the corridor and slump down on a bench and sit there watching the cloaks and the wigs and the suits walking by – *clackety-clack, clackety-clack . . . yackety-yack, yackety-yack . . . clack-clack . . . yack-yack . . .*

You know what? All this – it's all just a game to these guys, the whole bloody thing. The courthouse, the clothes, the wigs, the cloaks, the fancy words . . . it's just a bloody GAME. Like all this stuff I'm going through – standing up, answering questions, getting JUDGED – it's all bollox. It's POINTLESS. Henry knows Vine ain't done nothing. He knows it's a set-up. Coley knows. Donut knows. Callan knows. Even the judge probly knows. Everyone KNOWS. And they all know Vine's a badass, too. It's obvious. They all know he's a nasty piece of shit, and it's not like he *wouldna* killed the dead guy, cos he woulda killed him if he'd had to, it's just that he din't have to . . . not this time, anyway. But none of em gives a shit . . . cos it don't MATTER if he did it or not. It just don't matter. Not to them. They're just trying to beat each other, trying to win the game . . . and even if they don't win – who cares? There's always another game tomorrow, or the next Day, or the next Day. And even if they don't win *them* games, ain't none of em coming out losers, that's for sure.

Nah . . . the only loser round here is me.

Back in the courtroom . . . it's about 3.30 now. I ain't sweating so bad no more, cos it ain't so hot, but I don't feel too good. I got a thumping headache, one of them necky ones that squeeze the back of your head, and my chest feels all tight and achey. I think it's the air in here. It's stale and dry, kinda stuffy and still, like it's been breathed too many times and run outta life.

Henry's asking me about the stuff after the fight now, the confusing stuff when all the other guys came out the BMW. He's passed me up a copy of my statement, to help CLARIFY things. What he *really* means is, to help CONFUSIFY things.

'Page 3,' he says, '3rd line down. You say that 3 men exited the BMW, one from the front and 2 from the back. Have you got that? Page 3, third line . . .'

I look at my copy of the statement and find the bit he's talking about. 'Yeh,' I tell him.

'So, there were 4 men inside the BMW?'

'Yeh.'

'But earlier, when you first saw the car, you said there was only one man – the driver. Is that right?'

'Yeh.'

He gives me a dumb look. 'How can that be?'

'I dunno.'

'I'm sorry, I don't understand. Are you saying there were *4* men in the car, or just the one?'

'There was one when I first saw it . . . the other 3 showed up later.'

'They showed up later? From where?'

'The car – they musta been hiding, I guess.'

'Hiding? Why would they be hiding?'

'So no one would see em, I spose. That's usually why people hide.'

Henry steps closer, looking annoyed, but then the judge calls down to him, 'Mr Henry, you're edging into the realms of conjecture again.'

'Sorry, Your Honour.'

'And Mr Cole,' the judge says, looking at Coley. 'Are you still with us?'

'Of course,' says Coley, blinking the boredom from his eyes.

'Look after your witness, then.'

'Yes – thank you, Your Honour.'

'Continue, Mr Henry.'

Henry continues.

'All right,' he says to me. 'These 3 men who suddenly *appeared* from the BMW . . .' He looks at my statement again. '. . . page 3, 4th paragraph – would you read from your description please?'

I got the pages mixed up now, so it takes a while to find the right bit . . . and cos I know everyone's waiting for me, that makes it even harder. My fingers ain't working too good, they're all shaky and sticky with sweat – I keep flapping the pages around like an idiot.

'Page 3, Mr Nelson,' says Henry.

'Yeh . . . hold on . . .'

'4th paragraph.'

'Yeh . . . I *know* . . .'

'Can you see all right? Do you need any help?'

'No . . . I got it.'

'You've got it?'

'Yeh.'

'Would you read your descriptions, please?'

'OK . . .' My head's really throbbing . . . the writing's really small, photocopied, all squiggly and smudged . . . it's hard to focus on the words.

'Mr Nelson?'

'Yeh, yeh . . . OK . . .' I start reading. '"The man who came out of . . . from . . . the front of the car was large and heeve . . . *heavy*. He was wearing a white T-shirt. One of the men who came out from out of . . . the back of the car . . . had thing . . . *thinning* hair. He was wearing a zipper jacket. The other man was wearing a white T-shirt and jeans and a black Nike cap. All of the men were wearing gl—"'

'Thank you,' says Henry. 'Now, according to measurements taken by the police, the distance from the centre of the bridge to the verge where the incident took place is approximately 22 metres. Would you say you had a fairly reasonable view of these men?'

'Yeh.'

'Was it dark at this time?'

'Yeh.'

'But you had a reasonable view?'

'There's a light there, by the road.'

'The man in the cap,' he says, looking at the statement. '"White T-shirt . . . jeans . . . and a black Nike cap." Yes?'

'Yeh.'

'Would you read your description of the BMW driver, please? Page 2, paragraph 2.'

I flap through the pages again, then read. '"A white male, wearing a white T-shirt, jeans, and a black Nike cap."'

'No,' says Henry, 'I think you have the wrong page . . . I asked you for the description of the *driver*. Page 2—'

'That *is* the driver.'

He looks at me, like he don't understand, which he *does*, of course – he's just being a smart-arse. He looks at the statement again, does a bit of page-shuffling, then looks back at me. 'Yes, of course . . . my mistake. I do apologise. There seems to be a remarkable similarity between these 2 men – both white, both wearing a white T-shirt, both wearing jeans, and both wearing a black Nike cap.' He frowns at me. 'Is that right?'

'Yeh.'

He shakes his head. '*Very* confusing . . . you're sure you're not mistaken?'

'Yeh . . . no.'

'Yes or no?'

'Yeh – I'm sure. No – I ain't mistaken.'

Henry gives me a long hard look. 'This is very important, Mr Nelson. The victim of this incident, Mr Burke, the man who received the fatal stab wound . . . he was dressed as you describe. So it's vital for us to clear up this matter. Do you understand?'

'Yeh.'

He nods, very serious now. 'When the 3 men exited the BMW, where was the driver – the first man in the black cap?'

'He was lying on the ground.'

'And Mr Vine – where was he?'

'Kinda standing over him—'

'And the second man in the black cap?'

'He was on the ground—'

'I'm sorry? I though you said the first man was lying on the ground?'

'Yeh . . . he was . . . but then the other guy got into a fight with the bald guy and *he* went down—'

'You saw them fighting?'

'Well, kinda . . . they was between the 2 cars—'

'So you *couldn't* see them?'

'I could see they was fighting.'

'Could you see them well enough to identify them?'

'Yeh . . .'

'How? If they were hidden between the 2 cars—'

'I saw em before—'

'Before what?'

'Before they went between the cars.'

'I see – all right . . . so while these 2 men were fighting between the cars, the other 2 men, the 2 men in identical clothing, they were both lying on the ground . . . is that right?'

'Yeh . . . well, the first one got up . . . the driver—'

'The man in the black cap?'

'No . . . he din't have his hat no more.'

'I'm sorry?'

'When he got up he wasn't wearing the cap.'

'Where did it go?'

'I dunno – he just got up and started grabbing—'

'He suddenly got up?'

'Yeh.'

'He was injured, he fell to the ground, screaming . . . and then he suddenly got up?'

'I never said he was injured.'

'If a man falls to the ground, clutching his stomach and screaming . . . isn't it fair to *assume* he's injured?'

'Not if he's acting, it ain't.'

'Acting? Is that what he was doing?'

'I dunno. I was just saying—'

'Mr Burke died from a stab wound to the heart . . . that doesn't sound like acting to me.'

I look across at Coley. He looks at Donut. Donut looks at

Vine. Vine shrugs . . . like – who cares? Donut nods, looks at Coley, blinks, and Coley does nothing.

Henry goes over to his table and picks something up, then comes back and passes me a photograph. 'For the benefit of the jury,' he goes, 'I'm showing Mr Nelson a photograph of Lee Burke.' Henry says to me. 'Would you look at the photograph, please?'

I look at it – it shows this kinda dopey-looking guy with scraggy hair and a cock-eyed grin. Not much of a face, kinda blank, not much to it . . . just a face . . . you know, a part-time bad guy . . . a dead guy.

Henry says, 'Was this one of the men in the BMW?'

'I dunno . . .'

'The man in the black Nike cap?'

'I dunno . . .'

'The driver?'

'I dunno . . . I din't really see—'

'You were 22 metres away, Mr Nelson. There was a streetlight. You said so yourself, you had a reasonable view—'

'Yeh, but the light was kinda strange . . . kinda orangey and shadowy . . . and they had caps on . . . you know, with peaks . . .'

'But the driver lost his cap.'

'Yeh . . . I know . . . it was all a bit confusing then . . .'

'Confusing?'

'Yeh.'

'The sequence of events you witnessed – this was confusing?'

'Some of it – yeh.'

'Are you easily confused?'

'What?'

'Are you easily confused?'

'I dunno . . .'

'Have you ever met Mr Vine?'

'What?'

'Have you ever met Mr Vine? Have you ever seen him before today?'

My eyes flick across at the dock . . . a pretty DUMB thing to do . . . but I can't help it – I'm confused now. I got my mind working on the cars and the fight and all that stuff, then suddenly I'm getting asked about something else . . . something I ain't expecting. Which maybe I shoulda expected, I guess . . . but like I said before, I ain't DUMB, but I ain't no GENIUS neither. Anyway, I flick a quick look at the dock, and Vine ain't grinning no more . . . he's giving me the laser look, burning me down with his silent heat. I can hear him, loud and clear – *you better keep your mouth shut, fat boy, you better keep your fat mouth SHUT* . . . Above him, in the balcony, his 2 goons are burning me, too.

'Would you answer the question, please?' says the judge.

'What?'

'The question,' says Henry. 'Have you ever met Mr Vine before today?'

'No.'

The sound of my voice echoes round the room – *NO NO NO* – and I can SEE the sound of it flying through the air and zipping into the heads of the jurors, and I can SEE em watching my skin turn red, and I can HEAR their brains turning the *NO NO NO* into *LIAR LIAR LIAR* . . .

Henry steps closer and lowers his voice. 'I'll ask you again, Mr Nelson – and remember, you're still under oath.' He takes a deep breath. 'Have you ever met Mr Vine before today?'

'No.'

Henry looks at me. I look back at him – and I KNOW . . .

I know he knows I'm lying. He KNOWS . . . but I dunno if he's got any proof or not. I dunno . . . I'm trying to remember meeting Vine . . . where and when . . . trying to think if anyone coulda bugged us or took pictures or something . . . but I can't get nothing straight in my head. And Henry's still looking at me . . . and I'm thinking – maybe he ain't got no proof, maybe he's just taking a chance, betting I'm rattled enough to crack. If he is, he ain't far wrong. I flick another look at the balcony. Bowker's looking worried, Dorudi . . . I ain't sure about her . . . and Callan? Callan's looking the same as he always does – cold as hell.

'You've *never* met with Mr Vine?' Henry says.

'Your *Honour*,' says Coley, standing up.

The judge nods. He says, 'The witness has answered the question, Mr Henry.'

Henry looks at the floor, thinking. I fix my eyes on the wooden railing around the witness box, concentrating hard, trying to control my heart . . . *THUMP THUMP THUMP* . . . beating like a big fat drum . . . GOD . . . it's so LOUD it HURTS . . .

'Why are you here, Mr Nelson?' says Henry.

'What?'

'Why are you here?'

'Why?'

'Yes – why are you here?'

'I don't get you.'

'Why did you come forward as a witness?'

'I din't come forward – the cops saw me on the bridge. They come round my place and took a statement.'

'But you're not appearing as a witness for the prosecution, are you?'

'No.'

'You're a defence witness.'

'Yeh.'

'You were asked to appear for the defence?'

'Yeh.'

'By whom?'

'Whom?'

'Who asked you to appear as a witness for the defence?'

I point at Donut. 'Him.'

'Mr MacDonald?'

'Yeh.'

'How did he approach you?'

'On the phone – then I went to his office.'

'That would be the office of Hawks, Spalding, in Moulton?'

'Yeh, it would be.'

'You don't live in Moulton, do you?'

'No.'

'How did you get there?'

'They sent a car.'

'That was very kind of them. And what happened when you got there? What did Mr MacDonald say?'

'He said he was working for Mr Vine and he wanted me to appear as a defence witness.'

'And you agreed?'

'Yeh.'

'Just like that?'

'I din't think I had much choice.'

'Did you feel you were under any pressure to agree?'

Coley starts to stand up, but the judge waves him back down.

Henry repeats the question. 'Did you feel you were under any pressure?'

'No.'

'Who was present at this meeting?'

'Me, Mr MacDonald, and my mum.'

'Anyone else?'

'No.'

'Are you sure?'

'Yeh.'

'No one else entered the office whilst you were there?'

'No . . . well, only the girl . . .'

'The girl?'

I nod, thinking of Tracy . . . thinking of what she makes me think . . . and I start feeling embarrassed . . . oh GOD . . . why the hell am I feeling EMBARRASSED? They're only THOUGHTS . . . no one KNOWS . . . and anyway, it ain't WRONG to think stuff like that, is it? It's only natural . . . Yeh? So how come my face is bright red?

Henry's staring at me, the corners of his mouth twitching in amusement.

'The *girl*, Mr Nelson?' he says.

'Yeh . . . I dunno . . . she's the receptionist, I guess. She wasn't actually *there*, like not *in* the office . . . she just kinda popped in a couple of times.'

'I see . . . the receptionist. And she just popped in a couple of times . . .' He nods his head and looks at his papers. 'That would be a Miss Regan, I believe? Mr MacDonald's Personal Assistant – Miss Tracy Regan?'

'I dunno her name. Yeh, Tracy something . . .'

'A blonde-haired young lady?'

'Yeh.'

'Rather striking . . .'

I shrug.

He grins. 'You don't remember?'

I shrug again, feeling the red heat melting my face.

Henry smirks. 'But you remember her popping into the office a couple of times?'

'Yeh.'

He nods. 'All right – let's leave Miss Regan for the moment and turn our attention to your mother. Now . . . your mother was with you when you saw Mr MacDonald, yes?'

'What?'

'Was your mother with you when you saw Mr MacDonald? Yes or no?'

'Yeh, but—'

'She was in the office with you?'

'Yeh.'

'For the entire meeting?'

I glance across at Donut, but he ain't looking, he's got his eyes fixed on the table.

I clear my throat. 'Well . . . she mighta nipped out to get something to eat—'

'Might have?'

'Well . . . yeh, she did.'

'Was that *her* idea?'

'I dunno . . . I can't remember.'

'How long was she gone for?'

'I dunno . . . not long.'

'5 minutes? 10 minutes? Half an hour?'

'Yeh, maybe half an hour . . . something like that.'

'So you were alone with Mr MacDonald for at least half an hour?'

'I spose so.'

'Except for when Miss Regan *popped in* once or twice?'

'Yeh.'

'How did you feel about that?'

'About what?'

'Being alone with Mr MacDonald.'

'It was OK . . . I din't mind.'

'He explained things to you? About the trial, appearing as

a witness . . .?

'Yeh.'

'Was this before or after your mother went out?'

'I dunno . . . I can't remember.'

'Did you understand what was being asked of you?'

'Yeh.'

'You weren't confused?'

'No . . . why should I—'

'All this popping in and nipping out . . . it could easily confuse matters—'

'It wasn't like that—'

'So you felt quite comfortable?'

'Yeh.'

'You were treated kindly.'

'Yeh.'

'*How* kindly?'

At this, Coley gets up again. 'Your Honour, I must object to this line of questioning. It really is—'

'Sit down, Mr Cole,' the judge says.

'But there's no—'

'Sit *down*.'

Coley frowns, goes to say something else, then changes his mind and sits down.

The judge nods at Henry.

Henry grins at me. 'You were telling us how well you were treated by Mr MacDonald – please elaborate.'

'Ain't nothing *to* elaborate – he was just all right, that's all.'

'He provided a car to and from his office?'

'Yeh.'

'Refreshments?'

'Yeh.'

'Compensation for your time?'

'No.'

'Are you sure?'

'Yeh.'

'No financial compensation?'

'No.'

'Is your mother in court today?'

'What's that got to do with it?'

'How many times have you met with Mr MacDonald?'

'What? Hold on—'

'How many times?'

'I dunno . . . twice, I think.'

'And you've never met with Mr Vine?'

'No—'

'Never received any inducements, from either Mr MacDonald or Mr Vine, to appear as a witness?'

'I already *told* you—'

'No inducements, no pressure, no intimidation—'

'HOW MANY TIMES I GOTTA *TELL* YOU, YOU DUMB *SHIT*—'

'Mr *Nelson*!' the judge barks. 'I will *not* tolerate unnecessary language in my court.'

I look up at him, all sweaty and shaky and HOT. 'Yeh, but he keeps asking me the same questions over and over again—'

'I understand your irritation, Mr Nelson, but that's no excuse. You will not speak like that in my court. Do you understand?'

'Yeh, but—'

'Do you *understand*?'

'Yeh.'

'Good.' He turns to Henry. 'And as for you, Mr Henry, unless you're willing to offer anything factual to substantiate your allegations, I suggest you move on. And I would remind the jury that we're only interested in the facts of this case. *Facts*, Mr Henry – do you understand?'

'Yes, Your Honour.'

'Do you wish to continue?'

'Indeed.'

The judge looks at me. 'Mr Nelson? Have you calmed yourself? Are you ready to continue? Mr Nelson?'

I got my head bowed down, looking at the floor . . . I can't look up. My head's too heavy. My face is wet, streaming with tears . . . I dunno what's happening . . . I just can't do it no more . . . I've had enough . . . enough questions . . . enough. I'm sick of it . . . sick of being here . . . sick of being looked at . . . sick of being judged . . . sick of being messed about . . . sick of lying . . . sick of the TRUTH . . . sick of being called *Mr Nelson* . . . I'm just sick of the whole damn thing. And now I gotta look up . . . I gotta show my face . . . and everyone's gonna see me blubbing like a baby . . .

'Mr Nelson – are you all right?'

. . . a big fat baby . . .

'Mr Nelson?'

. . . dripping snot and tears . . .

'Michael?'

I raise my head and look up at the judge.

'Oh,' he goes.

And there's a whisper of RAIN around the courtroom . . . a mixture of PITY and scorn and embarrassment . . . then an awkward silence – the biggest silence I ever heard – like the whole WORLD's looking at me. A world of silent RAIN – silent as nothing. It's so quiet . . . I wanna DIE. I can't do nothing. All I can do is stare at the judge . . . not that I can see much. I'm looking through a wall of tears. Everything's liquid. The room's a blurry white sea. The judge ain't nothing but a shimmer of wrinkles and a dusty old wig . . . his dried-up mouth croaking like a fish . . .

'Hmmph . . . huh-um . . . yes . . .'

Then Coley's voice gurgles up through the depths. 'Perhaps now would be an appropriate time, Your Honour?' And the judge says, 'Hmm-hmm, yes – thank you, Mr Cole. Perhaps you're right. Members of the jury, we'll break off now and resume again at 10 o'clock on Monday morning. Let me just remind you again not to talk about this case to anybody outside your own number. Do not allow anybody to discuss the case with you at all. Have a very pleasant weekend.'

I can see myself **now** – walking back along the courthouse corridors, walking with my eyes down . . . dead to the world. Dying. The tears have stopped . . . I ain't got nothing left to cry. I can see the usher guy walking beside me, and Donut on the other side, scuttling along, trying to talk to me . . . but I ain't listening, I'm locked away inside my head . . . *I've had enough . . . I'm through with it* . . . and there's Anisha and Mum outside the office . . . asking me what's the matter . . . and I can hear a part of me saying – *nothing, it's OK, it's nothing* . . . and the other part, the INSIDE part, saying – *I ain't coming back, I ain't coming back, I ain't NEVER coming back . . .*

Then the picture goes outta focus, and the rest of it's a mixed-up mess.

Leaving the courthouse.

Getting in the car.

Driving the roads.

. . . I ain't going back, I ain't going back, I ain't NEVER going back . . .

Into the village.

Up the lane.

Stopping.

Comforting words – *we're nearly there, Mike . . . one more Day . . . get some rest . . . don't forget . . . don't worry . . . pick you up . . . Monday . . .*

Getting out the car.

. . . ain't going back, ain't going back, ain't NEVER going back . . .

Up to the house.

Through the front door.

Dad . . .

Mum . . .

Kissing . . .

Then – *ping* – the focus comes back, and Dad's squeezing my shoulder, saying – 'Hey, Moo – you all right? How'd it go? You look done in.'

'Yeh.'

'You hungry? I made some sandwiches.'

'Great.'

'You got a visitor, by the way.'

'What? What d'you mean?'

'There's someone to see you,' he says.

And just for a second my blood goes cold, frozen with the memory of a killing voice – *they're gonna find you . . . don't matter where you are . . . they'll find you* – and my brain starts to panic – *they're here, the tattooed guys with psycho eyes . . . they're HERE* – and I WANNA look round, I WANNA see where they are . . . but I can't move my head. My legs are jelly. I can't MOVE.

'You all right?' asks Dad, giving me a funny look.

'Yuh . . . wh . . . wh . . .'

'What?'

'Where?'

Dad shakes his head. 'He's upstairs.'

'Who?'

'You know, what's-his-name . . . he called round earlier. He's upstairs.'

'Who?'

'The short kid—'

'Brady?'

'Yeh – I said he could wait in your room.'

'*Brady?*'

'Yeh.'

'He's in my *room*?'

'I just said—'

'He's in my room right *now*?'

'*Yes* – what's the matter with you? You lost your brain or something? Go and ask him if he's staying for tea – cos if he is, I'll have to make some more sandwiches.'

My heart's beating like mad as I leave the front room and start climbing the stairs, and my legs are still kinda wobbly, but at least I can move again. Yeh, I can move . . . I can climb the stairs . . . up to my room . . . where Brady's waiting . . . Brady . . .

Waiting for me . . .

In my room . . .

The stairs feel incredibly steep.

Like I'm climbing a mountain.

19/ Kissing the RAIN

My heart's still thumping when I open the bedroom door. I feel really weird, like I'm all mixed up, my insides buzzing with fear and excitement and a strange kinda relief, like I KNOW this is it – THIS is the start of the end.

'Hey, Moo,' says Brady. 'How's it going?

He's sitting at my PC desk, playing *Grand Theft Auto 3*. He looks a lot better than the last time I saw him, but he still don't look too great. There's an ugly scar above his right eye, his jaw's kinda twisted and bruised, and there's a reddish black streak down one side of his face. Also, he's sitting kinda funny – all hunched over and leaning to one side.

'Great graphics,' he says, nodding at the screen.

'Yeh . . . you got the old one – *GTA 2*?'

'This is better.'

'Yeh . . .'

I walk over and sit down on the edge of the bed. Brady closes the game and swings round to look at me.

'Nice suit,' he grins.

'200 quid,' I tell him, taking off the jacket. 'Look at that . . .' I show him the plush red lining.

'Looks a bit sweaty.'

'Yeh . . . well, it's been a long Day.' I look at him. 'How you doing?'

He lowers his eyes. 'Well, you know . . .'

'Yeh . . .'

I lean down and start taking off my shoes, taking my time

. . . cos this feels strange . . . I need time to think. Brady's never been in my room before . . . NO ONE's been in my room before, apart from Mum and Dad. I dunno what to feel about it. It feels kinda weird . . . but kinda nice, too. You know? It feels OK. But I still dunno what to feel about it . . . and I dunno what to say to Brady, neither. I dunno if I oughta ask him stuff or not. I dunno if he wants to talk about it . . . I dunno what he's doing here . . . and another thing – I gotta get outta these clothes, but I dunno if I oughta get changed in front of him. Cos if I do, he's gonna see my big fat belly . . . but if I don't, like if I go and get changed in the bathroom or something, he's probly gonna think I'm some kinda ponce.

So . . . I take my time taking off my shoes – thinking, thinking, thinking – finally thinking – ah, just get on with it . . . and I get up and go over to the wardrobe and get out some clothes – hood, T-shirt, troozies – and I start taking off my shirt and tie, casual as hell.

Brady's still looking at the floor.

'You coming back to school then?' I ask him.

'Nah . . . not for a bit. Next year probly . . . I dunno.'

'What you doing?'

'When?'

'I dunno . . . schooldays . . . what d'you do?'

'Not much . . . I gotta see people sometimes . . . they said I gotta rest . . .'

Even though he ain't looking at me, I nod my head, like I'm listening to every word he's saying . . . which I AM, kinda . . . it's just that I got my suit troozies off now, and I'm feeling pretty bare . . . and I gotta concentrate on getting my normal troozies on . . . you know, I don't wanna go falling over or nothing. So, anyway, I get that done, then chuck the suit in the wardrobe, then go back over and sit on the bed.

'That's better,' I says.

Brady looks up, half-smiling.

'You want anything to eat?' I ask him.

'Nah.'

'My dad's made some sandwiches . . .'

He shakes his head.

'You wanna put some music on? I got the new Slayer CD – it's pretty good. You like Slayer?'

He don't answer.

'You OK?' I ask him.

He shakes his head again.

'You wanna talk about it?'

His shoulders slump and he lets out a sigh. It's a really sad sound. And he looks so small . . . GOD . . . he looks so SMALL, like he ain't got nothing inside him, like an empty sack.

'I got your emails,' he says quietly.

'Oh . . . right. I thought you'd gone away or something . . .'

'Nah . . . I got em. I just din't feel too good, you know . . . I din't feel up to talking much.'

'Yeh . . . I know what you mean.'

'Do you?'

'Yeh . . . I mean, I know you got it a lot worse than me, but I ain't been having a great time, neither. I been going through all kinds of shit.'

'Like what?'

I look at him to see if he's being sarky, but he ain't – he just wants to know.

'I dunno,' I tell him, 'all sorts . . . everything. Everyone's pulling me in different directions, trying to get what they want. Callan, Donut, Vine . . . do this . . . do that . . . don't do this . . . don't do that . . . one minute they're giving me stuff, being nice, then the next minute they're threatening me, whacking me, scaring me to death. Callan said he's gonna get my dad locked up if I don't do what he says, and Vine said he's gonna set his boys on me if I don't do what *he* says. I dunno *what's* going on . . . I dunno which way to turn. Then, today, when I get to court . . .' I look at Brady. 'You really wanna hear all this?'

'Yeh,' he says.

'OK – well, Donut drives me to court in his car—'

'Who's Donut?'

'The solicitor – the guy defending Vine.'

'Right.'

'He picks up me and Mum and drives us to court, and I gotta stand up in front of all these guys in cloaks and wigs, and it's really hot and I'm sweating like mad, and then they start asking me all these questions about what happened at the bridge—'

'What *did* happen?'

'Don't you know?'

He shakes his head. 'Not really – only what I read in the papers and what Callan told me.'

'It was some kinda set-up thing,' I tell him. 'The guys in the BMW cut up Vine so he'd stop his car and pick a fight with em, then they made it look like Vine stabbed this Burke guy—'

'But he din't?'

'Nah – it was one of the other guys. They got hold of Vine and stuck the knife in his hand so he'd have his prints on it . . . I think some of the cops was probly in on it too . . . I dunno . . . it's pretty confusing.'

'What d'you tell em in court then?'

'Well, the first bit was all right, cos that was the defence guy. He just asked me what happened, and I told him. But then the prosecution guy started having a go at me . . . like, *really* having a go.' I close my eyes for a second, remembering the courtroom, the sound of Henry's voice, the questions, the headache, the laughter, the sound of the silent RAIN . . . I rub my eyes, wiping away a bit of wetness, then open em again. 'This guy – Henry, he's called – he ripped into me about all this stuff . . . personal stuff . . . like being fat . . . lonely . . . getting *bullied* . . . shit like that. Bastad even asked me how much I *weighed* . . .'

'Why?'

'I dunno . . . to make me look pathetic, I guess.'

'What for?'

'So the jury won't believe me. I mean, who's gonna believe a pathetic fat guy who sweats all the time and can't even *talk* proper?'

'Not me,' grins Brady.

'Oh yeh?' I grin back. 'And what d'you know?'

'Not much.'

We smile at each other . . . but it don't last long. It ain't that funny, anyway.

'So, anyway,' I says, 'after this Henry guy's had a right old go at me, he starts asking me about Vine and Donut, like how many times I met em and how much money they gave me . . . stuff like that.'

'They gave you money?'

'Yeh, Vine did – 3 grand.'

'Shit – 3 *grand*?'

'Yeh – you wanna see it?'

'OK.'

I go round to the top of the bed and get down on my knees, then reach in and pull back the flap of loose carpet and take out the envelope that Vine gave me. It's looking kinda grubby now, all creased and manky and covered in dust. I stand up and go over to Brady and show him the cash.

'That's 3 thousand quid?' he says.

'Yeh.'

'Don't look like much.'

'I know.'

'He just gave it you?'

'Yeh . . . about 2 minutes before he threatened me . . . then he whacked me in the belly and threw me out the car.'

'Nice.'

'Yeh,' I says, putting the cash back in the envelope. I stand there for a second, just looking at it, then I fold it up tight and stick it back under the bed. 'The thing is,' I tell Brady, 'I reckon they musta known. Henry and Callan . . . they musta known all about it. They knew all about Donut, too. What he said to me and everything. I reckon Tracy told em.'

'Who's Tracy?'

I sit down on the bed again. 'Donut's receptionist – she's really hot.'

'Yeh?'

'Yeh . . . too tall for you.'

'Everyone's too tall for me.'

'You wanna get yourself some platforms . . . or a she-midget.'

'You're funny.'

'Yeh . . .'

I don't FEEL funny. Thinking of midgets has got me thinking of the Clark guy, the midget driver, and that's got me thinking of Donut . . . and Vine . . . and the way he looked at me in court . . . and then me breaking down and blubbing . . . and it all comes flooding back . . . how I never felt so bad in my LIFE . . . and *I ain't going back . . . I ain't going back . . . I AIN'T NEVER GOING BACK* . . .

'Moo?' says Brady.

'Yeh?'

'The emails . . . what you said about fixing stuff . . .'

'Yeh?'

'What d'you mean?'

I look at him. His eyes are set, like he KNOWS what I mean . . . he KNOWS KNOWS KNOWS . . . but he wants me to say it. He NEEDS me to say it . . . just like I NEED him to DO it.

'I got this idea,' I tell him.

'Yeh?'

'Yeh.'

And then I tell him about kissing the RAIN.

I start with the girls in the playground. Explanation-wise, it probly ain't the best place to start, but I been thinking about it a lot recently, and I reckon that's where it started for me . . . and that's probly where it's gonna end, too . . . so it kinda makes sense. And, anyway, you gotta start *some*where.

So –

'There was these 3 girls, right?'

'Is this a joke?' says Brady.

'No . . . I'm telling you about this idea I got. Listen – there was these 3 girls, OK? At school. They was hanging round that little corner near the science block, you know? Near the back gates?'

'Right.'

'This was a few years back – when we was in the first year . . . or maybe the second year. Something like that.'

'I don't get it.'

'Just *listen* . . . OK, these girls . . . I dunno who they was. I can't remember . . . Debbie Mason was one of em . . . but I can't remember the others—'

'Becka and Charlie?'

'No . . . yeh . . . maybe, I dunno. Anyway, it don't

matter . . . they was THAT kinda girl . . . you know what I mean? There was 3 of em, just sitting around yakking, like they do . . . picking on people, tearing em apart . . . that kinda thing. I dunno what I was doing round there . . . I think I'd probly sneaked off to the shop or something . . . anyway, I was coming round the corner when I heard em talking, and for some reason I stopped and listened.'

'Like you do . . .'

'Yeh . . . the thing is, they was talking about *me*.'

'Yeh?'

'They was doing this thing . . . you know . . . like what's worse – doing this or doing that? And one of em goes – "What d'you rather do? Kiss Moo or eat dog poo?" Right?'

'Yeh.'

'Then another one says, "Yeh – what d'you rather do? Kiss Moo or die?"'

Brady just stares at me, shaking his head in disbelief. 'And you're *listening* to this?'

'Yeh, I'm right there. I can't believe it – *what d'you rather do? Kiss Moo or die?* – like I'm some kinda DISEASE or something. And you know what the answer is? You know what the 3rd one says?'

'What?'

'She goes – "I'd kill him, then I wouldn't have to do neither."'

Brady looks at me.

I look at him.

He goes, 'That's shit, man.'

'Yeh, I know.'

'But I still don't get it.'

I think he's lying – I think he gets it all right. Like I said before, Brady's an idiot sometimes . . . most times actually. A small ugly idiot. But he ain't DUMB – he KNOWS what

I'm talking about. He just wants me to spell it out. And that's OK, cos I want me to spell it out, too. I wanna hear what it sounds like outside my head.

So I start telling him about the stuff I was thinking about the night after Callan met me on the bridge, when I was lying in the dark thinking up all the things I coulda said to him . . . like when he said that stuff about school, about me being a *protected species* . . . about me being scared . . . and how I LIKE being a protected species cos it *makes me feel big* . . . and the stuff about right and wrong . . . and JUSTICE . . . and him not being any better than the rest of em . . . all that kinda stuff . . .

And Brady goes, 'Yeh, I know what you mean. I been doing a lotta that lately. Lying in bed thinking what I'd do to them guys . . .' His eyes glaze over. He looks at me. 'It don't help much, does it?'

'I dunno . . . I din't *think* it did . . . not at first, anyway. I mean, when I was thinking all this stuff about Callan, I thought it was all a waste of time, cos he's like REALLY smart, so it wouldna made much difference *what* I said . . . but then I got this other idea . . .' I look at Brady to see what he's thinking.

'Yeh?' he goes. 'This other idea . . .?'

'It just kinda popped into my head. I just thought . . . like . . . spose . . . spose I'd just chucked him off the bridge?'

'What?' Brady grins.

'It was just an idea . . . you know, like he's so smart, there ain't no point in trying to outsmart him . . . so why not just push him off the bridge? Cos then it don't matter HOW smart he is . . . not with a 20-ton truck rolling over his head. D'you see what I mean?'

'Yeh,' says Brady, nodding his head. 'Yeh . . . that'd shut him up, all right. He wouldn't bother you much after *that*.'

'Exactly.'

'Yeh . . .'

We look at each other . . . still not sure . . .

'So,' I says, 'what d'you think?'

He chews his thumbnail, thinking it through . . . staring at the floor. Then after a while he looks up at me. 'You ain't talking about Callan, right?'

'Right.'

'And the girls . . .?'

'Think about it.'

He thinks about it, then shakes his head. 'Gimme a clue.'

'Callan and Vine.'

He looks at me, still looking puzzled.

'OK,' I says. 'Callan's gonna lock up my old man if Vine gets off—'

'What for?'

'It don't matter . . . it's nothing – all you gotta know is Callan's gonna lock him up if Vine gets off – OK?'

'Yeh.'

'But if Vine *don't* get off, if he goes down for stabbing Burke, he's gonna send his boys after me and I'm gonna get what you got . . . worse, probly.'

'Ain't *nothing* worse,' whispers Brady.

'Yeh, well . . . that's it anyway. I gotta choose between Callan and Vine . . . bad and bad . . . bad or bad . . . I gotta choose, see? It's just like them girls doing their thing with me . . . you know . . . like what's worse – doing this or doing that? What's worse – kissing Moo or dying? Now *I* gotta choose what's worse – getting wrecked by Callan or crippled by Vine.' I look at Brady. 'You know what the answer is?'

He don't say nothing – just waits, like he's been waiting a long time.

'Think of the girls,' I tell him.

'*What d'you rather do . . .*' he says, his voice a broken whisper.

'Yeh . . . that's it.'

'*What d'you rather do . . . get wrecked by Callan . . . or crippled by Vine*?'

'I'd kill Vine,' I tell him. 'Then I wouldn't have to do neither.'

20/ It's Gonna be Fine

We don't speak for a while, we just sit there – Brady at the desk, me on the bed, the room all quiet and still. Outside, the evening light's coming down, the summer sky turning pink on the horizon. The window's open. I can hear birds whistling on the roof, the muffled sound of the TV downstairs, and the distant rush of the road . . . the whisper of traffic, singing in the evening breeze . . . calling out to me – *get it done, Moo . . . get it done, get it done, get it done* . . .

Yeh . . .

Get it done.

It's OK.

I feel OK.

Now I said it, now it's out in the open, it feels OK.

It's gonna be fine.

I look across at Brady – he's got his stumpy legs crossed, sitting hunched over in the chair, one arm held across his belly. He's thinking . . . his eyes still, staring at the possibilities . . . his left hand smoothing the scarred skin of his face. I dunno what he's thinking, but I guess it's about him and me. If I was him, that's what I'd be thinking about. Him and me . . . yeh, it's OK for him, but what about me. Why me? What do I get out of it? What's in it for me?

He sniffs, wipes his nose, and looks up.

'That's it?' he says. 'That's your idea?'

'Yeh – what d'you think?'

'You mean it?'

'Yeh . . . I think so. I mean, it makes sense, don't it?'

'Push him off the bridge?'

'Yeh.'

'Vine?'

'Yeh.'

'Kill him?'

'Yeh.'

'Shit . . .' He shakes his head. 'What then?'

'What d'you mean?'

'When he's dead – what then?'

'Nothing – it's over. There's no trial . . . no verdict . . . nothing to worry about. Nothing's gonna happen.'

'What about the other guys? Vine's crew . . . the guys who got me . . .'

'They ain't gonna do nothing, are they? Vine's dead – they ain't getting paid no more. They don't do stuff outta the kindness of their hearts. They ain't even GOT no hearts . . . they ain't gonna do nothing.'

'You reckon?'

'Yeh – 100%.'

Brady thinks about it some more. I sit there watching him. His face . . . it looks really bad. It looks *permanently* bad, if you know what I mean. Like there's something wrong with the inside of it, like the skull's been mashed outta shape or something. And his eyes . . . they don't seem to fit the sockets quite right, like they stick out too much, or maybe the sockets are too deep . . . I dunno . . . it just don't look right . . .

'How you gonna do it?' he says.

'What – get him there?'

'Yeh . . . the whole thing – how's it gonna work?'

'Well . . . I got his mobile number. I give him a call, tell him I wanna see him about something, like something to do with the trial . . . you know, make out it's really important—'

'You could tell him you changed your mind . . . you're gonna tetsify against him or something—'

'*Tes*tify – yeh.'

'That'd make him listen.'

'Yeh . . . I tell him I'm thinking of doing what Callan wants, and I wanna see him about it before the trial starts again on Monday. Just me and him, somewhere nice and quiet. Which'll be OK with him, cos then he can push me around or offer me more cash or whatever.'

'And you suggest meeting on the bridge.'

'Yeh . . .'

'What if they trace the phone call?'

'Who?'

'The cops, the wiggies . . .'

'I got a mobile . . . Donut gave us one.'

'They can trace mobile calls.'

'Can they?'

'Yeh, I think so . . . I think they use statellites or something . . .'

'Well, I'll chuck it away after – just smash it up and chuck it away somewhere.'

He nods. 'Yeh . . . OK. Then what?'

'We meet Vine on the bridge—'

'We?'

Here we go . . . I knew it was coming . . . it had to come sooner or later – *why me?*

I lean forward, looking in Brady's eyes. 'Them 2 guys . . . the ones that got you in the woods?'

'Yeh?'

'They was in court. I saw em. What they done to you – they was only doing what Vine told em.'

'I know.'

'You said you wanted to fix him, din't you?'

'Yeh . . .'

I look in his eyes. 'I can't do it without you.'

He looks down.

'I need you Brady,' I tell him. 'I ain't got the guts to do it on my own. And, anyway, he's messed up both of us . . . we *both* gotta do it. You and me . . .'

'I dunno . . .'

'You gotta do it . . . make yourself better. Them things . . . you gotta get them things out your head . . . get rid of the bad stuff . . . wipe it out . . .'

'I guess . . .'

'Stand up and fight.'

'Yeh . . .'

'Make yourself feel better.'

'Right.'

'OK?'

'Yeh . . . OK.'

'You sure?'

'Yeh – what d'you want me to do?'

'OK – let's say we get him down the bridge, say tomorrow morning . . . early morning, when it ain't too busy. We get there before him, so we're already there when he shows up.'

'Right.'

'We're standing on the bridge, waiting for him . . . he's gonna come up the lane and park beneath the bridge—'

'We got masks on or anything?'

'Masks?'

'So no one sees our faces – just in case.'

'Vine's gonna be a bit suspicious if he sees us standing on the bridge wearing masks, ain't he?'

'Yeh, I spose.'

I tug my hood. 'You got one of these?'

He shakes his head. 'I got my parka . . .'

'Yeh, that'll do. Wear it with the hood up.'

'OK.'

'Right – so he gets out the car, comes up the steps, along the bridge . . . and then we start talking.'

'You and him?'

'Yeh . . . he ain't gonna like you being there, so you can kinda slope off . . . just move away a bit . . . behind him . . .'

'Then what?'

I'm thinking about it now . . . it's getting real. I'm picturing the bridge, trying to remember how high the railings are . . . seeing myself standing there . . . in my position . . . arms crossed . . . leaning over . . . looking down . . . feeling the railings against my chest . . . just below my chest . . . just here . . . above the belly, below the chest . . . yeh . . . that's it. And Vine's pretty tall . . . so if he's standing with his back to the railings they'll come up to about . . . here . . . on him . . . Yeh . . . that'll do.

'OK,' I says. 'I'll be talking to him, right . . . I'll get him so he's standing with his back to the railings . . . kinda close, but not too close . . . yeh . . . then I'll give you some kinda signal, and you start sneaking up behind him, like REALLY quiet, then I'll give you another signal, and you get right behind him, kinda crouched down, and I'll smash into him—'

'Like you smashed into Jicky that time?'

'Yeh—'

'Like Jumbo Stalloney.'

'Yeh . . . and when he falls back over you, you gotta stand up, kinda push him *up*, and I'll give him another shove, and we'll get him over the railings . . . what d'you think?'

Brady nods. 'Yeh . . . sounds pretty good. How big is he?'

'Big enough.'

'You think we can get him over?'

'Yeh, I reckon – he won't know what's happening if we do it quick.'

'You think that'll do it . . . you know . . .'

'Yeh – the bridge is pretty high . . . and even if the fall don't do it, he's gonna get mashed up by a lorry or something.'

'What if someone sees us . . . someone driving past . . .?'

'That's why we meet him early in the morning – so there ain't many people about. The road's gonna be pretty quiet. I'll try and push him over when no one's coming . . . it'll be all right.'

'You sure?'

No, I think.

'Yeh,' I say.

Brady looks at me again. I look back at him, trying to keep the doubts outta my face . . . cos I ain't sure about NOTHING. I been making up most of it as I go along. Will it work? Is it a good idea? I dunno . . . I don't care. It's the best I got – it's ALL I got. But I don't want Brady knowing that, so I look at him like I ain't got a doubt in the world.

'You worried about it?' he says. 'You know . . . killing a guy . . .'

'Nope.'

'Why not?'

'It don't mean nothing . . .'

Brady looks at me, drawn to the emptiness of my voice.

I smile at him, dead-faced. 'We're all just little things, B, ain't none of us mean nothing. Vine don't mean nothing . . . what's he ever done? He hurts people, uses em, abuses em, kills em . . . messes em up. Look what he done to you . . . you think he cares about that?'

'No.'

'He don't care about nothing, and no one cares about him. Ain't no one gonna miss him . . . ain't no one gonna care if he's dead. And it ain't like he's gonna suffer or nothing, is it?'

'I guess not.'

'So if no one's gonna miss him, and we ain't gonna make him suffer . . . what's the problem? He ain't gonna *know* he's dead, is he? He ain't gonna know nothing about it. All we're gonna do is take him out.' I snap my fingers. 'Just like that. He's gone. Wiped out. End of story.'

Brady nods. He probly knows as well as I do there's more to it than that . . . or maybe there ain't . . . I dunno. There probly is . . . but I ain't got the smarts to think about it. It's just something . . . I dunno . . . it's just something I gotta do – I gotta kiss the RAIN. I still dunno what it means . . . but I know I gotta do it.

I look at the clock – it's getting on for 9.30 now. Outside, the sun's gone down and the light's fading fast. It'll be dark soon. And I got things to do.

'You in or not?' I ask Brady.

He looks at me. 'You reckon it'll be all right?'

'Yeh.'

'Tomorrow morning?'

'Yeh – get it over with. Get it done.'

'When you gonna ring him?'

'Pretty soon . . . you staying?'

'Nah . . . I gotta go.'

'That's OK – I'll email you later.'

'You could phone—'

'Ain't safe – I'll email you.'

'OK.' He gets up, looking a bit nervous. 'You got the new address?'

'Yeh.'

He looks around, shuffling his feet.

'You want me to walk you back?' I ask him.

'Nah . . . it's OK . . . you gotta ring Vine, anyway.'

'That's all right. I'll call him on the way back. I can get rid of the phone then – smash it up and stick the bits in a bin or something.' I get up off the bed. 'Come on, I'll walk you back.'

'You sure?'

'Yeh – no problem. I'll just get my trainers on.'

He smiles. 'Thanks, Moo.'

'No sweat.'

21/ The End of the TRUTH

Walking through the village back to Brady's . . . the night's hot and sticky, the streets are dark, and there's a funny smell of burnt rubber in the air. The village is empty and quiet, like it's a ghost town or something, but every now and then you can hear the sound of shouts ringing out in the distance . . . you know, them tough-guy kinda shouts – *OI! OI! OI! YAH! YAHHH! AAHHHH!!* . . . the kinda shouts that crack the silence and echo hard around the streets, sending shivers through your belly. It's probly nothing, just people coming outta pubs or something, shouting and laughing, having a GOOD TIME . . . but it's a pretty NERVY kinda sound, and Brady's really edgy anyway – looking around all the time, jumping at the sound of cars, scuttling along at 50mph . . .

The funny thing is, though – I ain't WORRIED at all. I ain't WORRIED about NOTHING, cos I KNOW that nothing's gonna happen. I just KNOW it. I got this strange kinda feeling in my belly . . . a BIG warm feeling – like everything's gonna be all right. Nothing's gonna happen. And even if I'm wrong, even if everything AIN'T gonna be all right . . . who cares?

Not me.

Cos right now, everything's fine.

Walking Brady home . . .

It's just *fine*.

Under the stars, through the streets, into the village, up

around the shop, then across the little park and along the bank by the woods . . . we don't talk much, just walk the walk, you know, just keep on going. Brady speeds up as we're walking along by the woods, keeping his head down and his feet moving and his arms dead stiff, like a stumpy little clockwork robot. His breathing gets a bit funny, too. But when we're past the woods and heading off into the estate, he slows down a bit and starts breathing more normal again, flashing me an embarrassed grin.

'All right?' I says.

He nods but don't say nothing.

We keep walking . . . 2 sets of footsteps drumming along the empty streets – *tump, tump, tump . . . scuff, scuff, scuff . . . tump, tump, tump . . . scuff, scuff, scuff* . . . and I'm just kinda thinking about stuff, non-thinking stuff, stuff that don't matter . . . and it feels OK.

'You wasn't there, was you?' I says quietly.

Brady looks at me. 'Where?'

'At the bridge . . . you know . . . when it happened . . . the fight and everything. You wasn't there . . . you din't see nothing, did you?'

He shakes his head, shrugs his shoulders, and carries on walking. I follow him down a scratty little street into the heart of the estate. It feels kinda dark and closed in, like a concrete maze. All the streetlights are out . . . all except one at the end of the road that's stuttering on and off like a retarded lighthouse – *tickatickatickaticka* . . .

'It don't *matter*,' I says to Brady. 'I was just wondering, that's all . . .'

'What?'

'You know . . .'

'What?'

'Why you told Callan you seen what happened.'

He shrugs again. 'I dunno . . . no reason. I just felt like it, I spose.'

I can tell by the flick of his eyes that he don't wanna talk about it no more . . . which is OK with me. I was just wondering, that's all. It DON'T matter why he did it . . . it don't make no odds to me. He don't *have* to gimme a reason for nothing, does he? Why should he? He just FELT like it . . .

Fair enough.

We cross the road and turn into another little street. This one *looks* the same as all the others – flat, grey . . . houses, cars, nothing much – but I can tell it's different by the way Brady's walking. He's walking more upright now, less crouchy . . . less *scuttly*. And he's LEADING me, he's taking me across the street, then slowing down and stopping outside a squatty little terraced house. There's a jungle growing in the front garden and a rusty old Metro parked on the pavement outside.

'This is me,' Brady says awkwardly.

'Right,' I says, glancing across at the house. The walls look like they're made outta grit.

Brady sniffs. 'I'd better get going.'

'Yeh, OK . . . you all right?'

'Yeh.'

'Right, well . . . I guess I'll see you tomorrow then.'

'Yeh.'

'I'll email you later, you know . . .'

He nods, looking down at his feet.

'OK?'

He nods again. 'Yeh . . . thanks.'

Now it's my turn to nod . . . nod, nod, nod . . .

'All right, then,' I says. 'I'll see you later.'

'Yeh, see you later.'

I watch him walk up to his house, digging in his pocket

for the front-door key, then looking up at the window as a light goes on . . . then I turn around and start walking back again. Back through the streets . . . *tump, tump, tump* . . . under the lights . . . *tickatickatickaticka* . . . up to the bank . . . *tump, tump, tump* . . . along by the woods . . . *thump, thump, thump* – that's my heart, the thumping. Cos, now I'm on my own, the woods are looking a little bit colder than they was before, a bit darker, a bit more scary . . . but it's still OK, I'm still feeling all right, and they ain't bothering me *too* much. I'm WARY, but I ain't waried stiff or nothing . . . just normal wary . . . you know . . . *natural* wary . . . just in case. But it's all right, nothing happens.

Nothing's GONNA happen.

At the end of the woods I cut through into the park, then follow the hedge along the bottom of the field and head for the swings. I'm doing OK . . . feeling fine, feeling fine . . . yeh, I'm still feeling fine. Walking across the grass . . . sitting down on a swing . . . taking the weight off my feet . . . looking around . . . checking things out . . . getting the phone out my pocket . . . turning it on . . . checking Vine's number . . . punching the buttons . . . and I ain't even THINKING what's gonna happen if he don't answer, if I get his voicemail or something . . . it ain't even OCCURRED to me – it ain't an OPTION, if you know what I mean.

The phone connects.

Duuh-duuh, duuh-duuh . . .

He gets it after a couple of rings.

'Yeh?'

'Vine?' I says.

'Who's this?'

'Moo Nelson.'

There's muffled music in the background. It sounds like some kinda garagey stuff – big boingy drums, thumping bass, twiddly keyboards . . .

'Yeh,' goes Vine. 'What d'you want?'

'I gotta see you.'

'Why?'

'I can't say on the phone – it's about the trial.'

He covers the phone with his hand and shouts at someone in the background. The music goes quiet. Then his voice comes back on.

'What you talking about?'

'I just *said* – I gotta see you about something.'

'Shit – what's the matter with you? I told you what you gotta do—'

'Something's come up.'

'What?'

'That's what I wanna see you about.'

'I'm busy, chrissake . . . I don't need this shit.'

'OK – forget it. I was only trying to help. I'll see you on Monday—'

'Hold on!' he snaps. 'Just a minute . . . you still there?'

'Yeh.'

He sighs. 'OK – where are you?'

'Where are *you*?'

'*What?*'

'You know the bridge?'

'What bridge? What you talking about?'

'The bridge . . . the A12 . . . where it happened . . .'

He sighs again. 'Right – the bridge. Yeh . . . what about it?'

'Be there tomorrow morning at 7.30.'

'*What?* Who the hell d'you think you are? Telling *me*—'

'I'm Moo Nelson. I can put you away. You want that?'

'You *what*?'

'You heard me.'

The phone goes quiet. I look out across the park. The

grass looks grey in the darkness. Above the woods, a slice of moon is shining white in the sky. Empty crisp packets are fluttering in the breeze, catching the moonlight and the sodium lights of the street . . . shimmering silver . . . orange . . . like electric ghosts . . .

Vine laughs. 'OK, Fats – you there?'

'Yeh.'

'Tomorrow morning, 7.30. At the bridge.'

'Just you.'

'Just me.'

'Don't be late.'

He laughs again. 'I hope you know what you're doing, boy.'

'Yeh,' I tell him. 'I know what I'm doing.'

I switch off the phone and sit there for a while, breathing the cool night air, thinking cool night thoughts, then I drop the phone to the ground and stamp the shit out of it, smashing it to pieces. It cracks up pretty good. I pick up the pieces, put em in my pocket, and head for home. On the way back, every couple of minutes or so, I take out a handful of broken-up phone bits and chuck em away – in litter bins, wheelie bins, hedges, gardens, skips . . . wherever. I dunno if it's a smart thing to do or not. I'm probly wasting my time . . .

Who cares?

It's something to do.

Back home, the house is empty. It's Mum and Dad's night-at-the-pub. They won't be back until 11.30 or 12. It's about 10.30 now, 11 o'clock, something like that. A quick email to Brady, letting him know we're on, then I go into the front room and switch on the TV. *Friends* is on – it's a repeat, one of them old ones they put on later than normal when they ain't got nothing else to put on. It's one of them episodes where they go back to the old Days . . . you know, when they go back and show us what they was like before they was FRIENDS . . . which is pretty much the same as they are now, except for what's-her-name, the skinny dark-haired girl, cos she used to be REALLY FAT. So they dress her up and make her look REALLY FAT . . . they even make her face look FAT . . . and it's REALLY FUNNY . . . HA HA HA HA HA. And you know WHY it's really funny? Cos she ain't FAT no more. She ain't FAT *now*. THAT's why it's funny. Cos now she's really sexy and good-looking, so the idea of her being REALLY FAT and REALLY UGLY is REALLY FUNNY . . .

Anyway, I sit there for a while just staring at the pictures, flicking around to see what else is on. There ain't much. News, dirty stuff on Channel 5 . . . some crappy spy movie . . . ain't nothing I really wanna see . . . but I keep watching anyway . . . just staring at the screen . . . watching, watching, watching . . . drifting away . . . falling away . . . fading away . . .

And after a while, I realise I ain't feeling *fine* no more. I ain't feeling fine at ALL. The feeling I had when I was walking Brady home . . . that BIG warm feeling in my belly? It's gone. Disappeared. Snuffed out – *phhtt* – like the flickering flame of a stubby little candle. The light's gone out, smothered by the TRUTH.

And it DON'T feel *fine* . . .

It feels cold and dark and empty.

It HURTS.

The FAT stuff, the lies . . . the words . . . the RAIN.

Brady . . .

The TRUTH.

GOD.

It HURTS.

I gotta get rid of it.

I gotta get it all out.

I need to EMPTY it.

I NEED TO TELL THE TRUTH.

So I turn off the TV and go upstairs . . . go into my room . . . shut the door . . . lie down on the bed . . . and I just kinda THINK of someone to tell it to. I IMAGINE this person . . . I dunno who they are. They ain't got a face or a name or nothing . . . they ain't even THERE, really. They're just this thing . . . like a mirror inside my head . . . an echo or something . . .

An inside ME . . .

Or maybe an inside YOU . . .

I dunno.

Whoever they are – whatever WE are – I bring em on out, sit em down, and tell em the TRUTH.

Listen, I says, you wanna know the TRUTH? I'll tell you the TRUTH – I'm sick of it. Sick of all the FAT stuff and Callan and Vine and the bridge and the road and the cars and the eyes and the words and the lies . . .

And I just keep going, getting it all out before it all gets done, and the dead of night keeps dying, taking me away, turning months and Days into hours and minutes . . . turning time into nothing . . .

And the silence ticks away . . .

The Days fall . . .

The hours go by . . .

Until . . .

Here we are.

Here and **now**.

Scatterday morning.

6.30 am.

And we're dressed and ready to go.

I ain't feeling tired no more, but there's SOMETHING

inside me, some kinda worn-out feeling, and I ain't sure what it is.

It's just . . .

I dunno . . .

It's just the whole thing, I spose. Kissing the RAIN . . . killing Vine . . . pushing him off the bridge . . . the thought of actually DOING it. I mean, I ain't saying I'm SCARED of doing it, cos I ain't. I KNOW it don't mean nothing, and Vine don't mean nothing, and none of us mean nothing, and no one cares about Vine anyway, so no one's gonna miss him, and it ain't like he's gonna suffer or nothing, is it? He ain't gonna *know* he's dead. He ain't gonna know nothing about it. All we're gonna do is take him out. End of story.

Yeh, I KNOW all that . . .

It's just . . .

I dunno.

It's just . . . it's like . . . the closer it gets – the REALer it gets – the more it DON'T feel like nothing no more and starts to feel like SOMETHING.

I dunno what.

Good or bad, right or wrong, THIS or THAT . . . I dunno what none of it means, and I don't really care, all I know is – KILLING A GUY AIN'T EASY. Yeh, all right, it don't mean nothing when you think about it, but THINKING and DOING is 2 different things, and you gotta FEEL like nothing to actually DO it. You gotta be MADE of nothing – like Vine and Callan and Bowker and Donut . . . and I ain't sure I wanna be like them. I don't WANNA be nothing no more. I'm sick of being nothing.

I'm sick of everything.

I ain't even sure if doing it's gonna fix things anyway. I mean, it ain't like I really thought it through or nothing . . . it ain't exactly FOOLPROOF, is it? In fact, if you think about it, it's a pretty DUMB idea all round. GOD, there's about a THOUSAND things wrong with it . . . probly more . . . it probly ain't got a chance in HELL of fixing things.

The only thing it's likely to fix is me and Brady.

Which is OK, I spose.

I mean, that ain't such a bad thing, is it?

Anyway, it's nearly time to go now. The house is quiet. Mum and Dad are still asleep. All I gotta do is sneak out the bedroom, along the hall, into the bathroom, take a leak, then sneak downstairs, creep out the back, get my bike out the shed, then ride the morning streets – around the back of the village, away from the houses, away from the people, into the country lanes, then down into the dip and up the hill, pedalling hard, puffing BILLY, sweating like a pig, looking out for the bridge . . . the railings – dit dit dit – the steps, the concrete, the dull grey steel . . . the shape of it, the angles, the colour . . . the tide of traffic on the road below . . . the sound of it . . . the *uuurrrrhhhhhsshhhhmmmm* . . . the *swoo-ooosh-swoo-ooosh-swoo-ooosh* of the cars . . . trucks . . . lorries . . .

The song of the road.

Yeh . . . I can hear it now. Calling out to me – *get it done, Moo . . . get it done, get it done, get it done . . .*

Yeh . . .

Get it done.

That's all I gotta do.

Get it done.

Just get up and go . . .

Get out the house.

Get to the bridge.

And get it done.

That's all . . .

BOOF!! AAAHHH!! HOONKKK!! KER-SPPLATT!!

No Vine . . . no trial . . . no verdict . . . no worries . . .

That's it . . .

End of story.

Right?

Yeh . . .

I mean, what else *is* there? I can't just sit here for ever, can I? That'd be stupid. I'd end up thinking myself to DEATH. And for what? For NOTHING is what. Nah, it's too late for thinking and feeling and wishing things was different . . . it's too late for all that.

I just gotta DO IT.

Just get up and go . . .

Before it's too late.

Cos – look – it's nearly 6.45 now. The clock's tick-ticking. And if I ain't gone soon, it ain't gonna happen. It'll be too late. Cos if I ain't gone soon, I'm gonna chicken out. And THAT's the TRUTH. I'm gonna stay here for ever, stuck in this hole, and NOTHING's GONNA HAPPEN . . .

Nothing but time.

Tick . . . tock . . .

The Day's gonna end . . .

Tick . . . tock . . .

Tomorrow's gonna come . . .

Tick . . . tock . . .

Tomorrow's gonna end . . .

Tick . . . tock . . .

And what happens then?

Tick . . .

Tock.

GOD knows . . .

WHAT YOU GONNA DO?

WINNER of
THE BRANFORD BOASE AWARD 2002

SHORTLISTED for
THE CILIP CARNEGIE MEDAL 2002

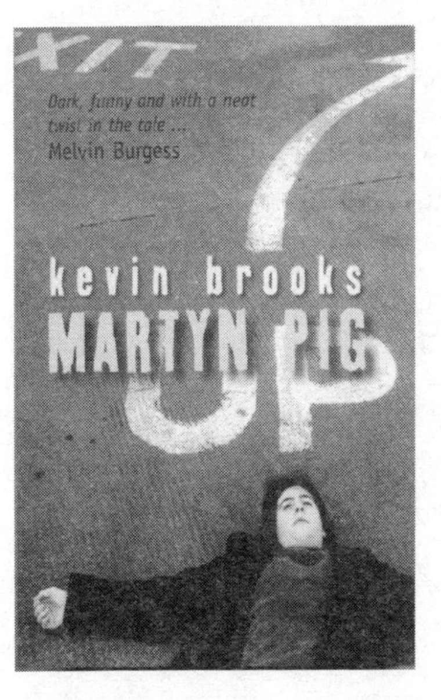

Martyn Pig is a boy with a miserable name living in a miserable world. His mother has left home and he lives with his father, a bullying, self-pitying drunk who meets an accidental and untimely death. What else can possibly go wrong? Try *everything*.

Martyn faces a stark choice as he stands over his dead father. He can tell the police what happened – that it was an awful accident – or he can get rid of the body and get on with the rest of his life. He decides on the latter and with the help of Alex, a girl he admires, he travels down a dead funny but dead frightening road.

AVAILABLE NOW

THE STUNNING SECOND NOVEL from
KEVIN BROOKS
Shortlisted for the
GUARDIAN CHILDREN'S BOOK AWARD 2003

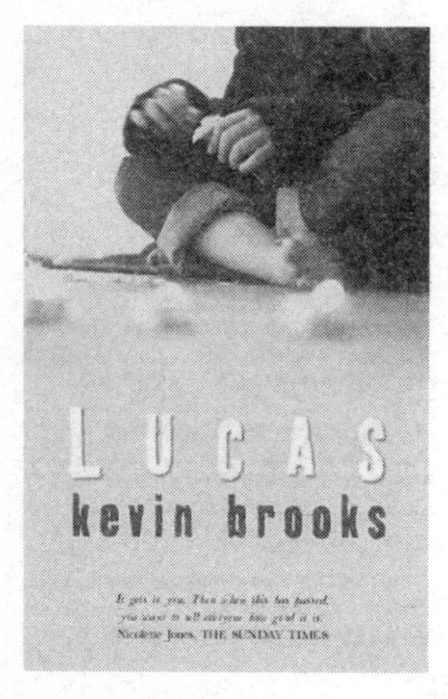

It was my dad's idea to write about Lucas and Angel and everything else that happened last summer. 'It won't make you feel any better,' he told me, 'it might even make things worse for a while. But you mustn't let the sadness die inside you. You have to give it some life. You have to ...'

'Let it all out?'

He smiled. 'Something like that.'

'I don't know, Dad,' I sighed. 'I'm not sure I can write a story.'

'Ah, now, that's nonsense. Anyone can write a story. It's the easiest thing in the world. How else do you think I make a living out of it? All you have to do is tell the truth, tell it like it was.'

'But I don't know *how it was, I don't* know *all the details, the facts—'*

'Stories aren't facts, *Cait, they're not* details. *Stories are* feelings. *You've got your feelings, haven't you?'*

'Too many,' I said.

'Well, that's all you need.' He put his hand on mine. 'Cry yourself a story, love. It works. Believe me.'

So that's what I did, I cried myself a story.

And this is it.

AVAILABLE NOW